**"Do you believe in love?" she asked, her
eyes wide in the hope that a flash of light
would reveal his face.**

She felt the bed give under his weight as he sat down
beside her. "Do you know what love is?"

"No." The revealing honesty of her reply started a quiver
at the corner of his mouth. If he laughed at her . . .

But he did not laugh, though his voice was now wistfully
amused. "Then if love came to you one night, out of the
darkness with all questions unanswered and all reason
against it, how could you welcome it for what it was?"

She stared into the gloom until her eyes stung, feeling as
exposed as if she lay naked to his gaze beneath a noonday
sun. She had the answer to his question. She knew what he
asked of her. She trembled on the edge of that knowledge,
now advancing, now retreating, but always trembling and
uncertain. If only she knew . . . if only she could reassure
herself . . . "If only I could be certain!"

"Nothing is certain."

Also by Laura Parker
FOR LOVE'S SAKE ONLY

LAURA PARKER

A DELL BOOK

Published by
Dell Publishing
a division of
Bantam Doubleday Dell Publishing Group, Inc.
666 Fifth Avenue
New York, New York 10103

ISBN: 0-440-20919-6

Printed in the United States of America

Published simultaneously in Canada

July 1992

10 9 8 7 6 5 4 3 2 1

RAD

For Anthony and Christopher;
the other men in my life

Prologue

DEVON OCTOBER 1845

It was the hour for lovers. A shower of feather-tailed stars momentarily silvered the night. Moon-flung shadows chased cloud patterns across the moors and up over the ancient walls into the rose garden where luscious fragrances of jasmine and rose scented the breeze. Tucked in indigo shadows, waxy bells of lily of the valley pealed in silence.

It was the hour for magic.

They came, the captain and his lady, with sighs softer than heartbeats, in silhouettes more delicate than fern-lace patterns upon the surface of a pool, their passage more tender than a lover's touch. Mere ether on the breeze, they were dressed in the fashion of more than two centuries earlier.

Their moods changed quickly. Their sighs grew less gentle, their silhouettes electric, their passage a burst of something more thrilling than the wind. Silent voices as strong and harsh as static broke the silence.

"It is desertion, madame! Nothing less! I knew it would come to this. Neither kith nor kin can be trusted!"

"Nay, Captain. 'Tis necessity that removes them from us. Their human frailties must be forgiven them."

"Must they? Even now the house grows cold and silent. Mortality plagues the emptiness!"

"Then you miss them too, my captain?"

"Madame, you presume too much. I reproach them not for their absence but for their cowardice. To shut the house up and turn the servants off without warning, without even coming to do the deed themselves; I'd have expected better of the Maxwell lad, though he is tainted with the Kingsblood line."

"Lad? Maxwell is three score and some years! As for the Kingsblood in him, he is your kin too."

"Do not remind me! He comes to it straight down the wrong side of the blanket."

" 'Twas your seed."

"In your sweet body. God's death! You've a sweet one still."

The potency of these mere wisps of ether shook snowdrops from branches and scattered blossoms on the shadow-strewn path.

"You are easily distracted from your anger, Captain."

"Love must divert any man worthy of his sex."

"Call yours lust, my captain, and I will agree."

"Agree to lift your skirts, madame?"

"Agree that lust addles your thinking, Captain mine."

"Then let them go! Mortals are an unreliable breed. As long as you to do not desert me, I cannot care too much what eternity serves me."

"And yet we are not what we once were. These last years, how swift the passage. Marriages, births, and death made purposeful the fleeting hours. What shall we do alone without them?"

"We will be alone, my lady. All alone."

There came a sudden whispering in the wet hedges, a sad sweetness sighing in the air. A forgotten nightingale piped its melancholy song in the hawthorn. Then silence rushed in to fill the void. Like a door abruptly shutting, they were no more.

DEVON JANUARY 1846

It was Mrs. Mead's least favorite task. Each day for the past three months she had made the long trek from the gatehouse where she lived with her husband to the deserted manor house. Though housekeeper of Blood Hall for more than twenty-five years, she was never comfortable alone inside the empty house. Glancing back uncertainly over her shoulder, she wandered with lantern in hand from room to gloomy room.

Everything that had happened since she had opened her eyes this morning seemed purposely designed to spur her unease. She had awakened to find a raven perched on her windowsill. Then Tom, her husband, had come to the breakfast table whistling. Later, as she tidied up, she had spilled the salt. Ill omens, one and all. If that was not enough, there was the day itself to further depress her spirit. The air was chill, wet, and sour. Though it was still midmorning, dark gray clouds lay so thick above the moorland that it appeared to be dusk. Yet she knew that the strangeness in the air about her had little to do with the weather outside. Odd goings-on were part of the lore of Blood Hall. The house was haunted.

It had all begun when a pair of ill-starred lovers lost their heads to Cromwellian forces on the very flagstones of the entry to the ancient house in 1649. There were those who swore that during the first hundred years following the beheadings, the entry ran with blood once each year in commemoration.

"Nonsense!" Mrs. Mead muttered to herself. Still, she would rather not have been reminded of the tale just now. In her long years of service, she had witnessed many a strange happening at Blood Hall. Presences were sometimes felt when, in fact, no one was there. There were tales of young maids who claimed they were pursued in dark hallways by a headless but lecherous Cromwellian soldier. Then there were the many incidences of rearranged furnishings. One painting in particular, a hunting scene, was forever popping up in the Great Hall though the marquess repeatedly ordered it to be stored in the attic.

Yet, in spite of its reputation, the ancestral residence of the Kingsbloods was not always so forbidding. When the Marquess and Marchioness of Ilfracombe were in residence, the house echoed pleasantly with the laughter of their children and grandchildren. The tall windows reflected the golden warm light of roaring fires and dozens of tapers and lamps. Any man, woman, or child who passed by knew that love abided there and that a hot meal could be had for a knock at the kitchen door. But the family was away this winter.

After the marquess's dangerous lung congestion of the previous winter, his doctors had recommended that he retire until spring to warmer regions in order to spare his health. But the marquess was a strongly opinionated man who had held fast against the entreaties of both the doctors and his wife.

Mrs. Mead smiled in spite of her uneasiness as she recalled the outcome. She had received the full account of the interview indirectly from the marquess, who had told it to his valet, who had then related it to the marquess's London butler, who had informed the London housekeeper, who had then passed the gossip on to Blood Hall's housekeeper in the form of a letter. The marquess prided himself on being the only noble in the realm whose entire staff could both read and write. Even the scullery maids and stable boys had to learn to make their letters. If they refused to learn, they were dismissed for laziness—and without references.

It was no wonder that the queen herself had had to intervene with so formidable and opinionated a lord. She had summoned the marquess to tell him that she would take it as a personal insult if he remained in England for the winter and died of an inflammation of the lungs when, come spring, she would need his good sense and cool head to help her control the House of Lords. And so he had retired to sunny Italy, and the marchioness with him.

Now, as Mrs. Mead finished her inspection of the house and crossed the huge entry toward the front door, she gave a deep sigh of relief. Her worries had been unfounded. The next moment, knife-blade chill suddenly careened through the closed house, lifting her woolen skirts. With quickened breath, she opened the front door and hurried out. Once outside, she made the finger sign to ward off the evil eye then fished the key from her pocket to lock the door.

As she turned the key in the lock, a sound like distant moaning caught her ear. Turning, she glanced toward the moss-laden stone wall that helped enclose a rose garden at one end of the house. The wooden gate set within it stood open on its hinges.

For a moment she debated what to do. More than any other place on the Kingsblood estate, the garden was known to be a ghostly domain. His lordship had a strict policy concerning the garden; none of the staff was allowed inside it except for the Hall's longtime gardener. But the gardener had died just before Advent, and because no one else could be induced to work enchanted ground, her husband had been doing the job. And Tom was miles away checking the copse for poachers. While she had no desire to set even a toe inside the garden, she knew it could mean disaster if an animal strayed in and ate the rare and wonderful plants that bloomed, remarkably, in all seasons.

As she reluctantly approached the garden gate, her lantern held high, the wind again carried the sound of a moan. This time it seemed to come from within the garden. After stepping cautiously inside, she glanced around but saw nothing untoward. Advancing a little, she noticed that several rose bushes had come free of their tethers, that other shrubs had grown reedy with neglect, and that weeds had sprouted up between the flagstones. Gazing farther afield, she looked for signs that a ferret or red deer or, perhaps, a neighbor's cow had taken the opportunity to slip inside. But the walled-in garden was even darker than the day outside, and within a few yards, her lamplight was swallowed up in deep shadows.

Then she heard it again, distinctly and quite close by. It was a man's moan.

"Who's there?" she demanded more bravely than she felt.

She felt a tug on her skirts and slowly looked down. Her eyes widened, her pupils dilated, and her mouth fell open.

A man had crawled within the ring of her lantern light, his face showing ghostly pale where it wasn't blackened by dirt or splashed scarlet with blood. His hand, grimy and bloodstained, gripped her hem. "Help me!"

The hair on her nape lifted as she realized they were being watched. She glanced up at the single second-story window that overlooked the garden. The window was dark but even as she started to look away, a pale rosette like hoarfrost or a frozen human breath suddenly stenciled the glass. An instant later a second blossomed. Then two pairs of disembodied eyes appeared above the frozen mist.

" 'Tis them!" Mrs. Mead gasped.

Even as the words left her mouth a howling wind swooped down over the wall and enveloped her in a frigid blast that seared her ears even as it froze her toes.

"Hast thou no shame?" a voice within the wind roared. "Fie on't! Fie! 'Tis an unweeded garden that grows to seed; things rank and gross possess it merely. That it should come to this!"

Cowering, she looked down and saw that the man had disappeared. With a cry of fright, she snatched up her skirts and rushed panic-stricken from the garden. It had all been a trick of the spirits. When Blood Hall's ghosts were disturbed, there was no telling what they might do.

As she disappeared from view, the mortally wounded man watched helplessly while his life's blood emptied into the rich, pungent garden soil. He had come to Blood Hall seeking refuge and safety and peace. Now he would die. Alone.

The shadowy figures who had appeared in the second-story window entered the garden. They bent over the prostrate man, felt his failing pulse, heard his shallow too-rapid breaths, saw the red sea foam of pain break over his white lips. In the indigo shadows nearby, Death waited patiently.

"Is he dead?"

"He soon will be."

"Then come away. 'Tis no business of ours."

"I wonder, Captain. Could he not prove a diversion to our solitude?"

"Confound you for a meddling wench! Death has come for him. We must not interfere!"

"Very well. But he will be on your conscience!"

Chapter One

It was February, an unfashionable month for a society wedding. Sleet rattled like impatient fingernails upon the diamond-bright windowpanes of the imposing mansion in Berkeley Square. Earlier in the day the wedding procession into St. George's Church had been plagued by high gusts that had threatened to overset the carriages of the bridal party and guests. To the satisfaction of the bride and groom, a significant number of London's *ton* had braved the elements to witness the ceremony. Their perseverance had nothing to do with the fact that the groom was the Duke of Montrose nor that the bride's father, the Earl of Stockport, was a well-known and well-liked man. They had braved the elements in order to be present at a ceremony that brought together the ancient houses of Montrose and Stockport. The burgeoning middle classes had begun to threaten the foundation of the aristocratic ruling class. Any alliance that cemented and perpetuated the ascendancy of the nobility was to be looked upon with great favor during these trying days. In a show of unity, the wedding was being celebrated in lavish style.

Even now, though the wedding vows were scarcely two hours old, the fashionable journals of the city had already allotted several paragraphs in their late editions to commemorate the event.

> At St George's Church, Hanover Square, by the Right Reverend the bishop of London, His Grace Lord John Dashmore the Duke of Montrose, to Philidia Twinning, eldest daughter of Richard, Earl of Stockport, K.G. The bride wore a lovely dress of entirely British manufacture . . .

The items continued to include a brief mention of the elegant déjeuner, given by the Countess of Stockport to celebrate the event of her daughter's nuptials. That reception had been under way for more than an hour, yet many carriages still ringed Berkeley Square, waiting to discharge their passengers. Those lucky enough to be inside were subjected to still more lines and waiting.

One among the newly arrived did not share wholeheartedly in the celebration. Accompanied by her cousins, Lord and Lady Cowper, Lady Julianna Kingsblood had come solely for the purpose of proving to herself that she could endure anything, even the marriage of the Duke of Montrose, the man she loved, to another.

"I don't know that it's necessary, Gillie," Lady Letticia Cowper whispered to her cousin as they mounted the grand staircase of the Stockport residence. It was a measure of her own agitation that she resorted to the use of her cousin's childhood nickname in public.

"Lettie's right," Lord Alfred Cowper chimed in. "You've seen them wed. What else is there?"

Deliberately pretending to misunderstand her cousins' concern, Julianna replied, "Nonsense. As Grandfather's representative, I must do my duty." Though tall for a woman, she lifted her dark head an elegant fraction higher to look up the staircase toward the ballroom where the wedding party formed a receiving line. "The line is moving along nicely. A few moments' wait cannot discourage me from offering my congratulations to the bride and groom."

"But, Julianna, are you really . . . ?" Lettie's voice trailed off as her cousin turned to gaze at her. Born with her grandmother's Gypsy-dark hair and brows that arched arrogantly over startlingly light eyes the shade of Chinese celadon, Julianna possessed a strong-boned face and determined intelligence that was quite daunting.

"Really, Lettie," Julianna said calmly. "One would think you were jealous of the duke's happiness." She smiled in a vague, distant manner. "Don't tell me that you, like half the other ladies in London, fell in love with a façade of good looks and charm? That would be really too boring of her, wouldn't it, Alfred?"

Lady Letticia and her husband exchanged glances. During the Christmas holidays two months earlier, they had engineered a meeting between the Duke of Montrose and Julianna at their country house in Hempstead. It was known that the duke was seeking a bride and Julianna, at five-and-twenty and well past the age when she should be wed, possessed the pedigree and dowry worthy of a duke.

It seemed, at the time, that Julianna and the duke agreed with this assessment of their suitability. During

the holiday, the two had been inseparable. Julianna, who
had never before displayed anything like genuine interest
in a man, or in what she had previously deemed the
"senseless pastimes" of cards, charades, and singing, was
suddenly present to be paired with the duke for every
activity. They had been discreet, of course, and no one
suspected what Lettie's keen eyes saw, the brief touch of
hands, secret smiles across a crowded room, and their
tendency to linger behind the others when each evening
ended. When their guests departed at the end of the
week, Lettie had confidently proclaimed to her husband
that the match would end in marriage.

Then, three short weeks ago, the astonishing an-
nouncement had appeared that Lord Dashmore, Duke
of Montrose, would wed Lady Philidia Twinning, daughter of the Earl of Stockport. Lettie had gone immediately
to the marquess's London residence in Kensington only
to be told that Julianna was indisposed by a "sudden
illness" and could not be disturbed. Left to her own de-
vices, Lettie had come to the only conclusion: Julianna
had been jilted. Yet when Julianna did receive her a few
days later, the young woman had displayed neither surprise nor hurt over the announced nuptials. But Lettie
was not fooled. While Julianna's expression seldom gave
away her feelings, the calm surrounding her that day had
been charged with the same vibrant stillness that de-
scends just before a storm. Yet nothing could have
shocked Lettie more than Julianna's suggestion that they
attend the duke's wedding together.

"Tedious things, weddings," Alfred offered as he surveyed the ballroom, which was near bursting with guests.
"Don't know that I'd even attend my own, given another
opportunity."

"Lord Cowper!" Lettie said in deep affront as she turned to glare at him.

"Don't mean that I wouldn't marry *you*, Lettie," he answered with a reassuring pat on his wife's arm. "It's only this deuced noise and folderol I object to. Making a nuisance of oneself with bands and fanfare, tying up traffic and freezing the—the nether regions of one's guests, it ain't right." He brushed up one end of his neat ginger-blond mustache with a forefinger. "Marry nice and tidy, I say. None of this pomp and circumstance for me."

"Well, that's all very fine," Lettie replied in a hushed voice. "But you, my lord, have a daughter scarcely four. What shall I tell her? 'Tis Gretna Green for you, my girl, or naught at all?"

"Now, Lettie," he began, only to have his speech cut short by another soft feminine volley from his wife.

Julianna turned away from the quietly bickering couple but not from dismay or embarrassment, for they never behaved any differently in public or private. She, Lettie, and Alfred were distantly related and had known one another all their lives. From earliest childhood, they were always more at home in one another's company than anyone else's. Lettie and Alfred's eventual marriage was a foregone conclusion from an early age. Julianna had often jokingly declared that, since she couldn't have Alfred, she would never marry. How those fateful words had come back to haunt her these last days.

Marriage! Marriage! The word fairly buzzed in her head as Julianna allowed her myopic vision to trail over the crowd ahead. For vanity's sake, her much-hated spectacles were never worn in public. They lay tucked away in a drawer in her bedroom. She recognized a few faces, but none in particular caught her eye. Yet it seemed that the entire world was composed of couples. She felt vaguely conspicuous to be without a gentleman at her side, but quickly brushed the thought aside. In the seven years since her debut, she had managed without a suitor's sleeve to cling to. She would survive today. Or would she?

Following her thoughts, her gaze swept forward until it came to rest on the tall figure of the Duke of Montrose. Though her eyesight was poor, she had quickly learned to spot him even at a distance. His exceptional height, which was accentuated by a mane of combed and curled black hair and a broad pair of shoulders, was distinctive in any setting. Dressed in formal black habit, he stood a head above those nearest him. Memory supplied what her vision could not, an image of his stupendous good looks multiplied tenfold by the contrast of his snowy linen.

With a tiny shiver of suppressed emotion, Julianna averted her eyes. For one short, precious interval, this handsome nobleman had made her love him. No one knew that she had continued to meet secretly with the duke after Christmas. No one knew that by the power of his charm he had made her feel all the things she had thought nature had denied her. She had felt beautiful, womanly, desirable, and wanted by a man. Then three weeks ago he had told her he would marry another and that their brief association must be forgotten.

To do him credit, Dashmore had been amazingly frank with her. He admitted that he had briefly escorted Philidia Twinning the previous autumn, though nothing had come of it. Yet, inexplicably, Philidia's father, a man whom the duke said he considered to be a little mad, had belatedly decided that his daughter had been slighted by the duke and had threatened to bring action against him in the form of a breach-of-promise suit. There was nothing to the claim, of course, but rather than allow his family name to be enveloped in scandal, Lord Dashmore had agreed to the marriage. Duty before dishonor, he had said.

Julianna drew herself up until it felt as if an iron bar had been thrust down her backbone. She understood the duke's devotion to his family and the notion that duty and pride were inextricably bound and above selfish considerations. Pride had driven her to brave the day rather than hide away in misery. She had been schooled all her life in how to behave in any and all situations. Only someone had forgotten the lesson that covered a broken heart.

Julianna smiled and shook the hand of the first member of the wedding party and was handed in turn to the next, and then the next. Following their lead, she smiled and returned the remarks of those who spoke to her, all the while acutely aware that each step brought her closer to the moment when she must look into the face of the man she was certain she would always love.

Finally her hand was clasped firmly by a masculine hand wearing a heavy ring with the ducal crest. Then the startled gray eyes of the Duke of Montrose were staring down at her. His face went white and then red and then white again. The handsome countenance that she had always admired was suddenly as hollow and unimpressive as a waxwork figure's. She wondered fleetingly if her own features were likewise affected. His lips moved, soundlessly forming her name. She waited for him to speak, to say something that would make sense of this impossible situation, so that she might breathe again.

The next instant he recovered from his surprise, and his expression changed. The handsome face lost its pallor and regained its perfection. Yet, though his lips smiled, his eyes frowned. "Lady Julianna, a pleasure as always," she heard him drawl in the bored tones of the *ton*.

"Your Grace," she heard herself say stiffly. "Congratulations and many happy returns of the day."

That was not what she had meant to say. She had prepared a hundred times. Her words were to have been witty, bittersweet, enigmatic, and most of all memorable. But now the moment had slipped by her, and he was speaking again. What was he saying?

". . . regards to the marquess and marchioness." He bent over her gloved hand to formally salute it.

The brush of his lips sent a tremor through her that seemed strong enough to shake the chandeliers. Surely he knew what his touch meant to her. He couldn't mistake the meaning of the fingers trembling within his. Yet when he straightened, he didn't look at her but turned quickly to the lady standing beside him. "May I present my bride, Lady Philidia Dashmore, the new Duchess of Montrose."

Julianna nearly cried out at the curt dismissal, but she was being handed along and then the lady's face swam into focus. In the church, Julianna had been too far away from the center aisle to appreciate the bride's beauty. Now it was dauntingly in view. Hers was a doll's face with soft daffodil curls framing a high round forehead and pansy-brown eyes. She wore a splendid confection composed of pale-blue silk trimmed with white velvet roses. Diamonds and fresh white roses wreathed her hair. The legendary Montrose sapphire-and-diamond necklace clasped her lovely throat. The duchess was the ideal bride: young, beautiful, healthy, and wealthy.

"Lady Julianna," the bride intoned coolly, and laid a limp hand in hers. "How kind of you to come."

"Best wishes, Duchess." Julianna hastily released the lace-gloved hand lying inert in hers.

And then it was over.

For a dazed moment Julianna stood staring at nothing, and then she moved away from the last member of the wedding party. Her thoughts careened back to the duke's glance of utter surprise. It was clear that he had not expected her, perhaps had not wanted her presence. Chagrin edged under her surprise and stung like a rash across her cheeks.

"Thank heavens, that's done!" Alfred said at her back. "Luncheon is being served in the next salon. Shall we try it? I understand that the chef's crab tartlets shouldn't be missed."

"You take Lettie in," Julianna replied, gazing out across the colorful blur of silks and satins and laces. "I must speak to a few of Grandfather's associates. They should be reminded that he's merely on holiday, not on his last leg." She moved sharply away before the cousins could detain her.

"Well, that's done." Alfred sighed again.

"Do you think so?" Lettie watched Julianna's stately progress through the crowd. Unlike many tall women, Julianna never slouched to hide her superior height. "She's not herself. She might do something rash."

"Gillie?" The notion of Julianna being unpredictable clearly astounded him. "Why, she's the most sensible lady in London. Just look how she's behaved. One would think she scarcely knew Dashmore. I suspect you've made too much of the matter."

"I wonder," Lettie murmured, unconvinced, though she was pleased to see Julianna chatting with an older gentleman.

"Crab tartlets, my dear," he reminded her.

"Very well." Reluctantly she followed him.

Once Julianna saw her cousins depart the room, she quickly broke off the aimless conversation she had been having with a gentleman who formed part of the marquess's opposition party in Parliament. She wanted to be alone to collect her thoughts, which the confrontation with Lord Dashmore had scattered.

She turned to scoop up a frosted champagne flute just as a footman passed her with a tray. By nature she preferred fruit punch to wine, but her heart was beating too quickly and her hands were shaking. Perhaps the wine would calm her.

Without thinking, she gulped it down. The chilled bubbles were like swallowing tiny slivers of ice. Almost at once, a shaft of pain shot up into her head, and with it came a threat of the release of the emotions she had been banking down ever since their gazes met.

Dashmore had nearly cut her dead! How dare he worry that Lord Kingsblood's granddaughter might not know how to conduct herself!

She quickly consumed the rest of the champagne to douse the agitation within her. When her glass was empty, she reached for another and moved silently to the periphery of the room to watch and listen. Glancing about, she thought once more that only she was without an escort.

No young man had developed a *tendre* for her during

either of her two London Seasons. The experience had left her with a distaste for the callous marriage-market principles that motivated the Season and for the more frivolous members of the *ton,* about whom she had not resisted commenting unfavorably. Whispers among the society matrons were that she was too caustic, too severe, too opinionated, and worst of all, too well educated to make a suitable bride. It seemed the male "flower" of London's aristocratic set was in agreement with that judgment. At least they had not openly called her too "plain."

Friends, embarrassed for her, had made bad matters worse by thrusting their reluctant brothers and male cousins upon her, much to her dismay and their acute discomfort. When her second Season was at an end, she determined to never again expose herself to such an ordeal.

Then two months earlier, first love had come to her just as she was resigned to spinsterhood. Falling faster than any green girl, she had begun spinning out the daydreams that she had always denied herself, dreams of marriage, and children, and most of all, of love. No doubt she had made a fool of herself over the duke. Her only comfort lay in the fact that no one else knew. She'd not confided in a single soul, not even dear sweet Lettie.

Across the room the orchestra suddenly struck up a tune. Moments later the duke moved from the sideline, leading his bride out into the middle of the floor for the first waltz.

Through her misted view, Julianna watched them embrace, bitterness and resentment twisting inside her. The wide skirts of the bride's pale-blue gown belled out gracefully across the mirror-bright floor as the duke swept her into a turn. The murmurs of approval from onlookers confirmed Julianna's hazy impression that no bride had ever looked more lovely.

It is just as well I will not marry, Julianna thought humorlessly as she reached for a third champagne, as I do not look well in pale blue. Nor did she look especially well in the gown she was wearing. Of the palest shade of gray, it made her complexion appear sallow. Beneath her lace cap, her heavy dark hair had been scraped back tightly into a chignon that offered no tendril to soften the effect of her prominent features. Yet what did it matter when there was no man to admire her?

The sensible Lady Julianna, who'd never sought to marry, thought suddenly of the babies that she would never have and hold, of all the slights and humiliations of spinsterhood that not even being a marquess's grand-daughter would buffet her from, of all the empty hours that would never be filled by a man's kisses and embraces, and unsensible tears flooded her eyes.

As the music and the applause of the wedding guests whirled about her, she moved away from the sight of the handsome bridal couple moving in perfect harmony and into the shadow of one of the Corinthian pillars that formed the galley ringing the dance floor.

At first she didn't notice the two gentlemen into whose vicinity she had drifted, but their conversation drew her interest when the Duke of Montrose's name was spoken.

". . . speak the truth!" said the first man. "Lord Twinning refused Dashmore's suit last autumn!"

"You don't say?"

"There's more!"

Her attention now riveted on their conversation, Julianna edged closer to the column that separated her from the voices. Though she could not see them, their voices came clearly to her ear.

"Why do you suppose the wedding is taking place now rather than at the end of the Season?"

A titter. "There was a threat of a breach-of-promise suit."

An answering chuckle. "A promise ain't what was breached, old man!"

"You can't mean . . . ?"

"Can't I just!"

As Julianna strained forward to catch those final words her glass struck the marble column, shattering into what seemed to her a dozen noisy pieces, yet the men did not seem to notice. Their voices grew louder as their conversation became more grotesque.

". . . Don't agree with his methods, however, Montrose Abbey's near falling down. For all he's played fast and loose with his inheritance, Dashmore knows his duty. Heard he set himself up with a well-dowered spinster when he thought his ploy hadn't succeeded."

The second man's chuckles grew heartier. "He can rest easy now. Twinning settled forty thousand a year on the happy couple."

"I ain't romantically disposed to vinegary old maids but I am partial to treasure! Perhaps I shall look up Dashmore's spinster."

"Owing to the delicate nature of the bride, you'd be well advised to wait. Nine months should tell the tale!"

At their burst of laughter, Julianna could no longer contain herself and stepped forward. "What do you mean?"

The two gentlemen looked around, their faces reflecting astonishment and chagrin to be accosted by an angry young lady.

"Lady Julianna, isn't it?" the first man began. Julianna thought she recognized him as one of the younger members of Parliament who occasionally visited her grandfather. He glanced at the column behind which she had been standing, and his eyes widened in realization that she must have overheard them. "I don't know what you think you may have heard, but—"

"I heard enough," Julianna answered impatiently, wanting him to take back every word but determined to learn the truth. "You said Lord Dashmore forced this marriage. How is that possible?" Their innuendoes were clear enough, but it seemed impossible that they were correct.

The two men exchanged pained glances. However frank they might be with one another, they were too well trained to admit such scandalous things to a lady. "It was nothing, nothing at all!" the first man said, and gave his companion a censorious glance. "In any case, we weren't meant to be overheard. Come along, Leslie. Our glasses need refilling. You will excuse us, Lady Julianna. And may I suggest that the talk of men in their cups isn't to be trusted." He bowed to her and quickly moved away.

The second man turned to him to murmur under his breath but Julianna only caught the words "Bad form."

For a dazed moment Julianna watched their retreating backs, and then she jerked her head toward the pair who were still waltzing alone on the dance floor, eyeing them with new knowledge. Lady Philidia was so beautiful she might have had any man she wanted. Why had she allowed her father to bully the duke into submission, unless things were as she'd just heard, the bride carried his child?

Though the bridal couple were beyond the scope of her keenest vision, she noticed how well they moved together. The tilt of their heads as they gazed into one another's faces revealed an intimacy she had missed before. Suddenly she knew the whole horrible truth. They were not victims of an enraged father but a pair in triumph of their duplicity to outwit a father who had once refused to give his consent to the marriage. Like a roaring in her ears the gentleman's voice came back to her: "Nine months should tell the tale." Lady Philidia carried the duke's child!

Lurking always in the back of her mind had been the suspicion that the duke's attention to her was too wonderful to be genuine. Why should he have chosen her when there were so many more beautiful and younger ladies to choose from? Now she knew. It was because he needed a handsome dowry for Montrose Abbey. The marquess's promised gift to her of a lavish dowry had been the talk of London two years earlier. It had been his blustering but loving way of hoping to tempt a man to offer for her. Though she loved him, she had hated the blatant tactic. Now she knew how horribly it had rebounded on her. She was to have been Lord Dashmore's last recourse.

Memory flashed through Julianna's mind, of the fool she had made of herself the evening Lord Dashmore had come to tell her his news. How she had clung to his sleeve and begged him to reconsider, offering to go to her grandfather to enlist his aid. She had thought then that his angry rebuff was born of pride. Now she knew

that intervention was the last thing he wanted. He had
gambled and won his prize. If she had been less cautious,
she might now be in Lady Philidia's place—but without a
duke as her groom.

Julianna felt flushed and then chilled and then flushed
again. Every nerve in her body was screaming, the silent
shrieks running up and down her arms and legs like
swarms of ants. And beneath it all was the bracing chill
of the champagne she had imbibed. She felt suddenly
reckless, giddy with grief and shame and a rage so strong
she trembled as she stepped forward to lift yet another
glass of champagne from a passing tray.

She had always been good sensible Julianna, the one
who could always be counted on to do what was right.
She had never in her life done anything reckless or rash.
Yet as she took another long sip of courage in the form
of champagne, she felt an alarming tendency toward
recklessness flowing through her.

Lifting her eyes from her glass, she focused on the
happy couple still twirling about the floor. How certain
they were of themselves and their position in the world.
No matter what they had done to attain this moment,
simply by marrying they had become respectable in new
and inviolate ways. The sham was beyond her power to
tolerate.

Feeling humiliated, cheated, and goaded by the courage of wine, Julianna stepped out onto the dance floor
and into the path of the bride and groom as they would
have spun past her.

She smiled as they stumbled into her, heard their startled gasps, and felt more than saw dozens of eyes turn
curiously toward her. Let them stop and stare, she

thought. She had eyes only for the deceitful duke and his duplicitous bride.

As if he guessed what was coming, Lord Dashmore put out a hand toward her and said in a warning tone, "Julianna!"

Lady Philidia's gentle gaze suddenly sharpened and her mouth thinned at his use of her Christian name.

Julianna realized that even a beautiful woman could be made less so by ugly thoughts. Smiling a smile that had no connection to her heart, she lifted her nearly empty crystal flute. "I wish to make a toast!" she said in a rich, carrying voice. "To the Duke and Duchess of Montrose. To the smug certainties of marriage! And to all the happiness that can be bought at the expense of genuine love and true feelings for forty thousand pounds sterling a year!"

Over the collective gasp of outrage that came at her from all sides, Julianna trained her gaze hard upon the duke's shocked face and whispered, "You were my last hope for happiness." She said it because she had no pride left and no hope of any future she cared to think about.

Turning, she walked out of the ballroom, uncaring for the whispers that followed her.

Lettie came hurrying toward her. "My dear! You shouldn't . . ."

Ignoring her cousin's distress, Julianna turned to Alfred. "Will you fetch my coat? I believe I've done quite enough celebrating for one day."

Behind her, she heard the incredulous voices of the *ton* and knew that she would never again be invited to any fashionable event in London. But, amazingly, she did not care. Like the champagne rushing hotly through her veins, she felt warm, strong, and inviolate. Tomorrow, when she and world were sober, she would no doubt regret every second of the last minutes. But not now. And maybe not tomorrow.

Chapter Two

❦

Seated in the main salon of her grandfather's Regency-style mansion in Kensington, Julianna passed a cup of tea to her cousin and smiled as if there were nothing unusual in her inquiry. "What news do you bring, Lettie?"

Lettie gave Julianna a considering glance as she accepted the refreshment. A week had passed since the duke's wedding, but the shock of her cousin's behavior lingered. Gossip ran rampant in the best salons, gentlemen's clubs, and gaming halls; and the scandal showed no indication of ebbing. She and Alfred had come to the conclusion that Julianna should be confronted with the results of her conduct and made aware of certain inescapable facts. However, now that she faced Julianna, Lettie didn't know where to begin.

Often there was no clue to Julianna's state of mind revealed in the face she put upon the world. She kept her emotions penned up as neatly as her dark hair. Yet today there was a hectic color in Julianna's complexion and a burning intensity in her light-green eyes that betrayed emotions barely contained. Tact seemed in order. "There's nothing to tell, Gillie, really."

Julianna lifted one dark brow imperiously. "If you won't tell me the truth, I shall simply ask someone else."

Lettie pinkened at the set-down. "Very well. There are those who think you were wronged by Lord Dashmore and thereby provoked unendurably."

Julianna blinked at the mention of the duke's name, but her voice remained calm. "Who, pray tell, are these superior beings who dare to defy common gossip?"

"I for one. Alfred for another. Though you won't admit it, I suspect Lord Dashmore gave you to expect certain things. To withdraw so suddenly, and then marry—"

"That's quite enough." Julianna's rich voice cut incisively through her cousin's speech. "However well meant, your opinion is the least useful to me. Surely there are other opinions?"

Unable to contain her own emotions any longer, Lettie burst out, "Some of the most vicious, unkind rumors I've ever heard are circulating about you, Gillie! They say that you are deluded, that you've been made hysterical because . . ."

"Because?"

Lettie's small mouth quivered dangerously, "Be-because you misunderstood Dashmore's show of kindness over the Christmas holidays. They are calling him a victim of his own good intentions and selflessness."

"Selflessness?" Julianna swallowed the temptation to tell her cousin the extent of his "selflessness," that he had been willing to marry anyone, even a vinegary old maid, in order to save his estates. "Because I'm a plain, middle-aged spinster, I'm damned from the beginning!"

"Gillie! Your language!"

Julianna smiled tightly at her cousin's shock. "It's a

nasty habit I picked up from Grandfather. No doubt he'd disapprove if he knew, so don't tell him."

To distract her cousin from what was certain to become a lecture, Julianna turned to squint at the Empire tabletop upon which a pot of fiery red geraniums sat beside the tea service. With an impatient sigh, she whipped a pair of spectacles from her pocket and perched them on her nose. Instantly her vision improved and every detail of the early-nineteenth-century room came brilliantly and clearly into focus. Bending forward, she snapped off a yellowing leaf from the geranium and dropped it in an empty hand-painted candle dish.

"There. One must keep up appearances. Mama cares so much for appearances. I wonder what she'll say when she learns what I have done?" Julianna smiled a tight, uneasy smile. "Thank heavens she and Papa are in Bombay. The news won't reach them for at least a month. By then it shall be old hat."

From anyone else, Lettie would have been shocked by such callousness, but she knew Julianna's indifference to her parents' opinion was the result of her unusual upbringing. The marquess and marchioness had taken Julianna in at Blood Hall when she was less than two years of age so that her mother, their son's wife, would be relieved of caring for a small child during a difficult confinement that resulted in twins. That arrangement had lasted nearly four years. Ever since, Julianna had felt closer to her grandparents than her parents and five younger siblings. When her father received a diplomatic post in Bombay eight years ago, Julianna had begged to be allowed to stay in London with the marquess and marchioness. The only reason she was not now with them in Italy was because her grandparents insisted that she accept social invitations for the Season, in the hope that she would yet make a match.

Lettie sighed softly. She and Alfred had promised the marchioness to do their part in seeking out a suitable husband for their cousin—with the present disastrous results.

Julianna turned to Lettie with a slight frown, momentarily having forgotten her. "But where were we? Ah yes, my unforgivable behavior. I could blame it on the champagne," she said airily. "I drank three or four glasses. Never do that. A dreadful head results. I should have known better. After all, I'm said to be quite intelligent though, God knows, it didn't show in whom I chose to love."

Lettie held her breath, for this was the first time Julianna had made such an admission. She might impart more if not interrupted.

"I quite forgot myself when Dashmore glanced my way," Julianna continued, her tone becoming self-mocking. "Why do you suppose I thought he was enamored of me? My features are too bold even for my taste. Mama says I inherited my looks and temperament from the male side of the family, neither of which does credit to a lady."

"You are too hard on yourself," Lettie temporized. "Some men—"

"Some men!" Julianna's voice crackled with contempt. "That is just the point. *No* man would joyfully choose such a wife as I would make." Her voice broke on the final word. "Oh, but it hurts, Lettie!" Her green eyes grew suspiciously bright behind her lenses. "How it hurts to be ignored by all the gentlemen! I've never said this to anyone, and you must never remind me of it. But it hurts most damnably!"

"Oh, Gillie!" Lettie reached out and grasped Julianna's hand, shaken to see her strong, proud cousin brought to tears. The common consensus was that Julianna was not a beauty. Yet Lettie thought that it was a shame some eligible young gentleman could not see Julianna as she appeared now. Emotion had brought color to her face and an inner light to her eyes that Alfred had once admiringly called a "magnificent wildness." Surely it was a sin—abet a small one—that Julianna so seldom revealed glimpses of the passionate nature she possessed. If she had showed this side of her nature to Lord Dashmore, she might not have lost him. "Gillie, you mustn't be bitter. Nearly every lady has lost a gentleman she admired."

"Not *you*," Julianna answered quickly, wiping suspicious moisture from her cheeks with a finger. "You've always had Alfred."

Lettie quickly blotted out an eight-year-old image of her handsome Italian music teacher. The memory of their brief, chaste kisses was the only secret she had ever kept.

"So, what am I to do now?" Julianna asked, recovering her composure as quickly as she had lost it. "Must I retire from society? Marry a country curate? Go into a cloister? Ah, perhaps I should become a governess. What about your home? Your children might need me." When her cousin didn't respond, Julianna drew in her temper a fraction. "Forgive me, Lettie. You were telling me the news. Surely there's more."

Lettie moistened her lips nervously, for she had not yet told the truth. "It's said the gossip has quite upset

Lady Philidia." She paused, watching for signs of another outburst. When it didn't come, she continued. "Lord Dashmore is taking her to the continent. They leave at the end of the week."

"How convenient I've made it for them." Julianna paused as once more tears stung her eyes. She had wondered how they would keep the public from learning their little secret. "Yes, I played into their hands very nicely."

Lettie moved forward on her chair. "Did you love him so very much?"

"Love?" The question struck Julianna as irrelevant, considering the outcome, and sparked the wit she often used to protect her true feelings. "Say rather that I was 'misled by fancy's meteor ray.' " She frowned as the rest of Burns's lines came to mind: *By passion driven;/ But yet the light that led astray,/ Was light from heaven.*

Did she believe that? If so, then why did her heart resist it? For, astonishingly, it seemed to whisper, *Not passion driven. There's more to love than that. Believe it!*

She looked at her cousin. "My feelings for Lord Dashmore were the last delusions of a put-upon-the-shelf spinster. I was infatuated, dazzled, flattered. No doubt we'd have been miserable within a year had we wed. If you recall, we argued in your home within five minutes of our first meeting." She refused to add that it had been the most exhilarating moment of their association. "Unlike you, I can't keep silent when I see or hear wrong."

Lettie smiled knowingly. "You could become accustomed to it."

Julianna looked askance. "You mean I would be forced to bite my tongue a dozen times a day. That would leave me raw and bleeding each nightfall. No, I've given the matter some thought these last days, and I've decided that the only sort of spouse I could endure would be one who appeared at my whim." She laughed as the fanciful notion took instant root in her imagination. "I would conjure him up like a genie at the dinner hour for genteel conversation. Then, if he began to bore me, *poof,* I'd make him disappear. That way I should be free of the encumbrances of being a wife in every way that displeased me."

"You'll regret your sharp tongue one day," Lettie warned. It had never occurred to her that any woman should ever want to do anything else but marry and raise children.

Julianna gave her cousin an affectionate glance. "Women like you are fortunate, Lettie. You have looks, charm, and a pleasant, biddable disposition. Grandfather is the only man I know who prefers me as I am. He once said that the *ton* had yet to produce a gentleman my equal."

Cheerfully Lettie seconded, "Perhaps he's right."

"In that case," Julianna replied, "I shall never marry. For if the right man were to be born today, I'd be some years past fifty by the time he was ready to wed!"

"You mock me when I'm being kind!"

"Then go and be kind to those who would appreciate it!" The words were scarcely out of her mouth before Julianna realized that, deplorably, her temper had again gotten the better of her. "Forgive me, Lettie! I'm in the foulest of moods. My tongue should be cut out."

"No doubt you would kick and bite instead," Lettie answered cautiously, yet Julianna's rare apology pleased her no end. There was another subject upon which she and Alfred had agreed Julianna should be informed. "I must tell you, Julianna, that you may expect to be snubbed by all those with high codes of behavior, Dashmore's and the Earl of Stockport's friends, and anyone else who seeks to be in their good graces." She paused but her words seemed to have had no visible effect on her cousin. "Have you thought of leaving London? You could come with me to Hempstead. It would do you a world of good and I could use the company."

"I love you too much to subject you to my temper on a daily basis," Julianna returned, "but I've already decided to leave London."

"Where will you go?"

"To Blood Hall."

The mention of the Kingsblood ancestral home did not reassure Lettie. "But that's miles away from what anyone would call civilization. Besides, the marquess closed the house. There won't be any servants about. The place will smell of mildew and dust."

"I like solitude. As for cobwebs and dust, I'm not afraid of things that can be remedied by a broom. I won't require a full house staff, nor do I want them. I wish to be alone."

"Mr. Owen won't like it one bit."

"Mr. Owen may go to the devil!" She smiled at her cousin's gasp of outrage. "Though he's Grandfather's solicitor, Mr. Owen doesn't govern my comings and goings. When Grandfather left I promised that I'd continue to see to his personal correspondence and keep him abreast of the news. Naturally I'd like to visit his holdings so that I may give him a firsthand report."

"It will be cold," Lettie countered. "Winters can be particularly cruel on the moors. You'll catch frostbite and chilblains." She added under her breath, "And what of the ghosts!"

"What a pleasant picture you paint, Cousin. The cold, the loneliness, and hauntings! I've never actually witnessed a manifestation, but the experiences of others have made for wonderful stories. I can hardly wait."

"This is most unlike you," Lettie replied, ruffled by her cousin's refusal to be serious. "You must be reasonable."

"But I am," Julianna answered, though until this moment she hadn't given Blood Hall a thought. She had decided to join her grandparents in Italy. "I should also visit Little Hangman Mine. Grandfather has received considerable correspondence as a result of an incidence of violence there several weeks ago."

Lettie's eyes grew round. "You mustn't become involved with radicals!"

"Whyever not?" Julianna asked in a maddeningly reasonable tone. "As Grandfather's private secretary, I'm well versed in his position concerning many matters. He believes in working by strictly constitutional methods. He says if Unionists are to succeed, there must be laws to regulate them. Yet those who would most benefit by such laws are threatening, by their violence, the possibility of them being enacted."

"I won't pretend to understand you," Lettie admitted with a sigh. "Even Alfred says that you quite perplex him with your persistent interest in politics and government."

"It's in our blood, Lettie. We are Kingsbloods."

"*You* are a Kingsblood. I'm only a distant relation. I wish you'd come home with me and forget unions and strikes. If miners will murder their own, what makes you believe that they will blanch to do violence to you?"

"They've no grievance against Blood Hall, dear

Cousin," Julianna replied. "They know the marquess champions their cause. A show of family force could be useful in keeping down mischief just now."

The words, the very sound of them, and the possibility of being useful made the blood pump through Julianna's veins more strongly than it had in weeks. She stood up abruptly. "I don't mean to rush you, Lettie, but either eat your cake or put it down. I have much to do and very little time left in which to do it."

Insulted, Lettie put down her china plate with such force the silver fork jumped off it and onto the floor. "Very well! See if I come to cheer you up again!" She snatched up her purse and stood.

Ignoring her thorny glance, Julianna hugged her cousin about the waist. "Oh, but you have, Lettie! You've given me an idea for something to do, and I did so need it! When the weather warms, you must come and bring the children to Devon. The sea will be calm and trout fishing in the streams spectacular! But go now, for I've things to do."

Lettie was bundled out so quickly she left behind one of her favorite lace mittens. Julianna spotted it on the chair and picked it up to admire it. It was a tiny thing, so small it seemed made for a child. Julianna pressed it between her hands for comparison. While her palms were no broader than Lettie's, her fingers were much longer. Julianna stared at her hands. They were strong and capable, the sort of hands that seemed fashioned for work rather than lace mittens. The smooth skin and perfect white crescents of her nails were the only indications that the hands belonged to a lady.

She had made a fool of herself in the pursuit of a man. A latent but desperate envy of other women with their suitors had moved her to abandon all good sense when a handsome man had at last smiled at her. The thought of being loved by a duke had made her proud, and that false pride had brought her lower than she had ever thought possible. She would never make that mistake again.

She turned and rang for Chapman. By the time he came in answer, she was half finished with a note for Mr. Owen. Once the note had been passed to a footman for delivery, she went to stand at the window and look out on the snowy day where the last light ebbed away before her eyes.

Another life, far removed from balls and parties, and romance, awaited her at Blood Hall. She was not afraid of the loneliness nor the difficulties that lay before her. But she shivered with the thought of living the rest of her life in the absence of love.

How did one survive, she wondered with renewed trembling, when one no longer believed in love? It was as if a great door had slammed shut inside her, and nothing of light or gaiety or sudden joy would ever escape from behind it.

Julianna walked down a long, darkened aisle. Like a tunnel tapering away toward infinity, there seemed to be no end to it. Softly at first and then gradually rising, she heard whispering voices at the edges of the darkness on either side of her. She could not understand them but the hair at her nape bristled.

Suddenly a pin-prick of light appeared ahead of her.

Panicky thoughts whirled through her mind. Where was she? Why was she here? She clutched her hands only to realize that she carried a bouquet of flowers.

The light grew. Like a lantern's glare, its intensity blocked out all before it.

She turned to flee but there was nothing behind her, no way back from which she had come. Turning around, she faced the widening circle of white light.

The voices became more distinct now. In the darkness beyond her view she knew that she was being watched.

"Poor Lady Julianna, so eager to believe him!"

"Who can blame a man for trying to save himself?"

"But to think she believed his suit sincere!"

"A homely spinster. He'd find her embrace colder than a witch's teat!"

Her mouth worked spasmodically in protest but her words made no sound. Who were the disembodied voices who jeered at her? Perspiration broke out upon her upper lip and brow.

The light burst upon her with blinding suddenness. There before her was a church altar. Every pew was filled with people craning forward eagerly for a better view of her.

Her heart pounded in heavy, slow strokes that tapped at her temples with a pressure bordering on pain, but her eyes were fixed on the man at the foot of the altar, his back to her.

Love, pure and unfettered, burst from her, but her hands were shaking as she quickened her step. Lord Dashmore waited at the altar rail to marry her!

She called his name, unmindful of the new rumblings of the crowd. If only she could reach him in time, no one would ever be able to take him away from her again. She stumbled as she reached him, her hand groping awkwardly for his arm.

He turned and looked at her. Contempt, pity, and distaste marred every line of his handsome face.

She recoiled from the intensity of his gaze. And then she noticed that he was not alone. Beside him stood Lady Philidia, all beauty in pale blue. Upon her finger was a gold wedding band so bright it hurt Julianna's eyes.

Soft despair and hopeless grief roiled up from her bowels as she turned away. The jeering faces, leers, and knowing smiles of the gentlemen pressed in on her. The simpering smiles of the ladies grew to grotesque proportions, crowding out her view of the duke and his bride.

They knew! They all knew that she had been jilted. They knew that the Duke of Montrose loved another, had never wanted her, only the dowry he had hoped she would bring him.

She turned to flee, yet her legs wouldn't work. Laughter ricocheted off the vaulted ceiling and shook the lead-glass windows. Humiliation clawed at her, shredding her emotions into ribbons of shame, rage, and inexpressible pain.

No! she cried. *No! You mustn't laugh! Mustn't!*

Julianna jerked awake, gasping for breath as if she had run a long race. But she knew what had happened. She had fallen asleep in her hired traveling coach. Sagging weakly back against the cushions of the seat, she waited for her heart to cease galloping.

The journey westward had been no easier than she had imagined it would be. Bad weather had stranded her more than once, causing a day's delay each time. The rain had been incessant. Even now the wind pushed it past the coach windows in long, wet streamers, pervading every corner of the coach with a cloying chill. Her back

ached from the constant jostling, and her fingers were
stiff with cold. Even her shoulders ached from the effort
of sitting upright for long, tedious hours. But all the dis-
comforts of the daylight hours were better than the tor-
ments of the nights.

The nightmares had begun on the evening following
Lettie's visit. Each time it was the same. The long, dark
corridor, the watching eyes, the whispers, then Lord
Dashmore and his rejection. She had even awakened the
guests with her cries at the last roadside inn where she
had spent the night. Afraid to spend another night at an
inn, she had decided to travel the rest of the way straight
through. But even now, in the light of day, the nightmare
followed her. A tremor of the dream's aftermath shook
her. She felt both feverish and cold and in need of fresh
air.

After pushing back the curtain, she opened the coach
window in time to see a long gray-green hedgerow pass
in a blur as the coach swung off the main highway that
led to Ilfracombe and into the narrow rutted lane that
led to Blood Hall. She recognized this place as one her
grandparents had often pointed out to her. It was the
spot where, forty-five years earlier, her grandparents had
met on a day very much like this one. One overturned
carriage, one bedraggled fiancée, and two people whom
fate had designed to be together; that is how the
marchioness had described that first meeting with her
husband. Her grandfather had leapt into the road like a
highway man of old to stop her grandmother's coach. It
was the stuff of romantic dreams and fairy tales, only
theirs had come true.

Julianna closed the window and lay back against the
cushions. She was nearly home now. In less than an hour

the chimneys of Blood Hall would be visible in the distance. In less than two hours she would be inside its thick walls, dry and secure. But fate had not connived a wonderful future for her. No man would cross her path through happenstance. No unexpected meeting would blossom suddenly into romance. No . . .

"Fiddlesticks!" Julianna muttered, and scotched her thoughts. Was she to become maudlin at every reminder of love? No! The dreams would end. They must!

Seeking what little comfort there was to be had in the small interior, she wound her fur rug more tightly about her legs. To further distract herself, she pulled from her fur muff a pair of letters that she had brought with her from London. Both missives were several weeks old and were addressed to the marquess. She had read them when they arrived and then dutifully recounted the contents to her grandfather in her weekly correspondence. But now seemed a good time to refresh her memory about the particulars.

The first was in the childishly round hand of Mrs. Mead, Blood Hall's housekeeper. She'd written to inform her employer of the fact that her husband was on the lookout for a new gardener and that they eagerly awaited the marquess's return in the spring.

Julianna's gaze lingered a moment on the phrase "have every hope that the garden will be in good condition. . . ." Why should they not? Surely the servants would not have allowed anything to happen to the rose garden? It had been the talk of Devonshire for two hundred years because it remained in bloom year-round. In any case, she would soon learn the answer.

She read the second letter more slowly. Its contents were grave and potentially more harmful than a neglected garden. It was from Jed Coleman, the manager or captain of Little Hangman Mine. It told of a thwarted plot to blow up the Kingsblood engine house near Little Hangman bluff. The constable believed the miners were to blame for the attempt, while the miners blamed outside agitators. Jed gave credit for averting the disaster to an anonymous note that gave the location and time set for the explosion. He went on to say he feared that the informant "could not be relied upon in future" but that firm steps would be taken avert further trouble. In the meantime, he awaited the marquess's advice in the matter.

Julianna folded the letter and smoothed it carefully with her fingers, wondering what her grandfather had written in reply. Despite the constable's doubts, she believed the miners' claim that they weren't responsible for the attempt to destroy the engine house. Its destruction would have put them out of work. Winters on the north coast of Devon were difficult enough without adding starvation to the hardship. As for outside agitators, she wondered who they were and why they should choose Kingsblood's mine as their target.

Finally her thoughts turned to the informant. Whoever he was, he must be educated well above the average miner, who often went to work at age six, in order to write a note. Perhaps he was kin to one of Blood Hall's servants. The marquess believed that an educated man was a reasonable man, and so he provided basic schooling for his servants. Then too, the informant must have the confidence of the troublemakers, or how else would he have known of their plot? Was he secretly working against them, or was he merely a coward among their number? Though Jed Coleman thought he could not be relied upon in future, she wondered if that was true.

By the time the coach swung through the iron gates and onto the cobblestone carriageway that led to the entrance of Blood Hall, the sound of the gale coming in off the North Atlantic was no more than a distant rumble. The rain had ceased. The sun had not yet set, and the sunset colors seeping through the heavy clouds on the horizon heralded a clearing sky. The light spread over the granite walls of the ancient house, turning its porch, oriels, and many chimneys sienna red.

When the coach came to a halt on the drive, Julianna opened the door and stepped wearily down before the coachman could aid her. The first thing she noticed was that the house was dark. Not a single flicker of light could be seen from any window. Disappointed that there would be no great roaring fire to welcome her, she turned to look back up the lane and saw two well-bundled figures hurrying up the drive. She knew at once who they were and forestalled their apologies as they reached her. "I assume you didn't receive my message."

"No, Lady Kingsblood," the groundskeeper and his wife, the housekeeper, chorused in surprise. Their gazes went immediately past her to view the dark interior of the coach. "Be the marquess with ye, yer ladyship?" Tom Mead asked, doffing his cap to reveal a thatch of graying hair.

"No. I'm quite alone," Julianna answered, and turned to the housekeeper, whose face was bright red from her exertions. "I'm sorry my message didn't reach you before I did. However, that's of no importance now. You may go in and light a fire in the Great Hall. No, on second thought, I'll eat in the kitchen." The Great Hall wouldn't warm quickly, and she was much too exhausted to wait. "Do you think you can manage a cold plate and a small glass of cherry cordial? I'm chilled to the bone."

"Of course, my lady," Mrs. Mead answered, curtseying in response to the tall young lady's regal tone. "Only—"

"That will do, I think," Julianna said abruptly, cutting off what she knew would be some excuse. She was too tired and sore to consider anyone else's needs just now. "Tom can take my things upstairs while the coachman sees to the horses. I trust there's fodder in the stables and that a bed can be found for the man?"

The Meads exchanged glances. "You weren't expected, my lady," Mrs. Mead replied, the better spoken of the two. "Which ain't to say you won't be well taken care of. Tom'll make a place for the coachman. There's always the Chinese Room for your ladyship."

"I trust it's in better order than the rose garden," Julianna responded with just a hint of her usual wit.

"The garden's comin' along, me lady," Tom quickly offered. "Got a new man to do the work. A rough 'un but good with his hands, he is."

At that moment a gust of wind careened around the corner of the coach, its force staggering Julianna. The Meads came quickly to her rescue, but the deep-down shivering she had been holding at bay broke loose, making her teeth chatter.

"Come along, yer ladyship," Tom urged as he and his wife steered Julianna toward the door. "Ain't a fit night for decent folk to be out."

Thirty minutes later, Julianna sat at one end of the thick oak table in the cavernous kitchen of the old manor house, her shivering body wrapped in the two woolen blankets Mrs. Mead had brought down from upstairs.

Idly running her fingers over the glossy surface of the worn, sway-backed table, she watched as the house-keeper poured steaming water from the kettle into a teapot.

"I don't suppose the house has been aired since autumn," Julianna said, recalling the faint, musky smells that had greeted her at the door.

"No, my lady," Mrs. Mead answered. She set the teapot on the tray she had prepared and brought it to the table along with the decanter of cherry cordial Lady Julianna had ordered. "Tom thought we'd best keep the windows shut, what with just the pair o' us to see to it all. O' course, once your maid arrives, we'll be turning out the whole."

"My maid won't be coming," Julianna answered, feeling under no obligation to explain that her maid had been "ruined" by one of the marquess's London footmen, and that though a wedding had been arranged hastily, the pair had been turned out—with references.

Julianna glanced down at the thick slice of ham set before her. Far from being appealing, the dark pink meat looked difficult to chew and more difficult to swallow. Because Mrs. Mead was hovering about, she picked up a piece of bread, surprised to find that it was tough and dry, lathed it with butter, and took a bite, grimacing at the rancid taste.

After dropping it back on her plate without comment, she reached for the teapot, but Mrs. Mead was quicker. "Allow me, my lady."

Sugar and milk were added, Julianna noting gratefully that the milk didn't curdle in the tea.

Mrs. Mead watched in concern as the young lady picked at her dinner. She had noticed first thing the dark

circles under her ladyship's eyes and the drawn look of
her cheeks. Unless she missed her guess, the young mistress was sickening. "I'm that sorry, my lady, there's
nothing better to serve you. I could run back to the cottage and fetch you a proper meal. Me and Tom was just
about to sit down to our tea when we heard your coach."

"Thank you," Julianna replied, "but I'll just finish my
tea and go up to bed."

"Ye were not thinkin' to stay here alone?" Tom exclaimed as he came through the kitchen door.

"Whyever not?" Julianna responded in frank surprise.

"Well, 'tis this way, my lady," Mrs. Mead began only to
be halted by her husband's frown.

"What with the house bein' all shut up," Tom cut in,
"and just Ellie and me to see to it, 'tain't fit for a lady."

"I'm not afraid of a little dust and disorder."

"We should tell her the truth, Tom," his wife said
firmly, and turned to Julianna. "Not above a month ago,
I come to the Hall and found the garden gate off the
latch. That's where I saw it."

"Saw what?" Julianna pressed in mystification.

"A dying man. At least, I thought it were a man.
Grabbed me skirt afore I could get away." The older
woman's face went quite pale. "When I come back with
Tom, it was gone!"

As Julianna turned a doubtful look on the groundskeeper, Tom only smiled and wagged his head. " 'Twas
her tale, all right. Only I said to her, 'Someun's played a
joke on ye, Ellie.' "

"Who would dare?" Julianna questioned, angered that
anyone would play so grisly a joke on an old woman.

"Some of the local lads," he answered. "There's trouble brewin', what with talk of un-ion-i-za-tion." He pro-

nounced the final word as if he chewed a hunk of tough meat.

"Why would miners upset a housekeeper?" Julianna asked.

"Mebbe it weren't the lads." Mrs. Mead's softly spoken words drew Julianna's attention. "Mebbe it were the ghosts!"

"Now, Ellie," Tom said. "Ye've no count to be frightenin' her ladyship."

"Having been reared at Blood Hall, I'm not likely to be frightened by ghosts," Julianna declared, relieved to be discussing something with which she was familiar. "If it was a ghost you saw, Mrs. Mead, then I'm relieved. Ghosts are old tenants and know they are welcome. That alone should keep strangers from breaking in."

She cast a wry glance at her dinner then picked up the decanter of cherry cordial. "If that's all, then I will retire before I fall asleep on my feet. You may consider yourselves dismissed for the night."

"But, my lady—"

"I insist!" Julianna said impatiently, her temper rising from exhaustion. She rose heavily to her feet, dragging the blankets with her. "Go home, both of you. You may come again in the morning to make my breakfast and light the fire in the Great Hall. Good night!"

As she left the room Julianna overheard the couple speaking together in low tones and paused to listen.

"Shockin', her travelin' about the countryside like a farmer's wife. She looks ill, if you ask me. Where is her maid?"

"Ben't none of yer business, Ellie. Her ladyship does as she sees fit."

Smiling at this judgment, Julianna continued up the

stairs, clutching the decanter of cherry cordial to her breast.

In the Great Hall, a flame suddenly flickered in one of the oriels. As mysterious as bog fire, the shimmering icy-green incandescence illuminated two shadows without substance but whose thoughts were as vivid as sound.

"Little Gillie. How she's grown!"

"Go quickly, Captain, and wake him!"

"Wake who?"

"Him!"

"Why should I?"

"Confound thee for a dullard, Captain. 'Tis plain as the wart on your face that she is the reason *he* resides at Blood Hall."

" 'Tis not plain to me. And I have no wart!"

"Then you have a bone to pick with your Maker, if ever you two should meet."

"Whatever do you mean?"

"That . . . ah, appendage, Captain, that which one could only in generosity call a nose."

"What's wrong with it? 'Tis a fine, manly nose."

"A trifle large, perhaps?"

"Say not, lady. 'Tis said to express a man's endowments in other parts."

"Another wives' tale laid to rest."

"Unkind, lady! Must I once again prove otherwise?"

"You may strive to, Captain . . . after you've awakened *him.*"

"He won't like it. He haunts this house more cautiously than we do."

"He is young and sad. Show him Lady Julianna. I predict a change."

"You predict mischief and romance! We cheated Death to save him. I don't like it. I've not felt the same since that night."

"Oh, but why were we able to save him if not for a purpose?"

"I don't know, madame, and that makes me uneasy."

"Go wake him, then I shall give you ease."

"Aye, madame. And then I shall prove that, like Pinocchio, my most cherished endowment can grow to impressive size!"

Chapter Three

He watched her a long while. He didn't know why he had come here. He had been sleeping, dreaming, and then something had awakened him, drew him to this room despite every reasonable caution to the contrary. Even now he could not say why he remained, just that the compulsion to do so was too strong to resist. The intuitive sense that something waited for him in this room, something momentous, soul-searing, and completely unknown, pushed him to learn its secret.

He stood in the shadow of her bed curtains, ready to disappear into the blackness upon the instant. How still she lay, quite like the dead. The thought amused him. For weeks he had been no more substantial in the world than a breath of wind, a bump in the night, a trailing afterthought, a glimpse of nothingness edging in at the corner of someone's vision. Now that might change. She was, after all, very much alive and thereby an intruder into his new existence.

The meager moonlight slanting through the window brought her features into relief, and with it the slight trembling of her parted lips as her breath came and went. He had not been about when she arrived. From what little he saw and heard later, she was no simpering beauty, nor possessed of what one would call a pretty disposition. Now he had the impression of youthful womanliness brought momentarily into submission by the gentle care of sleep. Yet there was a compelling quality in her face that even sleep could not erase.

She moved, turning onto her side toward him and drawing her legs protectively up to her chest. She must be cold, he thought. The errant desire to dive beneath the covers and warm her came unexpectedly to his mind.

He moved forward stealthily and, reaching out, almost touched the long, dark braid lying by her left arm. Like a switch of raw silk it was thick, resilient, and shone dully in the milky light. Just short of contact, he drew back his hand. After a long pause during which only her breath could be heard, he withdrew again into shadow.

Silly, foolish whim. It had been a long time since he had wanted a woman. Strange that he should now be moved by this stranger when he could not even divulge his existence to her. No doubt she was only another of the long line of smug, complacent aristocrats who believed that they had a right to the land and the labor of the people upon whose backs they earned their ease. Yet it was said that the Kingsbloods were different. The marquess certainly championed the common man. Still, that did not mean that every member of his household was like-minded. In his experience, ladies knew no more than was necessary to make them charming dance partners and attractive marriage goods. The issues of the world did not weigh down their minds.

In any case, she must go. Her unexpected appearance threatened his painfully gained solitude and peace. It was not safe for her here, or for him to allow her to remain.

He would see to it that she left quickly. For now, Blood Hall belonged to him.

Suddenly she twitched beneath the covers, her whole body shaking with spasms like an ague had come upon her. Her mouth opened and she breathed deeply. "No! Don't laugh!"

Her voice, though hushed and husky, had an urgent, desperate quality to it. Intrigued, he drew closer and saw that her eyes were still shut. She was dreaming!

"No! Please! Don't laugh! I love him!"

Her eyes flew open and for a timeless moment she lay staring up at him with strangely lit eyes that seemed to see into his very soul. "You came!"

She said the words so sweetly, so gratefully, that he did not even think to move away. And then she was lifting her arms to him. "Come, my love. Come and kiss me."

He smiled to himself. She thought he was someone else. Was she dreaming of an absent lover? How outraged she would be if she knew that a stranger stood by her bed to hear her lover's greeting. And yet, like an invisible hand at his back, something held back his retreat.

She sat up with a swift grace that quite surprised him. And then her hands were reaching out to him once more. She touched his shirtfront, her fingers curling into the fabric.

"Please, my lord. Don't you love me?"

He felt the hair lift on his arms. He knew he should simply back away, disappear before she awoke, but he could not, for at the touch of her hands a current of emotion passed through him like electricity.

She rose to her knees on the bed, her arms sliding up his chest and then around his neck. "Kiss me, my lord."

She leaned into him, bringing the full caress of her soft body into the persuasion of her plea. Through her nightgown her skin felt warm, and the womanly fragrance in that heat filled his senses, bewitching him. A steady warmth moved through him. He did not know her. He did not know her name, had never seen her in the light of day. But, suddenly, he wanted her with a directness with which only a man's body can manifest itself.

Just one kiss, he thought. He'd leave her after one kiss.

The first tentative kisses he pressed at the corner of her mouth brought a murmur from her. With a small movement of her head, she brought her mouth fully under his.

She tasted of cherries! The warm and sweet flavor from her mouth spread over his tongue. More magic! Lord, but he could not resist it. He captured her soft lips with his, blending their mouths together in kiss after tender cherry-sweet kiss.

She seemed untutored in kissing yet she followed his lead with an instinct that was deeply exciting. It was unlike any other feeling he had ever experienced with a woman. Was it the fact that she was a stranger, the stuff of every man's fantasy, offering herself to him without restraint or ties, or even knowledge of who it was she really held in her embrace?

"Sweet!" she murmured against his lips. "I knew! I knew!"

The vibration of her mouth against his sent a whiplash of feeling crackling through him. The old, long-absent pressure in his loins pulsated as she brushed innocently against him.

He reached out to touch her, drawing her in with a

hand at her waist. She came willingly against him, her belly a soft warmth pressing his throbbing loins.

She's had a lover, he thought in mild surprise. And then, What does that matter? She was so warm and soft and vibrant, like holding summer in his arms.

She moved restlessly against him. His lips moved from her mouth to her cheek and then lower into the slightly moist valley between her neck and shoulder where her pulse beat like moth wings against his lips.

When her hand moved tentatively to his chest, he closed his eyes. And then her gentle hand was delving beneath his shirt, seeking out planes of muscle and the ridges of his ribs. The spidery-light touch made his pulse leap and his belly quiver. He had forgotten what a woman's touch could do. Now that he remembered, his body began to ache with the effort to remain still. He promised himself that he would not take advantage of her, that at any moment she might awaken and see him for what he was, a stranger, and that would mean disaster.

But she would not be denied. Her other hand joined the first beneath his shirt, rubbing, soothing, pressing, and then skimming over his skin. Her fingers threaded through the fine hair on his chest while waves of sensation rippled through him, each lapping with ever more intensity at his groin.

His hands moved of their own will, moving up from her waist, molding her body in a heavy caress. He reached up to stroke one breast. The tip puckered instantly, and she shivered against him, her arms tightening about his neck until he could scarcely breathe.

"Easy, my lady," he said in gentle humor, and reached up to pry her arms loose. Her hands moved back to his shoulders and then to his shirtfront, impatiently working the buttons until it lay open. The heat of her mouth scorched his chest as she pressed kiss after kiss into his skin. Her movements quickened. She seemed suddenly anxious, almost frightened, as her lips moved up the side of his neck and then across his cheek to find his mouth once more.

A groan of pleasure was wrung from him. At his response, she tightened her arms to bring him closer than before. She pressed her full length into him, seeking to become a part of him. There was no pretense in her movements, no reluctance, no teasing. Just this great urgency that was melting his bones and stiffening his manhood. The long-buried emotions of sexual desire and sweet longing coursing through him were overpowering cold reason. She felt so right, as if conjured by his imagination for his own purposes. Did he dare accept this forbidden gift?

He caught her tightly to him, molding her hips to his as he ground himself slowly against her. She moaned in pleasure at his touch and turned her lips into his ear. "Love me, my lord," she begged softly. "Please. Love me."

"Oh, lady." He sighed softly.

What he was doing was wrong, so very wrong. But she was tugging at him, pulling him onto the bed, lowering herself back onto the bedding. And his body was following hers, loathe to lose even one moment of contact with her. He stroked her from shoulder to thigh, luxuriating in the incredibly sweet feel of her beneath her gown. He lifted the gown away and met heated skin, satin smooth and pulsing with life. She ached under his caresses, meeting the subtle pressure of his hand with her body.

Past consideration of any other thing, he divested himself of his own clothing quickly and stretched out again beside her. He enclosed her hip in a hand and rolled her toward him, searing and being seared by the touch of their naked bodies. When they were touching from shoulder to knee, he found her mouth again.

This time their kisses deepened until his tongue plunged in and out of her mouth in a sinuous rhythm as old as life. She drew shuddering breaths between kisses but she did not refuse him. When he tasted the sea salt of tears, he knew that she was as desperate for their joining as he.

Her thighs trembled on his as he turned her on her back and covered her with his body. He coaxed with his hands, and she opened to him. He touched her where she was melting, and she cried out in pleasure that was more flattering than any protestation of love he had ever heard. She was all heat and fire, soft and moist, and his.

His hands were on her hips, lifting her slightly as he found her. He entered her in one swift motion, propelling himself through the barrier of her maidenhead almost before he could record it. But she arched under him with a cry of displeasure that confirmed what his amazed senses could scarcely grasp.

He tried to stop the motion of his hips but the feeling of being inside her was indescribable and irrefutable, and his body had less compunction than his mind. The subtle rotation of his hips continued as he stroked her temples, feeling the soft pulse beneath the skin. "I'm sorry," he said softly, "I didn't know."

But she was no longer looking at him. Her eyes were shut, her face taut with passion. Her body fluttered low down, surrounding him in shock waves of pleasure that forced a tiny gasp from him.

Finally she arched under him, seeking the sensation he wanted so badly to give her. He felt insatiable, wanting to devour her and at the same desiring to be lost completely in her. He thrust slowly at first, questing the depth of her womanly body, until he was drowning in her. When her hands suddenly clutched him, he groaned in thankfulness.

His rhythm changed, becoming the all-consuming thrusts for pleasure. He heard her little cries of delight and then his own deeper moans as he realized the promise of her kisses.

He lay a long time upon her, resisting the moment when he must separate himself from her, when he must think again, when he must regret every second of this night. He felt her hand touch his face, skim the planes of his cheek before her palm settled caressingly over his jaw. "Now you know, my lord. I love you best!"

Her lord? Who was this man she had saved herself for and now, unknowingly, betrayed? His thoughts raced on to more personal considerations. He could not help comparing her with other women, wondering if they had been as pleased with his lovemaking. He knew the answer. No woman ever had. And yet her passion had not been for him. He had stolen what belonged to another man. He smiled. No theft could ever have been sweeter.

He rose from her slowly, afraid to wake her and yet dreading the departure. He felt like a thief, a cheat, and defiler . . . and yet he would not have done otherwise. What was he to do now? What would she think when she awakened? Would she remember? Would she be horrified? Who would she suspect of breaking in on her and taking such gross advantage?

He cursed silently as he searched for his clothing in the darkness. If things were other than they were, if *he* were other than he was, things might be different. But they were not. Perhaps memory would be kind and she would not remember.

As he turned back to her one last time, he spied a half-empty decanter at the bedside and reached for it. He sniffed the contents, and the aroma of fruit-flavored liquor filled his senses. Cherry cordial. Sweet but effectively potent. If she had drunk the missing portion, perhaps, his wish would be granted and she would not remember.

He left the way he had come, in secret, in silence, under the cover of night.

When he was gone, whispered laughter echoed faintly in the corners of the ceiling of the Chinese Room, sounding like dry husks stirred by a breeze.

"Now what do you make of that, madame?"

"I cannot say, my captain. They are strangers?"

"So it would seem."

"Mercy! How would they have behaved if introduced?"

"I do not think, madame, that we shall be bored any longer. It would seem courting customs have changed in London. I, for once, approve!"

The howling of the wind awakened Julianna. The only hint of light in the blanketing darkness came from the milky moonlight spilling across the windowsill. She rose at once and went to the window, barefoot and dragging the coverlet with her. She stood a long time at the window, looking out on the stark shadow-shrouded vastness of the night. The cold did not penetrate her half-waking state, nor did the darkness seem empty.

She was dreaming, a new dream this time, one that she sensed would erase forever the nightmare of the past. She dreamed of arms holding her gently and a deep, quiet voice speaking words of comfort in her ear. The blood rushed hotly through her as the dream images continued. She did not know where the sensations came from, but she felt different inside her skin. Her body tingled at all the pulse points. A man, a stranger with silver-streaked hair and eyes strangely bright, had come into her room . . . shared her bed . . . shared her body.

After a moment, she put her hand to the glass, surprised to find it cold. She blinked once, then again, her eyes focusing for the first time, awake. "Always dreams," she whispered sadly. "Always dreams."

She didn't see the shadows move behind her, nor hear the faint creak of old floorboards. When she turned toward her bed, she felt only the breath of winter blow softly against her cheek and then heard, from deep within the depths of the house, a clock strike three times, and thought she was alone.

"How long?" Julianna asked incredulously.

"Two nights and a day, my lady," Mrs. Mead repeated. "You slept the clock right around and then some. I was for sending for the doctor but Tom said since you weren't feverish we'd best wait and see." She peered at the young woman closely. "How are you feeling, my lady?"

"Amazingly refreshed," Julianna answered, and found that the statement was true. She felt that she had slept

away a full lifetime and that she had awakened to a new
world.

Looking at her flushed face and smile, the housekeeper decided not to mention the quantity of the
cherry-flavored liquor her mistress had drunk the night
of her arrival or how, when told of it, Tom had chuckled
and said it was possibly the best thing for her. The long
rest might well have saved her from a bout of pneumonia.

Julianna threw back the covers and stretched like a
cat. "I'd like a bath. Then I'll have my breakfast in the
Great Hall, if that's convenient."

"Very well, my lady. I'll just go and set the kettles on
for hot water for your bath."

An hour later the full light of morning revealed Blood
Hall's Great Hall in all its splendor. As Julianna sat
down to breakfast at the main dining area, she realized
anew that the oriels of the hall held a medieval majesty
that no amount of furniture coverlets, dust, or outright
neglect could diminish. From her vantage point, she
looked out and saw both the moors and, in the distance,
the silver-backed green expanse of the sea. Unlike other
houses erected in later centuries, the builders of Blood
Hall had not considered the sea to be too spectacular
and competitive a background for their own architectural
efforts. Built as a fortress against attack by hostile armies
and sea robbers and Atlantic gales, Blood Hall had stood
as the secure home for three hundred years of
Kingsbloods. Nothing short of an earthquake would ever
do it harm.

But that knowledge didn't stop Julianna from saying as
Mrs. Mead appeared with a bowl of porridge, "After

breakfast, you must get a broom and see to the cobwebs in the rafters."

"A few local girls could have the Hall turned out in no time," Mrs. Mead answered, thinking of the back-breaking effort cleaning the rafters would involve. "There's your old room to be sorted out as well."

Julianna turned back from the window. "Oh, no. I don't want a troop of maids disturbing the peace. Whatever you and Tom can manage will serve. Besides, I'm quite happy in the Chinese Room."

Mrs. Mead darted a cautious glance her way. "Then you don't hold with what they say about the room being haunted?"

Julianna laughed. "I felt perfectly alone, I assure you." Yet, even as she said the words, a fleeting, not-quite-forgotten memory of creaking boards and of skirting shadows in the night came back to her. Dismissing it as the vapors of dreams, she said, "If there are ghosts, they are as anxious for solitude as I."

"That's as may be," the housekeeper replied, not liking to speak of specters within their hearing. "When you've done, I'll just pop out and bring up a few more of me things to the Hall."

Julianna's first spoon of porridge paused in midair. "Why should you do that?"

"Why, so's I can continue to keep you company," she answered as she poured a fresh cup of tea for Julianna. "I stayed the night last night, what with you sickening, or so we thought. 'Tain't proper, you being all alone in this great place."

"But that's exactly what I want," Julianna said a little testily. Then she took a deep breath to curb the temper she kept losing too frequently these days. "There's no need for you to stay here," she continued more evenly. "As you can see, I'm perfectly fine. You should be with Tom, in your cottage."

Mrs. Mead folded her arms over her ample bosom. " 'Tis not like in times past, my lady. There be tramps and thieves abroad. Tom caught three poachers just last week."

"What happened to them?"

"Turned them into the magistrate in Ilfracombe," she answered proudly. "Been tried and sentenced to transportation."

Julianna frowned, remembering the shanties of itinerant workers she'd passed on the highway the day before. "Were they family men?"

"Most like." Sensing disapproval of her husband's actions, Mrs. Mead added, "That's the law, my lady. Poachers were once shot. Transportation's better'n that."

"I suppose you're right," Julianna replied, "but it seems a great price to pay for a man who wanted only to feed his family."

The housekeeper clamped her jaws shut. Quality liked things ordered to please them, but they seldom wanted to hear the details that kept their world spinning pleasantly. "Tom does his job just as the marquess tells him."

"I'm certain that's true," Julianna said, aware that she should not question her grandfather's authority with a servant. "I shall write the marquess this very day with news of Tom's good work. Thank you, that will be all. Oh, that's not quite true."

When Mrs. Mead had turned back from the door toward which she was headed, Julianna said, "I'm expecting Mr. Coleman today, although like you, he may not have received my note in time to arrive on the date I suggested. In any case, I'll receive him here in the Great Hall whenever he comes."

"Very good, my lady."

Mr. Coleman had received her letter and presented himself at Blood Hall half an hour later.

A big man with burly shoulders and the rolling gait of a sailor, Jed Coleman had been Little Hangman Mine's manager the last twenty-five of his fifty-odd years. He knew how to handle both men and mines. His shrewd, fair-minded, tough, no-nonsense attitude made him an asset and trusted employee. Julianna knew him only slightly, yet the fact that her grandfather trusted him gave her an implicit confidence in his honesty.

"Mornin', my lady," Jed began without waiting, as was proper, for the lady of the house to address him first. A big grin split his face. " 'Tis hopin', I am, that yer arrival means his lordship is soon to return to Blood Hall."

"Good morning, Mr. Coleman." Donning her spectacles, she motioned him closer so that she could more clearly see his face. "I'm sorry to disappoint you but the marquess won't be returning from Italy for some weeks yet. When he does, I doubt he'll visit Devon. Parliament will have begun and his presence is needed there."

She saw his broad face, permanently creased by age, sober. " 'Tis sorry I am to hear it."

"Why, Mr. Coleman? By the look of you, there must be something quite seriously wrong."

Jed shook his head as if trying to dislodge an unpleasant thought. He knew the marquess's granddaughter only to speak to, but he was surprised to see how she had aged in the last year. Her matronly mobcap and spectacles and navy dress with mantelet that hid her figure made her seem twice her years. Spinsterhood was not being kind to her, he thought fleetingly. No doubt she suffered from various nervous complaints. The last thing he wanted to do was upset her. "There be nothin' wrong I can't handle, my lady. Ye ben't trouble yer head about such things. Time enough when the marquess returns to set it to rights."

Julianna wasn't offended by his assumption that she wouldn't be interested in trouble at the mines, or that she couldn't possibly understand or aid them. But she wasn't about to change the topic. She glanced away to look out the window toward Ilfracombe to the northeast.

After a moment she said, "Lord Kingsblood left me in charge of his personal affairs." Strictly speaking, he had charged her with monitoring his personal affairs, *not* managing them. "I know something of your present troubles. If you tell me more, I may be able to help."

The burly miner looked distinctly ill at ease as he stood in the center of the room. " 'Tis like this, my lady," he began reluctantly. "Trouble been brewin' for months, ever since them Chartist agitators come into the area with their talk of union oaths and such like." His face suddenly turned bright red. "We've the Combination to do our talking for us, my lady, and that be enough!"

Under her grandfather's tutelage, Julianna had learned a great deal about labor disputes and issues. The Chartists, as they were known far and wide, were the first independent working-class movement in the world. Unionization of laborers was only one of its six-point political program, which included universal suffrage. Yet north Devon seemed years removed from such political strategy. "Why have they come here, to Devon, Mr. Coleman?"

He shook his head. "Who's to say? The cave-in last

year at Torrs Mine couldn't have been prevented by union oaths. 'Tis a hazard all folk face who work the mines."

"How many were killed and injured?" Julianna asked, realizing that she had forgotten the matter soon after she'd learned of it.

"Four good men were buried, my lady. The injured were children and were more easily replaced."

"More easily—" Julianna paused. She couldn't very well expect him to continue if she was openly appalled by his revelations. She knew children worked the mines. Many believed children were better suited than adults for jobs like hauling ore wagons through the narrow passages of the mines. Even so, the marquess was laboring hard in Parliament for the passage of the Ten Hours Act, which would restrict working hours of women and children. "How many injuries were there among the children?"

"Assorted broken bones, one boy lost two fingers, and a girl had her foot crushed. The doctor took it off."

"I see," Julianna said slowly, willing herself not to feel sick. "And you believe the agitation by these Chartists at Little Hangman Mine is a direct result of the Torrs Mine cave-in?"

" 'Tain't what I say. 'Tis what others say."

"Who are these men?"

"I couldn't name 'em," he answered, but Julianna noted his eyes slid from hers. "They came in as workers, sly as foxes. Now they've got local folk, good men, stirred up with talk of a union and, like as not, rousing them to violent action."

Sensing that something was being withheld from her, Julianna narrowed her eyes behind her lenses until they showed only slivers of green. "Mr. Coleman, I believe that you are omitting something important in this matter. What is it?"

He shifted uncomfortably from one foot to the other. "There was an attempt to blow up Little Hangman Mine."

"I know."

His bushy brows rose. "Well, now. Then you know how it come to naught."

She nodded. "In your letter to the marquess you said someone sent you a note, revealing the plot beforehand."

"Aye."

"Tell me what happened."

He smiled again. " 'Twas nothin', my lady. We discovered the gunpowder and confiscated it. A few days later there were a fight below ground. A few heads were bashed, a man or two laid up a day or two. One went missin'."

"Missing?" Julianna said in a choked voice. "Who went missing?"

Jed's grin turned sly. "Hard to say. One of 'em Chartists, I suspect. He were a newcomer."

"You tell me that a man may have been killed in a fight at a Kingsblood mine and that no one lifted a finger to find out?"

Realizing that her interpretation of his words sounded very much like an accusation of neglect, Coleman vigorously shook his head. "Now, my lady, I said naught. The man took a drubbin', no doubt o' it. But killed, well, there was no body found, and no one's come forth to ask about him. I say he just ran off. That sort would."

"What sort?"

Jed cocked his head to one side. " 'Twas a funny thing,

him. He looked too soft to be a miner. Talked rough and all, but not like a Devonshire man. He were a *furriner.*"

Julianna smiled at this description, for any man who was not West Country born and bred was considered a foreigner.

Jed leaned forward slightly as he imparted his final thought. "I think he were the kind what sets up mischief just to make someone else's head ache. Forgive me sayin' so, but strong men make enemies, and the marquess isn't a man to live his life without gaining a few."

Julianna agreed with this assessment. "If you know which men are agitators, why not get rid of them and all who side with them?"

"Only harm would come of it, my lady. There're good folk mixed up in the business. A man without wages is a dangerous man. It'd be like settin' a match to tinder."

"I see. So what's to be done? Surely you have an opinion."

Jed nodded slowly. The ring of authority in her voice was so much like Lord Kingsblood's that he didn't feel as awkward as he thought he might have in discussing mine business with a woman. "A raise in wages would shut them up. Nothin' grand, but enough so's there ben't any complaints. A man with a full belly is hard to rouse. That's what I'd tell the marquess to his face."

Julianna smiled as she gazed at this earnest man whose rough exterior hid a quick and sound mind. No wonder her grandfather relied on him. "I'll write the marquess with your recommendations. In the meantime, you must locate the missing man."

"I'd as lief not," he answered forthrightly. "Stirrin' up things won't help."

"Hasn't it occurred to you that the missing man might

have been your informer and that those who beat him
might have been trying to murder him for revealing their
plot?"

The mine manager went pale. "My lady, ye oughtn't
say such."

"Who else would benefit by the man's death?"

'Once more Jed's gaze shifted sideways. "What's become of him ben't yer concern, my lady."

"Mr. Coleman," Julianna said hoarsely, "you didn't—"

The older man's head whipped back to her. "I did not!
I'm the marquess's man. If I'd done wrong, 'twould look
to be by the marquess's orders."

Julianna believed him. "Then it's more important than
ever that this man be found. He might have saved Little
Hangman Mine from destruction. If so, we owe him our
protection. If he's dead, then we'll have the evidence we
need to move against the agitators."

Jed smiled broadly for the first time since learning that
the marquess was not on his way to Blood Hall. "I like
yer manner of thinking, my lady. Ye've a man's head on
yer shoulders, if ye don't mind me saying so."

"Why, thank you, Mr. Coleman." Though his compli-
ment wasn't the sort of flattery most ladies wished to
hear, it pleased her. "I shall expect to hear of your progress, say, within the week?"

"Yes, my lady. Should I send my report to London?"

"No, you may present yourself to me here."

His brows shot up. "Ye ben't stopping here?"

Annoyed to be asked at every juncture about her unconventional arrangements, she snapped, "Yes, not that
it's any business of yours!"

"Begging yer pardon, my lady," he replied, and began
backing away. "Until the end of the week."

When he was gone, Julianna's thoughts continued to spin with the events Jed had revealed to her. She'd been down a mine only once, and the dank, cold darkness had seemed to her more terrible than any image of Hell. The idea of being hurt and left below to die was too terrible to contemplate. If the man lived, he must be found. If he was dead, that must be known too.

Finally she stood and went to gaze out of the window. The window overlooked the back of the house where the gray winter landscape seemed barren and inert. Yet she knew within days the first wild daffodils and crocus would peek through the rough brown grasses, refusing to wither before the last cold breath of winter. Soon after the streams would begin to rush a little more quickly. The wild moorland ponies, growing friskier, would gallop across the new-sprung grass at a brisker, more playful pace. But not just yet. Now the earth seemed to hold its breath in waiting, everything still, lifeless, yet hopeful.

Like my life, she mused with a twinge of sorrow. Edging in and out of her thoughts all morning had been snatches of memory of a dream made all the more disturbing because it was so vivid. A kiss. A hand on a bare thigh. A warm embrace. Her own satin-smooth skin gliding over the dense velvet plush of a man's. A powerful throbbing invasion. From where had such scandalous thoughts arisen?

Suddenly a movement at the corner of her vision made her turn back from the windows. Before the oriel at the far end of the room, dust motes danced in the golden slats of sunlight. Even as she stared bemused by the display, their tempo picked up as they began to swirl ever more quickly in time to a melody.

She could hear music! She recognized it at once as a

childhood rhyme, yet she could not say whether it was
being played by harp or flute. The tune simply *was*.
Floating faintly like tingling glass in the rafters the melody brought back a deep swift rush of memories of this
house and the love that had always surrounded her here.

She remembered the one place where even in the
depths of winter, the joy of spring always held sway: the
walled rose garden.

Chapter Four

❧

She descended the steps of the main stairway quickly, not bothering to collect a shawl or cloak. The urge to be where things were alive and vibrant was too strong to be resisted. The bluster of the winter breeze took her breath away as she swung wide the front door. Leaves, gathered against the threshold, flew into the entry as she stepped out into the day.

Goose bumps pricked up on her arms beneath the long sleeves of her woolen gown as she quickly crossed the cobblestones toward the garden. She didn't care about the cold or the wind threading icy fingers under her mobcap to drag free tendrils from the tight bun she wore. The garden gate was on the latch, but it opened easily when she dragged against it and then slipped inside into the stillness and the surprising warmth.

For a moment she leaned back against the rough planks of the gate, breathless with laughter. She felt like a child who had sneaked away from her elders. When she had caught her breath, she opened her eyes to the miracle of the garden.

Winter sunlight shone against the opposite wall, gilding the gray stones with sunlight until it seemed they glowed with heat. Roses, newly trimmed and tied, bobbed resiliently upon their trellises. Nearby a lavender bush thrust pale-purple tongues of scent into the air. Spangles of yellow blossoms turned leafy green shadows into secret treasure hordes while those in the full sunlight shimmered like new-minted sovereigns. She breathed deep, smelling the pungent aromas of new-spaded earth, decomposing vegetation, and the acrid sting of manure. Someone had been hard at work within the garden.

Then, with a lurch of embarrassment, she realized that she was not alone. A man stood in a shadowed corner of the garden watching her. He held a spade. She knew at once that he must be the new gardener the Meads had mentioned.

Embarrassed to have been caught making a display of herself, she whipped the spectacles from her nose and tucked the much-hated emblem of her nearsightedness into the pocket of her gown. Smoothing the loose hair from her face, she stepped forward in greeting. "You must be the gardener. I'm Lady Julianna Kingsblood, the Marquess of Ilfracombe's granddaughter."

To her surprise, he remained silent and simply stared at her as he leaned upon his spade handle.

Assuming he must be shy, as many rural folk were when in the presence of nobility, she turned and pretended to look about. "Mrs. Mead tells me that you are new. By the appearance of things, you seem to know what you're doing."

His silence continued. After a moment she turned her head to look at him, but she couldn't tell much about him without her glasses, not even his age. Perhaps, she decided after more reflection, he was simple. Everyone said that those who were best at tending animals and plants were a bit fey. A simpleminded man might be afraid of her.

Smiling as one might to assure a small child, she moved toward him, saying "There's nothing to be afraid of. I haven't come to run you off. Your job is quite safe."

"Ah t' be grateful, Ah'm sur'." His thick accent was almost unintelligible but the arrogance in the masculine tone was unmistakable. This was no feebleminded person.

Julianna flushed, feeling even more awkward than she had before. "I'm sorry if I surprised you," she began, thinking that if he had any sort of intelligence at all, he would realize that she was pretending to find an excuse for his rudeness. "I once lived at Blood Hall and the rose garden was one of my favorite places."

"Am Ah t' cut ye a posy?" he asked, his posture stiffening as she took another step toward him.

"No, I just wanted to be someplace where . . ." She stopped herself before she said, "somewhere where there is life," for it was much too personal a thing to say to a stranger.

"Ye were after comp'ny with th' roses?" His tone was edged with amusement.

"Certainly," she replied, refusing to be further disconcerted by a mere gardener. "All ladies love roses." She walked to the nearest bush and cupped a fully opened deep-pink blossom. "It's a miracle that such a thing can happen in February, isn't it?"

He moved so quick and unexpectedly that she had no time to react. One moment he was yards away, the next he was beside her, brushing her hand away from the rose. "There'll ben't a rose for aught, ye handle 'em so freely!" he said in disdain. "Th' human hand murders 'em."

The word *murder* acted on her like a chill. She backed a little away from him, yet he remained so close that she noticed many things at once. Several inches taller than her five-foot seven-inch frame, he wore an old-fashioned wide-brimmed hat so low on his brow that his eyes were hidden, but she read defiance in the razor-sharp thinness of his taut mouth. His skin was sallow and tightly drawn like a man who'd suffered great pain. His britches were patched in a dozen places. His coat appeared never to have been cleaned since it was originally stitched together. One whiff of him carried by the changing breeze made her involuntarily take another step back from him. He smelled rankly of manure and sweat.

The corners of his mouth lifted, one side drawing up a little higher than the other. She knew then that he had wanted to intimidate her and that he knew he had succeeded. "What is your name?" she demanded to keep him from thinking that she could be bullied into a complete retreat.

"Jos." He waited three heartbeats before adding "Trevelyn."

"Well, Jos Trevelyn, you'd better get back to work. There are weeds in the far corner, and several paving stones by the gate are loose. I complimented your work because I believe in encouraging those in our service. However, I won't put up with laziness or the insolence of a servant who doesn't know his place."

She saw him recoil, and knew that she had wounded his pride. She had never before spoken to a servant in such a manner, but he had rattled her, and she could think of no other way of giving him a much-deserved setdown.

As she watched, her heart beating a little fast, his head

lifted a little, just enough so that his eyes were revealed in shadow. They were light, the chill bright blue of a winter sky. His stare, bold and decidedly defiant, moved slowly down over her, taking in every detail of her clothing. When he looked up again, she read in his eyes an unmistakable look of amusement. Sensing at once that it went far beyond the words they had exchanged, she felt the full thrust of his masculine contempt for her poor showing as a woman.

" 'Tis yer right t' sack me, my lady, ben't yer ghosts don't mind. 'Twas in their service Ah were hired."

His blazing arrogance struck her like a slap in the face. It seemed as if he wanted her to fire him. Suddenly, contrarily, it was the last thing she wanted to do. For if she did fire him, she might as well admit it was because she couldn't tolerate his poor opinion of her as a woman.

"I'm not an unfair mistress," she said as haughtily as before. "I intend to reside permanently at Blood Hall. There will be ample opportunity for you to prove your value. Then we shall see." Not giving him a chance to insult her again, she turned and headed for the gate.

"Ah would nae com' again without first ye sen' th' gatekeeper t' warn me. Still, it'd mean a lot o' work goin' wantin'."

She turned back in spite of herself, indignation firing her cheeks. "Just what do you mean by that?"

He smiled at her. It was a remarkably attractive smile without the benefit of the rest of his face, which remained shadowed, to aid it. "If yer t' come again, Ah'd as soon clear out before time."

"That's an excellent suggestion!" Julianna replied, stung to the quick by the implication that he didn't want to be in her company. "Good day to you."

"Bring ye a coat next time!" he called after her as she swung away. "Ah would nae waste th' time t' set a fire t' warm ye!"

Pricked anew by this insult, but well aware that she would not come out the victor in another exchange of words, she continued out of the garden. Marching back toward the house, she couldn't feel the sting of the wind for the heat of anger moving swiftly through her, but she heard his laughter above the pounding of her heart.

"Who is that person in the garden?" she demanded the moment she entered the foyer and spied Mrs. Mead on the landing.

One look at her mistress's scarlet face and mussed skirts, and Mrs. Mead dropped her load of linen. "Gracious me! What's happened? The lad didn't—"

"Certainly not!" Julianna countered, realizing with impatience which direction the housekeeper's thoughts had taken. "He merely insulted me at every turn. Who is he?"

The housekeeper's stricken look ebbed a fraction. "I couldn't say exactly, my lady. He ain't a local lad."

"That much I gathered. His accent isn't of Cornish or Devonshire origin. Do you recognize it?"

"Can't say that I do," Mrs. Mead replied, watching her mistress carefully. "He's got a rough tongue but he's a good worker. The garden's come alive again under his hand."

Julianna began brushing the leaves out of her skirt. "How long has he been employed here?"

"Little more than a fortnight."

Recalling his image, Julianna could only remember his hostile light-eyed stare and an arrogance one seldom encountered in a commoner. She couldn't even guess the color of his hair or if he was handsome or ugly. He had seemed thin beneath his baggy woolen britches and jacket but, without her spectacles, she couldn't be certain. Ragged though he was, he had commanded a kind of respect that had nothing to do with physical points.

"That man thinks entirely too much of himself," she said defensively, angry all over again that he had so affected her. Even now she was on the verge of marching back into the garden just to trade new insults with him. "Do you know what he said to me, that if I discharged him Blood Hall's ghosts wouldn't like it! Imagine!"

"He's no call to be rude to you, my lady!" the housekeeper responded in a scandalized tone. "Tom will turn him off, if you wish."

"I don't wish it," Julianna answered as she gave her skirts a last angry swipe with her hand. "But I should like to know more about him. Mr. Coleman told me that we must be careful in the company we keep these days." She turned deliberately away as she asked the next question. "How old would you say he is?"

"The gardener? Tom though he were an old man when first he saw him shuffling up the lane. Only he told Tom he were a soldier injured in them foreign wars. Said he were just released from hospital and needed work. Being that we needed a man, my lady, and what with few willing to work haunted ground, whatever the wages, we took him on. Did we do right?"

"I don't suppose you could be expected to do more," Julianna said. But the thought that the man had been a soldier made her less eager than ever to again be in his company. Perhaps his battle experiences had addled his mind. Or perhaps his injuries had embittered him.

"I suppose," she said, musing aloud, "that as long as I

don't have to associate with him, I can overlook his rudeness. After all, he has put the garden in order, and plants are blooming."

"Yes, my lady," Mrs. Mead answered, and gave up a small sigh of relief as her mistress started to climb the stairs to her room.

A faint tingling sound startled Julianna into glancing up at the hundreds of dusty crystal droplets that made up the chandelier hanging in the entry. "Do you or your husband play a flute, Mrs. Mead?"

"No, my lady. Whyever should you ask?"

"I heard music earlier in the Great Hall. A nursery tune being played on a flute."

"Might it have been a lute, my lady?"

Julianna's gaze moved downward to meet Mrs. Mead's. "Why, yes, I suppose it could have been. Who plays the lute?"

Her expression perfectly neutral, the housekeeper answered, " 'Tis said the captain were a master of the lute." She nodded in the direction of the painting that hung as one of a pair on the landing before her. "He were known to play when he were pleased."

Julianna's gaze followed her direction. The portrait was that of one of Cromwell's soldiers, Captain John Monleigh, dressed in leather jerkin, plain collar, and sword, and wearing a pirate's grin on his bruisingly handsome face. Beside it hung the picture of a remarkably pretty young woman, a Kingsblood daughter who had resided at Blood Hall the year the captain had come to north Devon to conquer in the name of the commonwealth. Instead, betrayed in forbidden love, the pair had lost their heads in this very place. It was their spectral presences that were said to haunt the house.

Not to be outdone a second time this day by the threat of ghostly doings, Julianna kept her expression sweetly blank as she turned to the housekeeper. "Then he should practice more. I fear he was slightly out of tune."

Without another word, she went quickly up the stairs and down the hall.

"The missus and me locked up everythin' right and tight." Tom stood at the doorway of the kitchen watching in faint disapproval as the Marquess of Ilfracombe's granddaughter consumed her supper in the servants' hall. "There be no need for ye to pass the night alone, my lady."

Julianna smiled at him, for it was not the first time this day that one of the Meads had tried to persuade her to come and stay with them. "Thank you, Tom, but I am quite content to be alone."

"It'd be no trouble, the missus and me passing the night in the servants' quarters."

"I wouldn't dream of dislodging you from your bed. I prefer solitude, and you deserve to rest by your own hearth."

Feeling that his duty toward her had been discharged, Tom didn't press the matter. "Best lock yer bedroom door, then, my lady. I'd rest easier were I to know yer were protected."

Julianna put her fork down. "Is there any new reason why I should feel threatened?"

Tom shook his head, unwilling to say what he thought: that after spending one night alone in this house she would see reason. Only time would tell about that. "No, my lady, given that ye have nay fear of the night and the silence."

"I have none, Tom, but I promise I'll lock my door."

"Aye, my lady." He tipped his cap to her. "Till morning."

"Until morning, Tom, and thank you." She rose to follow him to the kitchen door to lock it behind him. "Do you keep a key to the front door?" she asked as he stepped out into the chill night.

He turned back, shoulders hunched against the wind as he jammed his cap down on his head. "Aye, that I do."

"Then good night," she called. As he quickly set off into the darkness, she swung the heavy door shut. When she had set the bolt she turned back toward the table, but her meal of lamb stew and soda bread suddenly looked unappetizing. There were too many things on her mind for her to appreciate the country fare. Thus she left it, bowl still steaming, and picked up a candle to light her way up the main stairway.

As she gained the first landing, an intense depression settled upon her. She had spent the better part of the afternoon composing and revising a letter to her grandfather. She could not lie to him, but she feared that if she told him the complete truth, he would feel compelled to return before the end of winter. Her impression from her conversation with Jed Coleman was that the mine was a powder keg to which a long but unpredictable fuse had been lit. An explosion might occur at any time. On the other hand, things might smolder for months. Common sense told her that her grandfather should be fully informed of the situation. Jed Coleman had intended to do just that until she forestalled him. Everything in her rejected the idea of disturbing her grandfather's sojourn in Italy. If he came back now, in the midst of a very bitter winter, he might sicken and die.

As if to confirm the harshness of the cold, an errant breeze whistled up the stairway from an unknown source, flickering the candle in her hand and making her shiver. The house smelled of rain, of burning wood, and of that faintly disturbing otherworldliness of all ancient places.

Feeling silly yet unable to shake the sense of uneasiness, Julianna glanced about her. Though the rooms of Blood Hall were as familiar to her as the planes of her own face, that familiarity had receded into the darkness. The night surrounding her was far from silent. Magnified by the solitude, a dozen minor noises vied for her attention. The wind was a dull moan. Rain spattered against the windows. Above her the old house seemed to groan in protest of the wet weather. The walls were stone but the wooden-beamed floors creaked beneath her tread as she climbed.

Reaching out to a newel post for support, Julianna found the shape of a figure under her fingertips. Lifting her candle, she turned to gaze at the foot-and-a-half-high wooden carving of a knight. With a smile of remembrance, she traced a finger from the helmet down to the breastplate, marveling anew at the detail that had been worked into the oak wood by artisans three centuries earlier. The other newel post figures—the pirate, the courtier, the damsel, the hunter—were equally well designed and equally familiar. As a child, she had liked to make up stories about them. Sometimes she made the knight the hero. Other times the courtier or the hunter won the damsel's true love. Only the pirate, with his drawn saber, had seemed too menacing to be a hero.

Somewhere deep in the house, the muffled sound of a slamming door reverberated.

Startled, Julianna turned to look down the stairway,

but nothing appeared within the circle of candlelight cascading toward the entryway. "Of course not," she murmured aloud. Nothing could appear. She was alone, quite and completely alone.

The wind gusted again, throwing its full weight upon the main doors. The wood creaked and the hinges squeaked. It was then she saw something in the hallway below, no more than a flash of pearlescence in the entrance of a nearby salon.

Instinctively she stepped back behind the corner of the banister, as if its open-work pattern would offer her physical protection. Her hand stole into the pocket of her gown, but it was empty. Too late, she remembered that she had left her spectacles in her bedroom, next to the letter she had been writing.

Then she saw it again, no more than a quiver really, as if the darkness was possessed of the pulse of life. Someone or something was standing just inside the doorway of the downstairs salon.

"Who's there?" she demanded a little angrily, for she had always hated being frightened. "I don't care to be teased. When I find out who's doing this, you can be certain I shall take action!"

Her voice sounded loud and theatrical in the still air, making her feel suddenly foolish. Whom was she scolding? The dark, the silence, the stillness?

Suddenly a pane of glass near the door shattered. A dozen shards of glass rained upon the entry flagstones as a rock hit the first step then bounced back onto the slate floor.

Julianna flew down the steps and flung open the door. "Who's there?" she cried, not nearly as afraid as she had been. Vandals were a part of life in London. "Coward!"

she cried as she spied someone fleeing around the corner of the house. She waited a moment longer, but she could not tell if she had seen a boy or a man.

As she slammed the door, she swore against the damage that had been done to the lovely window. After locking the door, she set her candle on the floor and bent to picked up the rock. It was a chunk of mine ore about the size of a goose egg. But, unlike in novels, there was no message attached. But then, perhaps there was. Mine ore. Could this be a message from a discontented miner?

As she stood there, the certainty that she was being watched came creeping back over her. Poor sight, further hampered by the darkness, made her nearly blind, but her sense of another presence just beyond her vision deepened. Yet it was not the conventional form of sensing. Sensation was jumbled. She could almost "see" the thoughts of another, "hear" the gesture of the unseen.

The hair lifted on her nape as fear iced a path down her spine. The feeling was strong. Someone waited, holding his breath, afraid yet elated by her detection, aware of her in ways she could not be of him. She remembered then what Tom had said of desperate men and the marquess's enemies. Had someone been watching the house, knew that she was alone, and had now come to exact some kind of deluded revenge?

Fear of her own vulnerability, of being trapped and stalked by an unseen force, brought a cry to her lips. "Go away! Just go away!"

Turning, she scooped up her candle and flew up the stairs, feeling eyes on her back, her hips, her trembling legs.

When she reached her room, she threw open the door and then slammed it with a force that echoed throughout the house. She had been routed, completely and thoroughly, by her own cowardice, but she did not care. After she had turned the key in the lock, she pocketed it and then lit every lamp and candle she could find.

Julianna awakened as the clock in the hall below struck three. The room was not in darkness. She had made certain that there were enough candles lit and enough coal in the fireplace to keep the room bright and warm throughout the night. The warm reddish glow drew her sleep-filled gaze even as her heart began to hammer. The shock of fright she had received on the stairway hours earlier had acted like a sedative once she reached her room, and she'd fallen instantly into a deep sleep. But now an abiding sense of unease jolted her to full wakefulness.

Automatically her hand went to her bedside table. With a sigh of relief she felt her fingers curl about the wire rims of her spectacles. This time she would not have the disadvantage of blurred sight to further tease her imagination. She put them on quickly but furtively, curving the wires behind her ears with as little movement as possible.

The room came into focus, the images so crisp and clear that it seemed faint black margins had been drawn about each object in the room. The lovely bedroom, imaginatively decorated with all manner of Oriental commodes, porcelains, lanterns, rugs, and silk bed hangings, had not changed in more than a dozen decades. The hand-painted Chinese wallpaper depicted delicately branching bamboo with jewel-toned birds perched in its limbs. The faint, exotic fragrances of sandalwood and cinnabar wafted in the air. On the tiny black lacquer table beside the bed a cloisonné clock belatedly chimed the hour.

For reasons of which she was never certain afterward, Julianna sat up and, bending over, looked down at the floor. Showing dully upon the surface of the dark wood were fresh, muddy footprints. A man's footprints!

More astounded than frightened, Julianna whipped back the covers and, poking her feet into her slippers, crouched down by the bed to get a better look at this evidence of an intruder. She recognized at once that the prints had been made by heavy workman's boots. Gingerly she touched one. Her fingers came away with an oily stickiness that confirmed her suspicion that it was mud. But who could have left such marks? Had Tom come up to her room before leaving for the night? Even if he had, she couldn't imagine that he would dare mar the house with muddy tracks. Why, she had heard Mrs. Mead repeatedly warn him to wipe his feet each time he came into the house. Besides, she would have seen them when she came up to bed. They were fresh.

Julianna rose to her feet, her eyes widening behind her glasses as she followed the path of the tracks. They formed a perfect ellipse, beginning before the fireplace, moving to the side of the bed, then ending again right before the hearth. It was as if the person who had made them had come and gone by way of the chimney.

Perplexed, Julianna followed them until she stood before the roaring fire. Looking back, she noted that the door to her room was in the adjoining wall while the door to her dressing room was on the opposite side of the room. That left only the windows, but they too were not within reach or leap of the spot on which she stood. She bent to check the fender for signs that the mud had

been scraped off, but she found nothing. It appeared that
the owner of the mucky boots had simply vanished.

Her trembling took her by surprise. She had thought
she was perfectly calm, but suddenly she felt a scream
hovering in her throat, threatening to erupt in a loud,
terrified wail. "I'm not afraid," she gasped out. "I'm not
afraid!" But she spun about and ran back to the bed
where she scrambled under the covers like a frightened
child.

For several minutes she remained buried beneath the
covers, a trembling lump huddling in the middle of the
bed. Then reason reasserted itself and anger took the
place of fear, pumping courage through her veins. After
throwing back the covers in disgust, she sat upright in the
center of the bed and looked quickly about. Nothing had
changed. The candles and fire held back the shadows. As
she should have known all along, there was nothing and
no one there but her.

There was a simple explanation for the muddy prints,
she told herself as she arranged a pile of pillows for her
head. Someone was playing a trick on her. But who
would do such a thing? Tom Mead had warned her
against remaining at the house alone, but surely he
wouldn't try to frighten her into obeying him. The only
other man who worked at Blood Hall beside Tom Mead
was . . . "Jos Trevelyn!" She said the name aloud before realizing it.

He had shown himself to be a rude and inconsiderate
lout who thought nothing of tweaking the noses of his
superiors. It would be like him to try to frighten her in
retaliation for threatening his job. If, indeed, he was a
soldier, no doubt he had been drummed out of the service for insubordination. Well, no foul-smelling bully

would have the satisfaction of getting the better of her. If Tom denied leaving his bootprints in her room, then she would know whom to blame.

"I should dismiss him," she muttered, sliding again under the covers. But if she did that, he might cause further mischief. Despite his remarks, she had sensed that he wanted to keep his post. Then why would he break into her room in the middle of the night and leave mud on her floor? And how had he entered?

The last possibility, the one she had forgotten about until sleep drifted back over her, was that the ancestral ghosts were having a laugh at her expense. She had never before been the butt of their mischief-making, but that did not mean she did not believe them capable of it.

He waited more than an hour for her to fall asleep again. Not until her hands released their tight clutch of the coverlet, signaling that she had fallen into deep slumber, did he step forward into the room. He had watched her reaction to his prank with bemused interest. It had frightened her, all right, just as his appearance in the entryway had as she went up to bed, and the unexpected rock thrown by an unseen troublemaker. But none of those things had frightened her enough to send her screaming into the night.

He smiled. Perhaps he should not have expected that, considering that the night was so cold and damp. But he had hoped to move her to a vow to leave and never return. All he had likely done was cost the gardener his job. He could see now that if his goal was to be achieved, he would have to become more direct.

With deliberate care, he knelt and removed each bootprint, knowing that at any moment she could awaken and find him there. The danger was delightfully pleasant. What would she do if she awakened and found a man in her room? He smiled. What would she do, indeed?

When he had wiped up the last of the mud, he stood and found himself by her bedside. He had observed many things about her this day: that she had a temper, that she possessed a knowledge of politics and people that he would never have suspected; and that her eyes were a clear soft shade of green. He had always preferred blue eyes to any other color, just as he had preferred blondes to brunettes. But that was before he had held her in his arms, kissed her soft mouth, and made love to her so-willing body. If they had met in another time in another way, they might have . . .

His gaze strayed to where the coverlet lay folded back, exposing her throat. Even now his body chimed with the need to lift back the cover and slide down beside her as he had two nights ago. What had she thought when she awakened? Had she noticed the changes in her body, or had the deep sleep into which she had fallen for more than twenty-four hours erased her memory of their love-making?

He shook his head ruefully and, in doing so, was distracted by the glint of metal on the bedside table. Her spectacles. He picked them up and held them toward the nearest source of light. The thickness of the lenses told the story. She was quite nearsighted. Without them, she'd be at a great disadvantage. She might have to travel all the way back to London to get a new pair.

With a grin of satisfaction he closed his hand over them and backed away. No wonder she had not reacted more strongly to his appearance in the salon entry. It was a hoary trick but it should have been an effective one.

Undoubtedly she had not really seen him because she had not been wearing her spectacles. Next time he would use that to his advantage. Lady Julianna Kingsblood had just begun to experience the power of his presence in her home. One way or another, she must be convinced to leave Blood Hall.

His tread was soundless as his made his way back toward the chimney where, a moment later, he vanished.

Julianna opened her eyes to the night. The dream had come again, the new one that had replaced the nightmare once she arrived at Blood Hall. A man stood by her bedside, a man who loved her better than anything else in the world. He said the words she longed to hear, held her in his arms and made her feel things she had never experienced in her waking hours. If only it was real! Not a dream.

Tears slipped quietly down her face, staining her cheeks with sticky tracks. How empty life seemed when dreams were better than living. There, in the dark, with no one else to know, she wept in secret shame.

Chapter Five

❧

"Come in. Come in," Julianna murmured sleepily as the fourth knock sounded on her door.

"My lady?" came the faint reply through the thick door. " 'Tis locked."

Julianna reluctantly lifted her head and started to rise, but she had slept so fitfully that one sheet was wound about her waist while the another shackled her ankles. "Just a moment!" she called as she struggled to disengage herself from the bedding. Finally she succeeded, but her slippers and wrapper were nowhere to be found. Muttering, she marched to the door barefoot and unlocked it.

"Good morning, my lady." Mrs. Mead beamed, bearing a tray into the room. "I hope you slept well. 'Tis early hours yet, but I remember that you always were an eager riser. I've a special treat for you. I found a packet of cocoa in the pantry and made a pot for you."

The deep rich aroma reached Julianna's nose even as the housekeeper spoke, and her mouth began to water in response. "That sounds wonderful, Mrs. Mead. Thank you."

"Back to bed with you," Mrs. Mead said when she

spied Julianna's bare feet. "Wouldn't want you to take a chill."

Julianna obediently climbed back into bed as the older woman set her tray down and poured a cup of cocoa. "Now, my lady, what will you be wanting done this day?"

"We shall begin by removing the coverlets from the library and music room," Julianna said, and reached over to spoon two teaspoons of sugar into the cup Mrs. Mead handed her. "But, before that, there's broken glass in the entry that must be swept up."

"Broken glass?"

"Yes, someone threw a stone through the window last night."

"Oh, my lady!" Mrs. Mead turned on Julianna. "Who'd do such a thing?"

"I don't know." Julianna glanced thoughtfully at the older woman. "There's more. I think I saw someone in the entryway last night."

"You saw someone in the house?" Mrs. Mead's wide face went pale. "Why didn't you come for help?"

"Because I decided I must be mistaken," Julianna replied. "Just in case, I bolted my door and left the lights burning."

"I see." The housekeeper noticed now that a dozen tapers, burned down until they had guttered out, were stationed about the room.

"And another thing," Julianna went on. "I don't want Tom tracking up my room again. He must scrape his boots when he enters the house from now on. As for the mud on the floor, he can come and clean that up himself."

"What mud, my lady?"

"Why, right here—" Julianna leaned over the bedside

to point out the tracks but they had vanished. Her gaze swept in amazement toward the hearth, but not one single bootprint was visible. "But I saw them! Last night, when I awoke. A man's muddy work boots had left a trail from here to there." She used her finger to point out the path.

Mrs. Mead carefully lowered her gaze from her mistress's. "It were during the night, you say, my lady?"

"That's right," Julianna said defensively. "I saw them, plain as day." She knew her story sounded like the fragment of a nightmare when there was no proof to back it up. Yet she had gotten out of bed, studied the prints, even touched them.

She lifted her right hand to look at the fingertips and saw that they were dirty. "There! You see?" Triumphantly she held her smudged hand toward the housekeeper. "I touched one of the tracks and it left mud on my fingers."

Mrs. Mead frowned down at the floor and then made a low circumnavigation of the room before gazing up at Julianna again with eyes wide with open speculation. "Who cleaned them up, my lady, for ben't they no longer here?"

"I don't know." Defeated for the moment, Julianna leaned back against her pillows. "Never mind. I must be mistaken." But she was not, and she knew it.

"If that'll be all then." Mrs. Mead drew out the words encouragingly, obviously eager to be dismissed.

"Yes. That's all for now." She had made enough of a fool of herself for one morning.

The muddy prints had disappeared! Had they really been there, or had she only been dreaming? There was mud on her fingers, but perhaps her fingers were dirty when she went to bed. She had picked up and examined the rock thrown through the window. Besides, if there was mud, what had happened to it? She had not cleaned it up and no one else could have. She had been locked in. No one could enter or leave through locked doors. She must have dreamed it.

Half a dozen excuses flitted through her mind as she sought out a reasonable explanation for her experiences. For days she had been dreaming of a nightmarish wedding and then, more recently, of a lover who came to her under the cover of darkness. Ordinarily she was not given to such flights of fancy. Frayed nerves. The wretched journey. The aftermath from the shocks of the last weeks. Any of those things might have sparked her to an overactive imagination. Last, and reluctantly, she considered the possibility that had come to her in the middle of the night. That Blood Hall's ghosts had played the prank on her.

"Bosh!" Julianna murmured. Really, she was becoming quite tedious. If she was reduced to blaming ghosts for imagined incidents, she might as well take up residence in Bedlam. Resolutely she turned her mind to more pleasant thoughts.

It was a quarter past seven o'clock. It wouldn't be light for nearly an hour, yet she knew that the local miners were already on their way to work. The seamen of Ilfracombe and Bideford would be busily mending their nets if the cold windy morning had kept them from setting sail. In the better houses of the area, servants were up and working, lighting fires, baking bread, priming the house for their masters.

Yet Blood Hall was silent, so silent Julianna could hear the rhythmic *shirr-shirr* of her own blood through the arm on which her head rested. This evidence of her own mortality only magnified the disturbing quality of the dream she had had hours earlier. A man, a stranger, had bent over her while she slept. Had it been any more real than the imagined bootprints?

Belatedly she remembered her cocoa and picked up the cup and took a sip. With a gasp of surprise she spewed the mouthful back into the cup. It tasted terrible! She turned a suspicious eye on the sugar bowl. After wetting a finger, she stuck it in the silver dish and then brought it to her mouth. "Salt!" she exclaimed in surprise.

At that moment, Mrs. Mead came flying back into the room. "Don't drink, my lady! she cried. "I should have guessed when you told me about the bootprints. The captain and his lady have been at it again. They traded salt for sugar in the bins. There's starch where the flour should be and oatmeal in the yeast. Me morning baking is ruined!"

"Mebbe this too were a trick of the spirits," Tom Mead offered as he stood cap in hand before his mistress. Once the mischief in the kitchen had been discovered, Lady Julianna and Mrs. Mead had decided to investigate the larder and wine cellar, and there they uncovered a far more disturbing problem.

"Ghosts don't leave cheese crumbs and half-drunk bottles of wine in their wake!" Julianna answered indignantly.

"I'd not be knowin' anything about that!" Tom declared, growing red in the face.

"I'm not accusing you of any wrongdoing, Tom," Julianna replied in a more conciliatory tone. "I'm just enumerating the facts."

"Enum—?" The unfamiliar word got the better of him, and Tom shook his head in bewilderment.

"I'm merely listing our discoveries. The wine cellar's been broken into and a good number of the marquess's finest wines have been drunk. Obviously the villain didn't care that his presence would be discovered, since he didn't bother to hide the empty bottles."

She prodded with her shoe one of the numerous bottles lying about on the cellar floor. "As for the losses in the larder, Mrs. Mead says we are missing a smoked ham, a piece of salted beef, and several rounds of cheese, including the marquess's favorite Stilton. One must assume our intruders were great in number or that a single thief took up residence in the house for some weeks."

"That can't be, my lady. That careful were the missus and I to watch the house both night and day. Anyone sneaking about for long would have been spied."

"So it would seem," Julianna murmured, unconvinced by this statement. "And yet we have the evidence of an intruder before our eyes. How would you explain the losses?"

The question clearly troubled the groundskeeper, for he had no ready reply. Still, he knew that if he didn't offer some other suggestion, the finger of guilt would eventually point to him. "Them miners is a chary bunch. Mayhaps they broke in to do some mischief and settled for a meal instead."

"Miners?" Julianna arched a single brow. "Why it is that everyone I speak with berates the miners? One would think they had sprung suddenly to life by witchery rather than having grown up in Devonshire beside every

other man, woman, and child. Besides, if the intruders
had intended mischief, they might have caused a great
deal of it. Yet there isn't a single broken mirror or torn
drape, nor was a single piece of silver taken. Mrs. Mead
says there's some bedding missing and that a feather tick
has disappeared from one of the beds on the third floor.
No, I believe our mischiefmaker was simply enjoying
himself at our expense. And," she added dramatically, "I
think I know who it is! Where will I find Jos Trevelyn?"

"Beg pardon, my lady?"

"You needn't look surprised, Tom. I think our thief is
our new gardener. Where does he live? I mean to confront him myself."

"Now, my lady, ye'd ben't want to do that." Tom shuf-
fled his feet, thinking faster than usual. He had hired the
gardener. If the gardener was a thief, he would undoubtedly be held responsible for bringing him here in the first
place. Things would look better for him when the marquess found out about the incident if he could say he
caught the offender. "I'll see to it, my lady. Turn him off
right and proper, with a wallop or two to keep him company as he goes!"

Julianna sized up the man before her. He was an inch
shorter than she but with a wiry toughness gained from
years of work in the out-of-doors. He might be more
than a match for the gardener, yet violence was not her
goal. "That won't be necessary, Tom, but I would appreciate it if you would accompany me, just in case your
assistance is needed."

Mollified by her recognition that his presence would
be useful, he nodded agreeably. "Whatever ye say."

"He should be working in the garden. I'll just go up
and get my cloak and then meet you on the front steps."

But when she reached her room, Julianna didn't immediately fetch her cloak. Instead, she took the time to search once again for her spectacles. She thought she had left them on the bedside table when she went to sleep, yet they had not been there when she awakened. She and Mrs. Mead had searched the room, even going so far as to strip the bedding and turn the tick, but they had not found them. Was this more ghostly mischief?

"Devilish inconvenience!" she muttered, using one of her grandfather's more tame epithets. No doubt, since she was forever misplacing them, the spectacles would turn up. She would have liked to have a good hard look at the gardener's face when she accused him of the theft, but now that would be impossible. Giving up, she retrieved her favorite cloak, a plain red woolen one common in the West Country, and headed for the stairs.

As it turned out, she did not have to enter the garden to find Jos Trevelyn. He came around the side of the house, pushing a wheelbarrow of manure just as she stepped out the front door. He wore the same hat and rough work clothes of the day before but he'd shed his jacket. The sleeves of his shirt were rolled back to the elbows.

Not anxious to tackle him alone, Julianna realized in disappointment that Tom was not waiting for her as she had asked. Still, she supposed that she did not need anyone to help her in the matter. She had confronted more than one recalcitrant servant in her time.

Resolutely she stepped down onto the cobblestone carriageway to wait as Jos neared. In those moments she noticed that he had a decided limp, as if one leg was shorter than the other or a joint malfunctioned. She had not noticed this defect before and wondered if it was the result of the wound he had received as a soldier. The natural sympathy she held for any injured thing rushed to the fore, but she scotched the inclination. He was an ill-mannered, insolent thief who did not deserve her concern. Bracing herself, she waited for him to pause and doff his cap as custom demanded. Instead, he neither glanced toward her nor gave any indication that he saw her.

"Just a moment!" she was forced to cry, and rushed into his path when she realized that he intended to pass her by without any acknowledgment.

To her relief, he paused and set the load down on the drive then folded his arms casually before his chest, the thin faintly sallow lines of his face almost masked by dirt.

"I wish to speak to you." She felt his shaded gaze moving over her face and gown and was glad for the cover of her knee-length cloak.

"We're t' chat, yer ladyship? Dinna ye mind, Ah smoke?" So saying, he withdrew a clay pipe from his pocket, lit it, and began puffing away.

At that moment, Tom appeared from around the side of the house. Infuriated to see the man lighting his pipe in Lady Kingsblood's presence, he ran forward, pulled the pipe from the man's mouth, and threw it on the cobblestones where it broke into many pieces.

"What manners is that to be showin' her ladyship?" Tom demanded, his heavy workman's hands curling into gnarled fists in anticipation of the other man's retaliation. "Ye apologize!"

Julianna caught her breath. Seeing the two men side by side, she realized that her memory of the gardener had been at fault. His thinness had been an exaggeration.

Slender, yes, but with a competent strength of youth about him that boded ill for the older man.

Yet, even as she debated the outcome of a fight, Jos casually recrossed his arms and said, "She nae said it gave her displeasure, or d' yer speak for her ladyship?"

Tom glanced uncertainly at his mistress, conscious, suddenly, that he might have made a mistake.

Julianna smiled her reassurance. "Tom's right. I would prefer that you not smoke in my presence. However, I regret that your pipe was broken."

"Was ye wantin' somethin'?" Jos's eyes shifted from her to Tom. Beneath the brim of his hat, his mouth curved up in a insolent grin. "Goin' t' turn me off, were yer?" To Julianna's surprise, he sounded almost cheerful about the prospect. "Ye needn't o' brought a man t' protect ye. Ah'd nay set a hand on yer, for all ye may provoke me."

Refusing to be goaded into trading insults, Julianna decided to be as frank as he. "I intend to do more than turn you off, Jos. I've come to accuse you of theft. I suspect that before I arrived you broke into my larder and took wine that wasn't yours."

"Did Ah?" He shrugged his shoulders, and she noticed, despite herself, how the muscular contours reshaped his coarse workman's shirt. If he washed away the dirt that nearly obscured his features, he might prove presentable. "Ah wonder that Ah've no memory o' it. Were it a fair wine?"

"Don't be insolent," she snapped, annoyed with herself for being the slightest bit interested in a man who had robbed her. "I know you took it. You might as well say so."

"Ah'll say it, if ye wish, though ben't kind o' ye t' make o' me a liar."

"Are you denying that you stole food and wine?"

He didn't reply but simply stared at her in a way she was fast coming to understand was his habit when he was angry or considered the question beneath his regard. She grew even angrier. "Well, did you or did you not steal from me?"

"Am Ah t' have a choice? Then Ah muss think on it."

"You may do your thinking in the magistrate's jail." She turned to Tom. "Take this man to Ilfracombe and tell the magistrate that I wish to press charges of theft against him."

"'Appen ye'd better do th' takin' yerself, yer ladyship," Jos replied, his accent thickening with challenge. "Yer man will find th' takin' o' Jos Trevelyn som' doin'!"

"Are you threatening me?" Julianna asked in amazement.

He looked clearly amused. "Nae. Ah jus' find th' company o' a beautiful lady more t' me likin' than that o' a groundskeeper."

Julianna felt the color climbing her cheeks. He had called her beautiful. "If you didn't take those things, then who did?" She fully expected that he would turn the tables on the groundskeeper and his wife and accuse them. *Beautiful? Did he think she was really attractive?*

"Ah would say ye were pixied," he answered in a calm, direct voice.

The suggestion took Julianna so aback that she was momentarily speechless. "Yer missus"—Jos nodded at Tom—"told me a little while ago how as th' larder's been turned topsy-turvy. She thinks it were th' work o' spirits."

"Blood Hall's ghosts?" Julianna suggested. "Surely

you don't expect me to believe they drink wine and eat cheese."

"Ah ken naught o' that," he answered without a smirk. "It were only . . ."

"What?" Julianna demanded.

He lifted an arm and pointed at the main door of Blood Hall. "Ah respect th' spirits dwellin' within, an' they know 't. Ah keep a respectful tongue in me head when they're about strollin' in th' garden some evenin's, don't ye know?"

So that was to be his defense, Julianna thought in disgust. He must have known that they had trouble replacing the last gardener and hoped his mention of the ghosts would spook her into allowing him to remain. "Where do you sleep?" she demanded suspiciously.

He turned to her, his face glittering with wicked, unexpressed laughter, and she felt as hot and embarrassed as if she had made an improper suggestion. "You're insolent—"

"So yer said before."

"—and rude. Get off my property. This instant!" she cried, ending on a panting note.

"Nae, nae," he said quickly, and took a step toward her. Tom moved to place himself between Jos and the lady, but Jos halted well before they could clash.

Over Tom's shoulder he looked at Julianna, and she saw his eyes though the brim of his hat shaded them still. They were as softly colored as his voice had been hard. "Dinna turn me off for naught. It were only tha' ye were so certain Ah were yer thief, without so much as a shred of proof. 'Th' thief be Jos Trevelyn,' ye'd said to yerself, no askin' but tellin' me tha' t' me face. A man can stand only so much, after all."

Julianna stared at him in bewilderment, uncertain whether she or he had the right to be more insulted. He wanted to keep his job. She could see that much in his expression despite her blurred vision. But she also saw pride gradually stiffen his spine as the moments of silence stretched out between them, and she knew that he would not beg for it no matter how important it was to him.

She remembered the sallow thinness in his face and wondered if he was still ailing. "I understand you've been ill."

Jos made a sudden involuntary movement with his head as if to dislodge an unpleasant thought, but he did reply. "Hospital makes a Hercules sicken. It were nothin'."

Nothing? She had seen his limp and the yellowish tinge of lingering sickness, and wondered fleetingly what horrors he had endured while lying in a hospital bed waiting, perhaps hoping, to die. If she turned him off, how would he survive? "If you give me your word that you won't steal from me, I'll rescind my decision."

His expression changed, becoming forbiddingly cold. "Ah'll no do 't."

"Don't be daft, man!" Tom cut in, startled from silence at last.

"Why won't you make that promise?" Julianna asked in a genuine desire to understand.

"Yer ladyship made up her mind about me th' first time we met. Naught will change 't. Th' next trouble, and ye'll turn me off agin'. Tha's no way for a self-respectin' man t' live."

Julianna thought she understood at last. Proud yes, and arrogant, but with a set of ethics that set him apart from the ordinary man who would beg, grovel if he must, to keep his livelihood. Perhaps he had been a soldier of some rank, a lieutenant's batman. That would explain where he learned his arrogance and stiff-necked pride. "Very well. I take you at your word that you're a self-respecting man." She cast a meaningful glance on him as she added, "Who wouldn't stoop to thieving. You may stay. However, you may be certain that we'll see little of one another in future."

"Are ye goin' back to London, then?"

"No. Why do you ask?"

He shifted from one foot to the other. "Ah would no frighten yer ladyship, but this be troubled times. A bit o' flour missin', a bottle of wine drunk, 'tis nothin' compared to what might be. Ye'd do well to return to London. Ye can ask Tom there."

"What do you know of local troubles, Jos?" Julianna asked.

But he merely shrugged and turned back to his wheelbarrow.

"I hope yer ladyship doesn't come to regret her change o' heart," Tom said under his breath as they watched the gardener walk away, pushing his load.

"Neither do I, Tom, neither do I."

Julianna lay awake in the darkness, too proud to resort again to the blaze of candle and hearth to keep her fears at bay. The day had gone badly from start to finish. She and Mrs. Mead had uncovered the furnishings in the library only to find that the marquess's favorite settee had been nibbled at by mice. Immediately she had sat down to write a letter to the local furniture maker so that the damage might be repaired before her grandparents' return.

Later they had discovered mildew in the bedrooms on the third floor and carpet beetles in the Great Hall. Every room needed to be cleaned and aired. She had never realized the extent of care required to keep a house the size of Blood Hall in peak condition. Until this winter, with or without Lord and Lady Kingsblood in residence, the house had always been in the continuous care of a full staff. It was clear that she would need to hire a full staff in order to restore the house to its former glory by the time her grandparents returned, but she resisted the idea of having a troop of servants beneath the roof just yet. For the moment, peace and quiet were more important to her.

Still, those were not the concerns that kept her awake with late-night musings. It was something altogether more personal and dismaying.

She had made an error that morning in accusing Jos Trevelyn of theft. It was unlike her to make an accusation without proof. But there was something about him that raised her hackles each time she thought of him. She now believed him innocent, or at least she wanted to. Why, she couldn't say.

She sighed and shook her head. He was so sure of himself. He talked to her as an equal. It was not as if he seemed to think himself on a level with nobility, but rather that he felt she was no better than he. She had never given much thought to her aristocratic background, had always taken it for granted, as a matter of fact. Did she really resent his cocky self-importance in the face of her superior position? Or was her dislike of the man a more personal thing?

There was no use in turning over in her mind any of the rational explanations she had put in a letter to her grandfather. To her acute embarrassment, the one thought that remained when all the others faded was that Jos Trevelyn had done something she had never expected a man to do. He had called her beautiful.

Well, not precisely. And, of course, she knew he had said it with a calculation toward winning her over—which it had. But he had said it and, from that moment, she had known the battle was lost.

"Fiddlesticks!" she exclaimed. Rolling over, she shoved a fist angrily into her pillow. "I'll be no man's fool!"

Flattery was not about to turn her head, and certainly not from a common laborer. She had more pride than that!

Deeply ashamed of herself for having given his tribute a moment's consideration, she pressed her hot face into the impression she had made in the pillow and closed her eyes.

She was not aware of sliding into sleep or of the time that had passed.

The dream began as before, a vague stirring, a shaded awareness, a profile in the dark, familiar but unrecognizable. As he approached the blurred lines of his face sharpened into focus. Angles of strength met planes of determination. The mouth was straight yet sensitively modeled. His eyes were lost in shadow but moonlight turned his hair silver. As he bent slowly to her she raised her arms in welcome, knowing what was to come.

His lips were warm and firm, his breath hot and sweet in her mouth. Kiss played upon kiss, each more potent than the last. She felt herself melting, going down into the deep, delicious liquid center of herself where there was only pleasure. The gentle tug of teeth on her lower lip drew shivery sighs from her as she framed the shape of the man's shoulders within the compass of her arms. When warm palms moved down the front of her gown to trace the outline of her breasts, she arched against the pressure and heard his murmur of approval.

"Sweet . . . sweet," he whispered.

And she believed him.

The sweet sensation of desire was welling up in her. Her breath came more swiftly. Her skin felt brushed by flame. And still the kisses continued, hot, wild-honey kisses that brought tears of pleasure-pain to her eyes. If only it were real. If only she were loved. If only . . .

The clock chimed three times, awakening her. Unlike all the nights before, there was no vague unease as she emerged from the dream. The warning tingle of terror scudding along her bones was primitive and literal.

She was not alone.

She lifted her head, dreading what she would face yet unwilling to delay the inevitable.

Standing by her bed, within arm's length, was the shimmering image of a man.

Chapter Six

꧁꧂

He was in silhouette, a masculine image whose shirt-front gleamed faintly in the moonlight.

Julianna didn't move. There was some simple sound in the room, like the drip of rainwater from an eave, but softer. It was her own heart. Her spine tingled. Her palms itched. Her lids fell involuntarily shut. An urge shuddered through her to fling herself over the opposite side of the bed and onto the floor out of sight. Yet her body resisted. Her muscles were locked, rigid, incapable of motion of any kind. She felt hollow inside, scooped out by fear of the specter who hovered less than three feet away.

Her eyes opened.

He remained, indistinct to her nearsighted eyes, but more solid in her mind because the last dregs of sleep had drained away. He moved, as silently and bonelessly as a cat. The backward shift of motion carried him into the shadows at the foot of her bed. If she hadn't been watching him, she knew she would never have known he was there.

"Who are you?" She pushed the words past a terror-tangled tongue.

Silence.

Oddly enough, his silence made her braver. She understood that while there might be a threat in his presence, he was waiting, expecting something from her. She sat up slowly, feeling as awkward as an old woman whose joints had stiffened with time. "Are you a ghost?"

He extended a hand toward her, as if wanting her to clasp it in her own.

Julianna recoiled from the gesture, pulling the covers tightly against her breast as she came to her knees on the mattress. "What do you want?"

The room was too dim for her to catch his more subtle gesturing. "What do you want?" she repeated because fear had robbed her of her quick tongue and clever wit.

He swung his arm out. Squinting, she followed its direction until his finger was pointing at her bedroom door.

She half expected the door to be opened by supernatural power, or that someone would step through it. Then it struck her how ridiculous the expectation was. She was alone in the house, alone but for the shadowed presence at the foot of her bed.

Suddenly she wanted to touch him, to reassure herself that he was real, not a phantom of nightmare. Thief or robber, the thought of facing flesh and blood was preferable to the haunting, spectral figure whose image shimmered before her uncertain vision.

She pushed the covers aside and crawled slowly toward the foot of the bed, but he withdrew from her outthrust hand, the quick recoil of his body expressing eloquently that he did not want to be touched—if touched he could be.

Julianna's reason reasserted itself in a sudden blast of anger. Of course he must be real! Someone was playing a trick on her.

"Very well," she said more calmly than she felt. "If you won't speak then I'll see for myself who you are." She reached for the matchbox by her bedside and moved to strike a match.

The sound of his expelled breath hissed like escaping steam in the silence. "Don't."

The single word brought Julianna's head swiveling toward him. "What did you say?"

But he had moved again, farther away this time, until he was no more than a wavering shadow before her darkened fireplace. He pointed to the door a second time. "Leave here."

His voice was so deep, so hushed, so soft that the words seemed to register in afterthought. Had he actually spoken or had he placed the words in her mind?

Even in her amazement Julianna realized those words were a command. "Leave Blood Hall? Why should I?" she responded, preferring speech to the unnerving silence. "This is my home. You are the trespasser." Without another word she turned and quickly struck a match.

The saffron burst of the match catching fire momentarily blinded her. The next instant it subsided into a steady amber glow, and she glanced back over her shoulder. But he was no longer there. She quickly applied the match to the wick of her bedside candle, but as the candle spread its halo of light into the room, brightening it, she saw that she was completely alone.

"Who and what are you?" she called out, her voice echoed by the stone walls hidden beneath their rice-paper coverings. Beyond the candle's nimbus, the silvery murk at the edges of the room answered with silence.

There was nothing and no one there. No shadow. No footprint. No sound. Only the faint scent of roses dis-

turbed her senses. And a pervading chill that sent a
quiver of dread through her. He had simply disappeared!

Julianna caught her breath in a sob. Then, as on the
previous night, she heard the clock chime three times.

No one in her experience had ever simply disappeared,
nor moved so effortlessly or silently. Yet he had vanished
without a cry of hinge, a creak of wood, or a thud of
closure.

"That's not possible," she whispered to herself as she
struggled for control of her emotions. He must have
been real. He had spoken. She had seen the moonlight
on his shirtfront. Though he had moved with the soundless speed of a ghostly presence, she could not permit
herself to consider the possibility of having seen a phantom.

"I don't believe in ghosts!" she shouted suddenly.

In the backwash of the dying echo, she thought she
heard faint laughter.

Pulling the covers tightly about her once more, she
huddled back against the pillows, her wide and staring
eyes stripped of sleep and peace.

He stood behind the cold stones through which he had
passed, waiting with a trembling that had nothing to do
with the cold surrounding him. He wondered now if he
had been wrong to show himself to her. The thrill of it
had nearly betrayed him into making an error. Yet he
had not been able to resist touching her.

Watching her sleep, her soft mouth slightly parted, had
brought forth the memory of her kisses. The bedcovers
had fallen to her waist, and in the moonlight, the full
curves of her womanly figure had been revealed through
her sheer nightgown. The poker-stiff lady of the manor

who strode about Blood Hall during the day was more woman than she allowed herself to admit.

He had come to try to frighten her off, but the thought of touching her, however gently, had so strongly moved him that he had done just that. Her full lips had firmed upon waking, and their tantalizing taste had held him immobile so long he had nearly allowed her to capture him upon waking. Even then he might have stayed had she not struck a match and spoiled the mood.

Her face, though white with fear, had been extraordinarily strong and yet vulnerable. She was not beautiful but she had an air about her more compelling than superficial loveliness. She was so very much . . . alive. Yes, that was the word to describe her.

He preferred her as she had looked after her altercation with the gardener, her face flushed a quite lovely shade of pink and her eyes, Lord, her eyes blazing with green fire.

And yet there was an inexplicable sadness in her that only he had witnessed. No one else know that she cried herself to sleep each night, murmuring of broken promises and lost love. What man had spurned her? What man would?

He had seen how she conducted business and ran a household. She would make a dependable friend and dependable wife. As for love, only he knew the secret desire she kept banked down so tightly that he doubted even she realized its full potential.

A new thought struck him. Perhaps she could be useful to him. His use in the world had ended, but an emissary might take his place, go where he could not, see what he could not, speak where he could not.

Yet she was only a woman. The men who had bested

him were dangerous and ruthless. He could not ask her to risk her neck, but she could be his eyes in the world and, perhaps, with luck, point the way to those who could bring down the men who threatened Blood Hall and Little Hangman Mine. But first he must win her confidence. The question was, how did a ghost woo a lady?

The thought preoccupied him so long that the chill of the granite walls seeped deeply into him and the trembling of desire was replaced by a need for warmth.

Julianna knew that it was in the library somewhere. She had last seen it a year earlier when the marquess had been explaining its proper use to Edward, her younger brother, who had returned from India to attend public school.

She found the hand-tooled cordovan leather case in the right-hand drawer of his huge desk. After lifting it out, she lay it on top then flicked the catch with her fingernail. The top opened to reveal a brace of silver-inlaid pistols nestled in slightly faded wine-red velvet.

"Now then," she said softly, and closed her hand with satisfaction about the butt of one pistol.

She knew how to use it. The summer she turned eleven years of age, her grandfather had insisted, against her grandmother's wishes, that as a young lady who lived in the country, she should know how to shoot, both as sport and for her own protection. Ironically, it was during that first target practice fourteen years earlier that the extent of her impaired vision had been uncovered.

Julianna smiled to herself as she recalled her grandfather's astonishment when she could not only not hit a stationary target at ten yards but that she could not even *see* it. That very week, in the midst of the summer heat, he had taken her personally to London to have her fitted with a pair of spectacles. She detested them, but they had given her the ability to see and become a crack shot.

The exotic woods and polished silver that composed the butt gleamed with the deep sheen of long care as the weapon lay in her hand. It was one of a pair of dueling pistols given the marquess by a visiting Spanish dignitary forty years earlier. To her knowledge, they had never been fired to do mortal harm to another being. Strange that she should be the first Kingsblood to contemplate using them that way. Yet she intended to be ready if forced to again confront the intruder who had destroyed her sleep and peace of mind the night before.

She had had hours to consider her course of action. As time passed, her thoughts had become ever more dark, dangerous, and bitter. What would people think if she claimed that a man had entered her bedroom, spoken to her, then mysteriously disappeared? She could almost hear the snickering voices that haunted her nightmares.

Poor Lady Julianna claims to have seen a man in her bedroom.

A man in her room? What else but fancy—and wishful thinking!

Poor thing. Jilted she was. He married another. A beauty! You know what they say about spinsters. Sad, really.

She must be mad!

No, she would not allow that. The humiliation would be more than she could bear. She would handle matters in her own way.

"Oh, there you are, my lady, I—" Mrs. Mead came to a full stop at the sight of Lady Julianna with pistol in hand. "My lady, whatever are you doing with that?"

"I'm going to do some target practice," Julianna replied casually, placing the pistol back in the case. "I shall go out onto the moors after breakfast and see what I remember."

The housekeeper didn't ask why Lady Julianna had felt compelled to go downstairs in her bedclothes and bare feet to locate those pistols before breakfast, but it worried her all the same. There was something different about Lady Julianna these days. There was a peculiar look in her eye, a kind of feverishness that spoke of emotions barely in command. It was very unlike the Lady Julianna of old. "Did you sleep well, my lady?"

"Yes, of course," Julianna lied, for she had not slept a wink after three A.M. "I'm accustomed to more activity in London. After three days of lying about, I'm afraid I'm quite restless." Her smile was misleadingly bright. "The sun will shine today, thank Providence. Unfortunately, all the marquess's horses are in London so I can't indulge in a brisk ride across the moors. However, a good brisk walk should restore my spirits."

"Very well, my lady," Mrs. Mead replied, her mind going directly to the work before her this day, which included the pile of her ladyship's clothing that she had not yet aired and ironed. After a pregnant pause she added, "What would your ladyship think of me hiring a helper? I could get a girl in from the village who'd see to the keeping of your linen and the washing. She wouldn't be much good with dressing hair in the London fashion but she could learn, your ladyship having the patience to teach her."

The suggestion made such practical sense that Julianna was hard-pressed to resist it. "We'll see," she said evasively. Until she was absolutely certain whom or what she dealt with, she didn't want any extra people about. If she was losing her mind, she would do so privately. If she was being haunted, there would be plenty of time to seek corroborating witnesses. If a cruel trick was being played on her, she wanted to catch the culprit herself. Now that it was daylight, she was more disgusted with her own poor showing the night before than with the being who had frightened her. Well, she would not be found wanting in bravery a second time.

"You'll be wanting your breakfast then?" Mrs. Mead asked.

"Actually, I don't feel a bit hungry," Julianna replied. "If you'll pack a lunch for me while I go up and dress, I'll take it with me and dine on the moors."

The housekeeper kept to herself what she thought of the idea of picnicking on the winter moors because she could see that Lady Julianna was determined to have her way.

An hour later Julianna set off across the lawn, a basket on one arm and the leather case of pistols under the other. The pale early-morning sunshine promised to strengthen in the misty but clearing sky. By midday she was certain she could remove her cloak and be comfortable. In the midst of winter the rumbles of spring were beginning.

She skirted the empty stables, pausing only long enough to meet the new crop of kittens that came scampering from the main barn at the sound of her footsteps. There were six in all: two gray, orange, and white tabbies, three yellow ones whose fur looked more like the down of newborn chicks. The last, a black-and-white tom, had a smoke ring about one eye and three white socks and one black one. They tried to climb her boots with their tiny claws but failed, sliding down the smooth, shiny leather. Unable to resist them, Julianna squatted in the grass to scratch each and every one and didn't leave until she had parted with a fair portion of her lunch of ham and cheese.

After repeatedly shooing them away, she turned toward the open moorland, her back to the house. She ignored the sensation of being watched. It had become an almost familiar irritation, like an insidious itch.

From the oriel in the Great Hall two figures did, indeed, monitor her progress.

"What do you suppose she's doing?"

"Why, madame, she's proposing to blow her nightly visitor to kingdom come."

"Can she do that?"

"I should think she will try, providing she's the stomach to match the strength of her mind."

"But we must stop her."

"Whyever should we?"

"Because . . . well, because they've not yet been properly introduced."

"As I recall, that didn't stop you from taking a cock-eyed shot at me the first time I clamped eyes on you."

"That was different! All Roundheads were by definition my mortal enemies. I fully intended to kill you."

"I remember, golden-haired vixen that you were. God's body! If those heaving breasts of yours hadn't distracted the full company of my men, they'd have murdered you at once!"

"Then I must thank Providence for the endowment."

"Better to thank the yards in their codpieces! You shameless Kingsblood women know how to stoke a man's fire."

"I shall presently care to see a demonstration of it. However, what shall we do about Julianna?"

"Why, leave her to the lad. He's handled things quite well, to my way of thinking. None of Maxwell's niceties encumber him. Now, about that demonstration . . ."

"You must catch me first!"

Mrs. Mead entered the Great Hall at the exact moment a whirlwind spun past the entry, tossing her apron over her head and causing her to spill a good portion of the bucket of suds she had carried up to wash the windows with.

To the right and beyond a dip in the land, the lane running toward the highway to Ilfracombe stretched out before Julianna as a white ribbon in the brown and brackish landscape. Ahead, diaphanous curtains of mist cast faint, fleeting shadows over the day. Farther afield dark-gray granite tors thrust skyward from the boggy ground like pagan cathedral spires.

Julianna's spirits lightened as the sights and sounds and smells of the moors enveloped her. This was the land she knew and loved: difficult, changeable, unpredictable. Its wild and fierce beauty had nothing to do with fragile hothouse scents or careful cultivation and nurturing. Everything that existed on the moors earned its place by tenacity, strength, and endurance. If land could be proud, then the north Devonshire moors had much of which to boast.

She walked for a long time, past the tors and up over the ridges of hills. The grumble of the sea grew nearer, but she was not really seeking the sea. Her legs carried her over the ground, and she was without conscious thought. A thousand times she had come this way as a

child. In early summer she would pick wild lilies. Later in
the season she would bring home armfuls of heather for
her grandmother's bedside. She learned the meaning of
patience by sitting and watching the red deer emerge at
dusk from the trees in a nearby wooded valley. She knew
where to look for wild berries hidden among the bracken
on the hillsides and wild pears near the beach. Seeking
adventure, she would climb the cliffs that rose and fell
between Torrs Park just east of Ilfracombe. The steep
path led to Brandy Cover where, on a clear summer's
day, she could catch glimpses of the southern coast of
Wales. She knew a special spot where the path suddenly
descended into a tiny secluded cove of rocks and smooth
golden sand. Had it been summer, she would have gone
there to wade barefoot in the tide then sit in the sun and
eat her lunch. But today the fitful wind drove her to seek
the lee of a hillside.

Finally she paused in a place protected from the brunt
of the wind by trees and warmed by the sun, which had
now climbed nearly to its zenith in the pale-blue sky. She
went about her task very methodically, choosing targets
and measuring her practice distance from each by pacing
it out and placing a rock as a marker at each interval.
When she was ready, she placed the leather case on a
nearby flat stone, opened it, and loaded each pistol.

She began with the shortest distance, a pace of three
yards. Without checking her accuracy, she moved from
distance marker to distance marker, firing at what she
perceived to be the target. One. Two. Three. Four. The
sound of shots ricocheted under the canopy of nearby
trees, distorting the direction of the reports.

When she was done, she stood a moment, a pistol in
each hand. The violence of her actions momentarily

heartened her. At least she was prepared to respond to the threat of the unknown. Taking her safety into her own hands eased the humiliation of her fear, salved her wounded pride, and cooled the anger of impotence that had kept her awake and trembling half the night.

Yet, when she checked her targets, she found none of them marked by a bullet's passage. The new tremulous feeling of being in command slipped as she resigned herself to the fact that without her missing spectacles, she was nearly as blind as a bat.

"A man's a larger target than a leaf or twig," she murmured to herself, but then quickly shied away from the thought. She had no desire to shoot anyone. She only hoped to scare him away—if he dared return.

When she had cleaned and replaced the pistols in the case, and eaten her lunch, she moved on to where a huge flattened stone lay in the middle of a field of sheep. After taking off her bonnet, she stretched out on its warm hard surface and fell instantly asleep.

He knew the exact moment Lady Julianna returned to Blood Hall. He had heard the distant echoes of a firearm and wondered at the cause. Now as he watched her cross the carriageway toward the house, he spied the case she carried. Its shape and size were familiar. His father had owned one like it. He smiled at her audacity. Lady Julianna had been out on the moors practicing with dueling pistols!

What could her purpose be? He doubted she intended to challenge him. A smile eased into his face as he imagined her offering him his choice of weapons. Would she expect the gardener to be his second while Mrs. Mead acted as hers? No, more likely she planned a nasty surprise for him should he return to her room under the cover of night.

"The bloodthirsty little vixen!" he murmured in begrudging admiration. Once again he had underestimated her. The only thing he didn't understand was why she had not sent for the magistrate, or at least had the Meads search the house. Had Lady Julianna begun to doubt her own eyes and ears?

"Ah, Lady, you shall have even more reason to do so before the next sunrise," he murmured in good humor. She was not only smart, and passionate, she possessed the ability to surprise him continually. Before the next dawn he hoped to beguile her as well.

Her long midday nap had left Julianna too restless to retire early. Unfortunately, the country fashion of dining early had left her with nothing to do as the long evening stretched out before her. Eventually she would go up to bed and wait. But not just yet. Without any clear goal in mind, she drifted from room to room, candle in hand, pausing finally at the entrance to the music salon. As with most of the other rooms in the house, its furnishings remained covered, the fireplace closed, and the windows veiled by heavy draperies. Yet she entered.

She knew the room well. It was the only one at Blood Hall that her grandmother had remodeled. When free of its coverings, it was an elegant example of Empire styling. The huge Aubusson carpet's violet background provided a vivid setting for the harmonizing colors of lilac and green in which the rest of the room was decorated.

The piano was an Erard, a superb example of Regency styling. Beginning at one corner of the duster that covered the piano, Julianna rolled it up, careful to keep dust from sprinkling on the surface of the polished wood. When she had cleared the cloth, she went and brought over a candelabra from a nearby table. She pulled two extra candles from her pocket, set them in it, and lit them. Only then did she sit down and open the piano.

She didn't choose the music so much as she allowed the moment to direct her fingers into remembered patterns. After a few chords, a melody emerged as a memorized piece. She played two short pieces by Mozart. Then Mozart gave way to the more emotional Schubert, an étude followed by a serenade. She didn't think of the time or what might lay ahead. For the moment she was in and of the music, and her peace was complete.

When at last she closed the lid and rose, she was smiling. It had been weeks, no, months since she had felt like herself. She was now ready to face anything, even her intruder.

Julianna fell asleep after the second chime of midnight. Beside her bed a single candle burned steadily. It was the snuffing of that flame in the sealed room that quickened her senses to consciousness. A mysterious breeze, as cool as a human breath is warm, wafted across her cheek. Even in the instant her eyes opened she knew: He had come again!

He stood with his back to the fireplace where the glow of dying embers provided the only light. His very stillness radiated an impression of his masculine presence, a sensation not wholly unpleasant, but wholly unnerving for a spinster. A quiver began at the corner of Julianna's mouth as she moved a hand surreptitiously under the covers.

His image wavered as he moved, a solid shadow amid

night's less substantial ones. She heard one of the pokers
by the hearth being lifted. Did he mean to murder her
with a blow to the head? Her heart lurched as she
grasped the object in her lap. "You there! Stop!"

He stilled, blending instantly into the surrounding
gloom.

Squinting, Julianna tried desperately to separate his
shadow from the others but failed. Once more she
damned the loss of her spectacles. As little as she liked
wearing them, they would have been most useful just
now.

A few seconds later she heard the rattle of the poker
in the grate, the soft *clink* of coal as it was being shifted,
and then she saw the beginning of a reddish glow. The
fire blazed momentarily as fresh oxygen fed the thin
tongues of flame darting forth. Light licked his torso,
making bright his shirt and throwing his profile into
glowing relief.

The revelation took Julianna's breath away. The
sharply etched features were those of a young and very
handsome man. The next moment the scattered fire died,
leaving him once again in murky shadow.

Alarmed, Julianna called out, "Where are you?"

"Still here, madame." She saw indistinctly the wrinkle
of shading as one shadow slid over another.

He had shocked her more than he knew by having
spoken—in a thoroughly cultured voice no less!—but Julianna was determined not to show it. "Keep away from
me, young man!"

"Young man?" His tone was clearly amused. Her tone
suggested she was a woman twice his years when, in fact,
he was the elder. "Don't be alarmed, dear lady. I mean
you no harm."

"Don't talk to me!" Julianna snapped, preferring silence to this compelling masculine voice. This was clearly not Jos Trevelyn or any other common laborer or thief. Who was he? The glimpse of his profile had stirred her feminine appreciation of masculine beauty, and it immediately recalled to mind Lord Dashmore's handsome face, and his betrayal. That made her angry. "If you think that just because I'm a spinster living alone you can terrorize me, you are mistaken! I am not so easily frightened!"

"I can see that," he replied agreeably, his voice floating above the blanketing darkness. "Yet you are neither too sheltered nor too old to understand the inherent dangers of entertaining a man in your bedchamber." His voice drifted toward her in deep hushed waves of sound.

Julianna leaned forward, gazing intently at the spot from which the voice seemed to emanate. If only she could see him clearly, she was certain she would be able to give a reliable description of him to the magistrate in the morning. "Very well, disappear and don't come back, then I'll believe that you are no more than vapor."

"Is that what you really want?" His voice, rising from the violet gloom, teased her. The *swish* of fabric accompanied the parting of draperies and then moonlight spilled through a window, flooding the room with milky light. Yet he was careful to remain in shadow. "Do you truly wish to be left alone," he whispered, "alone and forgotten, to nurse your broken heart?"

Julianna gasped. "How do you know of that?"

"Ah, madame, a friend may know many things." His form detached itself from the darkness to become a well-defined figure approaching the foot of her bed.

Disconcerted by his action, she reached up with her

free hand to make certain that every one of the tiny pearl
buttons marching up the front of her gown was closed.
She thought she saw his silhouette quiver, as if in silent
mirth, and snatched her hand away. "I don't wish to be
haunted," she said in her most sensible voice. "Go
away!"

He paused at the foot of her bed, his silhouette blending into the bed hangings. "And do what, madame?"

"Find another place. England is full of ghost houses.
The West Country alone has hundreds of them. Every
valley, moor, and hill claims a specter. Haunt elsewhere.
We are full up!"

"You refer, of course, to the captain and his lady."
There was a short pause before he added, "We have
met."

Julianna stared at his opaque form, nonplussed again.
Either she was mad or dreaming, and she was not certain
which was preferable. "What do you want?"

"Why, no more than your friendship." He spoke as a
practiced courtier might, with just enough levity in his
voice to be flattering.

"Why should you seek my company?"

"Because you need me," he answered, his silhouette
more relaxed than before. "I know that you're sad. I also
know the cause of that unhappiness is a love affair that
could not be worth a single one of your tears."

Julianna jumped as if scalded. "You presume too
much!"

"In what way? Because I think the fellow, whoever he
is, was a fool to desert you?"

"I was not deserted!" she cried, shaken out of her self-
possession by his revelation that he was somehow party
to her most intimate thoughts and secret shame. It was

intolerable that he should know such things, say such things to her.

Then a new and horrible thought struck her. Could this man be a London wag who had come to Devon to play a practical joke on her? She knew that such things occurred. Gossip circulated in gaming halls by intoxicated gentlemen sometimes became the subject of callous bets and challenges. As she recalled the conversation she had overheard at the wedding reception, a stinging like a rash of nettle shot up her neck into her face. Someone might have bet a friend that he would be the first to "comfort" the spinster!

Julianna yanked the pistol up from her lap so quickly the intruder had no time to react before the barrel was level with his heart. "Now then!" she cried in an anger-husked voice. "If you truly are a ghost then my shot should pass harmlessly through you. If not, I'll have shot an intruder. What have you to say to that!"

"Your method would seem brutal but effective," he replied. Yet she detected a note of whimsy that betrayed that he was no more eager than she to put the matter to the ultimate test. "However, unless you're resolved to blow me to kingdom come . . ."

Julianna blinked back tears of outrage, struggling to maintain her dignity. At this moment there was nothing she would have liked better than to blow him to perdition. To think that anyone would stoop so low as to invade her home! The privacy of her bedroom! In the hope of winning a bet! "If you think that I won't fire a shot you're very much mistaken!" Yet her arm began to tremble with the enormity of the action she contemplated, and she had to add the bolstering of her other hand to keep the pistol aimed straight. "Who are you?" she demanded a second time.

"But I told you," he replied, sounding for all the world like a wounded swain whose beloved was taunting him. "I'm a friend who's come to help you."

"That's preposterous!" Julianna exclaimed. "I don't even know you."

"But you do. Twice, dear lady, you've welcomed me into your dreams," he said sweetly.

Appalled anew, Julianna could think of no reply. She could not decide which was worse, to be conversing with an audacious flesh-and-blood man or a spirit who seemed to have the power to see even into her dreams. Both thoughts were equally unnerving. His gentle laughter did not improve her mood, but it hardened her resolve to continue to believe that he was very much human. "If you are so perceptive, then tell me where I may find my spectacles?"

"In the pocket of your cloak," he answered promptly.

"Impossible. I checked there yesterday."

"Did you? Are you certain?"

"Of course I'm certain." Frowning in thought, she unconsciously lowered her pistol. "I looked through every pocket of every article of clothing I've worn since I arrived. It's not there."

"You may easily prove me wrong," he invited, sweeping a hand toward her armoire.

"Just so." Half turning away, she reached for a match and struck it. "We will settle this—" She glanced back toward the shadows at the foot of her bed, but he was no longer there.

"Wait!" she cried, turning to apply the lighted match to a candle wick. Yet, as the halo of light dispersed the darkness, she found only empty space where moments before a vibrant presence had stood. "Where are you?" she cried like a child deprived of a favorite plaything.

The voice was muffled this time, as if it traveled a great distance to reach her. "You will receive a visit from your mine foreman tomorrow. Give attention to what he tells you."

"Why?" she called, scrambling quickly from the bed to search for the source of the voice. "What interest can it be to you?"

There was no reply.

She rushed over to the fireplace, not knowing what she expected to find but half certain that the last words had come from that spot. Careful examination of chimney and hearth revealed nothing, not even a muddy footprint.

Almost reluctantly she approached her armoire. She stood irresolutely a moment before snatching open the door. When nothing leapt out at her, she set her candle on the floor and reached in to pull her cloak from its peg. She thrust her hand into first one pocket and then the other. With a cluck of her tongue, she withdrew her hand and stared down at the spectacles in her grasp.

"But I looked here before!" she murmured in mystification. "I'm sure of it!" She whipped around to face the room, but she knew, with the same innate sense that warned her of his coming, that he was now gone. "Friend?"

For the space of five heartbeats she stood absolutely still. With a speed that would have shocked her Cousin Lettie, she ran and jumped into her bed and threw the covers over her head.

Chapter Seven

Julianna awakened feeling distracted and confused. For a moment she did not know where she was. She had been dreaming the most fantastic things. Caught in the backdrift of the dream's aftermath, she stared ahead without seeing anything.

She had been in the rose garden on a summer's night watching as a pair of dancers swirled in one another's arms to the music of a lute. She did not know the tune, but the melody was so poignant that she teetered on the verge of tears. The dancers, unaware of her presence, had eyes only for one another. Their voices were whisperings that only they could share, but she heard the man's rumbling laughter and the woman's musical reply. A cloud drifted across the moon, dappling the garden in indigo. Then the pearl-white light reappeared and with a new sense of awareness moved in Julianna.

Someone stood beside her. She could not see him, but his shadow fell across her with the gentleness of a lover's caress. His hand lifted, grazed her cheek, then settled cool fingers against the nape of her neck. Her whole body began to tremble, but she could not look away from the dancers. There was something too compelling about them to be denied. A thumb touched her ear and began a mesmerizing circular path following its contours. Her lips parted involuntarily and a sigh escaped. His touch altered, his hand sliding forward to cup her chin and turn and lift her face toward his. Afraid, she shut her eyes, but the warm and searching mouth that descended on hers sent them flying open again. She blinked and, as Blood Hall's Chinese Room came into blurred focus, Julianna knew she was now awake. Turning her head on the pillow, she let her gaze drift toward the motes dancing in the sunlight streaming through the window. Who had drawn the draperies? Next her gaze lit upon the breakfast tray by her bed. She tentatively touched the teapot and found it lukewarm. The fact that it had been sitting there some while made scant impression. As she drew back her hand back under the covers, she brushed cold metal lying on the mattress beside her and her fingers closed round her grandfather's dueling pistol.

With a sigh of resignation she lifted her eyes to look up at the Chinese silk canopy overhead with its delicate embroidery in the purest shades of vermilion, sapphire, emerald, and gold. Though the silk and everything else in the room was more than a hundred years old, they looked as fresh and bright as the day they arrived. The room was said to be haunted, and last night the most remarkable event of her life had taken place within its walls. She had conversed with a ghost! At least, she could not prove that he was otherwise.

A light rap on the door was followed by Mrs. Mead's entrance. When she saw that Julianna's eyes were open, a smile broke over her face. "Ah, you're awake, my lady. Mr. Coleman is still waiting below. Has been this last half hour. Of course, I will tell him to come back later, if you'd like."

"No, no." Julianna sat up quickly. "There must be a problem at the mine for him to come here so early in the morning."

Mrs. Mead chuckled. " 'Tis midmorning, my lady."

"Gracious!" Julianna threw back the covers and slid from bed. "You shouldn't have allowed me to sleep so long, Mrs. Mead. Certainly you should have awakened me the moment Mr. Coleman arrived."

"I tried," the housekeeper answered with a wry expression. "And twice since. But you were sleeping so soundly I thought to myself that poor Lady Julianna must need her rest."

"Grandfather wouldn't be so tolerant of such laziness," Julianna answered, hurrying over to her washstand. "He once poured a pitcher of water over my head when I refused to rise. He says that an early start is the basis of competence."

In her haste, she splashed water over the side of the basin and soaked the toes of her slippers. "Oh, bother! Look what I've done. No, no, we haven't time to mop it up," she added as Mrs. Mead came toward her. "Please lay out my—oh, I see you already have." Her new brown silk gown and undergarments had been laid out on a chair.

"I didn't do it, my lady," Mrs. Mead answered with a puzzled look. "I supposed you had."

"Oh." Julianna glanced again at the clothing. She hadn't laid her clothing out the night before. Her scalp tingled. Was it more ghostly doings? "Oh yes, now I remember." She turned quickly away before the housekeeper could read "liar" in her face. "Just give me a moment to wash, and you may lace me up."

Ten minutes later Julianna swept into the Great Hall

in a gown the color of autumn leaves: brown India silk
with shimmering threads of gold and red. It was a gift
from her parents, but one she had thought styled too
young for her. The neckline was low and oval, framed by
a deep collar that fell over her shoulders in a manner
faintly reminiscent of the style of the seventeenth century. The bodice was close-fitting and deeply pointed in
front, which made her already narrow waist appear even
tinier. The flared oversleeves were trimmed in black velvet braid and cord. There was a matching cape collar that
would have made it more appropriate for day wear, but
she had not been able to locate it. Because the mine
foreman had already been waiting for a while, she had
forsaken her usual hairstyle, a complicated chignon composed of several intertwined plaits. Instead, she had
parted her hair in the middle and pulled it back with
combs, letting the rest fall in heavy waves down her back.

The effect quite startled Jed Coleman as she entered.
At first he thought another, younger member of the
Kingsblood family was now in residence. If not for the
spectacles perched on her nose, he would not have had a
clue to who she really was. Even so, his voice sounded
tentative as he said, "Good morning, m'lady."

"And a good morning to you, Mr. Coleman," she returned in a brisk but friendly manner. "I regret that
you've had to wait for me, but I see Mrs. Mead has taken
good care of you." She nodded toward the tray of tea
and sandwiches on the table by his chair. "I believe I will
have a cup. Ah yes, there is an extra setting."

While she helped herself to tea, Jed tried not to stare
at her. It wasn't only her appearance that had startled
him, though he had always thought she dressed too dow-
dily for so young a lady. There was something different

about her that defied the cut of a gown or the arrangement of her hair. She looked, well, younger, and prettier.

Unaware of his scrutiny, Julianna turned to him when
she had taken a first sip. "Now, what may I do for you,
Mr. Coleman?"

"The marquess always calls me Jed, m'lady. I came
cause ye ordered it. Come by the end of the week, ye
said."

"Yes, of course." But Julianna had quite forgotten her
request and had remembered only that the intruder in
her room had predicted Jed would come. "What news do
you have for me, Jed?"

"Little enough, m'lady. I didn't hear tell of the man ye
wanted me to find."

"Nothing?"

"Only that he were never seen again after the day o'
the scuffle."

"Scuffle." A man may have been murdered and he
called it a "scuffle." Julianna sipped a little more of her
tea in the hope that it would soothe her nerves, but her
cup rattled so loudly as she placed it back in its saucer
that she set it aside. "Very well. What do we do now,
Jed?"

"Nothin', m'lady. Just keep quiet and watch."

"What about the miners?"

Jed shrugged. "Same as before. No worse, no better."

"Then we can expect trouble at any moment," Julianna concluded, and rose to her feet. "I won't sit by
while others plot the fate of Little Hangman Mine. The
least I can do is meet the opposition. Who declares himself to be the leader?"

"There's a man by the name of Wheal. He's an underground captain, but he ain't the sort yer ladyship would want to meet."

"I don't plan to have him in to tea," she answered with a smile. "What sort of man is he?"

"He'd as soon wipe his boots on yer skirts as speak to ye, if ye take my meanin'."

"Then he'll have a surprise in store when he meets me," Julianna declared in a tone that erased the last doubt from Jed's mind about the usefulness of discussing business with a lady.

"If ye'd take me advice, m'lady, ye'll have no traffic with Rob Wheal." He looked her straight in the eye and added, "I'd give the same advice to the marquess, were he to ask it."

She held his gaze. "Would he accept it?"

Jed grinned, showing a newly broken tooth. "Nay, m'lady. I've nae doubt but he'd steer the opposite course."

She smiled back at this use of seafaring terminology in Jed's speech, for she knew that before he became a miner, he had been a seaman. "Grandfather says that more can be learned about one's enemy at the peace table than in the thick of battle. If it comes to war, then at least I'll have seen Blood Hall's enemy up close." She noticed that Jed was now staring at her. "What's the matter?"

Jed wagged his head. Her tone of voice and force of will were pure Kingsblood. The pretty gown and un-bound hair were mere distractions. "Ye cant yer head just like the marquess when he's displeased. Ye even nar-row yer eyes the same, like ye can see farther than mere mortals. It fair gives a man a chill."

The comparison pleased Julianna no end. "Don't be

deceived, Jed. I'm not the marquess, nor do I claim his place. But I'd like a look at this Rob Wheal. Can you arrange an excuse that will also allow me to visit the mines?"

Jed's brows lowered ominously. "Now, m'lady, I won't be tellin' ye yer business, but I can't have ye down me mines just now. In the best of times it's a dark, dirty business. As things stand . . ." Suddenly his heavy face cleared. "Aye, but there might be a way, for all that. 'Tis Shrove Tuesday this next week, a holiday."

"And Pancake Day!" Julianna exclaimed. "I'd forgotten. Will there be a festival this year?"

"Don't doubt there will, though what with the lean times, many will go Tiptoeing for their pancakes."

"Oh yes," she replied less enthusiastically. "Tiptoeing" or "Gooding" was the custom of the poor who would go from door to door to beg from their neighbors the needed ingredients for their final meal of eggs, butter, and fat before Lent began. She knew that a refusal often resulted in a shower of stones for the hard-hearted. Sometimes, though, the custom was used as an excuse for mischief. "I know what I'll do, Jed. Blood Hall will provide the foodstuffs for the miners' Shrove Tuesday celebration."

"M'lady," Jed cautioned, "that's nae small expense."

"It'll be less expensive than replacing the engine works of Little Hangman Mine." Or all the glass panes in the windows. "I don't want there to be any excuse for trouble. This celebration might be all that's needed to restore good feelings, at least until the marquess returns."

Jed grinned at her, his weathered face folding into deep pleats. "I said it once, and I'll be sayin' it again, I do admire the workin's of yer mind, m'lady."

She blushed, as pleased with her idea as he was. "Thank you. Tell Mrs. Mead before you leave which and how much foodstuffs will be needed. You may bring men on Monday to collect them. On Tuesday I'll attend the village celebration. I insist," she added when she saw him begin to frown. "A Kingsblood must be present to show we're not too good to eat with those we feed."

"I'm no likin' it, m'lady, but I'll come fetch ye, if ye wish it."

"No, you should be with the men to make certain that things are distributed fairly. Send someone you trust to escort me."

"Very well, m'lady." He glanced sidelong at the stack of scones remaining on the silver tray.

"Take them," she encouraged.

When he had stuffed his pockets full, Jed pulled his forelock in salute and left her.

As he walked down the hall toward the servants' stairs, he pulled a scone from his pocket and tucked it in his mouth. He had never had much traffic with the nobility, certainly not with ladies, but his opinion of their worth was steadily improving through his association with Lady Julianna. Oh, she thought too much of herself and her abilities, but didn't they all? She had a good heart and a sensible head. And quite a nice bosom, now that he had had a chance to look at her again.

A lewd smile stretched his lips. It was a real shame she was a spinster. A bit of "slap and tickle" was just what she needed to make her really blossom.

As he reached again into his pocket, he trod on a loose board at the top of the servants' stairwell. It suddenly swung up and smacked him smartly across the seat of his pants. The blow so surprised him, he nearly went head-first down the stairs.

He turned to examine the flooring but could not find the offending board. Yet as he turned away in puzzlement, he thought he heard the eerie echo of masculine laughter rising from the stairwell. Only then did he remember that ghosts were said to dwell within Blood Hall. Had they surmised his lecherous thoughts and sought to punish him for his impudence?

Though a brave man, he was Devonshire born and bred, with a hearty respect for things beyond his ken. Quickening his step, he descended the stairwell in record time, determined to keep his thoughts of Lady Julianna respectful from now on.

"That was unnecessary, madame."

"Do you think so? He's old enough to be her father, the lecher!"

"You've always held a fondness for lechers."

"I've a fondness for you."

Julianna had waited all day for an appropriate moment to ask her question. Now, as Mrs. Mead served her the evening meal, it seemed the moment had come. "I've been thinking of writing a history of north Devon and the Kingsbloods," she said by way of an opening. "We seem to have had more than our share of adventures and legends. For instance, what do you know of the spirits who are said to haunt this house?"

"Why, what anyone with ears knows," Mrs. Mead replied. "That the restless spirits of the murdered Cromwellian soldier and his Kingsblood mistress walk the halls."

Julianna picked up her fork and pushed a pea across

her plate. "Are there no other spirits who haunt this corner of Devon?"

The older woman eyed her cautiously. "What sort would you be meaning?"

"Oh, I don't know precisely," she dissembled. "Surely there are tales of other specters, a young man, for instance. Handsome, well spoken. A spurned suitor who committed suicide or died of a broken heart?"

Mrs. Mead's expression went blank. "I wouldn't be knowing about such."

"I see." Feeling that she had pressed the matter as far as she could without revealing a little of her nighttime adventure, Julianna fell silent.

"Oh, now that I think on it, my lady, I do recall a tale." Mrs. Mead paused to fill Julianna's wineglass. She smiled and rolled her eyes. "Only, 'tis a bawdy bit o' of a tale. 'Tain't the sort a lady should be hearing."

"Really?" Julianna chased a pea off her plate, and it rolled into her lap.

Mrs. Mead seemed to debate the matter internally before she said, "Have you ever heard tales of the Love Talker?"

"No, I haven't," Julianna replied, surprised by the quickening of her heartbeat. "What an odd name. Who is this Love Talker?"

"Well, 'tis like this. When a lass comes a cropper and there's no man willing to step forward to admit the deed, the lass will sometimes claim she's been seduced by the Love Talker."

"Seduced?" Julianna's fork plowed to a stop in the midst of her mashed potatoes. "Could a mortal girl be seduced by a spirit?"

Mrs. Mead snorted. "There's them as will say so, my

lady. Particularly if the lass's had no suitors or 'tis known she's fey."

"You mean feebleminded?"

"Oh, there's that too. But mostly the Love Talker is said to appear to lasses who are lonely or living alone. He beguiles them with flattery and wins their hearts."

"The poor girls," Julianna said softly, beginning to see a possible explanation for the past night's events that she did not like one bit. "What happens if the girl listens to him?"

"Naught happens if she only listens," Mrs. Mead replied with a chuckle. " 'Tis the doing of the deed that causes the mischief."

Julianna looked up. "What sort of mischief?"

Mrs. Mead gave her mistress a considering look before saying "Nine months and a new mouth to feed, that's mischief enough for any maid, isn't it, my lady?"

"Oh, I see." Julianna laid her fork aside and reached for her wineglass.

" 'Tis only a legend, o' course. 'Tis a bit of Celtic nonsense from the old days when folk believed in pookas and pixies."

"Thank you, Mrs. Mead. You've been most informative."

When dinner was finished, Julianna remained in the Great Hall with a book she had brought to read. After the Meads looked in to say their good nights before they departed, she remained, reading by the fire and sipping the cherry cordial she had poured for herself.

She did not look up when the clock struck twelve or one A.M. Not until it struck the second hour after midnight did she close her book and pick up her candle to light her way to bed.

She entered her room slowly but without particular fear. Her nightly visitor had made himself known to her only after three A.M. She had plenty of time to prepare.

When she had lit enough candles to her satisfaction, she folded back the bedcovers but did not get into bed. She pulled two pillows from the top and laid them end to end on the mattress and then covered them. Stepping back, she surveyed her handiwork and smiled.

She moved to her dressing table, intending to pick up the stool set before it, but when she saw herself in the mirror she paused. She had had no time to appraise her appearance that morning, but now she straightened and studied her reflection. Amazingly, she looked quite young and pretty. The rich golden-brown sheen of her silk gown added golden flecks to her jade-green eyes and turned her skin a soft peach shade. She reached up automatically to give her hair a pat, but the vanity of the action reflected in the mirror made her drop her hand.

"You mustn't flatter yourself," she admonished her image. She saw her faults for what they were: a long nose, a wide mouth, and hair so dark it would seem contrived with the aid of boot black. These were things that no cut of gown or curling papers could alter. She was too tall for fashion, too amply endowed for aesthetic tastes, and too restrained to suit others. No. She must become resigned to it, she was designed to repel the man who attracted her. As for the rest, men of small minds and great tyrannies, she would not have them!

This assessment seemed to release much of her pent-up frustration of the last hours. Feeling better, she picked up the little stool and carried it to the corner where an Oriental lacquer screen hid her washstand. When she was satisfied that she could see both the bed and the fireplace from this vantage point, she walked about the room dousing candles until only two remained lit, one on the mantel and one by the bed. Finally she went back and sat on the stool with her back to the wall and her spectacles firmly in place on the bridge of her nose.

She heard the clock strike three and then, much later, four. Tired, cramped, and numb from the cold, she forced her eyes to remain open until the clock chimed the next half hour. Eventually body won out over mind, and her head nodded forward onto her chest.

Once he was certain she was soundly asleep, he entered the room. As he bent and picked her up to carry her to bed, she turned her cheek into his shoulder as naturally as a child might. "Who are you?" she murmured.

"A friend," he said quietly by her ear.

She snuggled closer to his chest, mumbling "Friend."

Poor Lady Julianna, he thought, gently amused. She had hoped to trap him with her simple ruse, but sleep had been the more powerful lure. She could not know that he had watched her prepare her little deception, or that he had been with her in the Great Hall while she read, watching protectively and enjoying her silent companionship. She did not know that he had wanted to show himself to her there but had resisted the temptation. She did not know how she had begun to haunt his every thought, nor that the tenderness he felt toward her was the most disturbing and dangerous feeling he had ever known.

He crossed the floor noiselessly and laid her carefully on the bed. She murmured in protest as he released her, but her body was weighed by exhaustion and she went effortlessly onto the bedding. He reached down, plucked her spectacles from her nose, and placed them on the nightstand. Then, regretfully, he snuffed the bedside candle with his fingertips. Finally he pressed a knee onto the bed, turned her slowly onto her side, and began unlacing her gown.

She stirred again and he felt the tensing of her body as she strove to break sleep's embrace. "Who's there?" she asked again.

"It's time for bed, darling," he said, and smoothed her cheek. "Let me undress you."

She reached up and cupped his hand with hers, turning her cheek more fully into his palm. "Warm," she mumbled.

He stilled, waiting for the moment when her eyes would open. But she did not awaken. After a few seconds, it was clear that she had fallen into a deeper sleep.

Working quickly but with utmost care, he finished unlacing her gown and then slipped it from her shoulders. As a man, he had always been amazed by the amount of clothing women wore. All but the lowliest prostitutes wore stays and at least four petticoats. Lady Julianna appeared more modest than most. She wore an amazing number of layers under her deceptively frail silk gown. When he had tugged the fourth petticoat from her hips, he was tempted to find scissors to snip off the rest. But, finally, she lay in only her chemise, corset, and drawers.

In the faint light from the candle on the mantle, he saw that her undergarments were plain to the point of virginal prudery. Conversely, their purity inflamed his imagination. He had caressed and kissed but not yet seen what lay beneath those prim white garments. Now he would have that pleasure.

He gently loosened the drawstring round the neck of her chemise and drew it down, revealing the swelling fullness of her breasts above the corset. In another moment he had freed her of her corset. The sight sent blood rushing to his groin. Freed of restraints, her naked breasts lay full and proud against her slender rib cage. Candlelight bathed them in an amber glow, turning the soft nipples a dusky rose. Unable to stop himself, he reached out to touch her with his fingertips. At the touch of his chilled hand, she sucked in a breath and drew up her legs, shifting onto her side and trapping his hand between her naked breast and bedding.

For a long while, he allowed his hand to remain. She felt so warm and soft and alive. Her heart thudded with calm regularity under his fingertips. The weight of her breast trembled with each indrawn breath. His thumb brushed her nipple, and she shuddered.

The pleasure of merely caressing her was a pain almost beyond enduring, and so he withdrew his hand. He had taken advantage of her once, more advantage than he would have dared had he known she was a virgin. Now he could not, even in his own dubious conscience, find an excuse to take such advantage of her a second time.

When he had drawn the covers up over her, he melted back into the darkness from which he had come and from which he was determined never to appear again.

They watched him cross the yard and disappear in the direction of the coast.

"What pains the lad? Why did he not stay with her?"

"You surprise me, madame, for are you not the one who thought their meetings scandalous?"

"They are. Yet why do you suppose that should matter to him after all this time?"

"Perhaps he's playing a game with her. I tell you, I've not felt quite right about this from the beginning. We should never have meddled in this affair."

"How tiresome you grow. One would think you are losing your nerve after all these years."

"Tis a brave man who knows when to look to his back."

"You sound almost afraid, Captain."

"Cautious, lass, merely cautious. Where's the girl?"

"Sleeping, Captain, and dreaming."

Julianna dreamed of a scented garden, of a secret place where the sun shone in dappled pools, where leafy shade cast variegated shadows upon the path, where muted birdsong and the crickets' chirp vied with the hushed voice of the breeze.

He stood in leafy shadow, his hair a faint glimmer of bright gold among the stippled ferns and the deep, soft shade of trees. A breeze brushed past her cheek, carrying in it the scent of roses.

For one wild, heart-stopping moment, she thought she knew him, recognized in the tilt of his head, in the deceptive stillness of his figure, an intimate knowledge of him more complex than that which comes from the familiarity of features and speech.

He was her lover.

The sense, unmistakable, shook her to the soles of her feet. Then something stronger came wafting on the breeze, shouldering aside the body's knowledge of its possessor. As comforting and simple as the common scents of fresh earth, new-mown grass, and bouquets came the sweet and haunting surety of love.

Chapter
Eight

❦

With Lent close at hand, Julianna found herself sitting through a more lengthy sermon than usual at church. The comforts of the Kingsblood pew, which included a stove and lap furs for warmth and goose-down seat cushions and kneeler for comfort, could not dissipate the discomfort of listening to the sonorous tone of Parson Pollock. To keep from falling asleep behind her spectacles, she had so far counted all the angels on the altar (twelve), the number of pieces of red glass in the great lead-glass window beside her family pew (one hundred and sixty-four), and finally, the number of cross-stitches in the needlepoint plaque hanging inside her pew that read HE THAT IS WITHOUT SIN AMONG YOU, LET HIM FIRST CAST A STONE. She had lost count after five hundred and thirty-nine stitches.

He had not come!

That thought had tolled inside her head a hundred times since she had awakened the morning following her vigil and found herself sleeping in her own bed. That was three days ago. Nor had her nighttime visitor appeared either of the following nights. Perhaps it had all been a dream. She held a healthy skepticism toward the spirit

world. It might exist or it might not. What did it have to
do with her?

Should she tell Parson Pollock? If she dropped by the
vicarage after the service and admitted that she might
have been visited by a ghost, what would the consequences be? Less than two hundred years earlier, she
might have been denounced as a witch, expelled from
church, or, perhaps, even burned. But these were mod-
ern times. They no longer burned confessed witches and
familiars and devil's companions; they locked them in
the madhouse.

Reining in her straying thoughts, Julianna gazed toward the pulpit where the good vicar was leaning so far
out over it that she wondered how he kept from toppling
out onto one of the outstretched wings of the wooden
angel upon whose back the pulpit was borne. Known for
his sermonizing, Parson Pollock was about to launch into
yet another of the deadly sins—he had only covered four
in forty-five minutes—when suddenly he stopped, his
voice cut off as if by an unseen hand. His face, which had
already grown red with exertion, suddenly drained of
color as he grasped at his throat with his right hand. A
second later he burst into a fit of coughing.

Julianna turned her head as Mr. Crawley, the church
warden, rose in his place in the congregation and hurried
forward to aid the vicar. But Julianna's gaze did not follow him for, in looking in his direction, her gaze had slid
past him to the man who lounged against the wall staring
at her. His gaze was like the prick of a pin: sharp, piercing, and pointedly unpleasant. She did not know him, but
she knew what he was. Those who worked the mines had
a sallowness to their skin that betrayed the fact that they
spent their days out of sight of sun and fresh air. His face

was long, lantern-jawed, with several days of stubble that not even the thought of church had moved him to cut. His unkempt hair hung over his brow. As she watched he reached up and stuck his forefinger in his mouth, sucked hard on the tip, and then released it. Grinning, he slowly and deliberately licked his lips as he inclined his head toward her.

Shocked and appalled and angry beyond words, Julianna turned her head away so that the brim of her bonnet shielded her profile from his view. What he had done was lewd and deliberately meant to upset her. Who was he? Why should he pick her out? But she knew at least part of the answer. She was a Kingsblood, the lone bastion of nobility in a church where she was surrounded by both friends and unknown foes. There was no man beside her. She had come to church alone. Now she wondered at the wisdom in that.

Not wanting to give him the satisfaction of a response, she remained facing forward. Her face stiffened with the effort of not showing any expression, for she knew he was still watching. She wanted to leave the church at once, but that was impossible. Parson Pollock had recovered from his coughing fit, revived by a glass of water, and, to her dismay, he was mounting the pulpit steps once again.

Thankfully, however, the vicar found that he no longer had the wind required to finish his sermon. He consoled himself with a brief listing of possible sins that the congregation might repent of during the dark days of fasting and sacrifice ahead.

Only when the last hymn had been sung did Julianna allow herself to glance again in her taunter's direction, but he had disappeared. She swung her head toward the rear of the church, but the solid wall of the retreating parishioners prevented her from seeing if he was among them.

She lingered a moment, ostensibly to observe the new plaque that had been set at the end of the Kingsblood pew as thanks for the marquess's funding of the new church roof. In reality, she hoped that the crowd would thin and that he would be gone from the vicinity before she left the church.

But, to her dismay, when she reached the doorway she saw that not one single person had left the churchyard. In fact, they were gathered in groups of twos and threes. As she stepped out into the sunlight, all heads turned toward her. Then, quite unexpectedly, applause broke out across the scattered clusters.

"Lady Julianna, delighted, delighted as always," Parson Pollock said, coming up beside her. "As you can see for yourself, you are well thought of by my little congregation."

Julianna turned to him, perplexed. "I don't understand. It isn't at all unusual for me to attend services when in Devon."

"That isn't why they applauded you, my dear," Mrs. Pollock said as she appeared at Julianna's other elbow. A small, amicable woman with a smooth round face like a china doll's, Mrs. Pollock affectionately patted Julianna's arm. "They know what you've done."

"What I've . . . ? Oh." Evidently Jed had begun his campaign of good feelings by announcing her gift ahead of time. "It's little enough to ensure a proper Shrove Tuesday for the miners and their families."

"And may I hope that liquor won't be among your generous gifts?" the vicar said with a pointed look over the top of his spectacles.

"My family's gifts consist of butter, sugar, flour, and eggs," Julianna replied. After exchanging a few more pleasantries with the vicar and his wife, she moved down to the church steps and onto the road that would take her back to Blood Hall.

She smiled cordially at those she passed but did not slow her pace. All the while she watched for a glimpse of the man who had insulted her at church. More than likely he was one of those men who preferred to drink away their day off and had found himself in church this Sunday morning only because his wife had collared him before he passed out.

Unfortunately, her field of vision was hampered by her new poke bonnet. Chosen for her by Lettie, it boasted a brim so wide and inclusive that she felt like a horse with blinders. Unless she turned her head, she could see nothing but the narrow strip of road before her. She waited until she was out of sight of the church before reaching up to untie the silk ribbon that anchored it under her chin. She knew Lettie would be horrified, for no lady went about in public without a bonnet. But this was not London, and the winter sunshine was warmer than one might expect. The heat of it warmed her cheeks and cheered her considerably.

In fact, after a few minutes of solitary strolling along the empty road through the moors, she began to whistle, something a coachman's son had taught her to do when she was only five. He was fourteen, big and brawny, and called each horse in the marquess's stables by using a different whistle. She had thought him the most handsome and smartest boy in the whole world. Now she could not even recall his name, but she remembered his kindness, and how to whistle.

As she came even with a narrow stand of trees that flanked one side of the road, she was no longer thinking of ghosts or bullies or lewd men. Then she saw him, a lone figure cutting across the open moorland toward the road before her. She recognized him at once. His limp was identifiable even from this distance. Jos Trevelyn.

Her nerves contracted and she stiffened, coming to a halt. This was not the man she had feared running into after church, but he was nearly as bad. They had kept out of one another's path since the day she had accused him of stealing from the larder. Now, unless she deliberately dawdled, they would meet on the road ahead. Since they were both headed toward Blood Hall, they would then be forced to keep one another company the final mile.

Dismissing the impulse to strike out across the moor herself in order to prevent their meeting, she paused to replace her bonnet and retie the ribbon beneath her chin. As she was about to start off down the road again a man's voice stopped her.

"G'day, Lady Kingsblood. Or is it *lady*, I'm wonderin'?"

She guessed who it was before she turned her head toward the speaker. It was the miner from church who had insulted her. He was staring at her now as he came out of the shade of the trees. There was a shrewd, calculating look about him that unnerved her as much as his lewd gesture in church.

"Lady Kingsblood," he said again, smacking his lips as if those words contained a particularly well-liked flavor. "Swingin' her church bonnet by the strings and whistlin' like any brass tart."

He had come even with the road now, and Julianna surveyed him coolly. "Do I know you?"

"Nae, but that'll change anytime ye say, darlin'."

Julianna did not pretend to misunderstand him. They were past such niceties. "Good-bye."

She was surprised when he stepped into the road to block her path. It was noon on a Sunday with the sun blazing overhead. Did he not realize that at any moment someone could come up the road and see them? In just such a hope, she lifted her head to catch sight of Jos Trevelyn. The idea of his companionship was suddenly quite comforting. But the man before her moved again, blocking her view.

He reached out and took her by the shoulders. "Ye've nothin' to fret over, lass. There be only ye and me, and the shade o' them trees to hide us pleasurin' ourselves."

"Let me go!" Julianna demanded, annoyed by how frightened she sounded. But his hands were strong, and she was not nearly as much of an Amazon as she had always thought. In fact, she was shocked by how quickly and easily he dragged her off the road though she was struggling in earnest to prevent it.

"Come on," he said in a cajoling voice. "There's only ye and me to know what'll happen. I seen ye in yer pew, lookin' so right and proper, but there came a look in yer eye when ye seen me. There's a woman what needs a man, says I. I know the achin' when nothin' will serve but to have what ye need, in a bed or on the road. I'll ease thy achin', lady. See if I don't."

Julianna resisted the urge to scream, for she was not yet convinced that he meant to do more than frighten her. No man would rape a woman on the open road, she thought rapidly. It wasn't possible. But when he pulled her struggling body in hard against his and covered her mouth with his own, she realized that she was wrong.

The stink of his breath engulfed her and her stomach turned. He will smother me! she thought in terror. And then he was tearing at her cloak to reach her bodice. She heard fabric rip and then felt the pain of a hard hand closing over a breast. She cried out, slapping at the hand that grabbed her. Ignoring her protests, he ground his mouth against hers, bruising her lips. Enraged and repulsed, Julianna struck out wildly, landing a hard fist on his ear. With a muttered curse he swept the back of his hand across her face, bruising her mouth and knocking her spectacles from her face.

Suddenly she heard running footsteps close behind her and a man's shout. A moment later she was released as her attacker was torn from her. It happened so suddenly she lost her footing and fell backward onto the grass. She heard a fist connect with the solid thud of flesh, a man's *woof* of pain and then more scuffling. She sat up to see who had come to her rescue but her bonnet had come loose and slid across her face. By the time she righted it, the fight was over. The man who had attacked her was lying on his back. Jos Trevelyn, fists raised, stood over him.

The man on the ground reeled off a string of curses as he scrambled to his feet, but Jos merely stepped out of his way and lifted a hand to push his ever-present hat forward over his eyes. After an ugly glance at Julianna, her attacker stumbled off down the road.

For a moment Julianna felt only relief, and she realized that her heart was fluttering wildly and that she was breathless. When a hand gently touched her shoulder she jumped.

"Be ye all right?"

"Yes!" she answered, recognizing even in those brief

words that it was Jos who touched her. "Yes, I'm fine!" she said again. Keeping her face averted from him, she swallowed the taste of blood and pulled her cloak over her open bodice. "I've lost my spectacles. Will you find them, please?"

As he turned and stomped away, she wiped away a trace of blood from her rapidly swelling lip. Almost at once he came back within her view, two muddy boots planted squarely before her lowered gaze. "Ah found 'em, for all th' good 'twill do ye." He dropped a bit of broken glass and twisted wire into her lap.

She stared at the ruined spectacles in dismay. Without them, she was almost as good as blind. When she looked up at Jos she could not see him distinctly, for he was backlit by the sun. With his hat riding forward and his collar turned up against the breeze, his features were almost perfectly hidden from view. "Thank you, Jos. It's fortunate you came along when you did."

He shrugged. "Ben't no' my place to say, yer ladyship, but tha' man ben't no' sort o' companion for ye t' 'ave."

"Companion?" Julianna exploded, feeling the blood sting once more through her veins. "I never saw him before in my life!" She looked suddenly around. "Where did he go?"

Jos looked up the road in the direction from which she had come, a grim kind of satisfaction in his voice. "T' nurse an achin' head."

"You should have held him," Julianna said indignantly. "I want him turned over to the authorities."

"Ah well, so ye should o' said."

He extended his hand, reminding Julianna that she still sat in the grass. She took it and found his hand warm and firm and surprisingly uncallused for a laborer. A capable but sensitive hand, she decided, and then wondered why she thought that. When she had gained her feet she turned away from him and began adjusting her bodice. With relief she found only a small tear that would not be readily noticed if they did pass anyone on the way to Blood Hall. When she had straightened her clothes, smoothed her hair, and brushed most of the grass from her skirts, she turned to him once more. He stood so close her arm brushed his. Startled, she looked up and straight into his eyes.

This time his blue stare was neither mocking or hostile. It was blank, as if he deliberately withheld expression, but something about it caught at her heart and she felt herself blush.

Even as she stared the look changed, his eyes growing darker, if possible. He lifted a hand, licked his thumb, and then applied that moist finger to one corner of her mouth. The curiously intimate gesture made her insides tremble. When his gaze turned from her face, hers followed, and she saw that he was looking at the smear of blood on his finger. When he looked back at her again, her eyes widened in response to the intensity of his stare.

"Were tha' how ye looked at th' man?" he asked in his thick country vernacular. "Mebbe Ah should 'ave left ye t' work it out!" he finished, and laughed.

The insult had the desired effect. She stepped back from him as if from an adder. "I told you, I never saw that man before today. And if I ever do again, you can be certain I will set the magistrate on him."

She saw his grin blossom beneath the shadow of his hat that once more shaded his eyes. "Why were yer ladyship on t' road, were ye no meetin' a beau?"

"I was returning from church," she said stiffly.

"Alone?" He sounded skeptical.

"Church doesn't require a full company," she replied, annoyed now that he of all people had been the one to rescue her. "I prefer my own company when I walk to church."

"And tha' were a damned silly thin' t' do!" he said harshly. "Ben't there no carriage t' carry ye?"

"You know very well there aren't any horses at Blood Hall at present. In any case, I don't need to be accompanied to church like a child."

He looked at her, his silence a contradiction, and then turned and took a few steps only to pause and glance back at her. "Be ye comin' or no'? Ah've thin's need doin'."

"I—I . . ." Julianna bit her lip hard, for, to her shame, her body's reaction to the violence done it was not yet finished.

She didn't know if he took a step back toward her or if she made one toward him, but suddenly, thankfully, there was his firm shoulder for her to rest against and an arm to hold her steady as tremors shook her.

"So, th' lady has a heart in her after all," he said mildly after a moment. "Now her ladyship must pull herself together. Won't do for folks on t' road t' see Lady Kingsblood in her gardener's arms."

That was antidote enough for Julianna's nervous fit. She disengaged herself at once. "I'm ready to go on now."

They walked back to Blood Hall in silence. After the first few seconds it became impossible for Julianna to think of any way to start a conversation, and it seemed that he was content not to. When they reached the car-

riageway, he suddenly veered off toward the rose garden
without even a backward glance.

"Thank you!" Julianna hurled the words after his retreating back as if they were spears. She thought she
heard him chuckle but she could not be sure.

Though upon her return she had scrubbed herself
thoroughly and changed her clothing from inside out,
Julianna still could not forget the odious events of the
morning. After dinner she had intended to finish her correspondence to her grandfather, which included an explanation of her decision to provide food for Shrove
Tuesday. Instead, she ended up pacing the floor of the
Great Hall, her letter and pen lying forgotten beside her
place at one end of the huge dining table.

In spite of all that had occurred during the last days,
she realized she had never faced physical danger until
the moment that miner had stepped from the side of the
road and grabbed her. How strange that violence should
confront her on a mild February Sunday, upon an open
road, and practically within view of her own front door.
No spectral aberration had ever threatened her as much.

She shifted her shoulders in an unconscious attempt to
dismiss the remembered feel of those heavy hands upon
her. The more she thought about it, the less she liked the
idea of not having acted immediately so that the man
could be apprehended. Yet, once she was home, Jed
Coleman's warning against stirring up the miners came
back to her. He had said their emotions were like kegs of
dynamite, needing very little to set them off. If she, a
Kingsblood, accused one of their own of a crime, it might
well destroy the good feelings that had been demon-
strated in the churchyard that morning.

Still, Julianna thought as she rhythmically rubbed her hands up and down the sleeves of her gown, she would feel better if she at least knew the man's name. She would have no compunction about sending for the magistrate if he caused any more trouble. Perhaps if she described him to Parson Pollock, he would recognize the man.

As she paced, she began piecing together in her mind a description of the man, but she soon realized that she could be describing any of a dozen men who had been at church that morning. He was a miner: long-jawed, pale-eyed, stoop-shouldered, shabbily dressed, and hard-handed. If only she could think of more distinctive attributes.

Without a particular reason, she came to a halt before a portrait of her grandfather that had been done by Aiken many years before. It was a good likeness, showing his attractive strong features and vivid blue stare. Yet, to her way of thinking, it just missed capturing the spirit of the man, which showed in his smile. The marquess had a way of smiling that sometimes did not quite reach his mouth. It was more in the way his cheekbones became suddenly prominent beneath the piercing blue of his eyes when something struck him as humorous. If only the painter had known him better, he would have lifted the marquess's cheeks a fraction and . . .

One of the errant breezes for which the Great Hall was notorious wafted past Julianna, distracting her. As she turned, a sheet of stationery, lifted from her correspondence, sailed by on the draft. Thinking it was her letter, she snatched it from the air but, when she looked at it, her brows lifted in amazement.

The page was empty but for a single blot of ink. As she

stared at it, the shape of a human face came to mind. The ink blot bore an astonishing likeness to the profile of her nighttime visitor. The bold nose, the chiseled catch of his lower lip, every detail was visible. Having once seen it, she knew she would never mistake his profile for anyone else's. The only thing more amazing than the likeness was the fact that it had not been deliberately designed. She looked back uneasily over her shoulder at the vast empty room. Or had it?

As she glanced down again, inspiration struck her. "But of course!" she said under her breath. She could sketch a picture of the man who had accosted her. Then the vicar should have no trouble identifying him.

As if to confirm her thinking, a second piece of paper lifted suddenly from the table and came sailing straight into her hand. This time the breeze that accompanied it carried with it a sound like the rasp of dry laughter. Glancing up sharply at the portrait, she saw to her astonishment that the marquess's face now bore that elusive smile she would have sworn was missing seconds before.

"I don't believe in ghosts," she said firmly to the portrait, then turned and hurried away.

A satisfactory ink sketch emerged from her pen after several aborted attempts. By the time she had rendered the man's features in the right proportion and size, Julianna had gained more respect for portrait painters who had to contend with their patrons' desires as well as with nature.

Once she was done, she wanted to show it to someone, but who? She had deliberately avoided telling Mrs. Mead about the incident, feeling that the housekeeper would insist that she send for the magistrate. Then who? Jos Trevelyn! He had rescued her. He must have had a good look at the man. What better judge of her sketch could she wish?

Though several hours had passed, she found him near where they had parted company on the carriageway. He was not hoeing or weeding in the rose garden, but sitting on a stone bench in the full slant of the afternoon sunshine spilling across the top of the far wall. His hat completely covered his face, his shoulders were braced against the back wall, and his arms were folded across his chest. She decided that he must be asleep.

But the moment she came within six feet of him, he moved, tipped his hat back partway, and rose to his feet. "Afternoon, yer ladyship," he said gruffly.

"Good afternoon, Jos," Julianna began, inexplicably shy now that she faced him. "I hope I didn't disturb you."

"Ye ma' do as ye wish, 'tis yer garden."

So that was that, she mused in disappointment. He would behave as usual. So be it. That was no reason for her to be uncivil. "I didn't think to ask before, but I hope that you weren't injured in any way when you came to my rescue."

He had pushed his hat back a little more and she saw his lips curve into a oddly gentle smile. "A man likes a scrape now an' agin."

"Thank you for rescuing me all the same," she said politely, refusing to acknowledge his ungracious words.

The silence that fell between them seemed natural, but she was acutely aware of his perusal of her from beneath the brim of his hat. "Yer were after wantin' somethin' else, yer ladyship?" he prompted.

"Yes, as a matter of fact," she answered. "I want you to look at something." She held out the paper with her drawing but he did not take it.

"Wha' be it?"

"That's what I wish you to tell me." She tried to keep the testiness out of her voice, but his manner always made her feel like a cat who had been rubbed the wrong way.

"Ah can no' read," he said gruffly.

"It's not words, it's a picture." Again she held it out.

He took it, glanced at it so quickly that she was not certain he even saw it, then handed it back. " 'Tis a man."

Julianna bit her lip. "Of course it's a man. What man?"

"Ah did no' get his name."

"But you recognize him!" she said in delight.

"Aye. 'Tis the lad from t' mornin'."

She smiled at him. "Thank you."

"Why'd ye make th' picture?" He grinned. "Did ye admire him overmuch?"

Julianna squelched yet another inclination to stomp off in a huff. After all, she might yet need his help. "Exactly the opposite. I intend to find out who he is, and if he ever so much as approaches me again, I'll set the magistrate on him."

"Oh well, 'tis like tha'? Ye should go afore now."

Julianna thought of the long, lonely walk over the moors that she would have to make in order to take such an action. "Would you go with me to the magistrate?"

"Tha' Ah will no'," he answered so readily that she suspected that he had anticipated her question.

"Why not? I may need a witness. You were there."

He behaved as always, his silence more deafening than sound. A new thought occurred to her. "Are you afraid?"

"Why should Ah be afeared of th' law?"

"Oh, I don't know," she said impatiently. "Perhaps you are wanted by the authorities." She saw him flinch and narrowed her eyes against the blaze of the sun. In reality she knew little about him. What she did know he had told her. He had no references for his job, she had checked on that with Mrs. Mead after the thefts were discovered. He said he was a soldier, but he might be an escaped convict for all the proof he offered. "Where do you come from, Jos Trevelyn? Why aren't you working the mines or fishing like other able-bodied men?"

The moment she said the words, she regretted them. He turned and limped a few feet away, the display a rebuke more harsh than any words.

"I'm sorry," she said quickly. "I'd forgotten about your leg. Does it give you much pain? Is it healing properly?"

He half turned to her, a glance thrown over his shoulder. "Ye've no need t' be askin' after me. Ah can better care for meself than some wi' sound limbs."

She knew that he was referring to what had happened to her on the road but, curiously, she didn't mind his rebuff this time. He was a proud man, she had learned that much within minutes of their first meeting. It must grate against his independent nature to be hampered by an infirmity. "I apologize if I've offended you."

He shrugged. "Ah'm no' so. But Ah'll no' see th' magistrate with ye."

"Very well. I don't need your assistance. I can ask the vicar about this man. However, if he should cause further trouble, I'll be forced to press charges. You may then be called to testify in court." As she turned away, she thought she heard him mutter a curse, but she decided that it was better to pretend she had not heard it.

"Oh, by the way," she said, turning back, "I'd like you to cut and bring a bouquet of roses to the house. Mrs. Mead will put them in a vase for me."

"Ah will no'!"

The outright refusal drained the smile from Julianna's face. "And why not, Mr. Trevelyn?"

" 'Tis Sunday. A man's allowed a day off."

Julianna nearly offered to cut them herself, but she suspected that he would find another excuse to thwart her. Turning sharply on her heel, she marched out the garden, muttering "Odious man!"

Chapter Nine

~~~

Julianna decided to wait until morning to seek out the vicar. The thought of retracing alone her steps past the copse had shaken her resolve. After all, she reminded herself, Jed Coleman would be coming in the morning with some of the miners to pick up the food. She would show him her sketch, and he would doubtless recognize the man.

Once she had loosened her hair and thoroughly brushed it, she began undressing for bed. The candelabra on her dressing table provided enough illumination to brighten the room, but when she stood only in her drawers and camisole and corset, she reached up and pinched out all but one of the wicks.

Ordinarily, she would have completed her undressing quickly, but tonight she was conscious of herself in ways she had never thought about before. The lewd man on the road had repelled and disgusted her with his brutal attack. Yet, because of it, the thought lingered in her mind of what it might be like to be touched by a man whose embrace she welcomed.

Shyly she glanced at her reflection in the vanity mirror. What she saw was a tall, slender woman with a heavy cascade of hair tumbling over her shoulders to her waist.

Her plain calico camisole and drawers were devoid of
any decorative touch. Vanities such as lace and ribbon
encouraged depravity, her mother had informed her, a
sentiment echoed in nearly all respectable quarters. Yet
Julianna wished that a little frill of lace at the edge of the
neckline softened the effect of the utilitarian garment
she wore and made it, well, pleasant to look upon—not
that she ever expected anyone to look upon her most
intimate apparel but herself and her maid.

Yet an image of Lord Dashmore rose in her mind. In
spite of the fact she had once thought she loved him, she
could not imagine standing before him as she was now, in
her undergarments and unbound hair. Just the idea
made her cheeks pinken and her gaze slip from her mir-
rored image. Nor could she imagine him in a nightshirt
and stocking cap. The image of that handsome man enveloped in white linen reaching to his knees brought
laughter to her lips, which she stilled with her fingertips.

How awkward gentlemen and ladies must feel when
thrust into bed on their wedding night. It seemed impossible that the forbidden feelings she experienced in her
dreams could be conjured up by two people in nightdress. Rather it seemed they should shake hands and
then retire to opposite corners of the mattress.

Still tingling with forbidden thoughts, she recalled that
her grandmother's lingerie was always made of silk, elab-
orately embroidered and decorated with lace and ribbons
and tiny pink satin roses. As a child she had once asked
the marchioness about this and been told that the marquess preferred depravity to utility in the boudoir. She
blushed again. Now she understood what her grandmother meant. The chaste garments she wore would
never inflame a lover.

Urged on by the chilly February night, she unbuttoned
her camisole, disposed of it quickly, and then loosened
the laces of her stays and removed them. Modest by nature and reared in a strict household, she had never given
much thought to her body, even less to how it looked. No
one undressed in front of a mirror, and bathing was done
quickly and without lingering interest in the arms, legs,
and other portions of the body being washed. But tonight
she was feeling reckless, spurred on by the knowledge
that while she had nearly been violated, she knew very
little about her own body, even what she must look like
to another. On impulse, she glanced again at her image
in the mirror. What she saw quite surprised her.

Her skin shone faintly flushed and moist in the taper's
glow. Her slender waist and the flare of her hips were
revealed as the loosened drawers slipped down to her
thighs. Turning this way and that, she managed a complete survey of herself from head to knee. She was slender and full, the slope of her spine running into the firm
roundness of her buttocks, her thighs smooth and sleek.
She was, as nearly as she could figure it, as attractive as
any and more, perhaps, than most. Finally, lifting aside
her thick black tresses, she stared guiltily at her breasts.
Large and fully rounded, they gleamed with warmth. The
nipples were tinted a deep pink, fresh as rosebuds not yet
bloomed. The image of roses brought the garden to
mind. She was as lovely as any rose in Blood Hall's garden. Why, if Jos Trevelyn saw her now . . .

Sweeping her hair forward like a curtain, she banished
the thought abruptly. As if she would ever allow Jos
Trevelyn to see her naked, let alone touch her! Dirty
hands and all, he was the very last . . .

But shameful thoughts of Jos Trevelyn would not dis-

solve in her mind as easily as had the comical idea of
Lord Dashmore in nightdress. Instead, memory tricked
her into remembering the firm warmth of his hand when
he had helped her rise from the grass. She remembered
much too thoroughly the sensual touch of his moist
thumb as it grazed her lower lip.

She sucked in her lower lip, seeking the small cut with
the tip of her tongue. The tiny throb of pain also reminded her of Jos. What would she have done if, instead
of his thumb, he had used his tongue to remove the
blood from her lip?

The idea so shocked her that she turned abruptly from
the mirror. What was wrong with her that she was capable of such outrageous thoughts? It was as if the miner's
lewd behavior had awakened in her every sort of indecent idea. Was this how nice girls became loose women?
Did it take no more than the mere thought of indecency
to ruin a lifetime of modesty and reserve? As for Jos
Trevelyn, the less thought about him the better.

Yet her rebellious thoughts would not be controlled.
They moved on to the phantom visitor who had come to
her room more than once. Was he real? A dream?
Where was he? Why had he stopped coming? What if he
should appear at this moment? What would he say and
do? Would he think she was as lovely as she had just
come to suspect she was? Appalled once more, she
quickly slipped on her nightdress and buttoned it up to
her chin.

As she climbed into bed, she was unaware that her
every action had been observed, and that the witnesses'
conclusions had been even more generous than her own.

*   *   *

The third chime broke Julianna's dream as cleanly as scissors snipping a knot. At first she was only aware of darkness crowded in by the misty webs of after-dreaming. Then the room brightened as light appeared by her bedside. She heard the *ping* of a match being dropped into a china dish and turned her head toward the sound. Something brushed her cheek, cool and soft as velvet. An instant later the scent of roses wafted through her consciousness.

Startled, she sat up in bed. There on the coverlet were strewn several armfuls of roses: deep wine reds, seashell pinks, pure lily whites, and delicate reef corals.

Before she stopped blinking in surprise, a voice spoke to her from the darkness at the far corner of the room. "Is my lady pleased?"

"Pleased?" Julianna looked about for her spectacles before remembering that they were broken beyond repair. "Yes, I'm pleased." She reached out and picked up a coral rose. "But why have you done this?"

"To please a lady. Have I not said that I'm your friend?"

She lifted the rose to her nose. "A friend would show himself. Where are you?"

"Here, my lady." The voice, deep and gentle, directed her gaze to the alcove by the Chinese screen. She knew at once that this was his way of telling her that he had known of her attempt to catch him unawares several nights earlier. Yet she refused to apologize. "Why have you come back?"

"To bring you gifts." His gesture was no more substantial than a sweeping shadow. "I know how badly you wanted roses for your room so I stole them for you."

"Stole them?" She thought of Jos and how vexed he

would be in the morning. The thought that someone had bested him provoked laughter from her. "Oh, Friend, you've chosen for yourself an able enemy. My gardener thinks he knows better than half a dozen Kingsbloods put together how to run a garden."

"Then you're pleased."

Julianna had picked up another flower and held it to her nose. "Oh yes! They are a miracle. The roses in London won't bloom for another three months."

"A miracle," he agreed, thinking of the secret buds hidden now by her nightgown. "A lady clothed in roses."

Alerted by the change in his tone, Julianna pulled the covers protectively to her chest. "When did you return?"

"Oh, I'm never far away."

His voice held a lilt of amusement that made her blush. Her heart beat a little more quickly as she said, "Why have you come back?"

Nothing moved but the forlorn flame by her side that cast fretful shadows upon the walls and ceiling. He stepped forward, becoming the shape of a man just beyond the border of her keenest vision. "You know why I came, my lady," he said softly.

"I don't know what you mean!" she replied defensively, but she thought she did. He seemed to know too often for her peace of mind just what she was thinking. "I've had enough of mystery. Reveal yourself to me at once, or leave here!"

The faintest quiver of laughter came through his voice as he wondered how far he must push her before she realized who he was. "Very well, my lady. You've heard tales of the Love Talker?"

"But you can't—you mustn't!" Julianna sucked in a

quick breath, feeling suddenly heavy and full of dread. "Go away! I'll have no traffic with spirits! Go away!"

He was approaching the bed, moving with a graceful light tread that to her blurred vision seemed effortless and untethered by gravity. "Why send me away?" His voice, deep and hushed, was infinitely moving. "I mean you no harm. I offer only what every woman longs for." He paused at the foot of her bed, half hidden by the bed hangings. "What is it you long for, my lady?"

In the dusky shadows she saw a glimmer of fair hair and a profile worthy to grace an urn or be carved in finest marble. She was mad, that must be it. She did not believe in the existence of the Love Talker any more than she believed that goats could fly. Yet, if there were such a creature, surely he would possess the persuasive power of the man who faced her now.

But her secretmost thoughts of the night had stirred her, battering down all sense of shame and sanity, and of propriety. If she did not deny him, what would he do? Would there ever come another such moment in her life? "Are you really the Love Talker?"

For one awful, choking moment, she thought he would laugh at her. Her nerves felt as tight as new-strung wire, so taut that the mere quiver of laughter would be intolerable.

"Sweet Gillie," he whispered from the shadows. "As lovely as the flower for which you are named. Spice and sweetness are in you, Gillie. Douse your candle and receive a tribute to your gillyflower name."

She did as he asked without question. When the candle was snuffed, she lay back against her pillows unable to watch him any longer. Instead, she watched his long shadow, cast by the meager moonlight, move across the ceiling toward her. Finally he was there beside her, a black shape bending low.

And then he kissed her.

She did not know what she expected. The cold, dank touch of a corpse, the icy sting of death as it entered her through her breath, anything other than this blissfully stunning, warm human touch.

A shudder began deep within her, it shook and devastated her, and then she felt, to her astonishment, an answering shudder in him. She lifted a hand and touched his face. He did not move. Her hand seemed to burn where it lay upon his cheek. She felt the muscle tighten in his cheekbone. She moved her hand to his temple and met the pulse beating strongly there. This was no ghost or pixie. He was a man.

When he lifted his head, neither of them spoke. There was nothing to say. She was aware of his movements, of his withdrawal from her bedside, yet the taste of him lingered hauntingly on her lips and regret clogged her throat, keeping her silent.

"Friends?" she heard him whisper huskily when he had backed away.

"Yes. Friends," she answered softly.

For a long while she held her breath, and then his voice came again quietly. "You're in no danger from me. But there are others who don't want you here. Go back to London.

"Are you listening to me?" he demanded when she did not reply. "Stubborn!" she heard him mutter, then: "If you're determined to remain in Devon, you must stay at Blood Hall. You are protected on the grounds."

"By you?"

She thought she saw him shake his head. "By the powers that dwell within."

Reality was slipping from her grasp like water. Julianna clutched the rose in her hand, welcoming the prick of its thorns into her palm. "Are there really such powers?"

"I'd not lie to you about anything so serious."

"Then how was a thief able to break into the larder and take things?"

"What makes you think they were not responsible for that?"

"But why would spirits need food?"

"To save a life?" he suggested.

"Oh, I see." But she did not. She was beyond understanding anything but the moment, which might not even be real.

"Do you?" he said grimly. "I hope to God you do. In future, you mustn't venture from this house without an escort. Was your misadventure on the road not warning enough?"

The attack on the road had frightened her, but she was reluctant to admit it. "I'm not afraid."

"Then you should be. I'm afraid for you." His tone changed, became brusque. "Go back to London. It's for the best."

"No! I'm not in any real danger. You just said so yourself."

"I said you're not in danger within these walls. But what if I'm overly confident, or what if you take it into your lovely head to go off again half cocked—"

"I never go off half cocked," she said in affront. "Nor am I lovely."

"You both *do* and *are,* and stubborn into the bargain!"

"You're shouting at me!"

"I'd like to do more than that!"

Julianna stilled, for his tone had changed to one of
seriousness. Once more she was aware that she was not
conversing with a friend but with a mysterious, disturbing
stranger. Still, the question begged to be asked. "What
would you like to do?"

He was silent so long she began to squirm. "Make love
to you."

His words burst upon Julianna's senses with the force
of wind and flood and tide. The moment of reckoning
that she had vaguely felt stealing upon her for days had
arrived.

She knew it the moment he left the room. It felt
empty, barren of everything but the scent of roses and
the breath of desire.

Mrs. Mead stared at the arrangement of roses in the
blue vase that sat in the middle of the Great Hall's dining
table. "If you didn't bring them in, my lady, then how'd
they get here?"

"I've no idea," Julianna replied in round-eyed innocence. She did not add that the night before they had
been strewn over her bed, nor that she suspected her
visitor had gathered them up and put them in the vase.

"There they were, bright as May, when I first came
into the house," the housekeeper said. "Her ladyship's
cut herself a bouquet, I thought to meself. Only, if you
didn't do it, maybe 'tis the gardener's handiwork."

The mention of Jos annoyed Julianna. "Does he have
a key to the house?"

"No, that he hasn't," Mrs. Mead replied. "Maybe Tom
let him in when he came up to the house."

"Perhaps," Julianna agreed, but she suspected that Jos was more likely to send her a pound of manure before he cut even one flower from his precious garden.

When Mrs. Mead left, Julianna sat staring at the flowers but her thoughts were far away.

Every incredible, unbelievable, irrational moment of the night before came stealing back. And at those memories, an ungovernable happiness swept her. For a moment she had given herself up to a belief as old as the ancient misty land where she now lived. Once giant pagan gods strode the western moors and mortals shivered in the darkness of their rude huts, praying to live until another morning of light. Then the world had been held together by the uncertain powers of magic. In such a world one believed in spirits such as the Love Talker. But then he had kissed her, and she knew that he was real!

Yet many other questions remained. Who was he? Where had he come from? How did he come and go at Blood Hall without being seen or heard? Who could she tell about him? Or should she tell anyone about him? What if no one believed her? How could she prove that he was real?

" 'Twill be Bedlam for you, my girl, if anyone ever suspects you're entertaining the Love Talker," she whispered in amusement, and rose from her chair. She bent and picked a yellow rose from the bouquet, broke off the stem, and tucked it into the neckline of her brown silk gown.

No one must ever suspect who had brought the flowers into the house. Even she would not admit it, not when there was the least possibility that the roses had entered by other means. Why, they might not even have come from Blood Hall's bushes. Reluctant though she was, she knew a visit to the rose garden was the only way to satisfy her curiosity.

She found Jos trimming the hedge that grew outside the garden wall. The day was brisker than the one before, and he had wound a woolen muffler about his neck and added fingerless mittens to his hands. Julianna wrapped her red cloak closely about herself as she neared him, prepared to endure a wall of silence as she questioned him.

She need not have bothered. Once he looked up and saw her coming toward him, he swung around on her with a blast of words.

"Well, her ladyship's had her way! Ben't no' a bush in th' garden with more 'n a bud t' call its own. Hope yer satisfied!"

"I don't know what you're talking about!" she snapped back, more than willing to pick a fight with her gardener, for her tumultuous emotions badly needed some outlet.

"Do ye no'?" His voice dripped with sarcasm. "Com' on then." He waved her toward the garden, pausing only to allow her to enter it before him. "Now what do ye have t' say t' tha'?" He threw his arms wide to include the entire enclosure.

Sure enough, she could not spot a single flower when only the day before the garden was bright with roses. "Ben't no' a rose at all. Gone!" he shouted.

She took several involuntary steps back from him and his shears. He was in a rare fit of anger, even for him. She wondered if she should even mention where the flowers were. But then she remembered that he was an employee, and that the garden and all that was in it were at her disposal. "I don't know how they came to be there, but the roses are in a vase in the Great Hall."

"Hah!" He swung away from her. "Ah know how they come t' be there. Ye stole 'em!"

"I did *not* steal them!" she cried, and took a step toward his turned back. "I didn't take even one. But, if I had, my good man, you'd have no cause to quarrel with me. This is my garden. If I so wished, I could pick them all—but I didn't!"

He turned around and glowered at her in that characteristic way, from beneath the brim of his hat. It was a habit of his she had begun to detest above all others. "Th' roses, be they in th' Hall?"

"That's what I just said." The tone of combat was still in evidence in her voice.

"Ben't they in a blu' bowl?"

"They're in a blue vase," Julianna replied, "but how did you know that? Did you put them there?"

His body seemed to relax, the shears he had held aloft, now hanging by his side. To her amazement, a strange look came over what she could see of his face. "Oh well, that's different," he replied in a curiously mild voice.

"What do you mean?"

He shrugged, once again the reticent speaker she was more accustomed to dealing with. "You may as well answer me," she said, crossing her arms stubbornly. "I'm not leaving here until you do."

He seemed to debate the consequences before he said, "Ah'm no' afeared o' a man born but Ah'll leave off chasin' after spirits."

Julianna jumped as if he had poked her. "What spirits? What do you know of such things?"

Laughter exploded from him, loud and rude and wholly masculine. "Look at yer face!" he said between gusts of mirth. "Ah'd no' ken yer ladyship believed in pixies and such."

"What I believe is none of your business," she said haughtily, entirely insulted that he was laughing at her. "What do *you* believe?"

"Well, now," he said when he could contain himself. "There's no' many a man would take th' job. Ask yer housekeeper. Ben't because th' garden is pixied. But Jos Trevelyn stands a fair man with th' spirits. They want roses for th' house, they're welcome to all Ah can coax forth."

Julianna eyed him dispassionately. "You mean to tell me you think Blood Hall's ghosts took the roses?"

He shrugged, and she could only guess the expression in his eyes as he said, "Ben't ye no' done it."

She refused to respond to this jibe. "What do you know of a spirit called the Love Talker?" she asked instead.

He chuckled. "What's there t' know? 'Tis a pixie who woos silly lasses and lonely spinsters." His smirk returned. " 'Tis a common excuse given by lasses who'd no' th' sense t' know 'twas th' lads in their knickers what give 'em their bellies!"

The fire of embarrassment climbed her cheeks. She might have known he would find a way to insult her in his reply. "Odious man!" she muttered, and turned away.

An hour later Jed Coleman arrived with a wagon and two other men. Julianna watched him from an upper window until they had loaded the wagon and then she went down, catching him in the yard just as they were about to ride away.

"A good morning to ye, Lady Julianna," Jed called

when he saw her coming toward him across the kitchen yard.

"Good morning, Jed, men," she answered, nodding to the other two miners who pulled their forelocks shyly. "Do you have all that you need, Jed?"

"That we do, my lady, thanks to ye."

" 'Twill be the best Shrove Tuesday in years," one of the other men offered with a deferential tip of his cap.

"I'm pleased to hear that," she replied with a smile. "Now, Jed, if I may speak with you for a moment." She began to walk back toward the house. The mine foreman followed her after giving his men the signal to start back without him.

When the wagon had lumbered slowly out of the yard, she turned to him. "How are things at the mine?"

"Quiet as death, my lady," he answered, then grinned. "In a manner o' speakin'."

"Good. Now I have another matter for you." She withdrew her sketch from her pocket and carefully unfolded it before handing it to him. "Do you know this man?"

Jed took it and examined it. "O' course, I do." He looked up. "That be Rob Wheal."

"The underground captain?"

"The very one." The deep lines in Jed's face hardened into granite. "What, if ye don't mind me askin', are ye doin' with his likeness?"

Julianna reached for the sketch and held it up to the daylight, pretending to examine it. "I saw him in church yesterday and thought his features would make an interesting subject. Do you think I've done a good job?"

"Yer ladyship was kind to him, to my way of thinkin'. He's uglier than sin and a sneakin', connivin' devil into the bargain!"

"Why not get rid of him?" she responded.

To her surprise, Jed shook his head. "Best not, my lady. Only harm would come o' it. He's got the sympathy of the folk."

Though she sensed Jed's dislike, even contempt, for the man, she saw in his face a grudging admiration for Wheal's influence over the other miners. Jed was a foreman, a leader, but he was clever enough not to discredit or underestimate his challengers. "Whatever you say, Jed. I leave the management of the men in your capable hands."

He smiled at her with a rare ease. "Thank ye, my lady. I won't not fail ye, or the marquess."

"I believe you."

When he was gone, Julianna stood a long while in the yard watching the chickens peck at the scraps Mrs. Mead had scattered for them.

Her attacker had a name now. Rob Wheal. Had he known who she was? But of course he had. She had been sitting in the Kingsblood pew. But why had he accosted her when doing so was bound to result in trouble for him?

She tapped her fingers against the drawing, her mind sifting through the matter. The marquess had taught her that nearly all problems could be solved by subjecting them to logical, rational thought. In considering every possible motive behind seemingly irrational actions, the truth might be got at. Certainly Rob Wheal must have had something in mind when he attacked her on the road. What could it have been?

The Kingsblood mines were under siege by Unionists, a faction of which might be labeled outright troublemakers. According to Jed, Rob Wheal was one of those. His motive must have been to provoke trouble with the Kingsbloods. As she was the only Kingsblood in residence, she was the logical target. She had not forgotten the rock that had been thrown through the window shortly after she arrived but because nothing more had occurred, she had forgotten to be on her guard, until Wheal attacked her.

No doubt Wheal had chosen to use physical intimidation because she was a woman. But would he really have raped her, the granddaughter of a marquess, if Jos had not come along? She doubted it. So, what had he to gain by his action? It would be his word against hers that she had been attacked and was not the instigator in their tryst, as he had implied.

Julianna stumbled to a stop. His word against hers! If he had raped her, there would be no question of his guilt. But what if he only humiliated her? The courts would charge him, all the same, for no commoner could be allowed to lay hands on a daughter of the nobility. But then at his trial he would be allowed to make public his assertion that *she* had led him on. That would leave doubt in some minds. Too often in the past, the aristocracy had gotten their way, whatever the truth. That doubt might become a rallying point for his faction against the Kingsbloods, the needed tinder to set off the powder keg of rebellion.

She gazed down at the crude face in her drawing. Was this man smart enough to think through a scheme so subtle, or was he directed by a brighter, slyer mind?

"That, Rob Wheal, is something I intend to find out!" she murmured. Shrove Tuesday would give her the perfect opportunity.

Chapter Ten

❧

Julianna had dressed with particular care for her Shrove Tuesday outing. She wore a lilac gown of merino, its only adornment a set of black satin bows that marched down the front from chin to hem. Over her hair, parted in the middle and smoothed back, she wore a matching lilac bonnet whose black ribbons were tied at a jaunty angle into a puffy bow under her chin. Like the one ruined on Sunday, it had a deep brim that blinded her side view. In her ears she wore a pair of small black and white pearls, a gift from her parents in India. The face staring back at her in the mirror was bright-eyed but composed. No one would ever guess a half-mad eccentric spinster dwelt behind that placid green gaze. No shadows or lines betrayed the fact that she had spent another fruitless night waiting for the Friend who had not appeared.

When she was satisfied that she looked as dignified but festive as the occasion demanded, she slipped on a black cloak trimmed with gray fur and pulled on her gloves. Clutching a large matching gray fur muff, she descended the main staircase of Blood Hall. The entry was dark. Without her spectacles, it seemed she moved through air as murky as pond water. Yet she recognized a figure standing below even as he raised his head at the sound of her steps.

"Mornin', yer ladyship."

"What are you doing here?" Her tone was ungracious, but she could not help it. Jos Trevelyn was the last man she expected to deal with this day.

"I come t' escort ye t' Fassens," he answered, sounding no more pleased than she by the prospect.

"That won't be necessary. I'm going with the Meads." She continued descending, fully expecting that he would, as usual, swing away from her when she neared him.

Instead, he remained where he was. "Mr. Coleman said Ah'm t' see t' yer ladyship's comforts," he mumbled. "Brought around a wagon fer me t' fetch ye in."

"That was very kind of him," she replied, trying to place the source of the unease that had invaded her. "But what about the Meads?"

"Gone ahead." He said the words with finality.

She was struck by the fact that he had removed his hat, revealing fair hair that gleamed dully in the gloom. She had assumed it was dark. And he was staring at her again. His hot glance took in her clothes, her new bonnet, and her face. She stiffened, prepared to face another of his sneering comments, but, to her relief, he said nothing. He was too far away for her to see what his expression revealed.

He turned away as soon as she reached the bottom stair, and she followed him to the door. He did not precede her through it but stood back in an attitude that was almost deferential.

What Jed had sent by way of conveyance was a pony cart. Looking up at the narrow perch they would have to share, Julianna wondered how they would manage. Her

skirts were not as wide as fashion allowed, but they
would take up more than the room allotted for both of
them. She glanced uncertainly at him, but he had put on
his ever-present hat, obscuring his face.

Yet he must have been thinking along the same lines
as she, for when they reached the cart, he said, "Yer
ladyship must take th' seat. Ah'll stand behind in th'
cart."

He held out his hand to her and helped her up. She
would not have thought he had a great deal of experience in escorting ladies, yet he handled the maneuver
with amazing ease, taking care not to drag her volumi-
nous skirts across the muddy wheels. As she arranged
herself on the seat, he climbed in behind her to stand in
the cart, and she realized that he meant to drive the cart
standing up. This method brought him close behind her
and seemed rather more intimate than sharing the
wooden seat. She had no time to rethink her decision to
go with him, because he picked up the whip, flicked it
lightly over the pony's head, and they were off.

They drove awhile in silence. Julianna was vividly
aware of him each time his arm brushed her sleeve or a
rut in the lane jolted them so that her shoulder grazed
his chest. More gradually she became conscious of other
things about him. The first was quite pleasant. Unlike
other times she had been near him, he did not smell of
manure. His breath, coming warmly across her cheek,
smelled sweet, as if he had just eaten an apple. He was
very close yet she could not see him past the brim of her
bonnet unless she turned her head a full ninety degrees.
So conspicuous a gesture seemed uncalled for. Instead,
she glanced down at his hands, which held the reins beside her left shoulder.

She saw the cuff of a clean shirt peeking out from beneath the sleeve of a new tweed jacket. Or, if not new, at least it was not the dreadfully foul thing he usually wore. His hands were clean, the nails pared and unstained. They were good hands: square-palmed, lightly tanned, and lean. The knuckles of his right hand bore thin scabs from a recent skinning. She remembered then that he had struck Rob Wheal. He had fought another man for her honor. The reminder of his gallantry pricked her sense of fairness. However reluctantly she had come to be in his company this day, she had been grateful for his protection that day. Not wanting to seem churlish, she decided that polite conversation was called for.

"What did you call the day, Mr. Trevelyn? Fastings?"

"Fassens," he repeated, sounding annoyed. "Fasterns e'en, more properly."

"That's what it's called where you come from, I suppose." She gave him a quick sidelong glance but caught only a glimpse of his chin. He had shaved. "Where is that?"

"Where is what?"

"Where is your home?"

"North country," he answered, then barked a sharp order to the pony, which had begun to slow down.

It was not much of a conversation but she was determined to continue it. "I understand that you were in the army. Where did you serve?"

"East India Company," he muttered.

"Were you, perchance, a batman to an officer?"

"What's tha' t' ye?" he asked ungraciously.

"Nothing," she answered faintly, feeling like a child whose wrist had been slapped for a ill-mannered inquiry. "My parents are in India. I thought you might know of them, if you served an officer, or that I might know your officer myself."

"Ah doubt tha', he bein' dead."

"Oh!" Julianna swung her head toward him, but he chose that moment to swing off the lane into a path through the moors that was no more than two carriage ruts overgrown with weeds. As the cart jerked erratically, she had to grab the seatback to keep from being thrown over the side.

"Best watch the road," he directed as one hard hand came down on her left shoulder to steady her.

"May I drive the cart?" The question surprised her almost as much as it did him. Feeling that she could not back down now, she reached for the reins. "I often drove a pony cart across the moors when I was a child. My grandfather feared I'd break my neck on horseback so he brought me a jingle instead."

She was amazed by the heat of his skin when their fingers touched. Then his hands fell abruptly away, and she was left to grip the reins and feel the warmth of the leather where his own hands had warmed them. She felt the color flame in her face and was glad that he could not see past the brim of her bonnet.

Sensing a new grip on the leader, the pony tossed its head, nearly jerking the reins from her hands. Her hands tightened in response, jerking too hard on the reins, and the pony stumbled.

"Here, give a care!" Jos cried, and reached out, stopping just short of snatching the reins from her. "Th' pony's got clever feet, ye give 'im his head, yer ladyship."

"It's been a while," she offered by way of an apology, but she did not hand him the reins. That would be conceding defeat. Taking a deep breath, she loosened her grip, giving the pony the freedom to find its pace, and it quickly settled into an even trot. "There, I told you," she said in triumph, but received only a grunt in reply.

Falling silent, she watched the road before her, for her vision gave her an imperfect view of the ruts ahead. She had learned a little about Jos Trevelyn. Many country people were secretive about their lives. She had secrets of her own. He was welcome to keep his. She turned her thoughts to the land before her.

The moors were brown and sodden from the frequent rains. The sky was a high pure gray. It would rain again by nightfall, but for now it was only a purple smudge on the northwestern horizon. The wind sang past her ears, bringing fresh color to her cheeks and sparkle to her eyes, filling her lungs and quenching a thirst for traveling quickly over open places that had not been satisfied in years. After a few minutes she forgot about the unpleasant man at her side, about the troublesome moments that might lie ahead, even the small aches in her life. The clear, cold wind and the moors were solace enough.

The official festivities of Shrove Tuesday did not begin until two P.M., after a half day's work, but the village of Combe Martin had already begun its celebration. As they rode into town, Julianna saw that the square was filled with tables and banners and people. Every sort of carriage, cart, and wagon congested the lane, while people thronged the spaces between the cottages and stalls that had been set up for business. Apples and squashes were for sale side by side with rashers of bacon and last season's jams. The greasy brown smell of cooking sausages and the crisp-crust aroma of fresh-baked pastries vied for her appetite, reminding Julianna that she had been too excited to eat her breakfast.

When a market woman in a blue scarf and red woolen cape stepped into the lane with a basket of tarts on her arm, Julianna drew in on the reins and brought her cart to a halt beside her. "How much for a tart?"

"Tuppence, my lady!" the woman called back, her cheeks as red as her cape.

"I'll have two, please." Julianna extracted the coins from the purse tied around her wrist. As they exchanged coins for pies, Julianna discovered that the pastries were taken so recently from the oven that they burned her fingertips, but she didn't mind. Turning around on the seat, she held one out to Jos. "Don't add ungraciousness to your other sterling qualities," she said impatiently when he looked away, pretending not to notice her offering.

He looked back at her from beneath the brim of his hat. "Ah do no' like sweets."

"Liar!" She bit into hers and sighed with satisfaction, for it tasted as delicious as it smelled. "Everybody eats apple tarts. 'Tis Fassens."

His sudden grin moved her heart a fraction to the left. "Well, then, Ah'm no' a man t' stint a proper holiday." He took the pie from her and popped it whole into his mouth.

Julianna turned away to hide her smile, for she was pleased that he had taken it from her, even if he must be rude in his enjoyment of it. Something about him reminded her of the young groomsman who had taught her to whistle. He had been full of himself, proud, with a male aggression that even a girl of five could admire. Perhaps he would treat her with the same cocky rudeness as Jos if they met now. A male servant and his mistress could not be friends. What was there for them but this rough kind of bantering that was more than insolence but less than familiarity?

She stepped down from the cart near the tall steeple of the church and waved at Parson Pollock and his wife, who manned a booth in the churchyard. Jos took the reins from her hands and without so much as a word turned the cart back toward the square—and the tavern, Julianna suspected as she watched his back. He would be a hard-drinking man, she supposed, and wandered fleetingly what the trip home would be like.

For the next half hour, she conversed with the vicar and his wife, chatting of country matters, of simple times and simple pleasures. When she was done there, she strolled back toward booths set on the square. There were booths selling the bright ribbons that could not be worn until Easter. Others sold food or offered hand-knitted goods and lacework. Nearby were pens of hogs and chickens for sale. Farther on, the horse traders were doing a brisk business.

During the course of the morning, she bought a crock of wild clover honey, several jars of sloe-plum and rasp-berry jam, and finally, two laying hens for Mrs. Mead's coop. This last purchase was marked and would be brought to the Hall by the seller. The other things she carried in her arms, enjoying the bustle and chatter of the fairlike atmosphere.

People were merry, expending their last joyous hours before the forty dark days of penitence and sacrifice came down upon them. Everywhere she went, men tipped their hats while the women dropped a curtsey whenever they chanced to catch her eye. Everyone smiled at her, their benefactor for the day. She might have been a medieval noblewoman receiving tribute

from her vassals, Julianna thought more than once. Yet
that was not what she wanted. She had hoped to engage
some of the wives and, perhaps, even a few of the miners
in conversation. Her grandmother possessed what people
called the common touch. If the marchioness had been
there today, she would have learned how many children
each woman had, their names and ages, even which marriages and births were imminent.

But, Julianna thought with a burgeoning sense of inad-
equacy, she did not encourage that kind of familiarity.
While the people were all deferential, no one approached her, nor did anyone she spoke with spare her
more than a few shyly mumbled words. She was no more
one of the commoners than she had been one of the
London *ton.* For all the good she was accomplishing, she
might as well have stayed at home. She was, as usual, an
outsider looking with envy upon the lives of others.

Frustrated by repeated but ultimately futile attempts
to make friends, she turned her interest to other things.
There were street performers to entertain the crowd. For
more than an hour she watched jugglers and then Gypsy
fire eaters while she sucked on an orange. Later there
was a magician and, still later, a traveling band of mum-
mers enacted a Passion Play. The longer she remained in
the village, the more Julianna felt her sense of time slipping away, the years rolling back, until past and present
blended, and it might as easily have been 1546 as 1846.

"Pancake Races! Pancake Races!"

The cry echoed across the open ground to be picked
up by the holidaymakers. Finally the long-awaited event
was about to take place. It was one of the few holiday
games in which women played the central part. Following
along behind the stream of people headed toward the

end of town where a long, narrow valley fell away from the moors, Julianna glanced about for sight of Jed or Jos or Tom or Mrs. Mead, but none was among the sea of faces surrounding her.

The wind blew up in playful gusts, but people merely laughed at the chill as clouds played hide and seek with the winter sun. When she reached the meadow she saw that the racers were beginning to line up. There were a score of them, women and girls, each with a skillet in hand, wearing an apron and mobcap, with their skirts hiked up to give them the freedom to run.

"Well, her ladyship's come to Pancake Day," a man's voice said behind her. "I seen ye come ridin' into town with a man at yer back. Have ye been cheatin' on me?"

Julianna swung about. "Rob Wheal!"

"Ye've asked after me, have ye?" he answered low, his loose-lipped smile stretching into a sneer. "That's praise in a woman, ain't it?"

She felt the blood drain from her face, but she did not turn away from him. "I wanted to know the name of the man against whom I intend to bring charges," she declared in a low voice.

"Oh, well, then," he jeered, rocking back on his heels, "why ain't the magistrate come for me?"

She had not expected a bold challenge in the broad light of day with so many people around. Perhaps her reasoning had been correct; he wanted to provoke her into public conflict. That idea seemed to be verified by the way several people turned curious stares on them, pausing as they sensed something untoward was occurring. If he wanted a public exchange, then that was exactly what she would not give him. "Excuse me, I want to see the race," she said, and started past him.

" 'Tis yer portions in the pans." He stepped in close against her. "Why do ye no' run it yerself?" he challenged in a loud, carrying voice. "Or are ye too particular to run for yer supper like other folk?"

Julianna looked him straight in the eye, not bothering to hide her dislike. "I didn't know I could enter the race." She turned to the man nearest her. "Is it true that I may run the race?"

"Now, yer ladyship, who's got a better right?" answered the man, his grin a match for Wheal's.

All at once, Julianna realized that she had walked into some kind of trap though she did not yet know its purpose.

"Give 'er ladyship a skillet!" Rob Wheal cried as he turned to those about him for support. "Lady Kingsblood will run the race! Give 'er ladyship a skillet!" He swung back to her. " 'Ifin she's nay too dainty to join the game!"

A young woman thrust her skillet at Julianna, saying apologetically "Ye've nae need to do it, me lady, only I'd be that honored were ye to run in me stead."

" 'Tis never been done afore!" cried another of the women in protest.

Parson Pollock came rushing up to Julianna, his eyes wide in alarm. "My lady, you've no need to take up the challenge. Anyone can see that you're not prepared for the event."

Julianna felt the weight of dozens of eyes upon her. She could gracefully bow out and none would think less of her. Yet somehow, that did not matter. What mattered was that she had come here today to show that she was, in fact, one of the people and that she wanted to share their joy in the day. Until now she had been a bystander, a privileged onlooker to other people's pleasure. More than anything, she wanted to be a part of it.

"Of course I'll do it." She tumbled her purchases into the vicar's outstretched hands and began loosening the buttons that held her elegant cloak closed. "I was a fair runner as a child. Let's see what the years have done to me."

As she handed her cloak to the young woman who had offered her her pan, Julianna saw from the corner of her eye the briefest sketch of Jos Trevelyn's hat among the gathered crowd. She nearly called out to him for want of a familiar face by her side until she remembered Rob Wheal's first words to her. Any recognition of Jos on her part might spur Wheal to make other lewd comments that the crowd would hear. She was, after all, a spinster. Appearances must be maintained.

Instead, she turned away and began hiking up the front of her skirts as the other ladies had done. When she had turned her waistband several times, her neat black half-boots could be plainly seen. She gave only fleeting thought to the impropriety, or what Lettie would think if she knew her cousin was showing her ankles and a good portion of her calves to the entire village. One of the women handed her the traditional apron while another offered her a mobcap in place of her poke bonnet. Within minutes she was transformed from Lady Kingsblood into just another Devonshire lass ready to run a race as old as Blood Hall.

As the rules of the race were explained, Julianna observed that it was more a test of swiftness than skill at tossing pancakes in the air. In fact, she had to toss and catch her pancake only three times as she ran across to a point at the far of the meadow, circled it, and then raced

back. However, if the pancake was dropped, the runner
was disqualified. As for the midway point, a beech tree
standing alone at the far end of the valley, it might as
well have been on the moon for all Julianna could see of
it. After squinting uselessly in its general direction, she
decided to pace the other women.

The Pancake Bell Ringer came forward, a tall but
sheepish-looking fresh-faced young man who carried a
hand bell that would be used to begin the race. A kiss
from the bell ringer would be the winner's reward. After
the reverend's blessing, he stepped forward, lifted the
bell high, and rang it lustily.

The race began with cries from all sides as the women
struck out at a brisk pace. Julianna was inadvertently
jostled at the outset, knocking her off the pace, but with
her long legs and youth she was soon out with the front-
runners. The ground was wet. They kicked up mud and
water as they splashed through the meadow, but Julianna
did not mind. She had forgotten about the freedom provided by short skirts and how much fun it was to make
careless steps that soaked one's stockings. She nearly forgot about the need to flip her pancake until she saw the
woman ahead of her do it with expert ease.

Slowing down, she gave her iron skillet a flick of her
wrist. The pancake jumped like a landed fish and flopped
half in, half out of her pan. As the others sped past her,
she picked up the pace again, inordinately pleased that
she had not dropped her bread. It was not until she
reached the beech tree that she remembered that she
wore a corset. It was her oldest set of stays, nonetheless,
it was restricting her breathing. Slowing briefly to catch
her breath, she tossed her pancake and had the satisfaction of seeing it plop down squarely in the pan.

Once past the halfway mark, she again became aware of the cheering crowd. Their exuberance only increased as the runners neared the finish line. Names were called, hers among them, but she did not bother to try to guess who urged her on. Amazingly, she was in second place and gaining on the leader.

The cries rose to a crescendo as she sprinted across the last few yards. Suddenly she realized someone was shouting a reminder to her to toss her pancake a third time. As perspiration ran into her eyes, she tossed it, saw it rise higher than expected, and had to stop to catch it. As it flopped precariously across the handle and pan, she took up the race again. The pause cost her a few precious seconds, and she crossed the finish line a winded but pleased second.

"That made a fine showin', yer ladyship!" a woman said, and clapped Julianna familiarly on the back.

"Always said there's got to be good strong Devonshire blood running in the Kingsbloods' veins," said another. "Done a good job for ye today, yer ladyship!"

The crowd swarmed in around Julianna, offering their congratulations as heartily as if she had won. Mrs. Mead and Tom appeared at her side, beaming as if she were their own daughter.

Jed Coleman, having come in late from the mine, found her and pumped her hand. "Congratulations, m'lady. Ye showed what being a Kingsblood means in these parts."

Too winded to do much more than smile dazedly, Julianna accepted his and other accolades in silence.

Parson Pollock's praise was more restrained than the others, but she could tell that he was pleased by her showing in the event.

It was not until she spied Rob Wheal's smirking face that she remembered his challenge. "Well, Mr. Wheal," she said breathlessly, "as you see . . . we Kingsbloods are up . . . to any challenge." Not giving him a chance to reply, she turned to the young woman who had lent her the pan and said, "Have I earned a fresh stack of pancakes for my own?"

The young woman pointed toward the tent that been set up nearby. "As many as ye may wish to eat, me lady."

Julianna smiled at her. "Won't you join me? I hate to eat alone."

The woman smiled and nodded but her gaze slid away from Julianna's to the young man standing beside her.

"Is this your husband?" Julianna asked quickly.

"Aye, me lady." She reached behind her and drew forth a small child who had been hiding behind her skirts. "And this is me Bessie."

Julianna smiled at the little girl. "I'll bet you like pancakes, don't you, Bessie?"

The child nodded solemnly then burst out, "With honey on 'em!"

Julianna laughed. "I just bought a crock of honey. Shall we open it and eat some?" Bessie nodded a second time. Julianna held out her hand to the child then led the family into one of the tents that had been set up to serve pancakes.

The rest of the day was spent in eating and drinking and meeting all the people who had been too shy before to approach her. While she did not memorize the name of every child born in the area in the past twelve months, she did learn about Mrs. Wilkes's rheumatism and Elam Davies's leg, which was lost in a fishing accident, and then became involved in a lively discussion of the merits of Silas Archer's new heifer. Jed Coleman's wife had brought a batch of her apple cider with her. When everyone had had their fill of pancakes, cups of cider were passed around to take the nip out of the February wind. As the afternoon progressed, she began to feel that her grandmother would be quite proud of her. More than that, she had been so successful in making friends that the last time she saw Rob Wheal, he was frowning at her.

At the end of the day the wind suddenly rose. Rain could be felt in the wind gusting down upon the stalls and tumbling the contents off the tables. Laughing and jostling one another, people headed home in the purple dusk toward the dry warmth of their hearths. Soon to follow was the sobering realization that Lent was hard upon them.

Julianna found Jos in the doorway of a tavern, his hat cocked as always across his brow. "It's time to go home," she said in a voice mellowed by apple cider.

"Ye been drinkin', yer ladyship," he replied, his own voice smoother than usual.

"As have you." She smiled at him, wishing he would not always frown. And so mysterious he was. She nearly asked him why he never looked directly at her when she could see him clearly. Why had he had not come to the race and praised her as the others had done? Why could he not be kind and pleasant so that she might share her joy in the day with him? But she said none of those things. She said only, "You'd best get the cart. We've a long journey home."

As she stepped into the entrance of the tavern to get out of the windborne rain, he put out a hand to steady her. "Would ye no' stop th' night here?"

She felt the closeness of him, the strength in the arm

against which she had inadvertently swayed, and wondered again at the self-consciousness she felt in his presence. "No," she said huskily. "I want to go home. Now."

"Th' Meads are bidin' in th' village with friends." His voice was low, sweet, and compelling. His hand on her shoulder tightened fractionally. " 'Tis more bad weather coming in from th' coast. Can ye no' smell it?"

She did smell the salt in the wind. She could stay at the vicarage, but she had no desire to spend an evening with the Pollocks. The vicar had already expressed his disapproval of the imbibing of fermented cider. She was more than a little tipsy and in no mood for a sermon. She could not, like Jos, stay in one of the rooms above the tavern. Besides, though she had not allowed herself to think on it, she hoped her mysterious Friend would come again this night. For that she must go back to Blood Hall. "We'll go back."

"Ye'll be soaked through!" Jos muttered, but he swung away from the doorway and out into the lane to fetch the pony cart.

Unlike the ride to town, the ride back was a slow, laborious, and chilling affair. The wind blew more than it rained. Even so, Julianna's teeth began to chatter uncontrollably before they were even halfway home.

"Are ye cold?" she finally heard Jos call above the shriek of the wind. He stood behind her as before, driving the cart.

"Yes!" She sounded forlorn, but she could not help it. The fur of her cloak had become thick with mist, as cold and dank against her skin as the dead beast from which it had come. The world was all gray mist and darkness, and she had long since regretted her impulsive act of leaving the village.

The reins were thrust at her. "Take 'em!" he cried. As she did she felt him move behind her. There was a scraping sound in the bottom of the cart and then he was behind her again, his hands encircling her waist. "Move aside!" he called, showing her with his hands where he wanted her to go. Julianna slid along the seat until she thought she might slip off, but he climbed over from behind, his arm holding her away from the edge.

" 'Tis only th' pony's blanket," he said when he settled beside her and held up his find. "Ben't too mean for yer ladyship?"

"No!" She pushed the word forth with effort, for her throat had begun to ache from the raw wind.

"Good of ye!" His voice seemed inordinately cheerful, she mused, until the breath of spirits that accompanied his every word reached her. He had spent his day in the tavern. He was probably drunk though he seemed steady enough.

In his first show of kindness to her, he drew her tight against his side and wrapped the musky blanket about them both. "Ye be a stubborn woman, yer ladyship."

"I know," she answered, too chastened by the wind and rain to dispute him this once. She leaned against his shoulder, grateful for the warmth of his body, amazed by the strength that encompassed her, and slightly bemused by this intimacy with a man she neither liked nor trusted.

He held her all the way back to Blood Hall. There was nothing loverlike in the embrace, but it was strong and protective and she doubted he would have allowed her to move an inch away. By the time the dark bulk of Blood Hall loomed before them, she no longer cared who held her or why. Her ribs ached from the afternoon's exertions and her calves had begun to cramp. She had left this place a picture of patrician affluence and poise. She returned to it a bedraggled spinster no longer as young or spry as she once thought.

When Jos drew the cart up before the door of the Hall, Julianna resisted moving away from him for a moment. His embrace was so reassuring and warm. Even the odor of his body seemed comforting and somehow familiar. He was a man and she suddenly felt all the vulnerability of being a woman. She knew she should sit up, make her movements crisp and assured, show him that the journey had meant nothing but the necessity of sharing mutual warmth. But she could not move away. All her body wanted was to go on sharing the warmth, the extraordinary surprise of another human body so close to her own.

"Will ye be needin' a carry-up?"

She started at the sound of his voice, for it came to her ear through the walls of his chest, deep, full, and curiously alive. "A carry-up?" she repeated as she lifted her head.

It was dark. His face was no more than shadow. Something in her stirred, moved inexplicably by the moment. She felt his hand touch her bonnet, then his chill fingers lay against her face. In another moment she knew that he would kiss her. She lifted her face not knowing why.

He leaned into her. "There ben't none other to see to yer ladyship's comfort. Shall Ah then come in with ye?"

The oddly formal words were deferential enough, his voice quiet below the wind's howl. But she understood. The force and strength and animal fascination of him were things she had never before felt. This man, this stranger really, whom she could not sketch as easily as she had Rob Wheal, moved her.

The flicker of flame in an upper window caught her eye. It flickered in the oriel of the Great Hall, a steady burst of light so white and pure it could not be candle flame.

"Look!"

She pointed up but as Jos turned his head it died. "What do ye see?"

"A light." She glanced down at him once more, realizing who she was and where she was and with whom she was. A rolling cannonade of thunder shook the sky. An instant later rain hissed down through the darkness.

" 'Twas lightning on the glass," Jos offered, his voice grown distant.

"Yes," she whispered, but she did not believe it. In the instant before the light at the window had died she had seen a face, a woman's face, and the tread of the spirit world had marched lightly down her spine. She turned away. "Good night, Jos, and thank you."

"Ye mustn't do tha', yer ladyship," he drawled, his voice thick with his north country accent. He climbed down and came around to help her descend from the pony cart. When her feet touched the ground, he lifted his hands to frame her shoulders. As she prepared herself for his embrace, he merely removed the wet pony blanket from her shoulders. " 'Twas a pleasure."

She turned her back on him without a word and walked to the door. Once inside, she closed it after her, her heart thumping like some live thing trapped within her chest. She had nearly shamed herself with the gardener. Had he known how badly she wanted to be kissed by him, how much she longed to go on clinging to his well-muscled warmth? Had he known and been laughing at her?

Chagrin stung her cheeks and then a sneezing fit began. When it ended, she was beyond caring, for the moment, about anything but getting dry before pneumonia claimed her.

Chapter Eleven

A half-drowned rat! There was no more apt description of herself, Julianna decided as she lay awake sneezing and shivering beneath the covers. She seldom felt the need for pampering but tonight, when she was utterly alone and too bedraggled even to make herself a pot of tea, she longed for Mrs. Mead's attentive care. She had even begun to regret dismissing Jos's offer of assistance. If only she could have been certain he would not have taken her acceptance of his offer as an invitation of another kind. No, she was better off shivering than fighting off the unwelcome advances of a lecherous gardener.

The storm that had threatened all evening was now in full force. The room brightened repeatedly with the blue-white spears of lightning while the windows rattled with each crack of thunder. The hiss of rain pervaded every corner of the room, masking the smaller, more familiar sounds of the house. She heard, faintly, the clock strike nine P.M. and groaned. It would be hours yet before her mystery companion showed himself, if, indeed, he chose to come at all.

She closed her eyes, willing him to come as he had said she could. She did not believe him, of course, for he always came while she slept and could no longer summon him. Yet the wishing distracted her from the fact that she would most likely be ill by morning.

A sudden stillness roused her even as she drifted toward fretful sleep. In the blink of an eye something changed, changed so utterly that even the sounds of wind and rain and thunder were muted. She opened her eyes slowly, scarcely daring to believe what she wanted very much to be true.

He stood at the foot of her bed, a dark figure revealed by a flash of lightning.

"You came!" Her words were wistfully sweet.

He remained motionless so long she began to wonder if her eyes were playing a trick on her and that only shadow stood where she had wanted to see him. Then the sky, and the room with it, brightened again for an instant with sharp white light. The flash silvered his light hair and sharpened the profile that was both familiar and yet unknown.

In the backwash of the thunder's blast she heard his voice. "I've brought you a treat, my lady." He pointed and she turned her head to find a goblet on her bedside table. "Drink it. It will warm you."

After sliding up in bed until she was sitting, she obediently reached for the goblet and took a sip. "Cherry cordial! My favorite. How did you know?"

"Drink it all," he urged when she started to set it aside.

"I think not," she answered. The trembling inside her had altered at the sound of his voice, and she knew she would need all her remaining wits to deal with him. "Anything more and I might become intoxicated."

"Would that be so terrible?" he replied with a smile in

his voice. "Drink it. You don't want to be ill behind the day's adventures."

"What would you know of my day?" Suspecting that he would not answer her until she obeyed him, she brought the goblet back to her lips. When she had drunk a greater portion of the cherry-flavored liquor, she looked up as the lightning flashed again, hoping to catch another glimpse of him, but he had disappeared from the footboard. "Friend?" she called softly.

"Here, my lady." His voice now came from across the room, perhaps from the small chair beside her fireplace, but she could not be certain. "What is your desire?"

The question was phrased more provocatively than was necessary, but she was too pleased by his presence to quibble. She was also relieved to hear tolerant amusement in his voice. While she had never seen his face clearly, his voice was more expressive than any other she had ever heard. "I should like to know something about you. Your name, for instance."

He laughed. "We've had no need for names before. Why change?"

"Be-be-becau—*achoo!*"

As she sneezed into her handkerchief she heard him say politely, "God bless you. Now finish your cordial."

After she had daintily wiped her nose, she did as he directed. The cordial sang through her veins with a sugary warmth. Combined with the cider she had drunk earlier, the effect was quite soothing. But as her shivering lessened her heart began to beat faster.

She knew he was watching her. Each flash of light, gradually growing fainter, lighted her bed, whereas he was now in full darkness. Just because she was doing something as unorthodox as entertaining a man in her bedroom while she lay in bed in her bedclothes did not mean that they could not behave as correctly as if they were sharing afternoon tea in the Great Hall. "I think it's time we were properly introduced."

His deep chuckle eddied through the darkness toward her. "Would you feel safer if I were Mr. Green or Earl Brown or, perhaps, you'd prefer I was Lord White?"

"I would like to know the truth," she said with as much dignity as could muster between sniffs into her handkerchief.

"Why?"

She supposed it was a natural question, but she sensed that his reason for sparring with her came from another source. "It's only proper that I know something about my guest, who you are or once were, why you came to Blood Hall."

His silence was different this time. In it was an electric tension more vivid than nature's display beyond the window. "What would you have me be, my lady? I began as any other man."

"Where were you born?"

"Yorkshire."

"But that is miles from Devon!" she exclaimed in surprise.

"A man's travels may take him to China or the Americas. Surely Yorkshire is not so far compared to that."

"Of course, you are right. And did you travel to any of those places before you came here?"

"No, my lady." His voice was regretful. "The youngest son is always poor, and a poor man may seldom follow his heart's desire."

"You are poor?" She could not keep the disappointment from her voice though she could not have said precisely why.

"As poor as your gardener," he agreed, amused once more. "Men of little means are apt to follow where the fortunes of others lead them."

"So what did you do? You're educated. I hear it in your voice."

"Education has its virtues. It enabled me to find work. But my father didn't approve of my choice. Men of limited means never understand when their sons do not aspire to greatness. But poor men . . ." She heard him sigh as if the repetition had become a burden. "I worked, this and that, sometimes with my head, other times with my brawn."

"Surely you had some say in what you did?"

"Hardly ever," he confided with the careless humor of a man who accepts his lot. "Did you consider the desires of the man whom you ordered out into this stormy night? No. You pay Jos Trevelyn's wages, thus he must obey."

She gasped. "That's entirely unfair!"

"How so?"

"I'd had a long, tiring day and simply wanted to sleep in my own bed."

"Is that the only reason?"

She did not answer. She had come back in the hope of seeing him, but now that he was here she was suddenly shy and uncertain of herself. Proprieties could only be observed if certain matters were overlooked.

"Shall I tell you about your day?" he said after a moment. "You nearly won the Pancake Race. You admire jugglers more than one might suppose. And you enjoy being among people. Yet when you've had more fun than you think is right, you try to make up for it by becoming excessively conventional—and stubborn. The part of prim spinster misbecomes you almost as much as your choice of bonnets!"

His tone was different from all the times before, judgmental and disapproving. She wondered again how he knew so much about her. Was he spying on her, or could he read her thoughts? She was glad for the darkness that hid the deep, uncomfortable blush that climbed her neck. "I'm by nature a practical person."

"Was it practical to demand that Jos drive you home in the wind and rain when you might have found shelter in the village?"

She had no ready answer to that discomforting question and reached for the goblet only to remember that she had already finished the contents. "I didn't intend to put the gardener to any great task." She began spinning the goblet stem between her fingers. "How was I to know the storm would break so soon?" Impatient with the pricking sense of guilt his words had roused, she added, "No doubt Jos is at this very minute tucked tidily in his bed with a bottle of rum to keep him company."

"If he has yet reached his bed," he returned. "Do you know where he lives or how far away it is? Did you tell him to take the pony cart, or did he feel compelled to leave it in the stable and walk the rest of the way home in the storm?"

"I didn't think of that," she replied slowly, feeling her defenses erode like shifting sand beneath the insistent pummeling of his questions. "I will apologize to him in the morning."

"That should take care of your guilt," he said dryly.

She glared at him through the darkness, barely containing a harsh reply behind her clamped jaws. "Very well. I'll pay him for the extra trouble. Does that satisfy your sense of fair play?"

"An inquiry after his well-being might not go amiss."

"I can't very well do that, not after . . ." She left the thought dangling, remembering Jos's amused tone after she had rebuffed his advance. At least, it had seemed at the time like an advance. She had been certain that he meant to kiss her, but perhaps he had only been teasing her because of her skittish reaction to his simple offer of aid. If only she could be certain which was right. She set the goblet aside, more flustered than she had been at that moment.

"You've finished your cordial? I've brought more."

"I don't need it." She folded her hands primly in her lap and laced her fingers together. "I'm never ill. I—I—*achoo!*" She plucked up her handkerchief and impatiently wiped her nose. "Oh, why did you come? If it's only to scold me then go away."

She was too occupied with several more sneezes to at first notice his continued silence. Finally, when she seemed to be free of them, she peered hard into the darkness, but it was impenetrable. The flashes that had offered glimpses of his silhouette were now fainter and farther between. "Are you there?" she asked softly. "Don't go away. I didn't mean it."

More silence.

"Oh, very well. Go away, stay away! What do I care!"

His laughter riffed across the dark. "My lady has a temper."

"My lady is wretched," she answered, and sniffed again.

She was amazed by the brief touch upon her brow, for

she had not seen or heard him move. "You're trembling!" His voice sounded no less amazed than she felt.

There came another flash of lightning and then a deep roll of thunder that reverberated through the house, echoing and redoubling on itself again and again. She felt the modulation of sound deep against her bones, but that is not what sent primitive sensations jangling along her nerves. She was remembering this man's kiss, the stunning unexpectedness of it, the sweet anguish of its end, and knew that she wanted more than anything else in life to feel it again.

The acknowledgment tugged with equal amounts of excitement and shame at her conscience. She sat motionless as his cool firm fingers again traced her brow then skimmed the crest of one cheek. "You're cold, Gillie. I will warm you, if you let me."

Apprehension and joy quavered through her as his fingers traced the upward slope of her jaw and spread out through the damp hair over her ear then up behind until he cradled her head in his palm. She wanted him to speak again, to coax her over the edge of her misgivings. Yet she knew he would not do that. "I'm not brave," she said slowly. "I fear everything. But I want . . ."

What did she want? To be loved? To have a lover? To be persuaded that some man, any man, found her desirable? But what if she was only fooling herself again? What if this faceless, nameless stranger who stood beside her bed was someone altogether different from the man she imagined him to be?

Then again she felt his strength, his assurance, his ease in his silence. His fingers tenderly massaged her scalp. Where they touched she tingled. He was strong enough to be gentle, of that she was certain. What safer way to risk her happiness than with a stranger who had no future or past, no real existence beyond the hours they spent together here? Yet, always circling in her thoughts was the acute humiliation by the one man she had dared to love.

"Do you believe in love?" she asked, her eyes wide in the hope that a flash of light would reveal his face.

She felt the bed give under his weight as he sat down beside her. "Do you know what love is?"

"No." The revealing honesty of her reply started a quiver at the corner of his mouth. If he laughed at her . . .

But he did not laugh, though his voice was now wistfully amused. "Then if love came to you one night, out of the darkness with all questions unanswered and all reason against it, how could you welcome it for what it was?"

She stared into the gloom until her eyes stung, feeling as exposed as if she lay naked to his gaze beneath a noonday sun. She had the answer to his question. She knew what he asked of her. She trembled on the edge of that knowledge, now advancing, now retreating, but always trembling and uncertain. If only she knew . . . if only she could reassure herself. . . . "If only I could be certain!"

"Nothing is certain."

His reply startled her, for she had not realized that she had spoken aloud. She swallowed her pride and her fear, but she could not find the words to free herself from twenty-five years of morals and principles and the desperate suspicion that she was not like other women, not made for love.

She felt his hand slide away, leaving her scalp suddenly chilled. "I should leave you, my lady."

She knew he meant forever and not for the moment. She reached out in the darkness as the bed gave up his weight, but he moved away too quickly. "No. Wait. I want to understand."

"How can you when I scarcely understand it myself?" His voice came from above her, sounding as perplexed as she.

The uncertainty in his voice brought courage to her as she felt again a treacherous and intimidating tidal yearning for this man. "Why can't we continue to be friends?" Secret friends, she continued in her thoughts, who shared a few of the many lonely nights that stretched out before her into the foreseeable future?

"Because it's a fraud, a cheat." His voice was tight, withdrawn.

She wondered what he meant, for it occurred to her that there were several possible interpretations for his words. "I don't care," she said, and suddenly she knew that it was true. "If I'm mad and you aren't real, I don't care. Stay here, with me."

"Don't!" He sounded almost angry. "You don't know what you're saying."

But suddenly she did know exactly what she was asking of him. She was conscious of everything about her all at once: her skin puckered by the cold, the shift of her muscle inside it, the *shirr-shirr* of her blood, and deep down the hard support of her bones. Her eyes ached from straining fruitlessly against the dark. Her feet were cold, feeling like blocks of inert wood attached to her ankles. Her heart chimed in her chest and her lungs seemed cramped inside her ribs. But none of that seemed to matter any longer. All that mattered was the voice and man behind the voice, whoever he was, for she had a memory of him that was stronger than any dream. She had the memory of his kiss.

"The reality of this world is that I'm a plain spinster with no hopes of loving or being loved." She said the words slowly, testing each for the soundness of it, for it had never seemed more important in her life that she be perfectly understood. "It sounds mad, I know, but I thought in the beginning that I had dreamed you up to keep away the loneliness that stretches before me. Now I don't want you to be real because . . ." She breathed in a long, trembling breath. She had come this far. The moment demanded honesty. "If you were real then I would have to doubt everything: myself, my sanity, even my feelings."

His voice was hushed, deep, and tender. "What are your feelings, my lady?"

She began to reply but fell silent.

"Gillie?"

The tender question framed in her childhood name gave her the courage she had lost. "I think I could love you."

"Oh, Gillie." His voice sounded curiously forlorn. "You can't. You mustn't. You must love only what you see and feel and know is real. I'm only a shadow to you, a half-truth in the night."

"It doesn't matter." Her words tumbled out hurriedly, for she felt that there was little time left in which to persuade him, and herself, of this impossible possibility. "It's better this way."

"You prefer this trickery by moonlight to flesh-and-blood reality?" He sounded amazed, and not a little hurt.

She was silent a long time, not because she did not know how to answer, but because she did not know how to make him understand. Nor was she certain she wanted him to. A few short weeks ago she had shocked Lettie with the suggestion that the only man she could ever abide in her life would be one who was at her beck and call, only there when she summoned him. Now it seemed as if Fate had sought to make a fool of her. The gift was being offered. "Yes."

She saw his shadow shift, felt the quiver of indecision that held him vibrant to the spot. "You needn't grasp at shadows to find happiness, Gillie. You need only the courage to take what you need from life. The gulf that would separate you from me in the real world is no wider than the one that divides us now. It takes courage to cross the distance, but it is only a short distance."

Reason struggled to reassert itself into her thoughts. "The world would count me as mad."

"How does the world reckon you now?"

Of damned little worth, she thought bitterly. Oh, as a rich maiden lady she might eventually be married off to a noble widower with children who were in need of a mother, or an aging vicar in need of a younger companion to help with the shepherding of his flock. But always her life would be put to the use of another's concerns. If her life continued as it was now, conventional and correct, she would never know or possess anything that was her very own, of her own choosing. He was right. The poor, if only of spirit and heart, were condemned to follow where the will of the more fortunate led them. That was unfair, so very unfair!

Choose love!

The words came to her in a resonance that seemed to

have no sound before it. Less than a whisper, more compelling than motion, the words drifted like internal music through her mind.

Choose love!

She rose from the bed, feeling that her whole world was contained within the walls of the Chinese Room. Whatever happened here would affect the rest of her life, and more.

The air suddenly shivered under a breeze as cool as any February chill, yet it smelled of roses and violets, and hyacinths and lilacs. The distance between her and his black silhouette was only a few feet, yet closing that span took more courage than walking into St. George's Church to attend a wedding ceremony a fortnight ago. Perhaps, she thought suddenly, it was because she was going to meet something of her own choosing, not merely face the results of a situation over which she had no influence. Whatever happened here this night, right or wrong, it would be her own doing and her desire.

And then she stood before him, his image more solid than the lacy shadows in the room. "I have chosen."

His breath was sweet upon her face, real and warm and human. His hands lifted to stroke her face. His fingers were gentle. She felt them flicker over her brow and then her cheeks and then trace down her nose to follow the generous shape of her lips.

"My sweet Gillie," he whispered.

Light streaked across the sky. The brilliance of it took her breath away, but in it she saw him. The profile took for a moment the shape of muscle and skin, high cheekbones, a straight wing of nose, a tender mouth, and strangely light eyes in a pale face. He was beautiful, she thought, a man possessed of such handsomeness that she wanted to reach out and hold him to her breast forever. Then as thunder shuddered around them, she was in his arms, sheltered and shaken by emotions whose source lay in his kiss.

His lips covered hers gently, tentatively, as if posing a question. But his touch was a flashpoint of sensation. She melted in answer. Her body yielded, and she leaned into him even as his hands found her waist and drew her closer. Her arms went about his neck, her breasts flattening out along the planes of his chest. How sweet his mouth, she thought, how sweet and clean and natural it felt to be in his arms.

There had been the usual assortment of stolen kisses in her life from ruddy-faced boys when she was a child. Later, when she was thirteen, she had gone into the hayloft with a stable boy, but her grandmother had caught them before they had done more than press lips together. But now this man's kiss—and he did it so well, so well—seemed like the revelation of the first kiss on the first day at the beginning of the world. And yet it was so right, so familiar, so longed for.

His lips moved away, his velvet-rough tongue licking lightly at her cheeks and then her eyelids, flickering like candle flame over her face. Everywhere he touched her she tingled. She heard her own soft gasps and then his deeper sigh as his mouth settled over hers once more.

His arms tightened about her and he began to move, walking them backward like a pair of dancers toward the bed. As the mattress came up against the back of her knees, she sat down and he followed, pressing her onto her back as he moved to half lie over her. His hands found her breasts under her gown and began a gentle kneading. "Soft, Gillie. You're so soft."

Needing to steady her world, Julianna reached out to him and found the rough silk of his hair under one hand and the hard turn of a muscular shoulder under the other. She felt his fingers on the buttons of her gown and then the heat of his hand as his palm slid inside, over the narrow valley between her breasts and up onto one peak.

She shrank back into the bed, her body unsure of this new intimacy. She tried to push his hand away but he distracted her by kissing her again. This time he parted his lips on hers and ran his tongue along the closed seam of her mouth.

In half surprise, half pleasure, her lips parted, and his tongue slipped inside. His mouth was hot, his tongue a sleek wet flame as it moved sinuously in and out of her mouth. "So sweet. So hot. You taste like cherry pie," he murmured, and expelled appreciative chuckles into her open mouth.

She wondered if she was, perhaps, drunk on the cherry cordial, for his caress awakened in her body a fleeting resonance of memories of things that had never been. She no longer wished to protest his hand stroking her breast. There was only this heavy, full feeling in her pliant limbs and the desire to submit. It was as if her body had done this before, knew and welcomed what was to come. When his mouth left hers she felt momentarily abandoned, but then he delved into the shallow plane of her breastbone and his tongue lathed the delicate skin, plying slowly up and down. The hand on her breast moved to the outer side, urging it up until the hot cavity of his mouth enclosed her nipple and began sucking hard upon it.

Sensation streaked through her, impossibly exquisite pulses of feeling that made her moan. Ashamed of the sound of her own voice, she pressed the back of her hand to her mouth.

He lifted his head at once and reached for her hand. "No, love. Let me hear you." He brought her hand to his mouth and kissed her palm. "It pleases me to hear your pleasure cries." He curled her hand inside his larger palm, squeezing it tight, then stroked her fingers open one by one with his tongue. "Here," he said, drawing her hand down between them and pressing her hand open on his chest. "Touch me, Gillie. Make me moan too."

She did not know how his shirt came to be open, but the hard heat of his naked chest amazed her. She moved her hand shyly over the flat, firm walls of his chest, astonished by the lush density of a man's skin. He was all too real. How could she have ever thought otherwise? And so warm. It seemed impossible that his body could radiate such heat while she was shivering.

His hand, as it slipped back into her gown, felt like a branding iron on her cool skin. And then it slid lower, onto the concave skin of her belly. She quivered as his palm passed in slow circles over her, rubbing the pleasure deep into her skin. His mouth found her nipple again and he tugged at it with his lips. "Rosebud," he murmured, and flicked it with his tongue.

His words vibrated through her, sending new and strange messages deep down low, into places she had never known existed for feeling. A moan escaped her, followed by another as he took the tender bud between his teeth and rolled it ever so gently back and forth with his tongue.

Her hand clenched on his shoulder as her body arched under his mouth. Murmuring inarticulate words of gratefulness, she gave herself up to his desire when his mouth

slid in a slick path from one breast to enclose the other.
Freed of attention, the first breast began to ache. Either
he sensed it or simply knew. His hand rose from her belly
to encircle and massage it.

She flung a hand up over her eyes, lost and afloat in
the sea of dark sensual pleasures. Lower down where his
thigh straddled her hips she felt a building pressure, a
delicious growing tension and the hard thrust of his
groin. A wild hunger was building inside her. The deep
clamoring and tensing of nerves and delicate muscles
made her shift her body restlessly beneath the weight of
his.

She heard him chuckle softly and lift his head once
more. "You are very easy to please, my lady. So eager
and so womanly."

She wanted to ask him if that was good, because the
only veiled reference she had ever heard to "easy"
women was not good at all. But his hand was moving
downward slowly and she couldn't think of anything but
where it was going and what it might do next.

It brushed her waist, the flare of her hip, moving inward to lightly press her belly then sliding even lower to
press— "Oh!"

He caught her exclamation with a kiss, deepening it so
quickly she could only submit. What was he doing? The
sweet torment of being touched there, the slow circular
motions chasing pleasure before it. She sank her teeth
into her lip only to hear him grunt and realize that it was
his lip she bit.

He moved over her, pressing her body down into the
feather tick, but she did not mind. He was like a blanket
on her, heavy but warm and oh-so-pleasing . . . and fa-

miliar. The legs tangling with hers were bare and lightly furred. He had shed his clothing!

And then she stopped thinking, for his hand had found the secret center of her and instinct took over where reason retreated. Under the skillful tutelage of his fingers she quickly became all feeling, an incandescence. He had a perfect knowledge of what she needed and what she wanted. He touched her with his mouth and hands and body until the room receded, becoming less real than the secret dreams that had once possessed her in the hours of darkness. Her dream!

From the moment he kissed her, he had known there would be no going back. Now, as he lifted himself and gently parted her thighs, he smiled in the knowledge that he had been waiting for this moment to come again, ever since he had left her bed that first night. The other, the half-crazed lovemaking of her sleepwalking, had been a cheat. She had held her arms out for another man, offered kisses to him that belonged to someone else, had given her body into another man's keeping. Now she would belong to him in the full knowledge of that giving.

He smoothed his hands over the silkiness of her belly then framed her hips with his hands. How soft she was, and yet the bones of her pelvis were hard and solid, a perfect cradle for his. When a jagged burst of light filled the room, he saw her sprawled before him. She was a creamy flame in the eerie light but all too human. Her slender thighs lay along either side of his hips. The shallow indentation of her stomach quivered with tensed muscle. Her breasts tipped by dark, hardened aureoles rode the ebb and flow of her breath. But it was her gaze that compelled his response. Surrounded by an inky black cascade of hair, her eyes met his in a urgent need to match his own.

He entered her slowly, sighing as her swollen wet warmth enclosed him. So long without, and yet never quite like this. She arched intuitively beneath him, her hands coming up to brace against his chest. He bent the pressure of his hips upon her and heard her gasp catch in her throat. He was about to whisper a suggestion to her but, to his amazement, it was not necessary. She lifted her long, slender legs and wrapped herself about his waist, locking her feet together behind his back. He shifted, withdrawing slightly, and then arched his hips, threw back his head, and felt himself sink deep within her.

Her hands caught his shoulders, drawing him in for a kiss, then spread over his back in firm, smooth strokes.

More grateful than he had ever been for anything in his life, he began moving in and out of her, lifting her higher and higher with each thrust until her soft cries and his deeper grunts blended in perfect harmony, drowning out the night.

Julianna lay listening to the clock strike three A.M. Caught in a wonderment that had no name, she knew now that they had done this before, that in spite of the impossibility, against all reason, he had been in and a part of the dream that had invaded her sleep the first night she slept at Blood Hall. He had touched her, stroked her, made her different from what she had ever been before or would ever be again. And yet she had never seen his face.

Was she mad? Was this newly knit tissue of emotions nothing more than the wishful longings of delusion? But no, the leg lying alongside hers was warm, well turned by hard muscle, and pulsing with a life that needed no words to confirm it. He had been and was now real, warm, and solid. She cradled his head closer to her breast, and it rode the swell and ebb of her breathing, his own breathing a fiery bloom upon her naked skin.

They had made love twice this night, the second time without a single word being spoken. There was no need. Between them was this warm feeling of desires that flowed back and forth without the need of words to make sense of them. He had taken her even more slowly than the first time. None of the urgency or fear of the unknown that had accompanied the first time held her back the second. With lips and tongue and hands, he had possessed her in ways that left her writhing and pleading and delirious, then exploding and shuddering and sighing. He had stayed tumid within her for so long a time that she forgot where he left off and she began. And later, their bodies clinging to one another in the aftermath of passion's heat, they had subsided into tranquil sleep.

Whatever happened next, in the morning light or when he awakened and left her, she could face it now because she had something of her very own to hold on to and treasure.

He moved against her, the rough drag of his cheek abrading her tender, love-swollen breast. "Gillie?" His voice was low and sleep-blurred.

"Yes, my love," she answered naturally, and tightened her arms in expectation that he would move away from her.

But he did not. He surged forward to kiss her mouth and then suckle the tip of her tongue as if it were a nipple. Bending his head, he kissed the pulse beating in the hollow of her throat. As his lips lingered there in tiny nibbling kisses, he spread a hand through her heavy hair, his fingers combing it out on the bedding beside them.

She lifted her head and kissed his crown, wondering how it was possible to love him so much and yet know that she might pass him on the street on the morrow and not recognize him. Like one blind, she closed her eyes and ran her sensitized fingertips over his face. His brow was high and wide, the hair beginning thickly and suddenly at the hairline. His brow ridges were strongly defined, the eyes below deep-set and wide. His lashes tickled her fingers as she passed lightly over them, making her smile. The bridge of his nose rose prominently between those eyes and formed a strong wedge. Everything about him fascinated her. No detail was too small. She limned each nostril with a finger, causing him to shiver and laugh. She discovered the high curve of his cheek and felt it firm with his smile. She delved into the sharp, narrow hollow of a masculine dimple beneath and then quested out the gathered pleats fanning outward from the corner of his eye. His ear was as delicately modeled as a seashell and covered with skin as plush as the finest velvet. Last of all she traced the circumference of his wide mouth. The sharp definition of each lip rimmed the smoothest satin of his body's many textures. His was a sensitive face but a strong one. He would not be a bully or a brute, but the stubborn jut of his brow and the strength of his jaw spoke of a man of deep determination and resolute conviction.

"Now I know enough," she said when her hands stilled on him.

"What do you know?" He sounded pleased but cautious.

"I know your smell and your taste, the feel of you if

not your face. I think I will know you when next we meet."

He stilled. "Gillie, I must ask you something."

"All right."

"Tell me about the man who hurt you."

Chapter Twelve

✿

$\mathcal{H}$e nuzzled her where her arm joined her shoulder and the softness of her full breast pressed into the fold. "Gillie? Did you hear me?"

"Yes." Julianna had heard his question. *Tell me about the man who hurt you.* But she did not want to talk about that, or anything else that was real and outside the fragile peace inside this room. Hold back the world, her instincts warned. To speak of her past life might destroy the present one. No, she would not do it.

He slid a hand up from her thigh, across her abdomen, over her breast to her shoulder, then smoothed it down the long length of her arm to her hand where he threaded his fingers through hers. "You needn't be afraid to talk to me, Gillie. I know all I need to know to love you. I want only to know how to help you."

His gentle, ardent words shook her resolve more than she expected. She trusted him with her body, how could she not trust him with her secrets? After all, every London gentleman would know the details. Hundreds of people had witnessed her scandalous behavior. Where, then, was the harm? But she knew the answer to that question. The harm lay in exposing her shame to the one man who had accepted her for herself but who might then think less of her if he knew how the world judged her. And yet . . .

"There was a scandal in London." She swallowed with difficulty and felt him squeeze her hand encouragingly. "It involved a man who courted me and whom I thought loved me. He married another."

"Was it so terrible for you?" His tone was neutral, offering neither sympathy nor pity.

"It was unforgivable!"

"Why?" Again, only curiosity colored his voice.

"Because he made a fool of me, of my feelings."

"Why did you allow that?"

"I didn't allow it!" She tried to pull away from him but he held her fast with one leg thrown high over her thighs. The hand from the arm beneath her tightened on her waist. "He used me," she whispered, the old hurts eroding the pleasure of moments before. "He hoped to wed elsewhere but he needed a large dowry and, spinster or no, I have a sizable one."

"So?"

"So, he courted me while all the time he made love to someone else."

"But you must have suspected?"

Tears started in her eyes. "Suspected what, that he could never have truly wanted me, that I am too plain and unfeminine to attract the ardor of a duke?"

"That he did not love you." He brought their intertwined hands up and tucked them between their touching bodies so that the back of her hand was against his heart and the back of his pressed into her left breast. "You feel what is between us. Did you feel anything like this for your duke?"

"I don't know. Yes, I—no, nothing like this." She

shook her head distractedly. "But one has nothing to with the other. We never had the chance to be like this."

His chuckle disconcerted her. "Oh, Gillie, any man and woman who wish to be together as we are can find the opportunity. You didn't feel for him what you feel for me, I know it without you saying so. Thus the question becomes, had you no more sense than to allow a cad to woo you for your gold?"

His accusation took her breath away. "Are you calling me a fool?"

"Any woman knows when she is loved and when she is deceived, if she listens to her heart."

"How would you know?" she retorted, growing angrier by the heartbeat.

"Men are the same as women. The only people deceived by love are those who allow themselves to be."

"So you say I deceived myself." She jerked her hand free of his grasp. "Perhaps I did. Perhaps it was because I foolishly expected to be loved like any other woman that a man who had no scruples about deception blinded me. I was hurt because I let myself be!"

"There. Does that make you feel better?"

"It does not!" she replied with a catch in her voice. "It makes me so ashamed."

He cupped the breast nearer his mouth and lifted it for a kiss. "Then you aren't thinking of it in the right way. He may have deceived you about his intentions, but you deceived yourself about love. You're a strong and proud lady. You won't ever make that mistake again, will you?"

But a great dread was steadily growing in her. How confidently he talked, as if he had never known an indecisive or uncertain moment. How then could he understand her shame if he had never shared her weaknesses?

Now that she had begun the story, she saw no reason not to make her confession complete. "It would seem I have more pride than sense. Out of pride I attended his wedding and reception, even congratulated him on his marriage."

"Oh, Gillie!"

"There is more!" she said, flailing her pride with the shame of telling him what had occurred. "At the reception I learned what others already knew, that the duke had deliberately gotten his bride with child in order to force her father, a wealthy man, to agree to the marriage. He loved her, you see. With me he did not feel the same urgency for seduction!"

She sounded miserable and hurt all over again, but the emotions were no longer for the duke's desertion, only her own foolish vanity. "It was a shabby trick! I could not help myself. I had drunk too much champagne, and the lies hurt so much! I made a fool of myself before all the wedding guests by blurting out my pain and anger. But I wanted—"

"What every woman wants," he finished quietly, and turned her in his arms so that they lay belly to belly on their sides. Her breasts nestled in the light furring of his chest hair, and she felt the nipples pucker with the achy need only his touch could bring forth. "Come, Gillie. He's fortunate he did not seduce and abandon you."

"What did you say?" Surely she had not heard him right. "You mean I am fortunate."

"No," he said quietly. "Whatever he did, you would be all right. But if you'd told me just now that he had truly injured you in any way, then he'd now be counting his last healthy hours by the time it would take me to reach London."

"Don't be preposterous!" She laughed at the outrageousness of his implication. "You wouldn't—"

"Beat him to a bloody pulp? With pleasure," he answered with enough steel beneath his chuckle to make her shiver. "If he was blind to your beauty, your generosity and tenderness, then it is his loss. But if he had deliberately hurt you for his own selfish gain, then it would also be to his great regret."

"I've never had a gallant," she said in a small voice, inordinately pleased by his frivolous words.

"Then there are more fools in London than usual."

She could not tell him the rest, that she had never had a suitor before Lord Dashmore and that she only half believed what had happened in this room tonight. Perhaps she did hold the embodiment of the Love Talker in her arms, the spinster's perfect dream of a secret love. She curved a hand possessively about his cheek. "I didn't want to die without knowing a man's touch. You have changed that. Thank you."

"Oh, Gillie, I've done you no service out of kindness or pity. God! Don't you feel it?" He pulled her in so close their bodies touched from shoulder to knee. "It is for this that I lay with you." He kissed her so long and deep that their lips clung moistly together as he moved away. "And this." He smoothed a hand down the length of her spine and cupped a buttock with a force that made her gasp. "And most of all, this." He thrust his hips rhythmically against her, making the soft-hard tumescence of his manhood rub her lower abdomen. "Do you feel pity?" he asked.

She shut her eyes and shook her head, but he was not satisfied with that. He took one of her hands and guided it down between them until she touched his heated length. "Feel me, Gillie. You belong to me now. Tell me what you need."

Amazed at her own temerity, she opened her hand and took into her palm his hard-throbbing and strangely smooth flesh.

"Tell me what you need," he repeated raggedly, and half kissed the corner of her mouth.

"You," she answered, and gave herself up again to the pleasure and joy of his body's embrace.

Enraptured by love's perfect caress, they did not see that shadows walked or hear the creak of the floorboards in the corridor outside.

"Satisfied, madame?"

"I'm not certain."

"Even after that display? Jumping Jehosophat! What *will* satisfy you?"

"They play a game, my captain. What will happen when the daylight returns? I have an uneasy feeling about them."

"What? You, the matchmaker extraordinaire, are concerned about the outcome? God's bones! Look at them! They are like two young seals cavorting beneath the bedding. At least they came quickly to it, which is more to my liking than this infernal courtship that women will often insist upon."

"Just so, Captain. And that is what worries me. Their minds are clouded by smoky passion, but passion dissipates."

"Speak for yourself, Lady. I've fire enough for many years to come. Why, with very little encouragement I—"

"Don't touch me!"

"What's this?"

"I—I don't know. A feeling, a feeling like the gathering of a storm. Oh, but I am cold! Winds buffet me from all directions. Can you not feel the stillness?"

"You speak in riddles, Lady. One cannot be buffeted by stillness."

"Oh, Captain, you should believe. You should believe!"

"Madame? Lady? Where have you gone?"

"You're certain you're all right then, my lady?" Mrs. Mead's broad face was full of doubtful concern as she stood by Julianna's bedside. Her sharp gaze had already taken in the half-empty decanter of cherry cordial by the bedside. "No aching head or sour stomach?"

"I'm perfectly fine!" Julianna replied, stretching her arms above her head to the accompaniment of a huge yawn. She had expected to awaken with a cold or at least sore muscles and aching bones from the long, wet journey home. But as she stretched she realized she had never felt more relaxed or healthy in her life. She felt smooth as butter and as bright as the morning sky.

She saw the housekeeper cross the room to the pile of clothing she had left in a soggy muddle on the floor the night before and thought she should make some excuse. "I was soaked through by the time we reached home last night and I'm afraid I was too tired to do anything but strip and climb between the covers." She glanced furtively from her discarded clothes to scan the room for signs of her lover, but there were none. "Did you enjoy your night in the village?"

"Why, yes." Mrs. Mead bent to pick up the first of the wet clothing from the floor. "Me and Tom came home at first light. I was that concerned when I heard you'd come back to Blood Hall alone."

"I wasn't alone. Jos brought me back by pony cart. Speaking of which, do you know where he lives?"

"No, my lady. Tom told him he could have the old cottage when he hired him, but I don't know as he took it."

"What old cottage?"

"The former schoolmaster's cottage. 'Tis said the marchioness herself once lived there. In recent years the marquess allowed the gardener to stay there. We thought it 'd be all right, him having the cottage, since he was the new gardener."

"That's perfectly fine with me. I just wondered how much farther he had to travel last night."

"Not more than three miles," Mrs. Mead answered. "Jos can care for himself. Still, I was surprised to find him waiting by the kitchen door this morning, wanting a pot of tea. He's not the sort to beg the least favor. Only this morning he looked some the worse for wear. Spent the night in a rumpot, I'm thinking."

He would, Julianna thought wryly. No need to worry about him. Still, she had promised her Friend that she would ask after him. "Is Jos working in the garden today?"

"Couldn't say for certain but I doubt it. He said something about returning the pony cart to the mine, but I don't know that he's gone yet."

"Speaking of which, I've decided that we need transportation of our own," Julianna said. "I'd forgotten how much I enjoy riding over the moors."

"The marquess has carriages aplenty in the coach house. What you need, my lady, is a horse."

"Or a pony." Julianna smiled suddenly. "Now, why didn't I think of that yesterday? There was a nice little pony for sale in the village. He had a gray coat and handsome way of holding his head. I wonder if he was sold?"

"I remember him." Mrs. Mead shifted the armload of dirty clothes in her arms to one side so she could see over the top. "That'd be Tim Yellan's pony. Wanted twenty quid for it. He didn't sell. Times are hard for all, and no use buying what you can do without, I say."

"Do you suppose that he will sell it to me today?"

Mrs. Mead understood the question. It was Ash Wednesday, a day set aside for prayer and fasting, not finance. But she also knew that Tim had five children to feed and an ailing wife to see to. "I think he'd be grateful for the chance. He's more use for money than ponies just now. Would you like my Tom to do the bargaining for you? He's certain to get the pony for no more than twelve pounds."

"No, I think I'll make the buy myself," Julianna said as she slipped out of bed. "I want to see the pony again. It will take my mind off my empty stomach." And the incredible, inexpressible joys of the night!

After a quick cup of plain tea, Julianna dressed in her most somber attire, a tobacco-brown riding habit from which she had removed all lace and ribbons. Once her bonnet was in place, she scanned her image in the mirror for any sign in her face that betrayed the fact that she had spent a wanton, sleepless night in the arms of her secret lover.

The truth was, from the moment he had left her side as dawn grayed the sky, she had not been able to think of anything else. Deep within, her body hummed constantly. Her skin seemed newly alive. It was as if she had been given new sensory organs and what had once been normal and thus ignored was now heightened by her new awareness of herself. She felt the separate press of each corset stay encasing her waist and ribs as a sensual caress. The shift of her silk stockings as she walked reminded her of skin sliding on skin. When a kiss or touch was recalled, sudden flushes of delight tingled through her, making her breasts strain against her camisole.

Confused, delighted, and faintly alarmed, she could think of no better way to distract herself than to keep busy.

She went first to the rose garden, intent upon keeping her promise to inquire about Jos Trevelyn's health. But when she discovered that he was not there, she sighed in relief. She did not want to face him just yet, not when she feared that the experiences of the last hours might be too fresh to hide from his smirking gaze. Instead, she set off on foot for the village. Like all the other miners, Rob Wheal would be at work today, and she knew she need not worry about him.

Three hours later, she returned across the moors on ponyback, feeling quite pleased with herself. She had paid fifteen pounds for the pony because she felt sorry for Tim Yellan's family. He had been at the mine so she had had to deal with his wife, Sarah. Sarah was a thin, birdlike woman with eyes too big for her delicate face. Her gown had hung on her, betraying that at one time she had possessed a fuller figure. *Wasted*, that was the word that popped into Julianna's mind when she met the woman. Her racking cough had confirmed Julianna's suspicion that she was consumptive. Still, she had known it would not be wise to give the Yellans their asking price. Devonshire men and women respected a sharp bargain. Mrs. Yellan would have been insulted had she suspected that pity played a part in the transaction. Therefore, Julianna had offered twelve pounds for the pony and then allowed herself to be talked into paying fifteen. To even out the price, she had asked for the pony's harness and a blanket to be thrown in. She would find another way to help the Yellans, if she could.

The pony was not large. Her boots dangled only a foot above the ground as she sat astride. But he was broad-chested and not the least bit winded by the trot she pressed him to keep. When she had urged him up a rise, she paused to gaze about. The sky was clear and high and blue. Below them the ground fell away in a series of shallow, low hills. On her left Blood Hall crested the highest hill, its roofs, gleaming windows, and chimneys a heartening sight. Yet she continued to scan the horizon until she spotted a small, whitewashed thatched-roof cottage near a wooded copse west of Blood Hall. Could that be Jos Trevelyn's cottage? Letting curiosity get the better of her, she turned her pony into the narrow bridle path that led in the direction of the cottage.

It was only when she came within hailing distance of the cottage that it occurred to her to rethink the excuse she had for seeking him out. She could well imagine his smirking satisfaction if she stumbled over her explanation. Urging her pony forward before she lost her courage, she rode into the yard at a pace that alerted those inside of her arrival.

The white curtains at the windows were twitched aside and several pairs of eyes gazed out at her as she dismounted. She noticed the neat patch of garden and the fenced-in paddock behind which stood a pony, and she frowned. Parked outside it was the cart she had driven to the village the day before.

Even before she reached the cottage door it opened. A

young woman, really a girl of no more than seventeen, stepped through it, pulling it closed behind her. She wore a dark-blue gown with a scooped neck that quite flattered her high bosom and a white apron that emphasized her narrow waist. Her fair hair had been tucked with only limited success beneath a gingham mobcap, but it was the look of challenge in her large blue eyes that surprised Julianna the most.

"Hello," Julianna said, and nodded. "I'm sorry to bother you. I must have the wrong place. I was looking for Jos Trevelyn's cottage."

The young woman looked back over her shoulder as they both heard the window creak open. "Git back inside afore I wallop ye!" she cried in an angry voice. Immediately the window banged shut and the curtain was dropped. She turned a sullen look on Julianna and crossed her arms. "Why'd ye be wantin' Jos?"

Julianna was too astonished by the inadvertent admission that this was Jos's cottage to say anything other than "Who are you?"

"Ah may ask th' same o' ye," she answered spiritedly as she leaned a shoulder against the door.

Julianna recognized the accent now. Yorkshire, Jos had said. Reluctant to reveal that she was Lady Kingsblood just yet, Julianna replied, "Jos is doing work for me. I came to talk with him about it."

The younger woman looked her up and down slowly before she said, "Wha' sort o' work would tha' be?"

The door opened behind her that moment and a head covered by ringlets as bright as newly minted sovereigns poked through. " 'Tis Jessie. He's spilled t' milk."

"Git th' mop and clean it up," she answered, not even bothering to turn around to the child. "Now git inside!"

When she turned back to Julianna, the hostility she had been barely concealing erupted. "Jos works at th' great house, on yon hill." She pointed sharply in the direction of Blood Hall. "Ah know nothin' about him workin' for any else besides."

The challenge in her voice was clearly meant to intimidate her, but Julianna had come to some rapid calculations of her own and had decided that the moment for the truth had come. "I know," she said sweetly. "Jos works for me. I am Lady Julianna Kingsblood."

For the space of half a heartbeat, she thought the young woman had not heard her, but the enmity in her eyes was proof that she had. Almost at once, a shuttered look came down over her face and the sullenness resolved into a begrudging deference. She cast her eyes down as her shoulder came away from the door. "Good day to her ladyship."

"Is Jos here?" Julianna prompted.

"Nae. Ain't seen him fo' two days runnin'." She lifted her head, tossing a sullen glance at Julianna that suggested she thought the noble lady was to blame for his absence.

"Jos took me to Shrove Tuesday celebration in the village yesterday." She glanced at the cart in the yard. "I'm surprised that I didn't see you and the children there."

The mention of children made the young woman stiffen. "We've nae use for fairs."

"Not even the children?" Julianna asked in genuine surprise. "Jos had only to tell me he had a family and I'd have been happy to share the pony cart with you. By the way, I didn't hear your name."

"That's 'cause Ah did no' give it," she responded, sounding more like a petulant child than a wife and mother. She pushed out her lower lip and mumbled, "Me name's Tess."

"It's nice to meet you, Tess." Julianna searched her mind for something else pleasant to say. "You must have Jos bring you and the children to Blood Hall when the weather warms. We often have Sunday picnics that include everyone who works for Blood Hall."

"That's kind o' yer ladyship, but Ah do no' ken we'll be comin'."

Julianna didn't ask why. She suspected that Jos had married a very jealous and possessive woman who would not give him a moment's peace and every little joy beyond the obvious one her body would seem to promise. For reasons she did not probe, she felt sorry for Jos and thought more kindly of his drinking. Having met Tess Trevelyn, she wondered whether Jos had learned his manners from his wife or vice versa. "May I meet your children before I leave?"

Tess hesitated, then reached back and swung open the cottage door. "Cissie, come bring the babe with ye!"

Julianna smiled when the children appeared almost at once. Obviously they had been standing by the door in the hope that just such an invitation would be issued. The blond curls belonged to a small girl, no more than five, who carried a cherubic babe with the exact same hair and eyes as his mother in a round, apple-cheeked face. Tess bent down, picked up the baby, and slung him onto her hip, saying, "This be Jessie, Lady Kingsblood. The other be Cissie. Do yer curtsey, Cissie."

The young girl dipped awkwardly as she held out the skirt of her shift.

Julianna came forward and, having reached into her pocket, held out a shiny new sovereign. "Hello, Cissie.

This is for you. It's a magic coin that brings good luck. You must sleep with it under your pillow until you marry."

The child slanted a pleading look up at her mother and received a quick jerking nod of agreement from her. Then she snatched it with delight. "What do ye say, Cissie?" her mother snapped.

"Thank 'ee," Cissie replied, and ducked back behind her mother's skirts.

Smiling, Julianna shifted her eyes to Tess. "You've a lovely family, Mrs. Trevelyn. You must be very proud."

Cissie looked up in surprise. "Tess, why'd she—"

But Tess pushed the girl back inside and swung the baby from her hip to hand him to the small girl. "Take Jessie."

Julianna knew she was being impolite but curiosity was nibbling at her. "I'm amazed you have a child Cissie's age. You look too young to be her mother."

Tess turned a new scowl on Julianna. "Cissie ain't me child. She's me sister. Jessie's mine."

"I see," Julianna said, but the dozen other questions circled in her mind, their wings flapping loud enough to make her anxious. "I must be going now. You may tell Jos that I'll see him at the house."

As she turned back toward her pony, she was conscious of the fact that Tess made no reply. Here was one tenant who did not intend to curry her favor. In fact, she was certain the woman disliked her.

As she rode out of the yard, she looked back to find that the cottage door had been firmly shut, with no one in sight. It was almost as if she had stumbled upon a secret she was not supposed to learn about. Was that true?

Jos Trevelyn was married.

The idea should not have so surprised her but it did. Curiosity's wings beat hard against her mind. When had he married? The baby Jessie was a good six months old, yet Jos had told the Meads that he was a recently returned soldier. Did they know he was married? If so, why had they not mentioned it to her? Batmen who served the needs of officers were not encouraged to marry. Certainly their families would not be wanted on post. Perhaps he had not told the military he was married. Perhaps he had left a wife behind before he went to India. Six plus nine equaled fifteen. He could have been gone a year and returned to find a child born in his absence. Still, that did not explain why he kept them secret now. Or was it only as her Friend had accused, that she thought more about her own needs than those of the people who worked for her and so had not thought to inquire? Perhaps, if she had asked him, he would have told her he was married. If she had inquired before now, they might have been allowed to go to the Shrove Tuesday festivities. Still, she understood how he might have been reluctant to ask a favor of her. Before yesterday, they were scarcely on speaking, not to mention friendly, terms.

She pushed out of her mind the memory of his arm about her as they crossed the moors. She now understood that it had been a friendly, companionable arm. Nothing more. Other arms had held her with more passion and tenderness later that same night while, doubtless, Jos Trevelyn lay in some dark, damp corner of her stable huddled with a rum bottle. Why had he chosen to do that when, with a short journey, he might have spent the night in his wife's arms? Now that she knew how it could be between men and women, she wanted everybody to share that same joy. She would have to find a way to make up to Jos for her selfish behavior.

With her opinion of Jos Trevelyn tempered yet again, she rode back to Blood Hall with a smile and a secret longing for nightfall.

He kissed like a man born to make it an art: deeply, tenderly, completely—content with the act as a sensuous experience in itself. Open-mouthed, tongue deep, and warmly wet. His kisses reminded her of swimming in the ocean in summer. Warm waves of desire lapped at her body, trembling beneath her as cross-currents fed and blended, each rippling swell lifting her higher and higher, toward the back of the ultimate seventh wave moving silently, inevitably toward her.

Delicious, fragrant, enveloping kiss blended into kiss until her lips throbbed and her teeth tingled and her breath was lost. Then he moved lower, sliding his body slowly down along hers so that every movement, however small, communicated itself to her. The rasp of his body hair along her inner thighs, the heat of his skin baking hers, the all-too-new brand of his arousal pressing deeply into the shallows of her abdomen, all of it communicated itself to her in minute detail until he took a nipple in his mouth.

She had not known men did this, that women allowed it. But then, she had never considered, never even imagined possible much of what had taken place so spontaneously between them tonight and the night before. Were such things unnatural? But no—oh!—this feeling, so fierce and running so deep, could not be wrong.

Reaching down, she cradled his head to her breast,

brushing her fingers over the whisper of stubble dusting his lower jaw. How different he was from her, and how splendid. Did he know? Could he imagine how she felt now with his mouth suckling her and his body a living blanket upon her nakedness? Was it too good, too wonderful, the pleasure too exquisite to be real?

He had come to her tonight in darkness, as always before, but this time it was she who doused the light before she saw his face. The cover of night was her only protection, the final guard against what she already knew was a hopeless impossibility.

She loved him.

Without a name, a face, a position in life, without any reality and assurance beyond the flesh and blood stirring of the senses, she loved him with all her heart.

Emotions crested over her and battered her defenses. Her mouth twitched. Her eyes squeezed shut, but the assault of his tongue lower down was too much. Tears beaded up beneath her black lashes. Her mouth crumpled as soft catching sounds purled forth.

He slid back up on her, the drag of his body an all-consuming caress. "Hush, hush, love." He kissed the tears from her face and she tasted the mystery of herself in his mouth. "You mustn't be afraid. Don't fight the pleasure. Ride the joy, my love."

He entered her slowly, carefully, in regard for her newly opening body. "Feel how your body welcomes me? You are made for this, for me."

With a profound and joyous sense of wonder, she gave up the last resistance, the fear of herself, to this man whom she had never yet seen in the full light of day.

Later, when they no longer shuddered in love's climax,

they lay in one another's arms, silent, content, and perfectly attuned.

"Will it always be like this?"

He heard the doubt in her voice. "For as long as it pleases my lady."

She reached up and pressed fingers to his lips. "Don't! Don't tease me! I—I couldn't stand it if . . ."

He parted his lips and took her fingers into his mouth and nibbled them. "Have you so little faith in the power of your persuasion? Your charms are considerable."

"I am plain."

"You are beautiful."

"I have an intractable disposition."

"A maddening though ultimately charming stubbornness, agreed."

"I am old."

His laughter shook them both, reverberating through the vast emptiness of the room. "You are a coquette, madame, and I'll not feed your ego on demand."

But she only clutched him tighter. "Oh, please, don't be angry with me."

"Angry?" The surprise in his voice was complete. He felt her hands flex harder on his shoulders. "What is it, Gillie?"

"You won't leave me?"

"Not if you'll let me stay. I have yet even to see you properly."

"No, not that. I mean, will you come back each night, forever?"

He was silent, his deep, slow breaths sounding like a man who was mastering some impulse. "When will you trust me?"

"I do," she whispered, and turned her face into space

between his arm and shoulder. He smelled musky and damp from their lovemaking. Oh, but she loved his smell. "I don't want lose you."

"You won't lose me, Gillie, unless you refuse to accept all of me."

Bending over her, he reached for a match, but she caught his hand before he could strike it, begging softly "Not yet. Please. Not yet."

"Then when, Gillie? When?"

But she merely caught his face in both her hands and brought his chin up so that she could kiss him. "Soon," she whispered into his mouth. "Soon."

Chapter Thirteen

Julianna gave the huge rug slung over the clothesline a few more whacks with the metal beater before pausing to wipe the sweat from her brow. Her hair had been hidden under a large mobcap, but black tendrils had escaped and clung to her sweaty cheeks. This was no work for the granddaughter of a marquess, as Mrs. Mead had repeated pointed out, but exercise was the only thing that kept Julianna's nerves from snapping.

Several weeks had gone by, February slipping into the middle of March as spring began a gentle assault on winter. A soft sponginess had replace the sharp cold in the air. But that was not what had prompted this early bout of spring cleaning. It was the news that the Marquess and Marchioness of Ilfracombe were on their way back to London. The letter had arrived only the day before, but it was postmarked two weeks earlier. For all Julianna knew, her grandparents might already have reached their Kensington home in London. The marchioness might even now be on her way from London to Blood Hall, as her letter promised she would do.

Julianna blew out her cheeks and began pounding the dust from the rug once again. How quickly the days had passed. The letter had jolted her to a realization that was not altogether pleasant. She felt like someone awakening from a deep, lingering slumber that had left her unaware of time or place or anything else but the delirious dreams that had occupied her nights. Now she was awake to reality, and the realization made her as afraid and as happy as she dared be all at the same time. Everything was about to change.

She had sent Mrs. Mead into town to hire servants, men and women who would fill Blood Hall with footsteps, voices, and eyes. Her private retreat would soon be invaded. There would now be the need for furtiveness, secrecy, and cunning. The nights of abandoned lovemaking that she had shared with her secret Friend could be no more. Their pleasure would be constrained by waiting, listening, silences, and calculated sounds.

She opened her mouth to draw in breaths as she continued to add the full force of her power behind each stroke. She had known it must end sometime, but how soon it had come. And what now? Would her Friend simply go away? Would he come to her no more after she told him what was to be? Or would he reveal himself and possibly destroy her happiness?

She had never let herself think of who he might be. Once, on a very bad night when he was very late, she had fallen asleep and fretted that he was Jos Trevelyn in disguise. But once she jerked awake she had laughed at herself. He was not Jos or Tom or any other man she had seen with her own eyes. Of that she was certain. He must be a son of local gentry or perhaps his own master. Yet, perhaps like Jos, he had a family somewhere. But she never dwelt on that. If was she betraying some sad wife, she did not want to know it. Nor could she ask him about that without opening the path that might lead to learning exactly who he was. Sometimes he hinted and teased her with tidbits about himself, but she always stopped him with kisses. Once the world intruded she was sure that nothing between them would ever be the same again. And now that fear was coming true.

"Unfair! Unfair! Unfair!" She did not realize that she was muttering the word over and over until Mrs. Mead flew out of the back of the house, the door slamming after her.

"Oh, my lady! 'Tis terrible news!" Mrs. Mead's complexion was as pasty as bread dough beneath her bonnet as she came rushing up to Julianna. "I just come from the village. There's been a cave-in at Little Hangman Mine!"

Julianna went white. For anyone who had ever lived near or worked a mine, the worse news that could be heard was that there had been a cave-in. "How bad is it?"

"The man didn't say for certain but there's some trapped below. They're looking for every able-bodied man to help with the digging out. I came to fetch Tom. Jos ben't already gone."

"I must go too." Julianna dropped the beater and headed toward the Hall, tearing the apron from her waist as she went. "Tell Tom to harness the pony cart!" she called over her shoulder.

She hurried up the servants' stairwell to her bedroom, unrolling her sleeves as she went. There was no time for niceties so she did not tidy her hair or stop to wash her face. She just grabbed the first bonnet she found in her armoire and her red wool cloak. Only as she was descending the main stairs did she remember that it would do no good for her to come empty-handed. The injured would need blankets and bandages and medicines. After retracing her steps, she went to the laundry closet and pulled a huge pile of sheets from the shelf. When she had stacked them at her feet, she reached up higher to pull down the wool tartan blankets that had not been used that winter. Last she went to her bedroom and removed from her armoire the wooden medicine case with which she always traveled.

Mrs. Mead found her in the hall, trying to balance all her bundles. "I'll be taking that, my lady." She removed half of Julianna's armload. "Now then, Tom is readying the cart. He will drive us."

The day was bright. The sky shone a lovely shade of blue, the moorland grasses beginning to show green in places as they traveled along. It did not seem possible that anything could be wrong on such a day. It seemed impossible that men, women, and children might be struggling for their last breaths in the black earth beneath them. The steep climb northeastward offered some of the most spectacular views of the north Devonshire coast, but no one in the little party from Blood Hall appreciated that fact this day. Their hearts and minds were on the task before them. Long before they reached the cliff path, the sound of the sea surging ceaselessly against the coast below came dully to their ears. Then, finally, the chimney stack of the engine house came into view on the slope of the hill.

Still, a false sense of the ordinary pervaded the day until they were almost upon the mine works swarming with people. On a typical day, not nearly so many people would be gathered near the entrance of the mine. They'd be working in the ore dressing sheds and tips. Women in hobnailed boots, kerchiefed heads, and grimy aprons, their skirts hitched up to protect them from the worst of the muck, stood in silent knots as Tom maneuvered the cart into the center of the crowd. On their faces, Julianna saw the false calm of shock, but their eyes were hostile as she stepped down.

"Where is Mr. Coleman?" she asked the first person who passed her, but either he did not hear her or he deliberately ignored her.

"Best let me," Tom advised, and handed the reins to his wife as he stepped down from the cart and moved into the crowd.

Julianna turned toward a nearby group of women and recognized little Bessie's mother among them. "Hello. Can you tell me what has happened?"

The young woman turned a tear-streaked face to Julianna. "Oh, me lady, there's been a cave-in. Me husband's below." Her face spasmed as new sobs shook her.

"Now, now," Julianna said firmly, "you must be strong. I'm certain that all that can be done is being done."

"Such talk won't help Meg's boy," another of the women said, and nodded toward the edge of the cliff. Several yards away a man lay in the grass, his legs cocked at odd angles as a young woman knelt beside him holding his hand and weeping.

"There's others dead as well," the woman continued, her voice gruff with unfriendliness. "More to come, like as not."

Her final remark provoked a loud sob from Bessie's mother, who turned into the arms of the older woman.

"More deaths, did you say?" Despite her cloak and the sunshine, Julianna shivered. This was a small community where every birth and death comprised news for all the inhabitants. The shock of five deaths, possibly more, would have severe ramifications.

"Aye, two dead and nine more trapped below, me son Clem among them. What can yer ladyship do about that?"

"I don't know," Julianna answered the challenge that brought several new gazes her way, "but I intend to find out."

She walked briskly away from the women. Feeling their eyes on her back, she pulled her cloak close to her body and walked purposefully toward the woman whose man lay sprawled on the ground. But before she could reach him, a hand fell on her shoulder.

"Best not, me lady." Tom Mead stood beside her. " 'Tis bad, me lady, and gonna get worse. They were blasting a new level. Five men were brought up, only two of them likely to live."

Distress marred every line of Julianna's face. "What's being done for the others, the ones trapped below?"

He pointed to the narrow mine entrance. "A crew's gone back in, but they must shore up the weakened timbers afore they can begin digging proper."

"Are there enough men to see to that?" she asked, staring at the open hole in the ground where she knew men were letting themselves down by means of long ladders to the various galleries below.

"Aye, enough. But 'twill be slow going. And it depends on what fell between them inside and them what would dig 'em out. Can no' tell whether they'll be in time."

"What caused the accident?"

"Best ask the men when they're dug out." The gravity in Tom's expression didn't bode well for them, and Julianna suspected that he knew things he was unwilling to tell her.

Feeling useless yet wanting to do something, she turned toward the nearby dressing sheds where several men were carrying in one of the injured. "Has a doctor been sent for? Who's in charge of caring for the men who will be doing the digging?"

"Don't know about that, me lady, but ben't not hard to find out. I'll ask a few questions," Tom finished, and walked away.

"The diggers will need hot food and drink in order to keep up their strength," Julianna murmured to herself. Looking about for someone to say this to, she realized that unlike their shy but furtive interest in her on Shrove Tuesday, the female workers and miners' wives were consciously ignoring her now. Even as she searched for a friendly face, she saw that the crowd was swelling as they were joined by farmers and a fishermen from Combe Martin, the small nearby village on the rocky bay. One and all they had come to help. The women carried baskets of food while their menfolks brought crowbars, shovels, and other digging tools.

Mrs. Mead came up to her with a worried look on her face. "There's naught you can do, my lady. You needn't wait here. If you go back to Blood Hall, I'll come to you when there's word of those below."

"No. I want to remain," Julianna said firmly. "I can be useful. We'll begin setting up a shelter for the injured in one of the dressing sheds. We'll need help with the blankets and moving things to make a clear space. Where's Jos?"

"Why, below, my lady."

"What?"

"Jos was one of the first to volunteer, Mrs. Ames tells me. Seems he knows something of mining."

"Does he?" Julianna waited for her heart to settle. Why should she fear for Jos's life above any other man's? "Come along, Mrs. Mead. I'm determined to be as industrious as my gardener."

After soliciting the help of the women she had met on Shrove Tuesday, Julianna set about establishing a clear space for the injured miners to be placed. When the doctor arrived from Ilfracombe, she turned her energies to setting up a food tent. While her orders were heeded, she could not shake off a growing sense of wariness among the other women, nor the outright hostility of the few men who gathered to watch her as a soup line was set up, thanks to the offering from the womenfolk of Combe Martin.

The hours dragged by slowly. The only flurry of activity came whenever a party of excavating miners came to the surface to rest and revive themselves. Their clothes were wet and caked with dirt and their faces streaked with mud, making them appear to be exactly alike. As she ladled soup for the hungry, exhausted men, she could not keep herself from searching the faces of the crowd. Without her spectacles, she couldn't clearly see many of the people, but she was certain that if Jos was among the throng, she would recognize him. When he was not among either the first or second shift, she asked Tom about him and was told he was with Jed Coleman. The two men were attempting to unclog the air shaft that had fed the level where the missing miners were trapped.

The worst time came after the men returned underground. The dead had been removed to their homes while the injured were taken by carts to the village.

Those left simply stood and stared and waited. Julianna took up a lonely post on a large stone nearby the mine entrance, away from the wind and the others, but they occasionally raised their voices so she could overhear their conversations.

". . . dead men!"

"And boys scarcely more than children."

"Me Rob said 'tweren't time to blast. Too dangerous."

"Still, the owners will have their way."

". . . little less than murder."

"Us sweatin' while they make their fortunes."

"Union would've seen to better conditions for . . ."

"Money-grubbin' Kingsbloods! Let them toil for their . . ."

"Ain't like old times, when a man earned his own."

"Ye know who to blame for that loss . . ."

Julianna hunched her shoulders against the accusations borne on the wind, telling herself repeatedly that they were merely the vitriolic mutterings of people shocked and saddened by what had occurred. They wanted someone to blame their misfortune on, much like their ancestors had blamed the ancient gods and demons of the elements for everything from famine to flood to storm to earthquake. The fact was, and they knew it, mining was a dangerous business. Sometimes, in spite of every precaution, accidents occurred.

Yet, as the day dragged on and the beautiful sky began to gray with high clouds and the filtered sunshine turned watery, the feeling of oppression could not be so easily banished. More than once Julianna looked up to find one or two people standing nearby, their eyes trained on her in hostility. After the first few attempts, she gave up trying to speak to them. They were beginning to focus in on her as the source of their troubles. Let them, she thought, if it gave them something to do. Two other shifts of men rose from the mine and then returned, but neither Jed nor Jos came to the surface to rest.

"Break through! Break through!"

The sudden cry startled Julianna awake, for she had fallen asleep with her head bending forward onto her drawn-up knees.

The people rushed forward in a wave, all talking at once. Through the dim murmuring of voices, Julianna heard a man say "Some alive. Some dead. Can't say who yet. 'Twas another cave-in."

"What? What did you say?" She pushed her way to the front of the crowd.

The speaker, one of the miners who had been below, doffed his hat on which a candle burned. "Yer ladyship."

"Did you say there's been another cave-in?" she questioned anxiously.

"Aye, me lady. The air shaft broke through and some o' the men tumbled into the breach. But that were how the others were reached. They'll be bringing 'em to the surface directly. Ye must have a little more patience," he told a crying woman.

His counsel was scarcely adequate for the torturous slowness with which the men and bodies were borne to the surface. One hour passed before the first man, dead, was lifted from the mine. Half an hour later two other men, their arms dangling like unstrung puppets, were carried out. At least they were alive, though barely. As the crowd pressed in on the entrance, several more men and two boys were brought up. In all, seven men and three boys were found, six of them dead or dying.

The weather changed again, turning clammy and misty

with a fine cold rain. The distant moors turned dark and dangerous. The last of the rescue team came up only as the sun rode low on the horizon, their faces gray and haggard in the dim light.

Julianna stood anxiously by, watching each man's face as he passed her. She saw in their eyes exhaustion, resignation, and a deep rage at what they had seen and done below this day. One by one they blew out the candles that had lighted their way through the burrowing darkness. She looked again and again for Jos among the miners, but some of the injured were carried away so quickly she could not be certain whether he carried one of them or was one himself. It was only when the last man passed her that Julianna realized that Bessie's mother stood next to her.

Even as she turned to her, the young woman let out a high, keening wail. "Me Cal! Me Cal! Where's me Cal?" She rushed forth, intending to go down the shaft, but two men stopped her. She fought them like a wild person, clawing and scratching, kicking and wailing like some unearthly thing. When she was subdued, all eyes turned to Julianna.

Like a kick in the stomach, Julianna realized that they expected something of her, but she did not know what it was. She stepped toward Bessie's mother saying "I'm so sorry. We'll find him, I promise."

"Ye'll nothin' o' the kind!" Rob Wheal pushed through the crowd to reach her. "Cal was handlin' the explosive when it happened." He rushed right up into Julianna's face. " 'Twas ye who told yer foreman to blast today when ye was told it weren't safe!"

"I wasn't told any such thing," she protested, looking

about for someone to corroborate her statement. "Where is Jed Coleman?"

"Oh, now ye want a man to protect ye when ye had no need of a man afore." Rob stopped just short of touching her as he jabbed a dirty finger at her breast. "Worn-out old spinster that ye are! Have ye yet had yer fill o' bossin' about real men and woman what's got heart and blood and guts in 'em? Jus' look what ye done!" He flung a long arm about the now-weeping woman. "Poor lass, a child to raise and now no man to look after 'em. What are ye goin' to do about that?"

"I don't know," Julianna replied, choking back tears of frustration and weariness. She sent Bessie's mother a pleading look but it went unheeded. "I'll see that you and Bessie are taken care of, I promise."

But Rob Wheal was not to be mollified. He turned to the crowd, gesturing so broadly that the sides of his jacket flapped in the wind like the wings of some huge bird of prey. "We've nay need of me lady's hand-me-downs!" he roared to the other miners. "Let her take her scraps and used tea leaves and rotting linen to the alms-house! We want aught but what's due us!"

As the crowd mumbled in assent, he swung back on Julianna, grinning triumphantly. "Tell the marquess 'tis on his head, the deaths done this day! Proper management of the mines, better wages, and a decent care for the people who lie bleeding is what we need! A union, that's what we need!"

A sudden cheer went up as the crowd surged forward.

Julianna took a halting step backward, as afraid and yet unbelieving as she had been that Sunday weeks ago just before Rob Wheal had grabbed her. They would not attack, she told herself. She had done nothing but try to help them.

But as their blackened faces surrounded her she began to have doubts. Dirt and sweat streaked the men in equal parts, masking them yet making them part of one mass of shocked, angry, and dangerous humanity.

A lump of dirt suddenly arched out of the crowd and struck her skirt. The crowd's low grumbling rose several decibels, though in protest or assent she couldn't be certain.

She swung her head from side to side, looking for Jed Coleman or Tom Mead, but neither man was there. And Jos Trevelyn? Where was he?

The second lump of dirt struck her on the left shoulder with enough force to make her stagger. There was no mistaking the surge of anger rising out of the misery and despair that had weighted down the day. Like a pack of carrion scenting wounded prey, they seemed to close in on her. She held her breath, afraid that she would betray her fear in a scream. But her heart was beating so hard she could not keep it long.

"Get back!" she cried. "Let me pass!" The words sounded self-confident but she was backstepping, forced into an inevitable retreat she did not know how to stem.

"Yer ladyship!"

Julianna swung her head toward the sound of a man's voice, hoping it was Jed. Instead, she saw only another sweaty, mud-streaked miner. "Move aside!" the man called with authority to the crowd. As they parted for him, he drove Julianna's pony cart into the fray. He passed Wheal without a glance at the man. "Come with me, yer ladyship," he said in a flat, angry voice as he reined in near her, but Julianna shrank from him.

"Here! Don't I know ye? Who are ye?" Wheal demanded. He tried to grab the pony's bridle but the man
in the cart was quicker. He lifted his whip and cut Wheal
over the head with a stinging lash. With a roar of oaths,
Wheal swung away from the pony, clamping his hands to
his bleeding face.

The man with the whip turned again to Julianna and
said, "Will ye climb up now, Lady Kingsblood? Ah will
no' ask ye again."

"Jos?" In relief she rushed toward the cart. He helped
her up with a strong arm that practically lifted her from
the ground single-handed. And then she was on the seat
beside him and he was turning the pony.

The group of men, shocked and surprised by the sudden violence not of their making, fell back before Jos's
flicking whip, their thirst for revenge considerably, if momentarily, dampened.

"Hold on!" Jos cried, and cracked the whip sharply
over the pony's head. As Julianna clung precariously to
the cart seat, the pony picked a path through the mine
works yard at a trot, leaving angry shouts in the cart's
wake.

Only Wheal ran after them crying "Look! Look! Be it
her ladyship and her ponce!"

Yet even as they swung away in freedom from the
mine, a deep renewed sense of depression settled over
Julianna. Her family was responsible for the men and
boys who through their grim work made possible a
greater share of the Marquess of Ilfracombe's fortune.
This was only one of several mines operated on
Kingsblood land. If harm came to those men through
neglect, the Kingsbloods were at least partially to blame.
For the moment, that responsibility was hers, yet she had

been unable to stem the tide of anger and rage against her family because she did not know the truth of what had happened.

Julianna gazed back over her shoulder at the Little Hangman Mine only to spy the last of the supplies she had brought still in the back of the cart. "Stop, Jos. You must go back."

"Not for th' Devil himself!" Jos answered roughly, and flicked the reins on the pony's back to increase their pace.

"But they'll need these things for the injured."

He turned his head, showing her his dirty, blood-streaked face. "Better ye stay shod o' 'em, yer ladyship. They'd no' accept it from ye now. Let be."

And she knew then that he was right. *They hated her.* She had never seen undisguised enmity before. Their rage had been directed at her, and it had turned her bowels to water. All of the strides toward winning the miners' good wishes had been wiped out by a single accident over which she had no control.

"Do you know what caused the cave-in, Jos?"

" 'Twere an accident. Happens."

His words were few and small comfort but she clung to them as she clung to the cart seat. Mining was dangerous work. Accidents did happen. If this one was not caused by a deliberate or careless act, the miners would come to accept the bitter loss as a casualty of their existence.

Yet she could not shake the feeling that she had not acquitted herself well before their hostility. She had been weak, afraid, and run away at the first opportunity. Her grandfather would not be proud of her today.

She began to cry quietly, too sick at heart to hide her reaction.

"Nae, ye mustn't cry," Jos said, his accent thickening with what sounded suspiciously like tenderness.

The touch of his hand on her shoulder recalled her to herself, and she reached into her pocket for a handkerchief with which to blow her nose and wipe her face. When she was done, she did not look at him, and, after another moment, he removed his hand.

"Ah hate th' mines. Like workin' 'n yer own grave," he said after a moment in a low, quiet voice.

"You've worked the mines?" This was something she had not suspected though she supposed he must have known what to do when he went down with the other rescuers.

He turned to look at her, his blue eyes the only vivid thing in his filthy face. "Aye."

Really looking at him for the first time, she saw that at least one dark streak running along the side of his face was blood. "Oh, but you're hurt."

"Ah fell int' th' hole when th' wall 'n th' air shaft gave."

"You might have been killed."

"Aye." He had turned away from her so that she could not longer read his eyes, but his voice carried a careless disregard for the danger of which he spoke.

"Were you a miner before you joined the army?" she prompted.

She saw his profile tense. "So 'twould seem."

Julianna bit her lip, certain she should leave him alone. He had been through a lot this day, yet she wanted to know more. "Why did you quit the mines? Did your wife want a better life for you?"

He turned sharply toward her once more. "I heard ye came t' th' cottage some weeks back. Wha' did ye want?"

Now it was her turn to look away. "You've a handsome son in Jessie. You must bring him to ride the pony when he's a bit older. Cissie's welcome too."

He cocked one dirty brow. "And me wife?"

"Tess too, of course," she amended hurriedly.

"O' course," he murmured, and turned away, though she thought she heard him chuckle. "Yer ladyship's most generous."

Annoyed by his tone, she reached for the reins. "You must be exhausted. I'll drive the pony," she said crisply.

He released them instantly and leaned back, folding his arms before his chest.

"Jos?"

"Um?"

"What's a ponce?"

She saw him smile. "A kept man. A lady's paid lover."

"Oh." Abashed, she turned abruptly away. So that was what Rob Wheal had shouted at Jos. She was too embarrassed to ask Jos if he thought Wheal would be believed. No doubt Wheal would now continue to spread the rumor that she kept a secret lover at Blood Hall. If only he knew how close he had come to the truth!

The laughter that sprang out of her came as much from pent-up emotions as outraged sensibilities, but she did not try to stop it nor, thankfully, did Jos question her about the reason behind it. When the laughter subsided, she felt better than she had all day.

They did not exchange another word until they reached Blood Hall. Only when she turned to him to say her thanks once again did she notice that Jos's head had dropped forward onto his chest and that his shoulders were drooped in weariness. Exhausted, he had fallen asleep. For hours he had crawled about in the damp suffocating darkness, laboring to save the lives of men he had probably never met. He was a hard and difficult man to like but one possessed of a generosity of spirit that quite amazed her.

She reached out without thinking to touch the back of his neck. He jumped as if she had poked him, but even before she could withdraw her hand, he reached up and covered it with his own, holding her palm to his skin.

He turned to her with an expression the mud and blood could not quite veil. "Ye've a good heart 'n ye, yer ladyship. A man could look t' ye and ken he'd be fair treated."

She felt his light eyes like brands on her, but she refused the invitation she saw burning there. "You've a wife and family to look after you, Jos. Go home," she said, and slipped her hand free.

He stared at her a moment longer.

She said nothing, only stared back a little desperately into those blue eyes that seemed to gather the day's last light in their soft depths. Her hands trembled on the reins. And then he blinked, and the spell was broken. Looking away, she made a quick business of handing him the reins and then stepping down before he could alight and aid her.

When she stood on the ground, she turned to him with a subdued expression. "Good night, Jos. You may take tomorrow off. You've earned a day's rest. Say hello to your family for me."

"Ah thank yer ladyship." He offered her a snappy military salute and then flicked the reins gently over the pony's back.

As she turned toward the Hall, forbidden thoughts flickered in her mind like fireflies: beautiful, elusive, brightening but not eliminating the dark truth. For the space of a few heartbeats, she had allowed herself to feel the power of her desire for a man who by every law of God and man was denied to her.

Chapter Fourteen

Julianna made love to him in wild desperation. In the final moments, she raked his back with her nails and arched high off the bed, trying urgently to absorb him and his life force once and for all. But even as she relaxed beneath him, both gasping for breath, their bodies slick from their exertions, she knew a nameless despair. Always it came back to this, a return to oneself. This feeling of separation could be obliterated only for a few precious moments and then the world intruded, distributing back to her an arm and him a thigh, her an elbow, him a foot.

The poets were wrong. Lovers' hearts did not beat as one. In the hours of separation that made up so much more of their lives than their hours together, she did not even know where and how he lived in the world. There was no mystic bonding that kept them together even in parting. If he ever stopped coming, she would never know why.

That realization had come to her while she lay in bed waiting for him. He had been so late, hours later than he had ever been since they had become lovers. He might have died this day; been crushed in the mine, or thrown from a horse, or been tossed into the sea; and she would never have known but by his continuing absence that he would not be back. How did one manage to live and love when uncertainty hovered like carrion birds in the shadows?

Yet was not the same true of people who lived side by side? Today she had seen proof that openness and marriage offered no better certainty. Had not Bessie's mother waved her husband off that morning in the expectation that he would return? Yet he had not. Now there was not even a corpse to bathe and dress and bury. If loving a man meant such pain and anguish and sickness, she wanted none of it!

When he lifted himself off her and rolled onto his side, she turned away and drew her legs up protectively toward her chest, wanting desperately to separate herself from him when moments before she would have given anything to become part of him.

"Are you cold?" He sat up and reached for the covers to bring them over them, but when he tried to pull her closer, she refused to roll toward him. "What's this, Gillie? Did I not please you?"

"I thought you weren't going to come," she said in a small choked voice.

He kissed and then rested his chin on the shoulder hunched away from him. "I'm sorry. It couldn't be helped."

"Eight men died in Little Hangman Mine today."

"I know."

"One of them could have been you."

"Oh, Gillie! Is that what you feared?" His lips moved along her shoulder into the valley formed by the curve of her neck, but she hunched her shoulder, preventing his kiss from reaching the most sensitive spot. "I'm so sorry my delay frightened you," he whispered just below her ear. "Let me light a candle and end this charade once and for all."

"No!"

Her passionate objection surprised him, but he refused to acknowledge it. "What are you so afraid of? That I am ugly?" He chuckled deep in his throat. "I can't say how you'll judge me, my lady, but women have never yet run screaming at the sight of me."

"Have there been many women?"

There was a moment's pause. How does a man ever answer that question? he wondered. "Less than you might imagine. None like you."

"And what am I like? How am I different?"

Curiosity relaxed the barrier of her shoulder a fraction, and he began to nuzzle the tender skin of her neck. "I love you."

"You don't know me. These . . . these trysts . . . aren't a fair measure of my existence."

"Nor are they of mine. Yet, because of this"—he slid a hand over the generous curve of her naked hip—"I know more about you than you're willing to believe," he said low and possessively. "I know your passion and your tenderness, and I love you. What is there for you to fear in that, Gillie?"

She shook her head, digging her nails into the fleshy part of her upper arms. She needed time and distance from him to sort out her feelings. The day's events had brutalized her, leaving behind hurt, confusion, and fear. More than anything she wanted to be alone, away from the cross-currents of desire and dread in which his nearness was drowning her. There was nothing he could do to make that pain less. Knowing who he really was would only alter the context of their relationship. He could still leave her, or be taken from her.

She brushed his roaming hand from her hip. "This was a mistake."

"Never." He smoothed a hand down her spine, feeling her shiver, and then insinuated that hand up under her folded arms until he held one rounded breast in his hand. "Gillie, let me be real for you, a mortal man, not some phantom who is part shadow and all desire."

She shook her head. His talk frightened her. Could he not comprehend what she feared? "Mortal men die."

So that was it. He pulled her closer until, spoon fashion, they touched; her thighs bolstered by his, her bottom against his groin, the elegant arch of her back riding the muscular curvature of his chest. "All men and women die, Gillie, but first they live. I would live with you. Marry me."

She closed her eyes, fighting the terror and irrational anger that his words brought forth. She did not know if he was teasing her or in earnest, but neither was tolerable to her. In another moment she would blurt out the truth, that she loved him with an intensity that was a physical thing, a sick pain in her heart. "Go away. Please. Just go away!"

He was silent a moment. "I asked you to marry me."

"No!" She ground the word out through clenched teeth. "Is that what you want to hear? No, I won't marry you. I won't!"

He moved away from her slowly, turning onto his back, but he didn't rise from the bed. With a deep sigh of perplexity he squeezed his temples between thumb and forefinger. "What has happened, Gillie?"

"The marchioness is coming to Devon," she said in a

voice that did not sound at all like her own. "She's expected by the end of the week."

He thought then he understood. She was having very human second thoughts about her very unconventional behavior. After all, she was no wanton but a very proper young woman in love. The idea of her grandmother coming here must have shocked her back into a recognition of just how far she had come from the path of convention. "Tell your grandmother that I want to marry you. She will understand."

No, no, she thought wildly. That would be a trap. "I can't do that."

"Why not?"

She scrambled about in her mind for excuses. "I know nothing about you, not even who you are. You could be anybody. She might not approve of you."

"Is that the trouble?" His voice was challenging in the darkness. "Do you doubt I'm presentable enough for your titled grandmama?"

"Perhaps," she lied. "Are you a suitable marriage partner for the granddaughter of a marchioness?"

He turned his head and she knew his eyes were on her face, but she couldn't look at him. "And if I'm not?"

She flinched as his carefully enunciated words struck her like flicks of a whip. Why would he not leave? How much longer must she continue to push him away? "I never wanted you to be real. If you were mere imagination, I could summon you at will, and there would never be any need for interference by friends and relations." *Or death,* she thought with a quiver of fear.

"So you are a coward, after all."

Oh, yes, she thought. I'm the biggest coward of all, for I couldn't bear to know the hour when you no longer

walked the earth. Better to send you away while you have
no name or face than to give you reality and then be left
to wonder for the rest of my life if every parting will be
our last.

She turned to him in the darkness, hardly believing
that she was saying the words. "It is over. You must never
come back here. Ever."

His light eyes seemed to glow faintly in the darkness,
and she held her breath. "You can deny what is between
us, but you'll not succeed in changing it," he said ominously, but it was the hurt behind those words that made
her heart quake.

When he rose suddenly from the bed, she did not
speak. If she had, she knew she would have taken back
every word and begged him to remain.

She did not hear him walk away, but his voice came to
her distantly when he spoke again. "One word of advice,
Lady Julianna. Go back to London with your grandmother. It's not safe for either of you here."

She sat up, searching the darkness for his shadow but
even that was denied her. "How do you know?"

"Ask Jed Coleman. Good-bye, my lady."

"No. Wait!"

She thought she saw movement beside the fireplace,
but the fire had long since died and she couldn't be certain. "You prefer me to be a phantom," he said harshly,
"but I'm a flesh-and-blood man, which you cannot deny
each time you take me into your body. If you won't accept that, we've nothing to discuss."

She knew the exact moment he ceased to be in the
room beside her. Would it be the same when he ceased
to exist?

Turning onto her stomach, she succumbed to a stormy

fit of tears that did not end until her weariness overcame her misery.

The morning broke fair and crisp, the air so clean it seemed filtered though the cleansing power of amber sunlight. The elegant carriage barreling through the gates of Blood Hall was followed at a more sedate pace by two wagons piled with a vast arrangement of bundles and baggage, not the least of which was a sewing machine. Behind the wagons came two footmen leading half a dozen of the marquess's horses. As the horses' hooves and carriage wheels clattered up the drive, two pale faces appeared in the oriel window which overlooked the front of the house.

"Confound the Devil! What is this?"

"The Marchioness of Ilfacombe has returned. Look at the size of her entourage. Is it not imposing?"

"I'll not soon forgive her for what she's done, locking up the Hall and leaving us without a word. You, on the other hand, are too easily dissuaded from your anger. You always did possess a weakness for ostentation and vulgar display."

"Nay, Captain. I merely appreciate superb confidence on parade. Was I not impressed by your soldierly swagger?"

"That, madame, was the force of personality!"

"Oh, don't dissemble for my sake, Captain. With that conspicuously cropped head and leather jerkin stretched so tightly across your manly bosom that a lady might blush for the contours thereby displayed, you strutted and swaggered enough to make a cock blush."

"Better say, madame, that the cock made you blush!"

"Vulgar man! Cromwellian popinjay! Such arrogance!"

"Too true, madame, only too true. But you loved every moment of it."

"That does not absolve you. It makes you a knowing instrument of my seduction and disgrace."

"I should devoutly hope so! But enough of pleasant revelry. What, do you suppose, brings the marchioness hither in a caravan worthy of a sultan?"

"I suspect it has something to do with Julianna. Look, there's a London modiste in the carriage with her, several assistants, and a new lady's maid."

"How do you know that's a modiste? She looks like a crow in that black."

"That's how they look these days, Captain. Do try to keep abreast of changing times. And I believe the major portion of bundles in the second wagon is fabric. There're going to be dozens of lovely gowns fashioned beneath this roof. Oh, I do miss having a new gown now and then. This old rag—"

"Is the most beautiful rag fashioned since Eve felled Adam with an apple. The only thing I like better is your Eve-before-the-fall garb."

"Vulgar man!"

"Always, madame, always! Now come thee hither and charm my serpent!"

"A moment, Captain. There is other news, and not to my liking. Our young friend has taken flight."

"It was a necessary strategem, madame. Events have overtaken him."

"What events?"

"For once, you aren't privy to all? Nay, ask me not, for I shan't tell you."

"I don't like it. I've told you before, there are dark winds at our backs."

"Then we'd best huddle together for warmth, madame."

Lady Regina Kingsblood, sixth Marchioness of Ilfracombe, swept into the Great Hall with a step as light as a woman one-third her sixty-seven years. Favoring French fashion over English because it suited her taste for the dramatic, she wore a white ermine stole and muff over a deep-green velvet gown, a shirred and corded bonnet of green with green ribbons and green and gray ostrich feathers. The feather plumes danced gaily atop her bonnet as she gazed around the room. "Just as I remember it! As always. Nothing changes! Lord, but it's good to be home!"

Julianna smiled at her grandmother in awe as well as fondness. "Grandmama, you look as fresh as if you'd just stepped from your toilette instead of a traveling carriage. What is your secret?"

Lady Regina smiled warmly, the fine lines appearing on her face accenting good bones. "But, my dear, there's no secret. I have only to think of Blood Hall to feel as young as I was the day I entered this house in your grandfather's arms." She paused to arch a brow at Julianna, a mannerism she had unconsciously adopted from her husband. "Did I tell you that tale? Oh, but of course I have." She pulled loose the green bow beneath her chin. "Little did I know that day that I would soon become mistress of this great house. Did I ever tell you that your grandfather was engaged at the time to another lady?"

"No, Grandmama," Julianna fibbed because she loved to hear the marchioness's stories of her younger years.

"Well, he was, and he says now that he decided not to marry her the moment she announced he must change Blood Hall's name once they were wed. Of course it's a lie. I was there when she said it, and he gave no indication at the time that he was not totally besotted by the lovely twit. It was my fault, now that I think of it. I'd just told her in most grisly detail how the house came to have its present name. Unkind of me."

She lifted her bonnet, revealing a head of silver hair that was no less dramatic than the black tresses she had been born with. In fact, the pure brilliance of it underscored the personality of the lady whom time had aged in other ways less than most. The mother of six, she still showed the world a slim waist that needed very little boning and a bosom whose fullness was entirely her own.

Patting one of the braids looped over her ears, she continued in her rich alto voice. "I'd have repented the unkindness years ago had it not been the beginning of the end of that engagement. Not that Maxwell was aware of it just yet. But for me it was love at first sight. Or rather lust, if you will excuse the vulgar thought. Love came later."

She glanced back at Julianna, her creamy complexion blooming with a rosy blush. "I thought he was a highwayman, you see, bent on ravishment. Not that I would have allowed it. Ladies must not exercise their passions on whim. Good to have them, of course, and better to understand the workings of them."

"Grandmama!" Julianna protested, feeling the necessity to behave like the ignorant maiden lady the world thought she was. But, in her heart, she perfectly agreed with the marchioness's sentiments.

"I don't agree with this new age of modesty and excessive purity," the marchioness declared. "To know one's appetites is to control them."

As her grandmother paused to take a breath, Julianna waved in the housekeeper who stood in the doorway with a tray of tea and sandwiches. "Thank you, Mrs. Mead. Have the other members of the marchioness's entourage been looked after?"

"Yes, my lady. They are in their rooms unpacking. Tea will be served them directly."

"Good to see you again, Mrs. Mead," the marchioness greeted warmly. "I hope your Tom is well. And Agnes, Ruth, and Tim?"

"All very well, my lady. Married, they are, every one."

"Good. Productive lives are the best."

The next half hour passed conventionally enough, with the marchioness and her granddaughter drinking tea and discussing how one passes the time while spending the winter months on the Italian coast.

"Maxwell declares that he won't go back," the marchioness said in closing, "but he always has had an eye for the ladies, and those with Latin blood do seem more at ease in their gender than Englishwomen. Oh, he will bluster and fuss, but he'll succumb to my blandishments, especially when he learns that I've already invited a certain Signora Gucci to join us for part of the season. She's little more than a jade but, like Byron, your grandfather has a certain weakness for the type."

"Are you not jealous, Grandmama?"

The marchioness lifted her chin. "Dear child, any

woman who doesn't know how to keep a man too exhausted to stray isn't worth the starch in her petticoats."

Julianna didn't know where to look so she hid her smile behind her teacup. She knew her grandmother to be very prim and proper in public, more likely than her husband to be a stickler for manners. But alone, she delighted in shocking those nearest and dearest to her. "So, tell me, Grandmama, why are you in Devon when Grandfather hates for you to be beyond his sight?"

The marchioness smiled, her famous deep-green eyes made almost hunter green by the reflection of her green gown. "Why, because you weren't in London to meet me." Her perfectly arched silver brows winged up her brow. "What brought you to Devon, dear?"

Julianna's eyes, a paler version of her grandmother's, slid away. "You've heard."

"I've heard rumor, gossip, reckless talk, and scandalmongering," Lady Regina said forthrightly. "I've come to you for the truth."

Julianna reached for the silver teapot to pour each of them another cup, but her hands shook so badly, she gave up and folded them in her lap. "What you've heard is true. I made a spectacle of myself at the Duke of Montrose's wedding." She glanced from under her black lashes at her grandmother. "Too much champagne, I expect."

"And bile from a broken heart," the older lady replied gently.

Julianna's eyes widened. "What do you mean?"

Lady Regina reached for the teapot and poured two cups, added the appropriate lumps of sugar to each, and then a precise measure of cream. When she had stirred them, she gave one cup to Julianna and picked up her own and took a satisfied sip. "I've told you many things about my life, Julianna. Because you've been as much a child to me as your own dear father, I've treated you as my own. Yet, because you aren't my child, I've often treated you as my confidante as well, saying things to you that I would never have dreamed of revealing to my own children when they were your age. This is again one of those times. You mustn't ask questions about what I'm about to tell you. And, most assuredly, you must never, ever, speak to your grandfather about it. He must always believe that loving him overcame every sorrowful and awkward moment of my life since we married."

She set her cup aside and, instead of speaking again, rose and went to stand before the windows that over- looked the back of the house. Drawn by her grand- mother's sheer force of will, Julianna set her cup aside and followed her.

"It's the most beautiful place in the world," Lady Re- gina said of the moorland rolling away in static waves of green and brown. "Here I'm never afraid, or sad, or hurt. I would gladly have spent the rest of my life here. But there was your grandfather, and he is so good a states- man that I'd have been selfish, indeed, to keep him to myself at the risk of the country's gain."

Without looking at her, she reached over and patted Julianna's hand, which rested on the windowsill beside her own.

"Before I ever met your grandfather, I became em- broiled in a scandal that became so terrible and danger- ous that nothing you could ever think to do would com- pare to it."

Julianna doubted that but she squeezed her grand- mother's hand affectionately.

"I was married once before."

"Before Grandfather?" So startled was she by the admission, Julianna forgot that she was not to question what was being said.

Lady Regina turned to her and nodded solemnly. "He was an earl. I'd never met him. We were married by proxy while I was still a boarder at a convent in Italy."

Julianna's eyes widened to enormous proportions but she kept her mouth shut.

"The marriage was arranged by my uncle, who had become my guardian upon my parents' death. I was twenty-one, full of hope, and cowered by the world I didn't know or understand."

"That seems impossible," Julianna murmured under her breath.

"Oh, sheltered youth is so green and tender, Gillie. Too late I came to see that I'd been a dupe in the machinations of people I'd never met, to whom I was nothing but an instrument of devious and complex revenge. The earl, poor man, repelled me. By the grace of heaven I was spared the ordeal of the marriage bed. He died less than a week after I returned to London. I didn't welcome his death though I was glad of it. But his death unleashed the full assault of the brutal world against me. My mother-in-law hated me on sight. My husband's cousin, who'd lusted after me, thought to make me his mistress. My uncle, well . . . the less said the better. Because I was an orphan not of noble birth, the *ton* turned its back on me when accusations began that I was an adventuress, a calculating chit whose only purpose in marrying one of their own was to inherit his fortune."

Lady Regina's fingers tightened so strongly on Julianna's that the younger lady flinched, but she didn't pull away. "The scandal ran me out of London." She looked back at Julianna again and this time she smiled. "And straight into your grandfather's protective embrace."

She released Julianna's hand and patted it. "The details are unimportant, but even after the truth was made known to the public, at least as much of it as the public would understand, the scandal remained a lively topic for years. You see, my dear, most people lead such dreary lives that they'd rather dine on the sordid tidbits of others' misfortunes than nibble the thin crusts of their own sad existence.

"No one ever dared snub me outright once your grandfather and I wed, but I won't say I didn't suffer in private from the slights and thinly veiled ugliness that only women can mete out to one another. For, in marrying a marquess, I took yet another tulip of nobility out of the marriage market. Some ladies haven't forgiven me yet!"

An impish grin flitted across her patrician features. "They wanted him as a lover, you see. Lord, who can blame them? If you find a man who makes you quiver body *and* soul, then hold him against whatever the world may say of it."

"But why I have never heard about any of this?" Julianna asked, breaking yet again the condition of the confidence.

"It all happened years ago. Many of the gossipmongers are dead. The others have grown hard of hearing and short of memory, thank Providence."

"I see," Julianna said in a slightly dazed voice.

Lady Regina turned fully toward her granddaughter

and reached up to snare her by the chin and turn her face to hers. "Do you, child? Did you really love him?"

Julianna turned three shades of red before she realized that her grandmother was not speaking of her secret lover but the Duke of Montrose. "No, I never did. I understand that now." She lowered her lashes over her silver-green eyes. "I now know that being in love means pain and fear, and misery like a sickness in the soul."

"Oh, yes, there's that too. I won't lie to you. Great love requires great sacrifice. But, Julianna, when the right man comes along, it will be worth it."

Julianna opened her eyes. "But I don't want the pain. I don't want to wake up and wonder if he'll live another day. How could you bear it last winter when Grandfather nearly died?"

A spasm of pain as awful as it was swift entered Lady Regina's expression. "Oh, child, I was so very afraid. Not of his dying, but that he would leave me behind." A ghost of a smile played over her mouth. "I'm selfish. I don't want to be the one left. Not that I can bear any better the thought of him grieving over my grave. I haven't quite worked it out yet, but I should like us to go together, like our ancestress and her rascally captain. But not in violence. I detest violence. Perhaps in bed, or in the rose garden. One summer's evening, perhaps we shall simply fall asleep in one another's arms under the rose arbor and not awaken. Yes, I'd like that."

Tears pricked Julianna's eyes. "I wish I had your trust in love. But you've lived a long life together."

"That doesn't make it easier," her grandmother said with a small shake of her head. "It only gives me more to resent losing. But we are not such stuff as to endure like this house or the moors or the sea. When you find true love, the strength to endure the possibility of its loss will be there. You have only to accept one and the other will follow."

Smiling, she turned back from the windows. "I've never asked you directly. Do you believe that Blood Hall is haunted by Captain Monleigh and his Kingsblood mistress?"

Julianna slanted her grandmother a speculative glance. "Perhaps."

Lady Regina's expression turned roguish. "It is, you know. I met them once. They saved my life. Yet I don't envy our ghostly inhabitants. The longer I live, the less I approve of their continued abidance in this place. No, say that I pity them because they're bound to the earth by a sense of injustice that their mortal love lasted so short a time. Whereas I think they should be grateful to have known such a magnificent love, however short its mortal existence." She lifted her face to the ceiling. "Are you listening, Captain?"

The day was clear, bright, the sky as deep a shade of blue as March could invent. The clap of thunder that suddenly blasted the house, rattling windowpanes, trembling the tea service, and jarring the teeth in their heads sent both ladies scurrying for shelter.

When they reached the door it opened before them. Mrs. Mead stood blocking the entrance, her eyes as round as two bilberry pies. "Did you hear that, my ladies?"

"Indeed, we did," Lady Regina answered, and began to chuckle. "I fear it's my fault."

"Your fault?" Julianna and Mrs. Mead pronounced together.

Lady Regina put a finger to her lips. "Ghosts!" she whispered, and nodded, winking.

"Well, I never!" Mrs. Mead whispered, making signs to ward off the evil eye with both hands.

"Grandmother—" Julianna began in protest, only to be cut off by her grandmother saying heartily, "How I do enjoy pulling their proverbial beards now and again!"

Lady Regina chuckled and waved Julianna before her into the hall. "I will have to make it up to them." She looked at Mrs. Mead's ashen face, ignoring her fright. "Where is that horrid painting of the hunting party that the captain is so fond of?"

"Packed away in the attic. The marquess's orders," the housekeeper answered uncertainly.

"Have it taken down and hung in the Great Hall. That should please the old Cromwellian no end. Come along, Julianna. Nothing lifts the spirits like a new gown, and I've brought dozens of ideas for us to choose from."

When the two ladies had disappeared down the hall, Mrs. Mead stuck her head into the Great Hall and glanced suspiciously about. There was nothing at all to be seen and only a faint whiff of roses stirred the unusually cold air.

"Pesky ghosts!" she murmured, and firmly shut the door. If it weren't for the marchioness's presence, she would have given notice years ago. But if her ladyship wasn't bothered by pranks, then neither would she be. Still, she would send the new maid in to build a fire for the evening and retrieve the tea service. A body couldn't be too careful, after all.

The walls of the Great Hall misted over as the door swung shut. The darkness gathered quickly in to replace

the sunny afternoon's light. Pressing in on it was a deeper
darkness still. Boiling clouds of violet and gray roiled the
room with oppression. Angry sparks flickered in their
depths. A rumbling too low for the human ear trembled
the heaviest pieces of furniture and sent the mice beneath the floorboards skittering for the safety of open
places.

"She had no right to speak to us thus! A pox on the
meddling mortal!"

"After all that we have done for her!"

"Ungrateful! Disrespect! Defiant! I will not tolerate it.
Now and for all time, I withdraw my protection of Blood
Hall! I—"

"What is it, Captain?"

"Nothing, madame. Yet, confound it! I feel a weakness
I have not known since flesh held my spirit captive. It
must be her talk of mortality that caused it."

"I feel it too. A draft wafts across dead flesh. What is
happening?"

"Death still stalks us. We cheated him, and yet he
waits."

For a moment there was no sound at all. Then a new
and utterly unearthly voice rumbled down the chimney
and swept out as great tongues of flame from the empty
hearth.

"Someone must die! Someone must pay Death's debt!"

Like the fading wisps of dark at dawn, the effluence
receded, the darkness swallowing itself as day reappeared. A moment later the new housemaid appeared
with fresh fuel only to find a now-raging fire.

Chapter
Fifteen

"What do you think?" Julianna held her arms out and slowly whirled about so that the very full skirts of her new gown belled out above her crinoline petticoat.

"Ah, madame, *c'est très beau!*" Miss Sophie, the modiste, warbled in her fake French accent. She turned a sharp eye on her two helpers who then nodded in unison, murmuring in execrable accents.

"Magnifique! Magnifique!"

"Why, my lady, you look just like a painting," Mrs. Mead chimed in with an approving nod of her head.

"A new image, I knew it was just what you needed," Lady Regina pronounced in self-congratulation.

The five pairs of appreciative eyes turned on her made Julianna blush. "Well? When will I be allowed to view the great transformation?"

At Lady Regina's nod, Miss Sophie and Mrs. Mead moved to roll out the full-length mirror that had been pushed into one corner of the library–turned–sewing room.

In ten short days the marchioness had changed Blood Hall from a solitary retreat into a bustling home. A dozen servants had been hired for the much-needed spring cleaning. For most of this time Julianna had been measured, poked, prodded, occasionally pricked, remeasured, and fitted with piece after piece of material until she went to bed each night exhausted from the sheer idleness required of being a modiste's dummy. Though she loved her grandmother dearly, she was heartily sick of the entire affair. But at least the wardrobe sessions provided a distraction that kept Lady Regina from prying into other things, like affairs at Little Hangman Mine. For Julianna, they were an excuse to keep busy and away from depressing thoughts of her lover's continued absence.

"Where are my new spectacles?" she inquired only to see her grandmother pull them reluctantly from her pocket. Two pairs had arrived as ordered from London the day before but, for reasons not quite clear, they had both been in Lady Regina's possession ever since.

"You won't need them for dancing," Lady Regina reminded her, "But I suppose they won't entirely spoil the effect."

Julianna put them on, blinking as the world changed in an instant from a pleasant blur into sharp detail. With a flourish, Miss Sophie removed the canvas cover from the mirror and what she saw reflected there made Julianna forget every impatient, annoying, ungrateful thought of the past week. She scarcely heard the murmurs of agreement as she moved closer to inspect the fashion plate who gazed back at her.

She was dressed in a ball gown of white poplin patterned with tiny sprigs of the selfsame color. Crimson braid decorated the tight short sleeves that ended just above the elbow in a froth of lace. The tight-fitting bodice that delineated every curve of her bosom came to a point in front that emphasized her slight waist. The neckline was very low from shoulder to shoulder, showing off more of her than any other garment she had ever owned. From the dip in the middle, folds of material arranged *à la grecque* formed an off-the-shoulder collar that framed her shoulders. Much more sophisticated and daring than anything she would have chosen for herself, the style was more than becoming. She looked, well, positively splendid.

"So, Gillie, you too approve of my choice." Lady Regina beamed. "And what of your new coif? Doesn't it become you as well?"

Julianna lifted her gaze from her figure. Her dark hair had been parted in the middle, but instead of being smoothed back tightly over her ears, it had been poofed and draped to form curved wings on either side of her head. The rest had been fashioned into a thick plait and coiled high on her crown. A wreath of artificial roses and crimson and white ribbons fit bandeau-style over the whole. The effect was charming, feminine without fluff, elegant yet simple enough to do justice to her strong-boned face.

"You remind me of me at your age," Lady Regina said with a nod.

Julianna swung about, nearly oversetting a nearby tea table with the swish of her fashionably wide skirts. "Oh no, Grandmama. I've seen your portrait. You were beautiful."

Lady Regina's deep green eyes sparkled. "And what, pray tell, do you see in the mirror?"

Julianna turned back, prepared to tick off each and every one of her deficits, but, strangely enough, at the moment she couldn't find any. "I wear spectacles," she said at last.

"Is that all? They aren't a permanent fixture. You may remove them at any time. What else is wrong? Come, don't be shy."

Julianna frowned at her image. "My features have always been too strong for popular taste."

"Do you think so now?"

In truth, she did not. The new, fuller hairstyle softened the angles and gave her features a balance that had been lacking. But she was not about to give up her long-cherished prejudices against herself. "My hair is Gypsy dark and poker straight. It's impossible to curl."

"I've always thought your mahogany mane handsome and rather exotic. But if you'd prefer curls . . ."

"No," Julianna answered honestly. She liked the new style, which showed off the dark red and chestnut sheen of her thick hair as never before.

"As for my figure—" She had a sudden memory of her private assessment of her naked self in the bedroom mirror. Though it was hardly the same, she had the suspicion that, contrary to the yards and yards of fabric covering her, no man who saw her would be in doubt of the nature of the curves and valleys that lay beneath.

"Don't you think the style is too young for me?" she asked, stubbornly trying to contain her pleasure at her transformation.

"What girl of eighteen would be allowed to wear so revealing a bodice?" her grandmother returned. "No, the gown suits you, my dear. It's made for one of your height and figure. A shorter lady would look like an overturned toadstool. Come, admit it. You're pleased."

Defeated, she turned a wry smile on her grandmother. "You and Miss Sophie have worked miracles. I don't recognize myself."

"Let that be a lesson to you. You're what you believe yourself to be. You're a striking girl. For pity's sake, behave like one. No more gray, no more sickly yellows and fading pinks. Pure colors, Gillie! Mrs. Mead, you're to dispose of Lady Julianna's old gowns. Help yourself. The others will be distributed to the deserving poor."

"Very well, my lady," the housekeeper replied, thinking of one gown in particular, a gray alpaca with white lace at the collar and cuffs, that she just might, by taking material from the full skirt, make over for herself.

"There's just one problem," Julianna said with an apologetic smile. "The armholes are so narrow in all these gowns, I can't lift my arms high enough to pat my hair."

"One must suffer for fashion, my dear, but not too dearly." Lady Regina turned to the modiste. "You will need to put gussets under the arms of Lady Julianna's walking and traveling dresses. Now, the next gown if you will."

During the next two hours, Julianna slipped into and out of half a dozen other dresses and gowns made of printed calico, tartan plaids, check weave, and striped muslin. There were walking dresses and traveling gowns, visiting and carriage toilettes, and country gowns. Some had plain skirts, others had one or two wide flounces with pinked or scalloped edges.

As Julianna modeled each Lady Regina chose appropriate accessories and bonnet styles from those that Miss Sophie had brought with her. "No, not that one," she said at one point when the modiste was about to drape Julianna in a paisley shawl. "This one."

She held up an example of the finest work of needle- and loomwork in all the world, a cashmere shawl made of Tibetan goat hair worth several hundred pounds. Forming an "O" with her forefinger and thumb, she threaded one end of the shawl through it then easily drew the entire garment out the other side.

"A genuine cashmere shawl is so light it may be drawn through a wedding ring, Gillie. This one was given to me by the queen herself as an acknowledgment of Lord Kingsblood's valued service to her." She draped the gossamer weave about Julianna's shoulders and smiled in satisfaction. "My gift to you."

Much later in the day, Julianna sat in the Great Hall with her grandmother, looking out over the greening moors and drinking their Lenten tea—*sans* cakes and sandwiches. Both ladies were silent—Julianna musing over the continued absence of her secret lover and Lady Regina pondering the possible reasons why her granddaughter seemed distracted a good deal of the time.

Wearing a gown of stout cotton printed with bold pink stripes alternating with stripes of a red floral pattern, Julianna looked much younger and lovelier than ever, but Lady Regina had not missed the faint lavender smudges beneath her eyes each morning, nor her moodiness when Julianna thought no one observed her. The young lady was hiding something, Lady Regina was certain of that, and it had nothing to do with the trouble at Little Hangman Mine, of which Julianna was trying to keep her in ignorance. Now was the time to find out what this secret was.

"It's time we went back to London, Gillie," she began without preamble. "Your grandfather writes every day to say he's extraordinarily busy presenting a bill in Parliament that will mean the repeal of the Corn Laws. Yet he ends every missive with a complaint about cold rooms, cold feet, and cold sheets and . . . well, you understand, my dear."

"Yes, Grandmama."

Lady Regina's smile held all the charm of genuine age-less beauty. "Therefore, it's time we returned to London. I'll write tonight and tell him that he may expect us by the end of the week."

The moment had come to tell her. "I won't be re-turning to London."

"Because of that lack-a-wit Dashmore?" Lady Regina scoffed. "He should be grateful to you. Your imaginative toast made his wedding the social event of the Season, which is more than he could have accomplished on his own."

"It's not out of fear of facing scandal." She looked at her grandmother, realizing that she meant it.

Lady Regina regarded her granddaughter thought-fully. What she saw was the forlorn expression of a young woman hopelessly in love. Yet there had not been a sin-gle clue that there was a new man in her granddaughter's life. Shortly after her arrival she had wondered if Ju-lianna, in the throes of unrequited love, had formed a *tendre* for the new gardener, so vehemently did she dis-parage the man whenever his name came up. A discreet chat with Mrs. Mead had put that concern to rest. Still, she would have been happier if she could have set eyes on the man.

"When did you say the gardener will be returning?"

Julianna shook her head, unconcerned about Jos's whereabouts. "He's a law unto himself, Grandmama." She turned back to the window. "I wouldn't be surprised if he's gone for good."

"Without his wages?"

Julianna gave a slight shake of her head. "I sent Tom to inquire at the cottage about him, but Tess wouldn't say where Jos had gone, only that he will be back."

Wise in the ways of the world, Lady Regina bent a shrewd look on her granddaughter. "Who is Tess?"

"Jos's wife," Julianna said more wistfully than she realized. "They have a young son."

"I see." Lady Regina's mouth pursed into a troubled knot. "This young man, is he handsome?"

Julianna looked around in surprise. "Jos? I don't think so. Why do you ask?"

"Sometimes young men, if they're well favored and have too little to occupy them, will stray from their wives."

"I wouldn't know about that," Julianna said crisply, made uneasy by the recurring memory of Shrove Tuesday evening when she had thought he would kiss her. Wanting to change the subject, she added, "I hope Mrs. Mead is doing justice to the partridges Tom bought for supper. I'm famished."

Undeterred by the transparent attempt to steer her from her topic, Lady Regina reached out and took one of Julianna's hands in hers. "Attend me a moment, Gillie. It grieves me to see you silently mourning a loss not worthy of your consideration. Especially since you most certainly could have won the rotter if you'd wanted him."

Amazed and a little resentful to be so spoken to, Julianna pulled her hand free from her grandmother's light grasp. "I don't know what you may have heard in London, but I'm not pining for a lost love."

"Yet you blame yourself for Dashmore's desertion. He's nothing but a puffed-up self-absorbed dandy, as his poor wife will soon learn, to her sorrow. If he hadn't shown himself a cad before we returned, you can be certain your grandfather would have rejected his suit!

"I know you, Gillie, perhaps better than you know yourself. When you were younger you were never afraid of anything. Sometimes your grandfather and I would hold our breath for fear you would break your neck in some new scheme. I suppose that's why I never saw it coming. But one day, while you were away from us, you looked into your mirror and your courage failed. You should have confided in me your apprehensions when you came back to us for your first London Season. Instead, caught up in my own little world, I allowed you to stumble through two miserable Seasons that only left you more defeated and anxious for yourself than before. I blame myself for that. What a nincompoop I was!"

"You mustn't, Grandmama. I was too tall, plain, and vocal to suit any taste. Nothing you could have done would have changed that."

"Not true, child. You were as attractive as any debutante. This week has confirmed what I've suspected for years. I never should have let your dear mother choose your gowns. You look your best in bold colors and dramatic styling. Ruffles, flounces, and bows look silly on you. Even so, you might have been a success had you believed in yourself."

She placed a hand lightly over Julianna's heart. "Here is where you determine how the world will view you. It wasn't your face or intellect that drove the suitors away, Gillie. It was a failure of courage here." She patted Julianna's heart and then her cheek. "Harsh words from your grandmama, Gillie, but I feel I must speak the truth to you now. As it is, I've waited too long.

"Look about you. A lack of beauty never deterred any

true woman from obtaining the admiration she desired. Is our queen not a lovely woman? And what of the portraits you've viewed of Empress Eugenia and any of a half dozen of the late regent's mistresses? Attractive women, certainly, but exquisite beauties? Never! *They* decided they were beauties. The world merely acquiesced to their assumptions."

"You make it sound so simple."

"Do I? I think it is. The marquess says I came into his life and took it by storm, yet I seem to remember being very daunted by his then-fiancée's prettiness. Ever since, I've noticed that porcelain dolls are as numerous as tulips in Holland. Some become nonpareils, others languish in obscurity. It's a matter of character. You saw yourself differently for the first time today. All possibilities are now before you."

"Why are you telling me this?"

"Because I sense that you have found someone. Ah, how you blush! Then I am right. You needn't tell me about him yet. As long as it's not the gardener . . ." Her eyes narrowed to jewel-green slits. "It's *not* the gardener, Gillie?"

Julianna laughed. "No, Grandmama. It's not."

"Good!" She picked up her cup and saucer and changed the subject more deftly than her granddaughter had. "Now you may tell me what our mine foreman wanted this afternoon. Don't say it's nothing. I've been conversing with the housekeeper and the maids. What's all this about unions and unrest?"

Julianna took a deep breath and smiled. "Very well, only you must promise me that you won't say anything to Grandfather until Jed and I are convinced that his intercession is needed."

"Your grandfather and I have no secrets," Lady Regina replied promptly, but the ever-present mischievous twinkle came back into her eye. "Yet I always reserve the right to choose the time and place of my confidences. Speak up, Gillie."

Reluctantly Julianna told her grandmother all of the events that had occurred since she arrived at Blood Hall. The only things she left out were her confrontation with Rob Wheal after church and that she had been attacked by the crowd the day of the mine cave-in, and that both times she had been saved by Jos Trevelyn's intervention. After Lady Regina's probing question about him, it seemed that the less said about him the better.

"This is serious, Gillie. I'm more convinced than ever that you should return to London with me tomorrow. However," she continued with a hand held up for silence, "I won't insist. But, if there's any more trouble of any kind, I'm charging the Meads with putting you on the first coach for London, bound and gagged if necessity dictates. As for your mysterious young man, he can well come to London and present himself to the marquess and myself. He should do so in any case."

Julianna was painfully silent on that subject.

Julianna was surprised to find Mrs. Mead and one of the new maids hunched over a newspaper at midday. She was even more surprised when Mrs. Mead snatched up the paper and tried to hide it behind her back as Julianna entered the servants' hall. "Ben't there something you need, my lady?"

She smiled but her eyes moved suspiciously between the two servants. "Yes. One of the new maids was overzealous in her cleaning. She waxed the piano keys. I need a cloth to remove it."

"That'd be Nora's doing," Mrs. Mead said with a scowl of disapproval. "The girl can't do the simplest things. If she doesn't improve by the end of the week, she'll be let go. I'll take care of the piano right away."

"That won't be necessary, if you'd just get a cloth. Is that the weekly paper?"

Mrs. Mead started guiltily. "What newspaper would that be, my lady?"

Julianna struggled to keep her expression bland. "The one behind your back."

"Oh. This?" The housekeeper pulled the paper out from behind her back. "It's an old paper, my lady. I was just about to use it for kindling." She began wadding it up.

"Please don't. I haven't had time to read anything since the marchioness arrived. I shall miss her, but things will be calmer without her. May I see the paper?"

The housekeeper and maid exchanged doomsday glances before Mrs. Mead very reluctantly smoothed out the worst of the wrinkles and handed it over. "We didn't bring it in the house," she said quickly, and sent a warning glance on the maid. " 'Twas found shoved under the door this morning."

What could be so potent that it made her housekeeper afraid to show the paper to her? Julianna wondered as she unfolded it. The masthead read "*The Northern Star,* February 1846." She recognized the name at once as the Chartist newspaper founded in Leeds some nine years earlier. Though she had never read it, she knew the marquess kept abreast of Unionist doings by occasionally perusing an issue. She looked up and smiled at Mrs. Mead. "Did you think I'd be offended by this?"

"Did ye see the picture, yer ladyship?" the young maid asked, her dark eyes at once shy and sly. "I say it is too the gardener. Mrs. Mead says it ain't."

Julianna looked back down at the front page. In the center was a copy of a daguerreotype of a serious-faced young man with light hair parted on one side and swept forward over his ears, bushy side whiskers, stiff collar, and a jaunty polka-dot cravat tied in a bow knot. His light eyes looked strangely transparent, like glass. His unsmiling mouth was stern, his expression uncompromising. Something about the composition of features seemed familiar, but nothing about the dapper young man reminded her of the scruffy likes of her sometime gardener. Beneath the picture were the words "Sir Adrian J. Lyngate, lieutenant in the Chartist movement."

"A most attractive man," she said after a moment, "but he scarcely bears a likeness to Jos Trevelyn." She looked up. "May I read it before I return it to you?"

"Of course, my lady," Mrs. Mead replied, and seemed relieved. "I told Molly here that weren't Jos, but she were a silly lass."

Molly glanced uncertainly at the older woman. "Wot I said was, he looks enough like the man what's livin' in the gardener's cottage to be 'im. Ben't the same, yer ladyship. Leastways, on account Mrs. Mead says the man in the paper's a gen'man while the folks what's livin' at the cottage is common sinners."

Julianna smiled tolerantly. "What sort of sinners are they?"

The girl's black-button eyes brightened. "They ain't

married. Me ma says folks wot are livin' together and ain't married will burn in Hell."

But Julianna had stopped listening to the maid. She had opened the newspaper to an inside page and what she saw blotted out all other thought. It was a political cartoon depicting the usual callousness of the nobility to the common masses, but the characters were shockingly and humiliatingly familiar. It was a depiction of a wedding celebration, complete with bride and groom and wedding cake, across which the banner FRUITS OF OUR LABOR was inscribed. The groom held a huge knife marked ARISTOCRATIC PRINCIPLE, which he had plunged into the cake while his bride stood patiently beside him, her hands outstretched to catch the first morsel.

But that was not what made Julianna cringe inside. There was no mistaking who the figures were. The groom wore a ducal coronet tilted across his brow and the bride, dressed in a gown made up of sterling pound notes sewn together, appeared to be grossly pregnant. The third prominent figure was that of a female dressed as a "buddling" worker in clogs and shawl who held aloft a champagne glass. The legend beneath read A TOAST TO ARISTOCRATIC RULE, AND ALL THAT GREED AND WRETCHEDNESS FROM MILLIONS OF STOLEN WAGES CAN BUY!

"What is it, my lady?"

She looked up, white-lipped and visibly shaken. "Nothing. Nothing at all. I've decided not to play the piano after all. I need some fresh air."

"Would you like the stable boy to saddle one of the horses?"

Julianna shook her head, moving toward the rear door of the servants' hall. After lifting a shawl from the peg by the door, she went out into the warm April day.

The sun lay like warm hands where it touched her head, cheeks, shoulders, and back. The moorland was festooned for spring. Gorse and brambles were a healthy green, promising a surfeit of blossoms in early summer. The newly lush pasture encouraged foraging sheep that did not bother to scatter until she was right upon them. Even then they only gamboled a few yards away and returned to their grazing. Blackcaps sang richly in the woodland undergrowth as she passed a small gorge. Tomorrow was Easter. Nature had kept its tacit promise and was returning the world to life.

Yet she felt sick and cold inside. It had never occurred to her that gossip about her infamous toast might spread among people who did not know her. Or that they would find it a tale worthy of a satirical cartoon. But there she was in black and white, publicly and horribly lampooned for the sake of someone else's cause. As a miner, no less! How degrading.

Had Mrs. Mead seen the cartoon and recognized the source of the lampoon? Was that why she had tried to hide it from her? Who else had seen it and recognized her? Her grandmother had left behind a houseful of servants, a few trusted employees brought from London to see to the cleaning of the delicate chandeliers and the collection of valuable objects that filled the house. The bulk of them were local lads and lasses. Did the London servants know the gossip? If so, were they smiling behind their hands when she passed them, or was it only her imagination that she was being watched every moment of the day?

When she reached a rise, she paused to look down upon the land that sloped away from the sea toward the combe below.

She had told her lover to leave her and never come back. She had never thought he would.

"Stupid! Foolish! Coward!" She flung the words into the wind and felt better for having said them. Yet tears filled her eyes and then ran unchecked down her cheeks.

What else could she have done but send him away? Her grandmother was coming, the house was being opened. Their peace and solitude would have been destroyed in any case. She had never known or asked how he found his way into her room each time. She knew the house possessed secret passages, but her grandparents, fearing some adventurous child or grandchild might sneak into one and become lost, or worse, suffer an injury, had refused to acknowledge their existence openly. Had he come to her by that method? How had he found the opening? Who was he? Most important of all, would he come back? He had once said all she had to do was will it and he could come to her.

She needed him now, more than ever before. "I'm sorry! Please forgive me, Friend! Please come back to me!"

As she wiped the hot tears from her face, she suddenly saw a man's head rise above the precipice of the hill. He was very close before she spied him. He must have come along the near side of the hill, his approach sheltered by the outcropping of tors on her right.

He looked the same as always, scruffy clothes and the ever-present hat slanted down to shield his eyes. The only change was that he had raised a beard during his three-weeks' absence. It was thick and brown, and streaked with threads of red and gold. He carried a sack slung over one shoulder. When he looked up and saw her he did not stumble or hesitate. Had she not known about

Tess and Jessie, she would have thought him a man alone and on his own, and one who preferred it that way.

"You're back," she said when he paused before her, feeling surprise that her pulse had grown unsteady at the sight of him.

"Aye, yer ladyship." A boyish grin grew in the nest of Jos Trevelyn's new beard. "Ah'm back."

"You needn't sound so smug about it." His impertinent manner annoyed her as always. She wondered fleetingly if he had heard her cries. She certainly hoped not. "The marchioness was here in your absence, and she wasn't at all pleased to find the rose garden neglected for the fortnight she remained."

He shrugged and heaved his sack onto the ground. "Th' garden takes care o' its own this time o' year. Wha' with th' sun t' warm and th' rain o' winter t' moistenin' all."

"Even so, you should have asked permission to leave," she answered stiffly, for the sound of his voice had triggered the memory of her grandmother's inquiries about him. The marchioness needn't have feared that her granddaughter was consorting with the gardener. They could scarcely be civil to one another for five minutes running. "If the rose garden didn't require your services, there might have been other things that did."

His gaze slipped over her new gown, lingering boldly on her bodice. "Tha' ben't a fine new gown, yer ladyship." He tilted his head back when he looked at her this time so that she could not miss the devilment in his blue eyes. "What sort o' thin's would ye be wantin' tended?"

Her anger was quick and hot, a culmination of weeks of loneliness and frustration and misery over the latest

infliction to her pride—the cartoon—and the shaming
fear that he could read every thought that was in her
mind and was laughing at her. Well, she was not the only
one about whom rumors were circulating. "I've heard a
disturbing story about you, Jos. I'm told you're not married at all, but living in sin."

He didn't seem in the least surprised by her statement.
In fact, he grinned. "Ah'd nae thought a lady knew o'
such matters."

The sarcasm in his tone was meant to make her even
angrier, and the knowledge that he succeeded only dou-
bled her fury. "Never mind who told me. Is it true? Are
you married to Tess or is she your mistress and Jessie
your bastard?"

"What matter ben't of yers that a woman takes t' her
bed a man she craves for no reason than th' joy o' it? Are
ye jealous?"

For a moment Julianna could neither speak nor move.
She froze, battling some dark and dangerous emotion
within herself so powerful and violent that she dared not
give it life.

"You vile . . . despicable . . . !"

"And ye be cold-hearted and a hypocrite no' t' admit
ye know th' difference 'twixt a bit o' whorin' and th'
warm feelin' a man and woman may share tho' it be
unsanctified. Ah pity ye."

"You pity . . . ?" She took a deep breath, her hands
trembling so badly she dropped the paper she had been
carrying.

Suddenly his arms were about her, crushing her to
him. His mouth was on hers, hard and demanding. He
strained against her so strongly that for an instant she

was overwhelmed. Then she remembered who he was and who she was.

Just as suddenly, he released her.

She pressed her fingers to her bruised mouth, seeing through her own shock a reflection in his face of her breathless anger and passions dangerously aroused. When he made a tentative gesture toward her, his expression altering subtly, she snatched her hand from her mouth. "You're sacked! Do you hear me? Turned off!"

She caught herself on the verge of a sob and swallowed it back. The final humiliation would be if he saw that he had made her cry. "I want you and your doxy out of the cottage and off Kingsblood property by noon tomorrow. Tom will bring you your wages. Now get out of my sight!"

But it was she who swung away, half running down the back of the rise as if she feared he might come after her, to beat and hurt her for the grievance she had done him.

But he did not follow her. He bent and picked up the paper she had been holding. The masthead made his brows lift, and then he saw the picture. He studied it thoughtfully a moment and then opened the page. The cartoon on the inside page caught his eye. He read the inscription before he lifted his head to look after her. But she was far away now, a flash of bright red and black tartan on the green hillside.

"Poor Lady Kingsblood," he murmured, more in sympathy with her than she would have believed.

The small church was packed. It was Easter Sunday. Parson Pollock, inflamed and encouraged by the unusually large size of the congregation, allowed that gratification to urge him to feats of oration the duration of which

must be setting a new record, Julianna thought in weary
resignation.

She fanned herself ineffectually, growing somnolent in
the stagnant heat. Beside her, Mrs. Mead sat with hands
folded in her lap, wearing the new dove-gray gown she
had fashioned from one of her mistress's hand-me-
downs. She looked quite nice, Julianna thought, wishing
her own gown of bleached muslin with yellow and green
sprigs had not required such a tight lacing of her corset.
As it was, her heartbeat struggled against the stays
pressed under her bosom while perspiration trickled
down her spine.

It did not help her discomfort to know that she was
being silently watched, as she had been every Sunday
since the mine accident. Though she had not yet seen
Rob Wheal, she suspected he was there today. The congregation had been diffident in the marchioness's presence the previous two Sundays, for they knew that the
wife more than her granddaughter had the ear of the
marquess. But now that she was alone again, a hush that
came over the church when she entered it was as impenetrable as it was hostile.

The stares were not malicious, but today she felt them
on her like an oppressive weight. She shifted her shoulders as if by doing so she could physically throw off the
burden.

When the sermon drew to a close after more than an
hour and a song of praise was called for, she closed her
eyes in a silent prayer of thanksgiving. She reached for a
psalm book on the back of the pew in front of her, but
suddenly the distance seemed too far away, the effort too
great. She stood up but the church had become a ship,
the floor a deck pitching in a stormy sea.

She heard Mrs. Mead's voice rise in alarm but she did not try to answer it. Rather she slipped gratefully into a long, dark slide where cool shadows and forgetfulness waited.

Chapter Sixteen

"**H**ello, my lady. How are you feeling now?"

Julianna blinked at the man who stood nearby, but the room was too dim for her to see him distinctly. "Who are you?"

"Dr. McClintock," he answered, coming over to light the nearby lamp. A moment later the familiar surroundings of the Chinese Room were revealed. "Do you remember what happened, Lady Julianna?"

She nodded and slowly pushed herself up in bed. "I fainted in church a little . . ." She glanced toward the windows for verification of how much time had passed, but the drapes were drawn over them.

"It's late afternoon," the doctor supplied. "What else do you remember?"

"That Mrs. Mead can scream quite loudly when the occasion arises." She smiled faintly. "I'm not certain which embarrassed me more, the swooning or her reaction to it."

"Your housekeeper does possess a healthy pair of lungs," he agreed with a small smile. "I was present at the morning service. Do you remember that?"

"Of course," she answered, the events of the day falling back into place. "Would you mind handing me my spectacles, Dr. McClintock? They should— Oh, I hope I didn't damage them when I fell."

"Fear not," he said, and produced them from the vanity.

"Thank you," she said, putting them on. The doctor's face was quite clear to her now. He had a stern countenance: long and square of jaw, imposing nose, wide, near-lipless mouth, and gray eyes as pale as mist. A serious man, he always dressed somberly in brown or black, as if to confirm that medicine was a grave matter. Only a parson could look more righteous. No clergyman ever looked more self-assured.

His had been the face hovering over hers when she awakened on the church pew. "Now I remember. You came to my aid. You pronounced me fit but Mrs. Mead insisted that you follow me home where I could be thoroughly examined in private. You did that and then gave me a draft for the headache that came on. I must have slept, and here we are." She frowned doubtfully. "Why on earth have you remained when you've already assured me that I'm whole and healthy?"

The doctor took off his own spectacles and began to polish them with a handkerchief that he had drawn from his pocket. "Forgive me, Lady Julianna, but I took the liberty of remaining while you slept because I've known the marquess and your family some time." He smiled at her again, a tight give-away-little smile. "I delivered your mother of you, did you know that?"

Julianna shook her head. She knew she had been born at Blood Hall, but she had rarely been ill as a child. She had never really known Dr. McClintock other than to speak to in passing. She sat forward suddenly. "Is there something wrong, something to do with my head? The headache is gone." She smiled at him. "In fact, all I feel is hungry. I missed dinner, thanks to your draft."

"I assure you, there's nothing wrong with you or your head. Have you had any other unusual feelings in the last weeks?"

She dropped her eyes before his. What could he mean? Certainly a broken heart didn't come under a doctor's advisement, nor the weeping fits of self-pity that had plagued her recently. "I'm often hungry but yet sometimes nothing appeals to me." She looked up at him guardedly. "What sort of unusual feelings did you have in mind?"

"Are you easily fatigued?"

"Oh, I suppose I am. The marchioness was in residence until two days ago. She's a dynamo of no small order, as you well know. On the best of days I can scarcely keep up with her."

"Are you sleeping well?"

Julianna shrugged and smoothed a wrinkle of the coverlet. Some nights she did not sleep at all, for fear she would miss her Friend's visit. But he had not come again since the night she had sent him away. "Sometimes I sleep twelve hours together. Other times I'm too restless." She lifted her gaze. "Spring fever, I suppose."

"And what of your, um, personal regimen? Your monthly flux?"

She was not certain whether she or he blushed the more, but his expression remained serious. "Why, I—" She frowned, giving the matter consideration. "I don't remember. Perhaps not in two months. I was extremely fatigued when I arrived in Devon in February. That can affect it, I'm told. Why do you inquire?"

He put back on his spectacles and came over to the

bed to look gravely down at her. "Unless my examination is in error, my lady, you are with child."

When she did not respond, only stared blankly up at him, he cleared his throat in an officious manner. "I see," he said, tucking his handkerchief away and then, "I see," again.

He withdrew a small leather-bound note pad from his breast pocket and then a fountain pen. "I suppose your grandmother's recent visit was in connection with this turn of events?"

"No." Julianna shook her head slowly back and forth, now staring straight ahead. *I am with child?* "She had no idea. Neither did I."

Frowning, the doctor gave her a considering glance from beneath his bushy brows. "Come, come, Lady Julianna. There's no need to dissemble with me. I assure you, nothing you can tell me will be in the least bit shocking. Let's begin with the father's name."

She looked back at him. "I don't know it."

"Don't . . . ?" His brows shot up. "Dear lady, you weren't accosted by a stranger?"

The idea took root in her mind. Yes, she was accosted by a stranger, set upon and disgraced, and she'd been too ashamed to admit the attack to anyone until now. "I— I—"

Julianna shook her head. She could not do it. That would be a kind of cowardice that she could not grant herself. Her lover had called her a coward the night he left her. Her grandmother had called her a coward for not living and believing according to her heart's dictates. *A child. She was going to have a child.*

"I can't tell you the father's name." She glanced at the

physician. "I prefer not to tell you his name," she amended when she saw how oddly he was looking at her.

"Very well." He did not bat an eye. "We'll move on for now. Whom would you like me to notify in this matter?"

"No one." She sat up straighter, her bemused mind beginning to function more quickly. "No one should be notified, under any circumstances. This is no one's business but mine."

"I am to suppose, my lady, that you are not wed?" he asked in the kindest tone she'd heard from him yet.

"No, I'm not wed—"

"But there is someone—"

"—nor do I expect to be," she finished dully.

"I see."

She doubted that he did. Nor could she explain it to him. There was no one to wed. Her Friend had disappeared. There were no witnesses, no one who could corroborate her assertion that she had been seduced in this very bed by a charming nightly visitor. People would think her mad.

"Certainly your parents should be informed."

"They are away in India. No, I won't bother them."

"The marquess and—"

"Absolutely not!"

Dr. McClintock laid his pen and pad aside and reached for Julianna's hand. "Now, my dear," he began, patting the back of her hand. "You've had a shock. I suspected it might be. That is why I stayed to talk to you after you had rested. But you must be reasonable. I assure you, you aren't the first lady to find herself in like circumstance. There are many methods by which you may be helped through this trying time. But I must have your word that you won't do anything rash."

He bent closer so that she could see her image reflected in his lens. "Nothing drastic." He pronounced the four syllables as four separate words.

"I don't intend to do away with myself, if that's what concerns you," she responded with a twitch of her lips.

"Good." In his experience, those who talked so frankly seldom killed themselves. "Now, you're in fine health. There's no reason to suppose you won't bear a healthy child by . . ." He reached back to check up his pad. "by St. Nicholas Day." He gave her yet another slight smile. "Most appropriate, wouldn't you say, as he's the patron saint of children."

Does that include bastards? she nearly asked, for suddenly she was beginning to see this as one huge joke on herself. But she bit her lip and kept silent. *A child!*

"Now then, if you'd like, I will write to the marquess myself. I believe I can make the matter known to him in such a way that, well, feelings can be spared."

"Whose feelings?" she asked. "Not mine, certainly. And not my grandparents'. No, you mustn't write them. I forbid it." She rose to her knees on the bed. "I forbid it, do you hear me? If you write them, I will run away."

"Calm yourself, Lady Julianna," the doctor said in the same quiet voice he had been using all along. "You'll only make yourself needlessly ill." With both hands on her shoulders, he pressed her back up against the pillows. "This has been a shock. It would be better if you told me the name of the gentleman most concerned. I will see him personally, if you wish. He should come to see you so that you can talk the matter over."

The first genuine smile of the day lifted his features. "I assure you, many a good marriage has sprung from this

difficult beginning. No doubt he's a good man and will
see where his duty lies."

"No doubt you are right," she answered, fighting the
sensation of giddiness beginning to bubble up inside her.
"If you know the whereabouts of the Love Talker, you
might mention the matter to him and apply to his good
nature."

He had said that nothing she could say would shock
him, but she saw in Dr. McClintock's pale eyes a surprise
that he could not hide. Almost at once the look disappeared and he became brisk and businesslike again.
"Very well, Lady Julianna. You leave me no choice but to
do as I see fit."

Having no doubt that that meant informing her grandparents, Julianna reached out and caught him by the
hand. "No, please, Dr. McClintock. You must give me
time to accept this. I promise you, I'll contact someone."
She thought quickly. "There's my married cousin. You
remember Lady Letticia Cowper, do you not?" He nodded. "I'll write her and ask her to come. As for the rest
of my family, I need time to consider how to approach
them. You said yourself that you might be in error. However, if I am with child, there's no harm in waiting a few
weeks, is there? Why, if I hadn't fainted today, no one
would yet know, not even I."

"Very well." Dr. McClintock looked more at ease, perhaps because she was now making sense. "I'll be back at
the end of the week and we will talk again."

"What excuse will you give?" she asked, thinking of
Mrs. Mead and the two dozen other servants now in residence at the house.

He nodded in understanding. "I'll say that you're suf-
fering from a slight malaise. You're to be fed lightly and

only what lies comfortably on your stomach. You may take the air but no strenuous activity until I say differently." He bent a powerful look at her over the top of his glasses. "And may I expect that a letter to your cousin will be your first task?"

She nodded. She needed to confide in someone. Who better than Lettie? Poor Lettie, she would be scandalized.

Still, when the doctor had departed and Mrs. Mead had come in and clucked over her and then gone to get her a light supper, Julianna got out of bed and went to stand at her window rather than write the letter.

She knew she must be very careful about what she said. Nothing could be admitted in writing. She would tell Lettie that she had been ill and was in need of company. How much of the truth she would tell Lettie once she arrived, she was not certain.

The scandal of her pregnancy would be all the fuel Rob Wheal would need to rouse fresh enmity against her family. She'd be pilloried by gossip as another example of the vice that was rampant in the privileged class. Had he not tried publicly to label Jos Trevelyn her lover?

The thought of Jos Trevelyn learning of her predicament vexed her the most. She could well imagine his smirk when he heard the news. How he would gloat. Would he remember how she had looked at him on more than one occasion in recent weeks? Would he remember that though she said she had sacked him for his impertinence, they both knew it was his lecherous glances that had disturbed her more? He had called her cold and a hypocrite. Would he now think that she had turned him off out of thwarted desire for him?

She groaned and gently hammered her fist against the

windowpane. How would Jos react if accused by Wheal of being the father of her child? Would he succumb out of spite to the temptation to claim her as his conquest? It would make him something of a local celebrity. He kept one mistress. Why shouldn't people believe that he had a second? He'd spent nearly every day of the last few months on the grounds of Blood Hall while she had lived here alone. She was certain Rob Wheal had wasted no time in spreading his rumors. He was a Chartist. The next lampoon in *The Northern Star* might well have her name and face attached.

She dropped her flushed face into her trembling hands. Somehow the thought of becoming vulnerable to Rob Wheal, and thereby perhaps becoming the instrument of an attack on her grandfather, seemed much worse than her present predicament. My Lord! Such talk could jeopardize his standing in Parliament just when his voice of reason was most needed.

"Where are you, my love?" she whispered to the room.

A sensation as ephemeral as a breeze and as comforting as a mother's touch brushed her cheek.

Take heart, it seemed to whisper silently. *Take heart.*

Julianna stood on the front steps of Blood Hall to welcome her guests as the private traveling coach rolled to a halt on the carriage drive. A pair of leather trunks had been strapped to the top and the Cowper family crest adorned the doors. She had been surprised that Lettie was arriving only a week after receiving her missive. Lettie's response to her letter had made her feel a little ashamed of herself. Poor Lettie had assumed her cousin must be on her deathbed to have written asking for company.

When the door of the coach opened, Lettie's face appeared in the space. As she waved gaily one of the footmen lowered the steps. She alighted wearing an amazingly wide crinoline under a natural muslin gown printed in floral and coral stripes. She wore a drawn bonnet lined in tulle and trimmed with a wreath of flowers inside the brim, the effect making her appear more like a girl of seventeen instead of a matron of twenty-seven.

"Why, Lettie, you look like a walking garden," Julianna said as she came forward with arms outstretched.

"And you—" Lettie's blue eyes widened as she digested her cousin's new look. "You look positively wonderful!"

The cousins embraced tightly, both murmuring endearments and additional greetings.

"And here I half expected to find you in a dim room full of camphor smells and sickbed prayers," Lettie said as she leaned back to better observe her taller cousin's face. "Yet you look perfectly healthy."

"I am perfectly healthy," Julianna replied. "I never said I was ill, I said I was lonely."

"Dash it all, Gillie. Do you mean to tell me we've run pellmell halfway across England to grieve where there's no corpse?"

Julianna lifted her head in surprise to find that Alfred had come up behind Lettie. "Dear Alfred!" She flung her arms about him and placed a kiss on his cheek.

"Well—well, I say!" Alfred blustered. He reached up to adjust his top hat, which she had bumped, but he was obviously delighted by her enthusiastic greeting.

Julianna took each of them by the hand. "My dearest and oldest friends, what a joy it is to know what you care so much for my welfare that you'd drop everything to fly to my sickbed."

"Except there is no sickbed," Alfred said, needing to point out the fact. His amiable face was a bit flushed. "Suppose you tell us what this is all about."

Julianna looked toward the coach a bit doubtfully. "Did you bring the children?"

"Certainly not," Lettie answered. "We didn't know if what you had might be contagious. Mother came to look after the brood while we visit you."

Stricken afresh by the inconvenience to which she'd put her cousins Julianna said, "I should never have written if I'd known what trouble I'd cause you and Alfred. Please forgive me."

"I might if I was treated to a breast of squab and a slice of Mrs. Mead's bilberry pie," Alfred answered honestly.

"Oh, don't listen to him." Lettie poked her husband's rather ample middle. "He's begun to think that the only two pleasurable pastimes left in life are to be found on the hunting field and at the dinner table."

"Oh, there's one to two other places besides," he replied, and rocked back on his heels as he gave his wife a significant look.

The glance of affection that passed between her cousins reminded Julianna of how very alone she had been since her grandmother left two weeks earlier. And how very alone her nights had been since . . .

Lettie spied Julianna's wistful look but misunderstood the reason for it. "But look how we stand here keeping Gillie on her feet. I don't care if you do look marvelous, I'm sure you are newly risen from your bed and should be resting out of the sun and wind."

Not wanting to frustrate Lettie's maternal instincts too much, Julianna took her arm and said, "You're right. Let's go in. Mrs. Mead's been making arrangements ever since we received your letter telling us when you'd arrive." She glanced over the top of Lettie's bonnet to say to Alfred, "Bilberry pie is on the menu. Mrs. Mead remembered that is your favorite."

"Well, now, ain't that jolly?" Smiling, Alfred offered an arm to each lady to escort them indoors.

Lettie kept up a constant chatter throughout the rest of the morning and through the dinner hour. She seemed to know the business of every family member, no matter how distant.

"Lettie writes letters like some women knit," Alfred offered at one point with a resigned shrug. "She corresponds daily. Our postman has begun to complain about the sheer volume of our mail. Had to promise him a new nag to keep up our delivery."

Undeterred by his comment, Lettie immediately launched into a story about Aunt Flora's bout with chilblains, followed by a full account of Cousin Muriel's confinement and new baby, and finally the marquess's most recent speech in the House of Lords.

"Mercy!" Julianna exclaimed in true awe when Lettie's formidable collection of stories seemed to momentarily run dry as they finished their dessert. "You're more entertaining than any gazette. You should publish your own." She lifted her hands as if holding a banner. *Lettie's Daily.* What do you think, Alfred?"

"I'd call it *The Mouth*," he murmured, and ducked Lettie's retaliatory swat.

"Don't you have something better to do?" Lettie said, bending a meaningful glance on her husband.

"What could I have to do?" Alfred began in an offended tone. "After all, I've just been dragged—*ouch*. You needn't resort to violence, Lettie."

Julianna smothered her laughter behind her napkin, for she knew Lettie had kicked him under the table.

"Oh, very well!" In full pique Alfred flung his napkin on a table before rising. "If you ladies should again require my company, I'll be smoking my pipe in the library." He paused to look at Julianna. "The marquess still allows tobacco in the library, I hope."

"He does. Grandmama brought a new humidor with her and put it in there. Give the blend a try and tell me what you think. She said the marquess wasn't certain it was aged properly and that he wanted another gentleman's opinion."

"Alfred will have an opinion," Lettie promised, "though whether it will be useful to the marquess I couldn't say."

As Alfred scowled at his wife Julianna sensed for the first time that there was something more than the usual banter between them. But all he said was "Good afternoon, ladies," before walking out.

When he was gone, Lettie and Julianna moved from the table to a nearby settee where Lettie took out her fan and began applying it with some vigor. "That man. I'm fond of him but he can be the most abominable pest when one wishes to be alone. He insisted—absolutely insisted—that he travel with me, as if I couldn't find Devon without his help."

"If I remember our geography lessons together, he may have a point." Julianna chuckled. "He loves you so much, Lettie. You are so very lucky."

Once again that rare wistful note was in her cousin's

voice and Lettie could contain herself no longer. "What's wrong, Gillie? And don't tell me loneliness." Her blond curls bounced about her ears, the fashion too young for her but one that was nonetheless becoming. "Now that Alfred's left us alone you may speak frankly."

Julianna looked at her cousin squarely. "I have something to tell you, Lettie, but if you scream or faint I shall soundly smack you. Do you understand?"

Two bright spots of color appeared on Lettie's soft cheeks, for her cousin hadn't spoken to her in that tone since they were children. Julianna had, indeed, once smacked her for becoming hysterical after a frog had jumped at her from a pond and muddied her favorite dress. "Very well," she said, her fan dangling forgotten from her fingers.

"I will preface my revelation by saying you may not ask me any questions and that under *no* circumstances can you reveal to anyone but Alfred what I am about to tell you. No one!"

Lettie's chin bounced up and down.

Julianna squared her shoulders and captured her cousin's soft blue gaze in her vivid green stare. "I am with child."

For the space of five heartbeats Lettie did not breathe. "But—but—I don't—" She snapped her mouth shut.

"Of course you do, Lettie. You and Alfred have children. I am going to have a child."

"Whose?" Immediately Lettie clapped a hand over her mouth, her eyes growing so wide they must ache, Julianna thought.

"I'm not prepared to say," Julianna said calmly. "That isn't important just now. I want your company and your help. I know nothing about the process in which my body is engaged, and your experiences would be useful to me. Are you willing to remain now that you know the truth about me?"

"Remain?" Lettie blinked like someone emerging from darkness into sudden light. "Of course I'll remain. If you thought for one—I would abandon—in your hour of need . . . Well, well, I just wouldn't!"

Julianna enveloped her cousin in a tight embrace. "Oh, Lettie, you are so good. I had hoped—I didn't know—"

The two cousins held one another for a long while, emotions simmering dangerously toward a boil.

Julianna suddenly let her go and busied herself with finding a handkerchief in her pocket. When she found it she blew her nose then wiped it with quick economical gestures. "Enough of that. The doctor says I must not overtax my emotions, though the truth is, Lettie, I never seem far from tears these days."

She raised her eyes to her cousin's, the vulnerability she had refused to show anyone else plainly visible on her face. "You must tell Alfred. I don't think I can. Will he make you leave?"

Lettie, who had been making use of her own handkerchief, lifted her brows. "I should like to see him try! After all, we are family." Her smooth brow lowered ominously. "Only, Gillie, it's not Dash—"

"It is not. I haven't given Lord Dashmore a full thought since shortly after I arrived."

"Then who?"

The question hung between them. Julianna had asked her not to press her, but she perfectly understood that she had been expecting too much of Lettie if she thought that particular question would go unasked. "It's no one you know."

Lettie licked her lips. "He is a gentleman, of course?"

Julianna smiled. "Ask me about anything but this."

"But, Gillie, surely he must know and if he does, then he can be made to see where his duty lies."

Julianna rose to her feet. "You mean well, Lettie, and I do so appreciate your coming, but I must ask you not to mention this subject to me again. Now I'm going up to lie down. I have become uncommonly fond of an afternoon nap."

Lettie rose to her feet. "But of course you have. I nearly slept the clock around the first months with Charlotte." She took Julianna's arm. "You poor dear, let me help you upstairs."

Because she did not wish to rebuff her cousin any more than was necessary, Julianna submitted to the unnecessary escort.

Fretful shadows coiled in the back currents of the closing door as, one by one, the candles of the Great Hall were doused by an unseen hand.

"A child! Think, madame, what that means. A child from the loins of a man who's cheated Death!"

"Where is he? Why has he not come back to her?"

"A new life, het only darkness gathers in this place. 'Tis an ill omen, madame. I—"

"Yes, Captain?"

" 'Tis strange, this sudden weakness."

"I feel it too. It's come again. It's Death!"

Beside her in the glassy gloom she heard an expelled breath of pain. "What's wrong, Captain?"

"I grow colder with each moment yet a fever burns my eyes. A searing of improbable flesh tortures me!"

"I am afraid! Take my hand."

"No, madame! Keep your distance. I know the source of the cold wind at my back. 'Tis retribution!"

All at once, the darkness surrounding them writhed with menacing force. Nordic winds sliced the spring night with icy blades, scattering all before it until the night air chimed like a crystal bell. The earthy odors of a new-spaded grave and the faint fragrance of white lilies invaded the night. As the hour struck, the hands of the mantel clock suddenly froze and then began racing backward, unraveling time with each rapid sweep.

Opening up like the pages of the Doomsday Tomb, the Impenetrable appeared before them to fill the trembling air with the voice of Everlasting Silence. *A child from the loins of man who's cheated Death! Did you think to escape your actions? You've broached the demarcation between life and death once too often. So you must own the debt.*

As the silence echoed around the stone walls, she turned away. "Captain? What must we do?"

The faint spirit beside her flickered, more fragile than any flame. "I feel myself dissolving from this twilight world. Farewell, my love! May all the spirits that bind be merciful!"

Even as the shimmering died away, she thrust out her hands toward him and, for the first time in two hundred years, she clutched only the emptiness of mortal reality. "Captain? Captain! Dear God! He's gone!"

Chapter
Seventeen

❧

Julianna smiled in bemusement as Alfred gently pushed her in the swing that hung from the bough of a huge oak planted on the property two centuries earlier. "Isn't north Devon the most beautiful place in all the world?"

"Quite, quite lovely," Alfred murmured, wishing he could shed the jacket of his buff-colored, checked country suit in response to the May heat. But of course that was unthinkable. They were no longer children and propriety had to be maintained.

She looked back over her shoulder. "A little higher, please, Alfred."

"Do you think you should, Gillie, in your—er . . ." Each time Alfred was forced to mention her delicate state, he found his tongue unable to form the shape of his words.

Blushing furiously, he gave her another gentle push. He had just spent the two most uncomfortable weeks of his life here at Blood Hall, and he didn't doubt that the next quarter hour would be worse. But Lettie had charged him with a task which he felt, as the only male relative present, duty-bound to see through.

"Will you not rest a time?" he asked as Julianna came

swinging back toward him. "I—I would like to talk with you, Gillie."

Julianna lowered her feet to the ground, her soft slippers plying the grass and bringing her to a halt. As he held the ropes to assist her rise, she bounded easily from the seat.

When she saw how heavily he perspired her smile turned rueful. "Poor Alfred. You've earned a rest."

She caught him by the hand and began leading him back toward the house. She had a fair idea of what was coming. Lettie had made an unnecessary production out of the fact that she was going to be busy in the kitchen all afternoon with Mrs. Mead, who had promised to teach her the secret of her bilberry pies. That could mean but one thing: Alfred had been appointed as spokesman, a responsibility he was obviously dreading.

"We'll find respite from the sun in the rose garden," she said as they neared the walled-in space.

Alfred opened the gate of the garden, stepped back to allow her to precede him, and then closed it firmly behind them. "My, my," he exclaimed when he turned to view the full glory of the secluded garden.

A dozen varieties of roses burst forth in a riot of color and sweetness. Jasmine ran in a wild tangle about the roots of the single huge tree, its tiny blossoms filling the air with exotic pungent scent. Bluebells nodded on slender stems as the couple passed, and ivy carpeted the open ground. Everywhere the eye fell a new color and fragrance met the senses.

"It's like diving headfirst into milady's perfume bottle," Alfred said with heady delight.

"It's a very special place," Julianna agreed. She shed

her straw poke bonnet and shawl and placed them on a stone bench. "Haven't you ever been here before?"

Alfred reached up to adjust the barrel knot of his cravat. "Can't say that I have."

Julianna's mouth fell ajar. "Alfred? Don't tell me you believe the stories that say the garden is haunted?"

Looking even more uncomfortable than before, he made a dissembling gesture. "Not as a rule partial to flowers. But these are very nice," he added in afterthought.

"It is, you know."

"Is what?"

"Haunted," she replied, and sat down on the bench beside her things. "Blood Hall is haunted. Grandmama scolds them and they shoot bolts of lightning at her in retaliation."

"Of course she does. And no doubt the marquess plays chess with the captain," he said, and laughed. But the heartiness of conviction was lacking, and he sounded more like he had a bone stuck in his throat. He had known Julianna nearly all his life. Though recent revelations had shaken him to the bottom of his soul, he still thought of her as the most sensible, rational woman he had ever met. Then he recalled Lettie's reminder that ladies in Julianna's condition were apt to act and speak peculiarly from time to time. It was true. Lettie had been a veritable chameleon during each of her pregnancies, changing moods as often as she changed her gowns. Damn, but he resented the situation into which he had been forced by a sense of family fealty.

Julianna regarded him impassively until he sobered. "Why don't you just say what you wish to, Alfred?" she encouraged after a moment. When his startled gaze swung back to her, she patted the empty space beside her. "Come and sit. We're practically brother and sister. You may say anything to me."

"Very well." He came stiffly forward and sat down beside her. But he did not look at her.

The strangest thing had happened to him during the past two weeks. He could not keep from gazing at her. Yet whenever she looked at him, he felt so uncomfortable it was all he could do to keep from bolting from the room. She looked, well, different, prettier and more feminine than he had ever seen her. For instance, today she wore a most becoming Turkey-red gown that made him flush that identical shade whenever he allowed himself to think about her "condition." Circumstances that would have crushed other ladies had brought out in his cousin a new spirit and sensuality. It was written all over her that some man had had a hand in her transformation. Some scoundrel, rather.

Jealousy gripped him, the force of it so powerful it drove him to his feet and into speech. "You must know that things cannot continue as they are, Gillie." He stared straight ahead. "There are others to consider, your parents and grandparents. You've a duty to them as well as yourself and your—um—your child." He expelled a short breath. "You must inform the father at once. Before it's too late."

"Too late?" Julianna frowned. "Too late for what?"

He ran a finger under his high collar. "Too late for him to come forward and spare you the needless gossip of an abbreviated confinement."

She bent her head with a sigh. She had known what was coming but that didn't make it any easier. "Dear Alfred, I know you mean well but you don't understand."

He turned suddenly to her, his beefy, handsome face deeply flushed. "Explain it to me, Gillie. Explain to me how you, of all women, could so debase—" His color deepened alarmingly. He bit his lip.

Feeling sorry for him, she extended a hand to him. "Please don't hate me, Alfred."

To her amazement, he reached out and gripped her hand so tightly she flinched. "Forgive me, Gillie. I didn't mean it. It's just to think some rotter— No, no! I don't mean that either. But, dammit, Gillie, the man must be told."

She looked up into his distressed face and rose to her feet. "It isn't so simply done, Alfred. He's gone away."

"Gone? Gone where?"

"I don't know. He has simply disappeared."

"You mean the man seduced and then abandoned you? Good God!" His hand flexed on hers. "But there must be those who know him, where he's from, how to contact him."

Julianna shook her head. "It's not possible. Besides, I sent him away."

She looked up at him with pleading eyes and saw something she had never before seen in her cousin's face, a need to ease her pain and a readiness to shoulder her burdens. How easy it would be, she thought, to lean on him, to feel a man's arms about her again, if only for a second. She needed that much, just that much assurance of herself as a woman. "Oh, Alfred, I made a dreadful mistake." She raised her free hand to lay it lightly on the lapel of his coat. "The folly of Lord Dashmore was nothing compared to this. I should have had more courage." She lifted her eyes to let him see a little of the pain and doubts she had been holding inside. "Things will never be the same."

Gazing into her misty green eyes, Alfred felt his heart contract with emotions much more powerful and dangerous than sympathy and pity. "How wrong you are, dearest Gillie. You're a grand girl. I've always thought so. There's a magnificence in you that you've always kept hidden. But I've seen it bloom in you these last days, and I couldn't look away." His arm came up around her shoulders to draw her in against his chest. "Any man would be proud to claim you. Why, if it weren't for Lettie—"

Julianna realized in astonishment where his thoughts were leading him and, turning abruptly away, broke their contact. Revelations of this sort were not at all what she wanted from him. "Come now, Alfred, you know you have never loved anyone but Lettie."

She took a step away, her eyes averted. "You and Lettie are the only two I could have turned to precisely because you are both so sensible. If I thought that my difficulties would in any way drive a wedge . . ." She let her words trail away as she took another step away.

Please take care, Alfred, she prayed silently. Your continued happiness depends on your good sense.

"Do you remember that you once turned me down when I was so reckless as to propose to you?" She looked back at him then with a conspiratorial smile. "I was all of seven and you were ten. How noble and gentle you were in your refusal. For, even then, you knew that you and Lettie were better suited in temperament than you and I would ever be. I cherished your kindness then, as I cherish your kindness now. But do let's keep our wits about us."

Alfred, facing a shock to his system as great as any in his life, wandered drunkenly in his thoughts for a moment before saying distractedly, "You're right, you're absolutely right. Didn't mean, didn't mean to imply . . ."

"I know." She nodded, still shaken herself. "Your support is more than I deserve, but I cherish it." She looked him directly in the face. "Shall we go in and see how Lettie is proceeding? I think I smell pies cooking."

Alfred looked at her most gratefully. "A capital idea. Capital." He frowned suddenly, remembering that he would have to face Lettie. What could he tell her? "About the other matter?"

Julianna came forward and slipped her arm familiarly through his. "You may tell Lettie that I have promised that you will be the first one I confide in when and if the time comes. After all, you are my nearest male kin in residence."

Mollified by her offer, he patted her hand lightly. "Allow me," he said, and bent to pick up her bonnet and shawl.

As they strolled forth from the garden, no one seeing them would have suspected that a dangerous moment had just been narrowly averted.

While the incident had been averted, that didn't quite eliminate Julianna's lingering sense of guilt. She had given in to the temptation to lean on Alfred when she should not have. Even if he had misunderstood the kind and extent of her need for his strength, she had been a little unfair to him. She saw that clearly now, and something else quite remarkable besides: how easy it had been to persuade a decent man's feelings in her direction. Her grandmother had told her she possessed such power, but she had not believed it, until now.

After all these years Alfred harbored secret feelings for her. Why had he never acted on them while he was free? Perhaps, because he knew as she always had, they weren't suited emotionally to withstand the minor rubs and annoyances that made up everyday married life. She needed more stimulation than his amiable personality would provide, while she would soon have driven him mad with talk of philosophy, business affairs, and politics.

What had nearly occurred just now was a minor aberration. She had once loved Alfred, but not with the wild madness that had made her open her heart and body to a man whom neither by name nor face she knew. Now that she had known such a love, she knew she would never be able to live with anything less.

The pang that began just below her heart was almost comforting. That was where she ached for her lost love, there and in every pulse point of her body.

Julianna regarded her cousins thoughtfully across the remains of their supper. In the distance, thunder growled like a caged beast yet moonlight slanted in through the oriels. "They say when men hear thunder on the left, the gods have something special to import."

Alfred stared moodily into his empty wine cup. "I hope the news has to do with the arrival of a new bottle of claret."

"Whose left?" Lettie asked, ignoring her husband who had been strangely reticent since noon. "I mean, how does one determine on whose left the thunder is heard? For instance, any sound that is on your left is on my right."

Julianna shrugged. "I suppose the news will be for me then."

"There you go again, speaking of things supernatural," Alfred mumbled. He raised slightly bloodshot eyes to her. "Lettie, do you know what Gillie told me today?" He didn't bother to glance at his wife, who leaned forward expectantly. "Gillie says that the marchioness talks to Blood Hall's ghosts and they in turn throw cannon shot at her. Hah! How's that for sport?"

"I believe I said thunderbolts," Julianna replied, and winked at her cousin.

"Oh, right, right. Thunderbolts," he corrected, his speech clearly slurred by his generous consumption of wine.

"You are too wozzled to make good company," Lettie said censoriously. "You make take your second bottle of claret, or port if you prefer, alone. We are retiring to the library. Gillie and I have things to discuss."

Contrary to every other evening before, Alfred didn't protest being left alone at the table. A stickler for convention, Lettie seemed to believe that traditions, such as leaving the men at the table, should not be amended for the sake of convenience, or loneliness. In fact, Julianna suspected, Lettie was trying to keep up appearances for the servants' sake. After all, there had been enough whispering and knowing glances exchanged among the cousins this past fortnight to move Mrs. Mead to inquire if Julianna was really as healthy as she claimed to be. As the ladies filed out, he merely rang the dinner bell to order more wine.

"Now then, what shall we do tonight? A game of cards, perhaps?" Lettie said brightly when they had seated themselves in the library.

"I'd rather read, if you don't mind," Julianna replied, picking up the volume she had left by the chair earlier in the day.

"No, certainly I don't mind." But Lettie's pouty expression said she did. "I know what we can do. Have you given any consideration to what you shall name . . ." She looked toward the closed doors then practically mouthed the words "your child."

Julianna looked up from her book. "Don't you think it's a bit premature?"

"Heavens, no. Alfred and I argued for months about the name of our first. Charlotte was three months old before we settled on her name. Now, let's see." She pursed her lips together and knit her brows. "Boys' names. It should be a name you're particularly fond of. What about Charles? Charles is a good manly name." Julianna shook her head. "Or Reginald. Reggie. Doesn't that sound dashing? So like that cavalry officer we met last summer. Or Ian, though it is a Scots name. Edwin? Barclay? Somerset? Ah, I have it. Nelson!"

Julianna regarded her cousin with a jaundiced eye over the tops of her spectacles. "Now that you've put forth the Christian name of every man you can remember who ever stood even one dance with me in the past five years, I hope I'll be allowed to return to my book."

Instead of blushing as Julianna expected her to, Lettie blanched and then her lower lip began to tremble. "You are so unhelpful. You do it just to spite me. Whyever did you send for me in the first place?"

"To be a comfort, not a spy," she answered forthrightly. "I don't know when Alfred will forgive me for putting him through the rigors of the afternoon. You shouldn't have put him in that position, Lettie. It was unfair to him."

"I know." Lettie sighed impatiently. "But you will be so stubborn."

"One of my less endearing traits," Julianna agreed. "Is that more thunder or was that a knock at the front door?"

"I didn't hear anything."

But a short while later, Mrs. Mead knocked and opened the library door. She looked quite agitated. "Beggin' your pardon, Lady Julianna, but there's a man here to see you."

"Who is it?"

Mrs. Mead glanced at Lady Cowper before she said, "He didn't give his name, my lady, but he said it was very urgent he see you."

Lettie bolted to her feet. "Oh, Gillie, suppose—"

The quelling glance Julianna gave her cousin stemmed her words. With deliberate movements, she closed her book and set it aside. "Very well, Mrs. Mead. Send him in."

The housekeeper's discomfort drew. "Said he won't go beyond the entry until he's certain you'll receive him."

The hair lifted on Julianna's nape. "Do I know him?"

Mrs. Mead bit her lip. "It ain't my place to say."

With that cryptic remark to spur her, Julianna moved impatiently toward the door. "Very well, let's see this mysterious guest. Lettie, you'd better fetch Alfred. If it's a miner, we may expect a bit of unpleasantness."

For once Julianna resisted removing her glasses in order to make a better impression on a stranger. If it was Rob Wheal, she wanted every moment of recognition to prepare herself for their encounter. If it was another of

the miners, she wanted to be able to recognize him again
on sight. As for Lettie's hope, she didn't give it a moment's thought. There was only one way her Friend came
into her life, and neither Mrs. Mead nor Lettie was likely
to be present.

She descended the stairs slowly but didn't see him until she reached the first landing. He stood in the entry, a
top hat held between his hands. She took in his attire in a
single inquisitive glance in order to judge his social position. He wore a dark-blue coat, the fabric good but the
cut not of the latest fashion. It pulled a little across the
shoulders as if it belonged to someone else, or perhaps
he had outgrown it. His dove-gray trousers were neat and
clean, as were his shoes. He had ridden here. He was
certainly not a miner, but neither was he dressed as a
gentleman. He wore no gloves and his cravat was black
instead of the more formal white required for evening.
But when he looked up at the sound of her quiet foot-
falls, she forgot her critical examination.

It was a remarkable face, so familiar yet completely
unidentifiable in that moment. His thick tawny hair was
streaked with lighter shades of ash and silver. A single
strand fell across his high, wide forehead, nearly touching one strong-defined dark brow. A bold blade of a nose
balanced well-spaced eyes, sharply angled cheekbones, a
wide, straight mouth with well-molded lips, a clean-
shaven square chin and jaw. His face was a veritable cat-
alog of favorable masculine features. Yet there was nothing commonplace or vacuous about the handsome face
turned up at her, his light eyes burning with a fierce,
bright flame. She had seen this face before. On the front
page of *The Northern Star.*

"How are you?" Julianna said a little nervously, coming to a halt two steps above the ground floor.

He smiled at her, suddenly making her wish that vanity had prevailed where her spectacles were concerned. "Don't you know me, my lady?"

The well-modulated voice, an educated . . . She began to tremble from some uncertain chord strummed by his words. Why was he looking at her like that, as if he knew her, knew all about her? "Perhaps, if you will tell me your name?"

The tenderness of his smile was like a razor, cutting deeply into her before she felt the prick of pain. "Earl Brown. Lord White. Jos Trevelyn. Which do you prefer?"

She knew without knowing, knew even before he spoke again. But she could not accept it. Her legs were carrying her backward, up the stairs down which she had so confidently come. She grasped the rail.

His expression changed to one of concern. "What's wrong, Julianna? Don't be afraid. I've come back for you." He took a few steps toward her, wielding a beautiful, bright smile to cut through her defenses.

"No. No, stay away from me." She heard the ragged plea in her whispered words as he advanced upon her. "Please, go away!" She was shouting now but she didn't care.

"Gillie? Lady Julianna!" A man's voice and then a woman's. "What's wrong down there?"

Julianna whipped her head around to find Lettie and Alfred descending the stairs toward her. "No. It's all right." She felt the muscles of her face form an awkward smile. "It's just the gardener. I'll take care of it."

She shot the man below her an angry glance. He had paused at the foot of the stairs, his hand resting on the carved figure of the knight errant. How inappropriate, she thought, and had the irrational urge to laugh. Alfred and Lettie were descending toward her. She felt trapped, penned in by reality and nightmare.

The man below her spoke to Alfred. "Good evening. My name is Adrian Lyngate."

"I am Lord Alfred Cowper, Lady Julianna's cousin. If you have any business in this house, you must direct it to me."

The man's expression altered to one of tenderness as he looked at Julianna. "If that is Lady Julianna's wish."

Julianna turned on him, too agitated to respond to the plea for understanding in his expressive eyes. "Don't do this. If you've any Christian charity in you you won't . . ."

"It is because of that charity I must." He looked at her so sweetly that she felt ill. Had any hangman ever looked as tenderly upon his victim? she wondered despairingly.

"Come up into the library, Mr. Lyngate," Alfred was saying, his voice full of officiousness. "It will provide privacy. Lettie, see to Lady Julianna. Gillie, go with Lettie."

Julianna didn't answer. *He* was moving toward her, mounting the steps slowly.

"I hate you."

Her voice was so soft she did not expect him to hear her, but he flinched, a quick downward sweep of his dark lashes over lambent blue eyes, and then he was past her, climbing the stairs to meet Alfred.

A moment later, a hand touched her shoulder from above. Even as she hunched away, Lettie's voice whispered near her ear. "Is he the one, Gillie? Oh, he is so handsome. A gentleman, surely."

Julianna looked up at her, her face stretching to the

limits of her smile even though her world was shredding before her eyes. "No, Lettie. He's the gardener."

Betrayal. Utter and complete betrayal.

Julianna sat in one wing chair before the fireplace of the Great Hall, staring eyes ablaze at the stranger who had completely destroyed her life.

"I think we are all in agreement then," Alfred was saying in closing. Never more in his element than he was now, he presided over what he hoped would be a tidy ending to an unpleasant fortnight's adventure. Unfortunately, displaying all the worst tendencies of men too seldom in power, he sounded pompous and self-congratulatory. "Dear little Gillie's to be wed. We've worked that out nicely between us, huh, Lyngate? The details will be sorted out by the marquess."

"That's quite clever of you, Alfred," Julianna said now, speaking for the first time since she had been sent for a quarter of an hour earlier. The men had been closeted for an hour and she did not yet know what they had said, only that Alfred had informed this stranger that she was with child and that the man named Lyngate claimed the child was his. So simple. For their purposes.

She rose to her feet. "I see that you gentlemen"—she sneered the word—"have gotten on like a house afire. There is just one small item that you've neglected to tackle. No one asked me what *I* think of the matter."

She had moved around behind her chair, feeling the need for solid protection between her and the man who called himself Adrian Lyngate, who stood beside the mantel. She pointed at him. "I can't say that I know you at all, but if I do then it must be as Jos Trevelyn. In that capacity, Jos Trevelyn, I call you a liar. You are not now nor were you ever my lover. I don't know who put you up to this cheap trick, but I suspect that the reason behind it was an attempt to discredit my family.

"And you!" She swung about on Alfred. "Don't you know what you've done? You've given away my secret to a member of the Chartist Union. A spy, Alfred, a man who will publish my shame so far and wide that I doubt a single South Sea Islander will be in ignorance of it within a month!"

She paused to catch her breath, but her wild expression kept her audience of three silent. "You!" She pointed again at Lyngate. "You have more than you came for. Just go away. The game is finished. You've won. I give you the victory. But know I shall hate you every day of the rest of my life. And, if one can haunt the dead, I intend to make your eternity as miserable as you've now made my life."

"Gillie, think what you're saying." Alfred stepped fearlessly into the fray to try to save his moment of glory. "Mr. Lyngate has said he will marry you. Think of the child."

Julianna rounded on him. "Have you taffy for brains, Alfred? Of course he agrees to wed me. He wants to humiliate the Kingsbloods. What better way than to force me into a marriage with a common gardener and revolutionary? Think of the ramifications that would have on Grandfather's career, to be linked by marriage to the Chartist cause?"

"Well . . . I don't . . ." Alfred began, directing a hurt look at Lyngate. "I suppose if what Gillie says is true, then it puts a different complexion on things."

As the three cousins stared at him, the stranger in their midst spoke for the first time. "I came here tonight to see Julianna. I should have insisted on speaking to her alone, but custom dictates—"

"Custom?" Julianna cried, fighting the persuasion of that so familiar voice. "What do you know of custom, or decency, or right? You may end this sham. You aren't the father of my child."

He sighed. "May we speak alone?"

"Certainly not!" She crossed her arms protectively across her chest. "There's nothing you can say to further humiliate me. You were never my lover."

"Then who was?" Lettie burst out, unable to contain herself a second longer.

Lyngate ignored her question. "Julianna, we must talk in private."

"No."

He looked down a moment, as if in defeat, but when he lifted his eyes a challenge burned brightly in those blue depths. "I filled your bed with roses one night. Another night I fed you cherry cordial to ward off a chill. You called me Friend, and I called you my love. Believe it, Gillie. It was so."

He was a stranger. She gazed on a stranger, surely. And yet he knew things no one else could know. And his voice. When she did not look at him, she knew who he was. So many nights she had listened to that deep, rich voice with its throbbing undertone of emotion. But no, she mustn't succumb to the temptation to be understanding. He had betrayed her. All the weeks while he had shared her bed, he had also taunted and baited her in the guise of the gardener Jos. To think of their encounters was to remember his smirking and his insolence. Now she understood its source. While he remained a stranger to her, he had known and must have found amusing her

pretense at propriety. After all, he had freely possessed
every intimate inch of her during the dark, wild nights of
their passion. The realization brought a hectic flush to
her cheeks.

She looked up at him again, at the stranger's face that
she could resist. "Jos Trevelyn has a wife. And a son."

He held himself as proudly as any lord, she thought,
illogically pleased and annoyed by this new knowledge of
him. "You need not be jealous. Tess is the wife of a dead
friend."

"How convenient a lie," she returned coldly. "I don't
doubt you never married her, but she didn't deny it when
I asked her if the child was yours. He looks like you."

"Blue eyes and fair hair prevail in certain districts. Jessie is my godson, nothing more or less."

Julianna turned and left them without a word.

"Well, well," Alfred murmured when she was gone.
Folding his hands behind his back, he attempted men-
tally to wade through the morass into which his neat and
tidy plans had sunk. The recent exchange of words between Julianna and Lyngate had made the future as clear
as bog water. "I suppose you can verify certain salient
facts, Mr. Lyngate, to wit, that you are not married?"

He inclined his head.

"And this name business, which is it? Are you Lyngate
or Trevelyn?"

"Both. You will have to ask Lady Julianna to make the
choice after we have spoken in private."

"She doesn't want to see you."

His gaze was determined but amused. "She will."

"How can you be so certain?" Lettie asked, and took
several steps toward him. "You have no idea how difficult
these last weeks have been for her. She's so strong and

proud. I'm glad you've had the good grace to step forward in this matter, but if I thought for one minute that you would hurt her in any way, I'd—well, I'd take a whip to you myself!"

This impassioned speech from a lady who barely reached his shoulder made Lyngate smile. "You must love her very much. Julianna is fortunate to have family who cares so much about her. She'll need your support awhile longer. But, I assure you, I intend to take care of her in the future. Now, if you will excuse me, I have other matters to attend to. I will return in the morning. Good evening."

When he was gone Alfred and Lettie faced one another with doubtful expressions.

"I don't know what to think," Lettie began.

"It's a havey-cavey business, my dear," Alfred replied.

"The gardener," she whispered faintly.

"Exactly," he responded.

"A handsome man, to be sure."

Alfred remained silent on that topic.

"A commoner."

"Of course."

"There will be a scandal."

"Precisely."

"Oh, my."

Chapter
Eighteen

She knew he had come.

The clock chimed the third time before her eyes opened, but he waited, silent, sitting in the dark at her bedside.

She did not speak. She had prayed for nearly a month for this night. She would ask no more of him than that he be there with her. The rest, the lies and deceit and confusion of the evening, were erased from her mind. The gardener Jos Trevelyn and the Chartist Adrian Lyngate did not exist for her. Nothing more was real to her than this moment and this man, her Friend. Fierce recognition and tender welcome rose up within her.

She lifted her arms to him, desire a fluttering, shy expectant need inside her.

He rose slowly from the chair, his steps making no sound as he approached the bed. And then his hand was upon her face, his fingers brushing back her hair and pushing it gently over and behind her ear. "My love."

She felt all the oppression and apprehensions of the last weeks purling back away from her. His strong fingers moved over the contours of her face and the doubts fell away. And then his lips were on hers. She knew then that her memory had distorted the singular beauty of his kiss.

Her arms went about his neck to bring him closer. His hands found her shoulders, framed them for a moment, and then slid past them to draw her up against his chest. She came to her knees on the bed and his hands moved again, one to the small of her back, the other lower down to gather her body softly to his. She felt his heat, reveled in his taste, inhaled his fragrance. The sensations seeped deep beneath her skin, proof of his physical presence flooding her spirit with joy. For weeks she had not dared dream that he would return. She had steeled her heart against loneliness and uncertainty and fear of the future without him. But now those disabling emotions were melting away as tears before the persuasion of his kisses and his caresses.

They shed his clothing together, four hands making the work quicker than two, and then he was sliding under the covers beside her. They came together quickly. Their time apart had been long, their need of confirmation made more urgent by the events of the last hours. He touched her down low where the gift of life had begun, and then he moved over her. She sighed in relief, weeping when he entered her, and knew a joy so sharp and intense that it was almost pain.

Later when the whirlwind of emotions had been spent in physical expression, she lay upon his chest, her ear pressed to the rhythm of his heartbeat, and knew that she had never been more at peace or secure in the world. It would not last. They had not yet exchanged more than murmurs of ecstasy. She dreaded that moment and so she put it out of her mind. In his arms, against his heart, surrounded by the circle of his body's warmth, she fell into a deep, carefree sleep.

* * *

Julianna woke slowly, reluctant to leave the deep contentment of her slumber. She stretched in lazy wonder, feeling different from how she had all the mornings before. And then she remembered why. Everything came back to her at once.

She sat up quickly, the sheet sliding to her waist as she reached for her spectacles. The room was bright, the drapes drawn to let in the strong sunlight of midmorning. She felt a vague unease as she looked toward the door. She had assumed that Mrs. Mead had been the one to open the windows, but she saw in surprise that a chair back had been wedged under the latch to prevent its opening.

Then she heard footsteps, the ring of them like boot heels on stone. Frowning, she looked toward the hearth. The sound seemed to come from there, but she was not prepared when a door-size panel in the wall beside the mantel swung open silently and without warning. She made a desperate attempt to pull the bedding up over herself but it was too late.

The stranger from the night before entered her bedroom, closing the secret panel behind him. He was dressed in the same blue jacket and gray trousers, but his cravat was missing and his shirt hung open, revealing the strong column of his throat. His hair was mussed. A light peppering of beard speckled his cheeks and chin. He carried a breakfast tray, which he set on the night table before turning to her.

The face that looked upon her was that of the Chartist lieutenant Adrian Lyngate, but when he spoke it was in the broad country syllables of Jos Trevelyn. "Be ye cold, Gillie? Ah mun a fire would no' go amiss."

She could think of nothing to say, even if she could

have managed her voice. A hidden door. A secret passage. That is the method he had used to come and go all those weeks without her understanding how it was accomplished.

He went to her armoire and removed a paisley shawl, which he brought back to the bed and slung about her shoulders. She shrank away but he did not try to hold or kiss her. Instead, after a quick burning glance, he turned away and went to stir the fire.

When it had caught to his satisfaction, he came back to the bed. "You should take better care of yourself, my lady. Now there's two for you to look after. You mustn't take a chill."

The voice of her nightly visitor. She leaned back weakly against her pillows. He was like a chameleon, ever-changing before her bewildered gaze. "Who are you?" she asked softly, filled with a renewed sense of confusion and wariness.

He watched misery and bewilderment change into apprehension in the spring-green gaze behind her spectacles but steeled himself against pity. That could not help them now. There were many things he had to say to her before he left her again. But first she had to be rational enough to take it all in. He reached for the teapot and poured her a cup, adding cream and sugar before he handed it to her. "Drink up, my lady. I may not be Mrs. Mead but I brew a decent cup."

She took the tea because it seemed easier to do so than to argue. When she had sipped a little of it, he took the cup and saucer from her and set them aside. Then he sat down on the edge of the bed beside her.

"My real name is Adrian Joshua Lyngate, third son of the Earl of Bleaklow. It sounds forbidding, and is. However, a moor-bred lady like you would appreciate the wild beauty of Derbyshire."

She averted her eyes for she could not think if she were looking at him. "Why did you change your name?"

"As I said, I'm the youngest son. Other than the title 'Honorable,' there was nothing my father had to offer me. Tobias will inherit the title. Christopher has become our politician. That left only a military career for me."

She looked up him. "You were a soldier?"

He shook his head. "Father balked at the cost of buying colors for a recalcitrant son." He smiled ruefully. "I was never any good at appearing properly humble. You must have realized that from the first."

She shied away from the intimate smile that urged her to join in his little joke about the character of Jos. "What did you do?"

"The usual. I went to college and stayed until they expelled me, drank away a small inheritance from my mother, gambled too deeply once too often and found myself arrested for debts. Father would have nothing to do with me, publicly denounced me as a disgrace. I was sentenced to the poorhouse."

His revelations astonished and tantalized her, as she suspected they were meant to. At least they kept her talking to him. "What did you do there?"

"Learned to fight and steal, a very useful education." He grinned at her like a little boy, boasting of his disreputable achievements.

"How did the youngest son of an earl sentenced to the poorhouse become Blood Hall's gardener?"

He turned his head to look toward the window. Looking at his profile shaped and shadowed by the morning light, she felt a swift pang of longing so great she clenched her fists.

After a moment he reached for her cup and drank down the rest of the contents in a long, thirsty gulp. When he was done he turned and swung his feet off the floor, moving back to lean against the headboard beside her. She inched away from him, keenly aware that she was naked beneath the covers, but he didn't move toward her, only stared straight ahead.

"The poorhouse is a remarkable place. Nowhere else will one meet characters of more variable abilities and virtues. There were farmers who had been turned off land their families had cultivated for generations, men imprisoned for debts amounting to no more than the price of your breakfast, and enough painters, writers, and poets to fill a university. Of course, the usual collection of cutpurses, thieves, whores, and flash Gents fallen on bad times rounded out the number."

He turned to her. "Do you know what I learned? The poor are mostly poor out of necessity . . . for the benefit of the nobility, people like you and me."

"That's not fair or entirely true," she responded.

"Oh, but I said it again and again, to whoever would listen." He smiled at her. "It was a novel speech, especially from the son of an earl, even the youngest son. Many thought so. By the time I had perfected it, I was sprung from debtor's prison by people who wanted me."

"Wanted you?"

"To make my speech to people outside the prison walls. I was put up before any rally or booth or platform where common men and women could hear 'an earl's son' plead their case for them. I made a little money. Then I began ending each little oration in the broad speech that every Derbyshire man could understand: 'Tha' ben't nowt a man t' stand agin' me!' "

The soft country speech made her tremble inside. This was truly Jos Trevelyn. "Is that when you joined the Chartists?"

"No." He turned back to stare at the opposite wall. "I soon grew bored. I was twenty-two. I went to Paris. I wanted to walk the streets that gave purpose to the likes of Voltaire and Rousseau. Don't laugh. I was quite distressingly earnest. The common battle against tyranny in politics! Dogma in religion! Prejudice! Hypocrisy in morals! These became my addiction and my cause. Nothing is so earnest as a young man with a mission."

She wondered why he was telling her all of this when it had nothing to do with the moment, or the fact that he had quietly reached out and covered her hand with his as it lay on the bed between them. She tried to draw away but he would not release her. She gave up. "How did you live?"

He chuckled. "A revolutionary speaker will always make a living in this century. A handsome young foreigner with the air of a gentleman and the manners of a noble can live even better."

She longed to ask him if he had lived that better life with women, but she refrained. She glanced at his profile, thinking that she had never seen so magnificent a man. "What brought you back to England?"

"I grew lonesome for home and eager to try out my speeches about what I believed to be the new order that must rise from men able to earn wages."

He turned to her, his strong features reflecting a little of the eagerness with which he spoke. "I'd come to understand that when men earn money instead of merely raising what they need to survive, they also gain a chance to advance in the world. Wages can be set aside, accumulated, invested. Factories and mills and mines were making possible a new life for the masses, but only if the wealth was fairly distributed."

"You *are* a revolutionary!" she exclaimed in faint alarm. He squeezed her hand, but the gesture was far from reassuring. It made her uncomfortably aware that they were only inches apart.

"I believe political power should be given to working men. The right to organize and strike and have differences fairly arbitrated are necessities for balance in this new economic system."

He spoke quietly but passionately and eloquently. Yet she had a far grimmer experience of this new reality. "Are blowing up mine engines and threatening the owners also fair tactics?"

He picked up her hand and brought it to his lips. The kiss was warm and dry. "I joined the Chartists to lend a creditable public face and an educated voice to the cause. But I'm only one man. The factions quickly became mixed, the distinctions blurred."

He stroked her hand with his lips and then lowered it to his lap. The backs of her fingers felt the shift of the heavy muscles of his thigh as he crossed his booted feet on the coverlet. "It was at about that time that I was also recruited by the government as a spy."

"A spy? Why?"

His blue gaze was shockingly sensual. "There are those who would prefer a revolution as bloody as anything France saw fifty years ago to quiet social reform. They infiltrated the Chartists, stirring up trouble. My recruiter convinced me of the necessity of policing our own quarters or losing credibility.

"I'd worked the coal mines in Yorkshire, to better understand what people endured. So when the government sent me to Devon to track down a troublemaker, I became a miner." He laughed, the sound of it better and finer than it had any right to be.

"What happened next?"

"Oh, I found my man, but he found me too." He shrugged. "I spoiled one plot but before I could catch him red-handed, someone informed on me." He spoke of intrigue, spying, and danger as easily as she might have spoken of a ride across the moors.

"You wrote the note to Jed Coleman?"

"I told Jed. We decided on the ruse of the letter so that he wouldn't be compromised if I was found out."

"Jed knew who you were?"

"Don't look so surprised. He's a good man."

"He let me believe that you—the informant—were dead!"

He smiled at her sense of outrage. "It was only a small lie. Wheal turned the tables on me, told some of his men I had tried to blow up the mine engine. They cornered me below then left me for dead. I managed to crawl out after dark. Knowing that Blood Hall was vacant, I came here." His gaze slid from hers. "I ate the cheese and drank the wines. I felt entitled to some amenities. After all, the marquess had recruited me."

"Grandfather?" He had shocked her yet again. "You should have told me who you were that first morning in the rose garden."

He looked at her with a mixture of sympathy and amusement. "Should I have said to you, 'By the way, your ladyship, the man you welcomed into your bed the night before was I, the new gardener and your grandfather's spy?' "

It was the first time he had admitted what she had always suspected. "That was a despicable thing to do!"

"I agree, as outrageous as it was for you to welcome me." His grin broadened. "But I forgave you, for you were nothing like what I expected in the light of day."

Julianna bit her lip. "I'm sorry you were disappointed."

He touched her cheek. "Not I. You. You didn't like the man I was. From the first you detested Jos Trevelyn. Admit it."

She lifted her chin. "You were rude."

"And you were supercilious!" He chuckled. "But that's not the reason I didn't tell you."

"Then why?"

"Because it might have put you in needless danger. Wheal thought I was dead or had run away. The job of gardener was an excuse to remain in the area until I had healed. Jed didn't even know I was here until he came to see you and we talked."

"Jed knows you've been living in this house with me?"

"It needn't be said, but he doesn't know that I was ever here alone with you like this."

Julianna looked away. This was too much to digest at once. "Yet you never changed your mind about telling me."

"Unfair, Gillie. More than once I tried to light the lamp, but you wouldn't allow it. That night when I drove you—madwoman that you are—home in the rain I nearly told you. You looked at me then and I thought, She knows, and she welcomes my kiss, but your courage failed you."

"Courage had nothing to do with it. I thought you were Jos Trevelyn."

"Did you, Gillie?" He sounded amused. "And still you wanted me to kiss you." She glared at him, her cheeks flaming. "What of the day of the mine cave-in? Do you deny that you wanted Jos Trevelyn that night as well?" She hunched her shoulders against his onslaught. "And again, on the hillside the day you cried out 'Please come back to me.' I thought you must have seen me. I climbed that hill faster than ever a man did, only to find you staring at me like I was something you'd scrape off your shoe."

Deep in her bones she knew he was right, but it only made her feel more misused and angry. "You tricked me. You used my feelings against me. You let me believe that Jos Trevelyn was a married man and still you tried to seduce me." She looked back as him defiantly. "Didn't you?"

He shrugged. "Perhaps I wanted a little revenge. You denied me everything but my manhood in this room. I had no name, no face, no past, no connection with the world."

"It was first at your choosing," she shot back.

"And it suited your needs to continue it," he returned with equal enmity.

"You left me!"

"You sent me away!"

For a moment they regarded one another warily, each angry, each feeling a little betrayed, each uncertain how to bridge the span that separated them.

"What will you do now?" she asked, her voice low.

"Oh," he said lightly, "I'm thinking of marrying. I'm twenty-eight, and it's time. It would please my father to see me settled. Marriage to a daughter of the aristocracy couldn't but sweeten matters between us."

Her cheeks grew hot. "Is that what you'll do, marry an aristocrat . . . to please your father?"

He looked at her in a way that made her forget to breathe. "Most certainly, but not to please my father. I picked her out the night she welcomed me into her arms and into her bed."

"It was a lie," she said softly, holding his gaze through the sheer power of will. "I pined for another man that night."

"No. You cried for a love you'd never known. You said those words aloud. You found it that night."

"I do not know the man you are."

"Then learn me."

She glanced away. "I'm not certain I want do."

He smiled. "Marry me and then decide."

"No."

"Gillie?"

"I thought you weren't coming back," she said carefully.

"Someone betrayed me to Wheal. The copy of *The Northern Star* you left behind on the moors told me the method by which I was found out. How did you come to possess it?"

"Someone slipped it under the door at Blood Hall. Mrs. Mead found it."

"Wheal recognized me the day of the cave-in. I thought he might have the day I saved you from his assault, but he was too angry to take a good look at me. Once he knew I was alive, everyone close to me was in danger. I had to watch and make certain that Tess and the children could get safely away."

Tess. Julianna caught her lower lip between her teeth. It was none of her business. She had no right to ask him about Tess. But she was a woman and could not keep silent. "What about Tess?"

"Tess?" He sounded genuinely surprised. "She's a woman of great spirit and no little courage." She could tell nothing of his feelings from his voice.

She turned to him in indignation on behalf of her own adversary. "She loves you."

He put his hand over hers again. His face was grave but his eyes were smiling. "Tess is the widow of Jesse Cox, my partner in the mines in Yorkshire. He died just before I came to Devon. I brought them with me because there was no one else to look after them. For convenience, we lied about being married. After I disappeared, to protect herself, she let people in Combe Martin believe that I had simply deserted her. When I was able I got word to her." He grinned. "She and the children moved into the cottage to get away from Wheal, but she'd already found herself a man."

"Someone she prefers to you?"

The incredulity on her face was balm for his pride. "Tess was rude to you the day you came looking for me because she was entertaining her man in the cottage and was afraid you'd see him and run her off. Have no fear, I'm yours for the taking."

He lifted his arms to embrace her but she gave him a shove that nearly knocked him off the bed. He recovered and caught both her hands in his. "I agree that it's a wonderful feeling, knowing that no one stands between us."

She tried to pull away but she only succeeded in loosening the shawl. It slid from her shoulders, exposing her naked breasts. He looked at her for a long while, his eyes roving slowly over her tousled mane and flushed face down over where a pink blush mantled the lush velvet skin of her full breasts, turning her nipples a deeper shade of rose. When he lifted his gaze to her face once more, his smile was devastatingly brilliant, at once bold and tender. "We've yet to make love in the light of day. But, alas, we've no time for it today."

"Insufferable man!" She snatched her hands back and fumbled for the shawl, but he caught her by the shoulders and drew her quickly in, kissing her long and deep. She did not struggle. She did not even whimper. The touching was somehow less daunting than the look of desire that she had seen gleaming a moment before in his bright blue eyes. Yet the familiar power of his kiss astonished her all the more for being delivered by a stranger. She shut her eyes, willing herself back into darkness. And with its return came her courage.

She lifted her hands, fingers spreading through the silky hair at his temples. She felt herself being turned and lowered until the mattress was at her back and he half lay over her. She welcomed the weight of his body. It made it easier to give in. From the beginning, she had not been fighting him but herself, and the fear that she had come to depend on him for an essential element in her happiness. For now, she gave up to the hot and heavy passion drumming in her blood and beating in her ears like the roar of the sea. To her surprise, he did not continue to make love to her. He suddenly broke off the kiss, his breath coming quick and hard in her ear. "You want me, Gillie, just as I want you. Have the courage to admit it."

For a moment she forgot to be angry. He was smiling down at her easily, confidently, supremely in command of himself and the situation. The fact that he knew his mind so completely when she had never been more confused seemed the most unfair thing of all. This wildness in her blood, this thumping of her heart under the pleasure of his touch, was something she could not master.

"I want you. I admit it," she said in a calm-shattered voice. *But I want the passion too,* she thought silently. *I want you to always look at me like you are now, and I don't know if you will.* How easily he had dismissed Tess's feelings. When he was certain of her as his wife, would he lose interest? The thought of him gazing at her with the same benign look of tolerance that Alfred sometimes revealed for Lettie made her heartsick.

She might be new to her role as temptress, but she understood instinctively that part of the charm she held for him was because she presented a challenge. Perhaps the only way to keep his interest was to flee and defy him. She shifted her head to look him in the eye. "I may have your child but I'll not have you."

"Those are hard words," he said mildly, his eyes lowering to the place where her shawl revealed the inner curves of her breasts. He moved a hand to rub one crescent with tantalizing slowness. "I could so easily change your mind, Gillie, but I haven't the time."

As he sat up, she caught up the edges of her shawl, tying them in a knot between her breasts. "Go away, Jos Adrian Lyngate Trevelyn, and let me be," she said in a tight voice.

He rose from the bed, a regretful smile on his face. "Ah must do so, m'luv. But fear ye no', Ah'll be back."

"You won't be welcome." She lifted her head, her green eyes defiant in her pale face. "I won't marry you."

He regarded her at length in silence. "You have nothing to fear from me. You never did."

Just then footsteps sounded in the hall outside her room and then a light rap sounded on her door. "Lady Julianna?" It was Mrs. Mead's voice.

Jos glanced at the door. "I'll be back."

"Don't bother!" she snapped at him as he walked toward the fireplace.

He ran a finger along the edge of a length of molding about eye level. A moment later the panel swung silently open. He winked at her. "Tonight!"

The three cousins eyed one another warily. "Leave us alone until I ring for you," Julianna told the servant who bore away the final dishes from their tea. "Now then," she began crisply. "We must talk."

"Yes, he came again," Lettie said, her alert gaze focused on Julianna.

She didn't pretend to misunderstand who it was Lettie referred to. She had been informed that Mr. Lyngate had come to the front door shortly before noon, and she had marveled at his audacity after having spent the night in her bed. "I refused to see him."

"We didn't." Lettie shot a conspiratorial glance at her husband. "Alfred and I agree that things must be settled quickly."

Julianna smoothed her napkin in her lap, struggling to keep her temper. "I won't have you talking about me behind my back. I'm not ill nor are my wits impaired. What did you say to him?"

"Now, Gillie, we felt it was our duty to make certain

that the man would not try to take advantage of your . . . condition."

She pinned him with a level gaze. "Thank you, Alfred, but I believe that any taking advantage of on his part has already been accomplished."

Alfred blushed furiously. "Really, Gillie! But, to the matter at hand. Lettie and I thought it prudent to inquire into his prospects. He is, after all, proposing to wed an earl's daughter."

"He's an earl's son," Julianna responded.

"How did you know?"

She lowered her gaze before his amazed stare. "I have my sources."

Disappointed to have been outmaneuvered in his hope to impress her with his keen inquiry, he moved on to his next point. "Then you know that he freely admits that he is impoverished."

"Younger sons usually are," she answered. "Now, if you are finished with your discussion—"

"Perhaps he's after your fortune," Lettie interrupted. "Alfred and I think it's a distinct possibility."

Julianna turned to Alfred. "Did you mention the matter to Mr. Lyngate?"

"Indeed I did!"

"And how did he reply?"

Alfred looked exceedingly uncomfortable as he said, "He suggested a marriage contract that will preclude him from touching your dowry or anything that you might inherit during your lifetime. After your death, all monies and land would go to your child." He pinkened. "Or children."

"How noble of him," Julianna said mockingly, but the

knowledge brought a softening to her eyes. Somehow she had known that would be his reply.

"Alfred says such a stipulation might not hold up in a court of law," Lettie cautioned. "Mr. Lyngate might change his mind after you are wed."

Julianna smiled. "Which worries you more, Cousin, that I will or won't wed him?"

"We're only trying to help you choose what is best for you."

"The great majority of people would agree that a woman in my position should wed, whatever the sacrifice, isn't that so, Alfred?"

Alfred puffed out his chest. "That would seem to answer the most immediate need."

"Yes, well, I'm not governed by majority rule. I don't wish to be wed, not to Adrian Lyngate or Jos Trevelyn, or the man by any other guise and name. Now, to my needs." She looked at each of them in turn. "You have been a great source of solace to me these last days. I love you both dearly. But it's time you went home."

Lord and Lady Cowper protested in one voice, "Absolutely not!"

Julianna raised a brow. "That's enough. I intend to remain in Devon until summer. In the meantime, I suppose I must write my parents. If they'll have me, I'll travel to India to have my child there."

Lettie's eyes begin to shine with tears. "What if they won't? There are your younger sisters to think of," she said gently.

"In that case, I'll ask Grandfather if I may remain here."

"The marquess will demand to know who the father is," Alfred reminded her.

"He won't learn it from me, or you. You swore your loyalty."

"*He* may tell them," Lettie ventured timidly. "I've seen his face when he talks about you, Gillie. Mr. Lyngate loves you."

"That changes nothing," Julianna said decisively. "Now, since dinner is over, I think you might want to begin your packing. Your children must be longing for the sight of you."

Lettie and Alfred exchanged glances, but neither of them felt able to withstand their cousin's willpower. "Very well, we'll go but we'll be back."

"But not before I send for you. Understood?"

Insulted to their shoe tips, both cousins gave her a tight-lipped nod.

Chapter Nineteen

※

"London? Why?"

He let his gaze wander lovingly over the figure of the lady confronting him. She had waited up for him but, unlike other nights, she had not gotten ready for bed but met him fully dressed. At least the half-dozen lit candles gave proof that she no longer needed darkness to welcome him. He wondered how many petticoats she wore under that yellow muslin gown. And her hair, how long would it take him to unbraid the coronet? "I must see someone in London," he replied.

"My grandfather?" Her voice was lifted in challenge.

"Since I have been in his employ in one fashion or another for nearly a year, he would seem to be the logical choice. You've nothing to fear in that."

She wanted to tell him how it was with her, why she did fear his association with her grandfather, how she knew it meant that it would make it so easy for the marquess to accept him as his grandson. Once he learned she was expecting a child, her grandfather would demand that she marry Adrian Lyngate.

The two men she loved best, deciding together her fate. The thought was intolerable precisely because it was so very tempting to let them do it. Then she would not be responsible for anything that happened afterward. If marrying turned out to be a mistake, she could always console herself with the rationalization that she had had no choice. She had spent her life being patient, sensible, and wise. But when she was with this man, as now, she no longer knew herself. She wasn't Lady Julianna, proper spinster; nor the Marquess of Ilfracombe's granddaughter; nor the selfsame independent being. When she was with him, she felt as strange and wild as the winds on the moors, as unpredictable as an Atlantic gale, as helpless as a rudderless boat on the tidal passion he evoked simply by entering a room. She didn't want anything to change that. Not even marriage.

She only said, "Promise me that you won't tell him about us."

He said nothing for a moment, his face somber. "No. I won't promise that. I'm not ashamed of us. If you are, then learn to live with it."

"I'm not—" She paused as a cocky grin broke the stern lines of his face. She lifted her chin. "Do what you must. My grandfather knows I'm not to be moved when I've made up my mind."

He smiled slightly. "It's time you learned the same about me. But I didn't come here for that. I came for a proper good-bye." He took a step toward her only to chuckle when she backed away. "What's this? For weeks I've been welcomed ever more readily each time I enter this room. But tonight you back away."

"Those nights you were welcomed as my Secret Friend. Tonight I see you are the Honorable Adrian Lyngate."

He chuckled. "Then blow out the candles, mistress, and let us to bed."

She shook her head. "No."

He came toward her, daring her by the power of his gaze to shy away. But she had no intention of simply succumbing to him. When he was within arm's length, he put his hands on her shoulders and drew her in against him. She was only a few inches shorter than he, no tiny thing to be tucked under his chin and pressed to his heart. He pulled her in close and put his cheek to hers. She smelled the clean scent of his skin and felt the warmth. His nearness made her want to touch with her lips the planes of his face, to kiss his cheeks and eyes, to feel the hot persuasion of his mouth on hers. She struggled against the almost irresistible urge and his arms tightened, bringing her whole body into alignment with his. She felt his heart beating against her breast. His hands were on her back, not to loosen her gown but simply to smooth caresses from her shoulders to her hips.

Surrounded by the heat of his body, communicating itself to her through their clothing, she felt a melting away of resistance and the awakening of her vulnerability to him. His very tenderness, his gentleness, was a more terrible weapon than any threat. She had been afraid of Rob Wheal's violence, but she hadn't known this feeling of utter surrender to a superior power. Wheal might have bested her for the moment, but he would never have won from her this desire for possession that this man wrought by a simple touch. And how he loved the challenge.

She caught back the sudden urge to laugh at herself. "You play unfairly at love, sir. I may swoon in your arms for an hour, but then you shall be gone, and I'll be free to do as I please."

He heard the implied threat and loosened his hold

enough to lean back and look at her. "Don't be foolish while I'm gone. If I thought you hadn't the sense to take care—"

"You needn't worry on my account," she answered. "I'm perfectly safe within these walls."

He nodded. "I believe that. If there should be trouble, send word to Jed Coleman." He looked at her, his pupils expanding to blot out the blue. "But in the end, it will be the same: You and I will be together."

"I'd not be so sure of it," she replied in a more subdued tone. How he looked at her, as if he wanted to swallow her whole!

"To prove to you my confidence, I'll not press you tonight." He released her.

She took a step away from him, unable to think clearly when he was within arm's reach. "When are you leaving?"

His smile quickened her pulse. "Miss me already?" He glanced deliberately at her bed before bringing his hot gaze back to hers. "I'd planned to spend the night but, unless you can provide me with a compelling reason, I'll be on my way."

"I wouldn't dream of delaying you," she said sweetly, and primly folded her arms across her chest. "Safe journey," she added in afterthought.

"With such sweet thoughts to comfort and warm me, the journey should pass like a dream," he said sourly. "How about a final kiss?"

"Absolutely not."

He reached into his coat pocket. "Ye try a man, lass," he said, falling back on the Derbyshire vernacular. "Ah mus' luv ye better'n ye deserve." He held out his fist, palm down. "Ah've nae violets for remembrance. This for the luv Ah bear ye."

Julianna held out an open hand and received a thin splash of gold into her palm. It was a bracelet, each of its dozens of links a tiny hollow heart. She looked up at him, a little amazed. "It's beautiful."

"I bought it for another lass but you may as well—" The look of hurt entered her face so quickly he regretted the tease even before it was complete. Yet her rejection had bruised his pride more than he was willing to admit to her.

He reached out and closed his fingers over hers. "That's a lie. I bought it for you when I took Tess back to Yorkshire." He took the chain from her palm and fastened it about her left wrist. "Now you may think of me as often as you look at it." He lifted her hand and kissed her wrist where the gold fell in a stream of hearts across her pulse. "Promise me you'll wear it?"

Julianna nodded, not trusting her voice.

"Then I'll be going."

He crossed the room and found the latch that opened the secret panel. "Wait!" He paused as the door swung open, turning an inquisitive glance on her, and she said, "I don't know what to call you."

He smiled at her. "Call me your love, Gillie." He shrugged. "What is easiest for you?"

"Jos?" It was more a question than an answer.

He laughed softly, exultantly. "Trevelyn is my mother's maiden name. She's a Cornish lass. Joshua was her father's name. So it is. Jos."

"Godspeed, Jos," Julianna called as he disappeared into the gloom of the passageway.

He ducked his head back into her room. "A week, maybe less, Gillie. Be careful." And then he was gone.

The next few days passed in a strange kind of lethargy for Julianna. After weeks of continuous house guests, she was suddenly bereft of company and things to do. The fact that a steady spring rain moved into Devonshire the morning after Jos's departure did nothing to bolster her spirits. Confined to the house, she finished several novels before the clouds broke and the morning of the fourth day dawned bright and promising.

After breakfast, and much against Mrs. Mead's wishes, Julianna had her pony hitched to a cart and set off over the moors. Because she was taking the cart out alone, she had loosened the tight lacing of her corset that would have restricted her movements and abandoned the heavy crinoline that would have weighed her down. As she rode along, the skirt flounces of her lavender-and-white striped gown floated about her like the huge petals of a flower.

In a few short days the earth had blossomed from a thin linting of green into a full carpet dotted here and there by clumps of heather and gorse. The moorland breeze bore in it the tang of earth and the brine of the sea. Cloud shadows chased themselves up and down the distant expanses while overhead the bright blue of the sky vied with the memory of Jos Lyngate's blue eyes for her attention.

Jos. He had been much on her mind these last days. She glanced down at her left wrist where the gold chain peeked out from beneath the lace of her sleeve as she handled the reins. He had bought the bracelet for her before Alfred informed him that she carried his child.

She realized that the moment she had time to think about it. He had asked her to wed him before he left the first time too. He loved her for herself, despite the deceit and make-believe that had formed the basis of their relationship until now. If only she could be certain that he would always feel the same. Yet she knew she couldn't. And that had kept her from saying yes to his proposal. But, perhaps when he returned . . .

Giving her pony its head, she sat back on the seat and removed her bonnet. She loved the feel of the wind on her cheeks and the sun on her head, but rarely indulged herself because the former chapped one's cheeks and the latter encouraged freckles.

She rode for hours with no general direction until she found herself within sight of the chimney stack of Little Hangman Mine. She paused before she reached the narrow path that led down toward the shore and the mine proper, not wanting to intrude upon a place that held frightening memories. She had told herself a dozen times that they wouldn't really have stoned her, that the tragedy of death had momentarily stirred them to a fury of grief. She was only a convenient target. But goose bumps lifted her skin as she remembered that dark afternoon, and she pulled a little roughly on the reins as she turned her cart away.

Only after she had made the complete circle did she see Rob Wheal. He was coming up the path toward her. She knew that she could have touched the pony with her whip and set him off at a pace that would have precluded their meeting, but she resented the thought of actually running from Wheal now that he'd seen her. Instead, she set the pony on the path toward him, intending simply to ride past him. But at the last minute Wheal put up his hand to hail her. As she hesitated she saw his hand move out as if he would grasp the pony's bridle. To prevent this, she reined in.

"Good day," she said with the regal tone she often used when confronted with an unpleasant task.

"Yer ladyship," he answered, and pulled his cap from his head. "A fine day for a little chat, I'm thinkin'."

She met his gaze unflinchingly. "If you want to discuss your work or conditions at the mine, you should speak with Mr. Coleman."

He shook his head but his eyes narrowed as his smile grew cunningly. "It's not about the mine, not that a lady would be knowin' anythin' about that." His contempt was barely disguised.

"Then what do you want?" She hoped her nervousness sounded like impatience.

He folded his arms lazily. "Due consideration."

"You're getting top wages."

"That's not what I'm talkin' about." He reached out and petted her pony's neck, but she sensed he was readying himself to prevent her from bolting. "I know thin's ye might find useful."

"Such as?"

"Such as that man ye got workin' for ye. Calls himself a gardener."

Julianna's brows lifted. "What of him?"

"I seen him close up the day o' the cave in. He ain't a gardener. He's a spy."

"I beg your pardon?" She hoped her bluff of ignorance would hold.

"He worked this mine till some o' the men ran 'im off."

She frowned. "Why would they do that?"

" 'Cause he's a troublemaker." He ran his ran over the pony's back and down over one flank, moving closer to her as he did so. "The mine cave-in were no accident. It were set by explosion."

"That's a dangerous accusation," she returned. "If you believe it why haven't you reported your suspicions to Jed Coleman or the magistrate before now? The accident is a month old."

"Aye, 'tis so." His eyes narrowed in calculation. "Only who'd believe a man like me against her ladyship's gardener?"

Just the way his said the last two words made her heart beat a little faster. "Your logic escapes me."

His grin turned sly. "I seen him hangin' around ye. I seen ye that day on the hill a few weeks back." His grin widened with lasciviousness. "I seen ye kiss him."

Julianna felt a chill run over her like a cloud passing before the sun. "You've a lewd mind and a troublemaker's eye for deception," she said contemptuously. "If you saw anything at all, then you saw him kiss me and me push him away. I fired him on the spot for the insult. He's not been at Blood Hall since. Ask anyone."

"I know what I seen," he maintained stubbornly. "And there's them as would wonder about a lady ridin' round the countryside with her gardener. Twice folks seen ye ride off after dark, just him and ye."

She felt a little sick at the lurid interpretation he presented. "I can tell tales too. For instance, a few weeks ago you accosted me on the lane after church."

He laughed. "Aye, ye tell that, after I've had me say, and we'll see who's believed." He big dirty hand began to caress the pony's flank once more, and the pony flicked his tail at him. "How come ye didn't tell on me when ye had the chance? Be it ye had a likin' for Rob Wheal?"

He looked at her bare head, at the open buttons at her throat, and at her bosom rising and falling under the strain of their encounter. "Mebbe I should've gone at ye another time. Mebbe 'twas only on account of yer kept man sneakin' about nearby that ye fought me. Was ye going to meet him then, to lay in the heather and lift yer skirts for Trevelyn's pleasure?" His mouth went slack. "Mebbe that should be me consideration, a bit o' yer pleasurin'."

She snatched up the whip and cracked it smartly over his head, but he had a moment to realize what she intended and flung himself out of her reach.

"That'll cost ye!" he cried, adding a curse behind the words when he'd righted himself. But he didn't draw close again and she knew she would be able to get away when the moment came. "Ye think ye'r so high and proud, an aristocrat. But ye weren't too proud to open the gardener's britches when the need rose up in ye. So ye'll be listenin' to what Rob Wheal says now."

She didn't want to hear another word but she had to know what his intentions were. "Why should I listen to you?"

"There're thin's ye don't know. Thin's I can tell ye. Like, Trevelyn's a troublemaker, for one. 'Twas him set to blow up the mine works last winter. Caught him at it."

He mustn't suspect that she had learned the truth from Jos. "Are you the one who reported the attempt to Mr. Coleman?"

He shrugged. "We like to take care o' thin's in our own way. Only Trevelyn turned up in yer pay." He eyes narrowed again. "I represent the Chartist cause in this part of Devon." Regaining his confidence, he set a fist on each hip. "The marquess ain't made himself clear on how he stands on unionization. How do we know he didn't hire Trevelyn to blow up the mine so he could blame it on union folk?"

Wheal's wild conjecture was the opposite of the truth, but, strangely enough, if Jos's spying for the marquess was ever made known, people might believe Wheal's version. "I'm listening."

He nodded. "That's better. Trevelyn's a known traitor, and there're those willin' to come forward and swear that he laid the powder that caused the explosion in the mine. How will it set with folks to know the marquess's granddaughter's consorted with a murderer? Might think to take matters into their own hands. Close down the mine, string up Trevelyn. Any number of thin's might happen of a night on the moors."

Julianna bit her lip. If she protested Jos's innocence, Wheal might realize she knew he was behind the attempts to close Little Hangman Mine. "Surely you've thought of a method to prevent that, Mr. Wheal."

He was grinning now, fully confident of himself and the situation. "I have at that."

But the sound of bootsteps ringing on the rocky ground made them both glance in the direction of the mine. Coming up the hill in the distance was a shift of workers returning home. Not wanting to be found in prolonged conversation with Wheal, Julianna turned quickly back to him and said, "Finish what you have to say."

He nodded. "First off, I want Jed Coleman's job. Being I'm in charge o' most o' the men already,"

"That's not my place to order. Jed works for the marquess. You'll have to see him about that arrangement."

Wheal scowled but he was smart enough to realize that she spoke the truth. "Ye'll know to put the word in for me when the time comes, then. Second, I want money to keep quiet about yer ponce."

The offensive word made Julianna flinch but she set her jaw against her anger. She needed time more than a release of her anger. "How much?"

"Two pounds a week."

"Two—but that's over a hundred pounds a year. It's not possible! I don't have access to that kind of money."

"That ain't my worry. Ye get it!" He looked over her shoulder as the footsteps neared. "I want two weeks' worth by the end o' the week. I'll leave word when and where 'tis to be paid." He tipped his cap and set off at a brisk pace down the lane.

Without looking back, Julianna whipped up her pony and set off in the opposite direction.

Wheal had had the last word, something she had not liked conceding to him. Nor did she like the fact that his half-truth and outright lies could stir up trouble or even danger for the two men she loved most, her grandfather and Jos.

She loved Jos. Why did that thought surprise her? She had loved the Friend who had come to be everything she needed and wanted in a man. Now that her lover had a name and a face and a past, it did not follow that anything important had changed. With that thought to keep her company, she hurried home.

When she reached Blood Hall she did not go directly into the house. Instead, she found herself walking toward the rose garden. She hadn't been there since the day she talked with Alfred, but now it seemed to beckon her as the only place where she could feel near Jos while he was more than a hundred miles away in London.

She found it difficult to open the gate. At first she thought it had somehow been bolted from the inside. Even after it gave under the full force of her weight, she felt as if something had resisted her entrance. Yet when she slipped inside there was nothing to warrant her feeling that she was not welcome. Instead, the sudden wonder and surprise of the garden in full bloom had never been more beguiling. She shut the gate and leaned back against it, reluctant to stir a single petal of the perfection arrayed before her.

Awash in spring sunshine, the colors bursting forth from every stalk, stem, and vine evoked the riotous display of a summer fair. Every hue of shrub rose—yellow, apricot, pink, red, and white—vied for the eye of the beholder. Whenever the eye might think to linger, the tease of something more beautiful drew it on. Pink oleander, china-blue plumbago, white and purple lilac bushes, borders of red geraniums, and the velvety indigo of hydrangea blossoms all provided a feast for the senses, filling the air with a mixture of summer scents. In cool corners, slender stems of lavender and pansies nodded among the lacework ferns. Retiring night-scented stocks, sweet meadow rue, Queen Anne's lace, thyme, rosemary, and forget-me-nots provided soft rain-washed color and country-garden scents.

In a nearby shaded bower, a tangle of wild roses and honeysuckle provided an oasis of fragrant exotica that drew Julianna to a stone bench dappled by sunshine. The bench was warm to the touch, its heat seeping through the layers of her petticoats to provide a sense of comfort and welcome that had been lacking before.

She spread out the skirts of her gown and, feeling very like a flower herself, removed her bonnet and gloves and turned her face up to the filtered sunlight.

But the mood of contentment did not last. There were too many troubles circling in the back of her mind that even the beauty of an enchanted garden could not dispel.

Each time she thought she could not sink lower into trouble, a new dilemma confronted her. She had never felt more alone, nor felt more keenly the distance that separated Blood Hall from London. Even if she wrote a plea for aid to her grandfather, it would take two or three days for it to reach London and as many for him to reply. A week. Could she hold Rob Wheal off for a week?

Revulsion shivered through her at the thought of how Wheal had looked at her, like a starved wolf that had spied prey at last. She detested the thought of him imagining her in Jos's arms, naked and sated from their lovemaking. It made it somehow tainted, wrong, ugly.

Wheal's threats were real. She could not forget the look on his face, the calculating shrewdness of it. Once she had not thought him smart enough to devise a subtle plot. Now she believed it. If he could, he would enjoy destroying her life and the Kingsbloods' public standing for purely malicious satisfaction of it. Yet if he possessed the wit to rise above his station in life, was there not a way she could use that to her advantage? Perhaps if she offered him something he thought never to have. But no, that was impossible. Only the marquess could offer Wheal the kind of position of authority that he craved. But it would take time to contact her grandfather and for him to decide on a plan of action. In the meantime, if she

could not think of a way to stall Wheal, she had no doubt
he would act immediately.

Then there was the other matter, the one she had yet
to tell her grandparents about. Even now, as she sat in
this garden, Jos might be meeting with her grandfather
to apprise him of the fact that, among other things, he
had seduced the marquess's granddaughter and, what's
more, had gotten her with child. How could she write her
grandfather about another trouble without mentioning
her own?

The idea of carrying a child was strangely unreal to
her. Other than the occasional moment of giddiness, she
felt no difference in herself beyond a slight soreness in
her breasts and the elusive sense of a filling low deep
down. Yet a night of joyous lovemaking with Jos had left
her feeling much the same. Her gowns still fit. Other
than Dr. McClintock's confirmation of her condition, she
would not yet have suspected the trap in which she was
caught. Even without Wheal's lurid tales, the result
would be enough to hurt her family's social position.
With child by the gardener. She was not ashamed of what
she had done, but neither would she be forced into marriage for propriety's sake. After all, marriage would not
protect Jos against Wheal's accusations. If the miners
found out Jos had been a spy in their midst, they might
not stop to consider that he had been hired to protect,
not harm, them.

"Where is my courage?" she murmured forlornly.
Generations of Kingsbloods had faced worse trials. Their
triumphs in the face of defeat were legendary. The story
of the captain and his lady was only the most revered.
The marchioness had recently told her of the scandal

that had nearly destroyed her even after she met the marquess. Yet she had survived it.

Julianna gazed about this quiet corner away from the cares of the world. It was said to be the captain and his lady's favorite place. The marchioness had talked confidently of lying in her husband's arms here and silently leaving the world behind. Why did she not feel their supreme confidence in themselves and the future, whatever it brought?

The drone of insects, the subtle whispering as leaf shifted over leaf, the warm sunshine, and the effects of her brisk ride on the moors combined to weight Julianna's lids. To drowse in the shade became a necessity, and she drifted off.

She had slept a long time. She knew it even before she opened her eyes. Sunlight no longer reached into the corner where she was. Her body felt heavy. And she was cold, so cold that in every limb she felt the tingling of her blood as numbness vied for mastery. She had slipped from the stone bench onto the flagstones, her head resting on one arm stretched along the seat.

She opened her eyes slowly, amazed to find a heavy gray mist had infiltrated the garden, draining away its color and heat. The vapor drifted in about her, its edges ruffled like the eddies of cross-currents. The air smelled of rain and clouds and the sharp tang of vegetable decay. Her face suddenly felt damp with dew. Blinking against the stark lack of color, she did not at first notice the changing shape of the drifting haze. But the curtain before her eyes was thinning, leaving behind drifting silvery flecks as the effluvium parted.

All of sudden she heard something. It was not a natural sound, like dripping water or the scrap of leaves on the paving stones. It was more than a sigh. A shiver of human breath released in deepest sorrow brushed her cheek. The touching reached down deep into her, alerting every human instinct for self-preservation. She was not alone.

The first distinct sob drove her to her feet. A human sound, a real moment of mortality that was not her own was almost comforting, yet frightening. She took a step toward the sound. It had come from the hedge row of yews that flanked the far wall. "Who's there? Are you hurt?"

The mist shifted, drifted across her face like veiling. She reached into her pocket for her spectacles but they weren't there. As she was about to turn back in search of them, the fog parted and she saw the indistinct figure of a young woman standing with her back to her.

She was tiny, no more than five feet, with an amazingly slender waist from which the yards of her gold silk skirt billowed out over a frame whose form was two hundred years old.

Julianna knew who it was even before the figure turned, revealing her perfect features and cascading tumble of pure gold curls. But the most astonishing thing of all was that Julianna could see imperfectly but clearly the shape of the yews through the figure. It was, indeed, a ghost.

More excited than frightened, she released her breath, unaware until that moment that she had been holding it. "Lady Kingsblood?"

She didn't know why she addressed the apparition, for surely ghosts didn't converse with humans, her grandmother's eccentricities aside.

But the figure held out her hand and opened her palm. A flame of silver-white light emerged.

Fascinated, Julianna approached, feeling as compelled to do so as if the figure had beckoned her. Only when she was a few feet away did she suddenly realize how dark the day had become. Beyond the perimeter of the flame the world had faded, turning as insubstantial as the darkness behind closed lids.

It was not until she was within touching distance of the magic flame that Julianna saw the lady's face with perfect clarity. The painting of her in the entry of Blood Hall had been done in the style popular during the years of the reign of Charles I. But the captain's lady—how strange that none ever mentioned her by name—was more beautiful than any flattering depiction could make her. The tender curve of cheek, delicately proportioned bones, the simple beauty of the lines of her brow and jaw seemed too pure for human demands. Yet Julianna never doubted that the apparition before her reflected an absolutely faithful rendition of the flesh-and-blood lady.

It was that very perfection that frightened her. "What do you want?" she asked quietly, hoping that she could not be heard beyond the garden wall.

The lady curled all but her forefinger inward. The hand that held the flame became an accusing finger. "You must help me. You sent him away! He must come back!"

There was no sound but Julianna heard the words like hammer blows against the inside of her skull. Anger buffeted her like a series of storm-driven waves. Hurt followed close behind it, a pain so acute Julianna felt her heart contract in empathy. "Who must come back?" she asked, her disquiet becoming alarm.

"My love and yours!" the spirit answered. "Death waits. And must be paid. I saved his life for you. Now you must repay the debt!"

Again the spirit's anger rushed over her like frigid waves and Julianna's flesh shrank against her bones. This was no malicious venting of rage. She understood instinctively that the anger was directed deliberately at her. "Whose death must I pay for? Is it Jos's?"

"You must cheat Death or we will be lost forever!"

Tears started in the spirit's eyes and, to her astonishment, Julianna felt them course in frigid rivulets down her own cheeks. "Forgive me," she whispered, good and truly frightened. "I didn't mean to disturb you. Tell me what to do to right things!"

But the spirit backed away, taking the light in the darkness with her.

"No! Wait!" Julianna started after her. "I need to know how to right my wrong."

For a moment the spirit stood perfectly still. Julianna strained for the sound of her voice within her mind, but it did not come. Instead, the lady curled her fingers over her palm, eclipsing the light and leaving Julianna in complete darkness.

It was then she heard the wind. It sounded at first like the distant rumble of the ocean as it rushed onto the beach. But gradually it rose in volume. Julianna remembered that she had heard this sound only once before, a night twenty years earlier when a vicious gale had battered the coast, uprooted trees, and destroyed homes.

Even as it gathered in the inky blackness about her, she turned and ran blindly for the gate. But the frenzy came too quickly. The wind shouldered her roughly side, knocking her to her knees. And then it was upon her, an

immense surf of noise and wind and dust. Like the
pounding of a thousand iron-shod hooves and the keening cry of a million lost souls, the icy fury stung her with
numbing cold.

Swamped by the sound and fury, she crawled along the
stone path until forced to stop and cover her head with
her arms as the churning, choking, shrieking darkness
enclosed her. The screaming was both in and of her.

And then there was nothing.

"My lady? My lady?"

Julianna heard her name being called from a great
distance. Between the words was a silence so complete
her ears rang with it.

She heard the creak of the gate and then Mrs. Mead's
startled "My lady!"

A moment later, warm human hands touched her
cheek and then the pulse in her throat. "Oh, my lady,"
she heard the housekeeper say. "What have you done to
yourself?"

Julianna opened her eyes to sunlight and the patch of
blue sky not blocked by Mrs. Mead bending over her as
she lay on the path. "Are you all right, my lady?" she
inquired anxiously.

"Yes. Fine." Julianna raised herself into a sitting position slowly, conscious of how her muscles and bones
moved to accomplish the task. She raised a hand to brush
the loosened hair from her eyes, and the scraped heel of
her palm left a streak of blood on her face.

"You've hurt yourself," Mrs. Mead exclaimed, reaching out to take Julianna's bleeding hand and wipe it
gently with a corner of her clean apron.

But Julianna felt no pain, only a numbness and confusion after her encounter with the apparition. "I must

have fallen asleep," she murmured through stiff lips, dazed to find that it was still afternoon.

"Why would you chose this place to rest in?" the housekeeper asked, glancing about. "It's run to rack and ruin since Jos left it."

Julianna blinked and looked about her. The profusion of color of moments—or perhaps hours—before was gone. There was only a confusion of overrun vines, untrimmed shrubs, and tangled canes of budless rose bushes. "Where are the flowers?" she asked in bewilderment as she gazed up into Mrs. Mead's face. "There were flowers. So many flowers."

Mrs. Mead helped her to her feet, saying in a soothing voice "Now don't you worry yourself about such things. 'Tis early days yet. The garden will come round. Wait and see."

Julianna's feet were as cold as ice blocks and she stumbled against the housekeeper when she tried to take a step.

"That's right," Mrs. Mead answered, putting an arm about Julianna's waist. "Let's go in now, my lady. 'Tis late. You missed your dinner. 'Tis teatime."

But only one thing was clear to Julianna. "I must find Jos. I have to talk to Jos."

"He's gone away," Mrs. Mead reminded her gently. "But we'll find another gardener, a better gardener."

Julianna pulled away from the woman. "No." She took a deep breath, remembering far more than she would ever tell the woman beside her. "No. I mean, I must send for Mr. Lyngate."

"You come inside with me," Mrs. Mead replied in a tone she'd use with a confused child. "Then when you're feeling better, you can send for anyone you please."

She gave a silent prayer of thanks when Julianna nodded and took the arm she offered in support. The last few weeks at Blood Hall had been the most confusing the housekeeper had ever lived through. She knew times were changing, and folks with it. Still, when gardeners changed their names and started walking through the front door bold as brass to visit the lady of the house, it was time to write the marquess.

"What's that you have, my lady?" she asked when she saw that Julianna was staring at her fist.

Julianna opened her hand and out fell a dozen rose petals as fresh as if they had just been plucked from a flower.

Chapter Twenty

KENSINGTON PARK, LONDON

The Honorable Adrian Joshua Lyngate was shown into a room that had been in the height of fashion half a century earlier. From a coved ceiling richly ornamented with graceful geometric designs, to the pale-blue damask wall covering, to the gilt settee and chairs, to the elegant tables specially designed by Morel, every detail of the Regency-style London town house had been beautifully realized.

"My lord marquess will be down directly," the butler said formally. Then with a slight bow he backed out of the room, pulling the door closed behind him.

Jos smiled as he observed himself in the mirror that hung over a commode. He was dressed for the city in a deep-blue frock coat, striped silk waistcoat, light-gray trousers, top hat, black silk neck cloth, gloves, and new boots. His hair had been trimmed but still brushed his collar as was the fashion. He looked for all the world like a young gentleman about town. Yet even a day ago he had not expected to be bowed into the salon of the Marquess of Ilfracombe, a favored and trusted member of

Queen Victoria's inner circle and renowned member of the House of Lords.

He had expected that the letter he had left with the marquess's aide at Parliament the day before would gain him a summons into the marquess's private chambers, but he was abashed to have received an invitation to Lord Kingsblood's home for tea. The invitation had caused him to spend the morning on Savile Row purchasing appropriate attire.

The salon doors opened suddenly, thrust apart by vigorous hands, and the Marquess of Ilfracombe entered. Tall and broad, he moved with the vitality of man a quarter of a century younger than his seventy-odd years. A handsome man whom time had treated well, he retained a full head of hair liberally threaded with silver. Dressed in black from his frock coat and trousers to his neck cloth, the marquess's only concession to vanity was a silk waistcoat of green-and-white check.

"Lyngate!" he intoned warmly, striding forth to shake the younger man's hand.

The grip Jos received made him wonder how anyone could be concerned for this man's health. "Good afternoon, my lord. I appreciate your taking the time to see me."

"Not at all." Maxwell Kingsblood took in the young man and his new attire in one shrewd glance. He had met Lyngate once before and that nearly a year ago, after the recommendation to recruit him for "a delicate matter" had come through other sources. At the time he had been more interested in the young man's ability to be useful to him. Now he had other, more personal concerns. Not that he was about to admit that his wife's frequent remarks concerning Julianna's reaction to any mention of Blood Hall's new "gardener" had piqued his curiosity. But it was at the back of the decision to entertain Lyngate where he could observe him without interference. Something was afoot. Regina was never wrong about these things. Julianna had become involved in one scandal over a man while he was absent from London. Her reputation might not withstand even the breath of gossip about another.

"I read your report with a great deal of interest, Lyngate. Yet I'm aware that there are things you left unwritten." He nodded in satisfaction. "Wish I could teach discretion to a few other young men but, alas, diplomacy is a part of character. Either a man has it or he has it not. Suppose you sit down while I pour us each a whiskey. Lady Regina will see we are shortly served tea but"—and he winked at Jos—"I've a thirst for something stronger."

"Fine." Jos stood politely while the marquess served them both from the cut-glass decanter set on a side table.

"Now then, have a seat," Maxwell said when he had handed Jos a glass.

For the next few minutes the two men were content to sip their whiskeys and exchange inconsequential chatter about the merits of north Devon. Jos quickly came to realize that the marquess had sorely missed spending the winter in his ancestral home and that doubtless he would not be spirited away from England again.

"Now to the matter at hand," Maxwell said suddenly. "Tell me everything that transpired from the moment you arrived in Devon last fall."

Their tea was served and consumed before Jos drew to a conclusion. "It's now my belief, my lord, that Wheal acts alone. The talk of unions is only a lever by which he hopes to raise his own personal desire for recognition.

I've worked beside him. He's a natural miner, smart, has a way with men. With an education, he might have risen quickly through the ranks to be one of your best men."

"But because he never received the education I offer to the children of every man who works for me, he's capable only of making trouble," the marquess mused.

"He's cunning."

"The young and hungry are always the most dangerous. Add cunning to it and there are bound to be difficulties. Somehow we must find a way to thwart him."

"My thoughts exactly, my lord. But I must bring to your attention a more pressing matter." He met the marquess's thoughtful gaze. "You've a traitor in your ranks. Someone who knew I was a spy. I've been to Leeds and talked with the editor of *The Northern Star*. I'm satisfied that they did not deliberately seek to harm me by publishing my picture. Yet the timing was suspicious. That leads me to consider other possibilities."

"Such as?" the marquess prompted mildly.

Jos rose to his feet, thrusting his hands into his trouser pockets. "I don't excuse myself for the poor showing I've made. I should have been more wary. The information about blowing up the mine engine came to me so easily I never thought to question the reason why. Now I know it was a trap." He turned sharply to the marquess. "I failed you, my lord. I feel ten kinds of a fool for allowing myself to be caught so easily."

"Not at all. I highly esteem your abilities." Maxwell stared up into the serious face of the young man confronting him. The first time they'd met, Lyngate had been thin and pale from his months in the mines. Now he didn't appear to have spent the last months recovering from a near-death beating. There he stood: tall, brown from his work out-of-doors, and muscular. Even in his city best there was something alert and urgent about him, something that would never allow him to lead the easy life of a town toff. That Lyngate was impatient with his shortcomings was a measure of his integrity. Something in Maxwell responded to that physical need for action. He had been very like that at this man's age. Time had mellowed the urgency but not the need.

"You won't come right out and say so but you think I have a spy in my office. Whom do you suppose it might be?"

Jos smiled easily, impressed that the marquess took his hint so quickly. "You overrate my abilities if you think I can answer that question."

"It's not so strange as you might first suppose. You don't know the players by name but you must have an opinion of some sort."

Jos frowned. He had come to several conclusions on his journey from Devon, but he hadn't been certain that the marquess would appreciate his opinion. "How many men knew of my purpose in Devon?"

"Three," the marquess replied, his cheeks rounding in the amusement his mouth did not yet share.

"The first would be yourself, the second would be your aide." Jos suddenly smiled. "The culprit must be the third man."

"Why the third man? Surely my aide is better informed?"

"Perhaps, but he knows your lordship's thinking in matters so well that he couldn't be persuaded to act against you. He can rise higher by remaining with you. I do not know who the third man is, but I would guess that he does not share your full confidence. He is a political necessity, perhaps?"

The marquess's lips parted in a genuine smile. "I like you, Lyngate. We think alike. You are correct. My spy is a fellow member of Parliament whom necessity required that I take into my confidence." He paused thoughtfully. "He's about to learn that my confidences aren't to be mistreated, but that is not your concern. So, what shall we do now?"

"We?" Jos registered surprise. "I don't think you need my services any longer. You must be satisfied that the Chartists are not, of themselves, dangerous subversives."

"I am. I'm thinking of other matters." Maxwell reached for his teacup, affecting a casual manner. "What will you do now?"

Now it was Jos's turn to be amused. "Oh, I don't know, my lord. A bit of this, a little of that." He subsided back into his chair. "I'm thinking of marrying."

The marquess's cup never reached his lips. "Marriage? Isn't this sudden? I understand the widow's a handsome woman but—"

Jos's startled glance stopped him. "How many spies did you have in Devon?"

Maxwell chuckled. "Besides you? Only my mine foreman."

"Jed told you about Tess? Didn't trust me, was that it?"

Though the younger man retained his careless tone, Maxwell knew that he was suddenly very angry. "It wasn't a matter of trust. I seldom employ men I don't trust, and never when there's much at stake. Jed mentioned the woman because he thought she and the children might make things more difficult for you. After Jed thought you were dead, he wrote me wanting to know what to do about them."

"That was considerate of him," Jos answered, but the knowledge that he had been watched still smarted. "It's not Tess I'm thinking of marrying. It wasn't like that between us. She has gone back to Yorkshire."

The marquess understood that though Lyngate might never have promised her more than what he had given, the woman must have held out hopes of capturing so handsome and vigorous a man. Poor Tess. "Well, in that case, if you've no special lady chosen for the role of bride, I'd like to offer you a position in the government. You've shown yourself to possess the two skills I most admire: a level head and the ability to reason."

Jos smiled at the older man, more touched than he would admit. "I thank you for the offer, my lord, but you'd best hear the rest of my plans. You may wish to change your mind."

Maxwell chuckled. "I doubt that. But tell me your plans. Perhaps I can dissuade you from them."

"You may very likely try, at that."

When Maxwell's shrewd glance met the frank blue gaze directed at him, he felt a force of personality seldom met in his lifetime. He had underestimated this young man at their first meeting. He would never do so again.

"The plan is personal but it concerns you." Jos came to his feet slowly. "I'd like your permission to marry Lady Julianna."

Maxwell thought he was prepared for every eventuality, but that one caught him with a surprise that made his heart pound a bit faster. He knew that surprise registered on his face before he could mask it, but his tone was bland as he said, "Suppose you begin by telling me how and when you met my granddaughter."

Jos thought it best to omit the truth, that they had met when he sneaked into her bedroom and she had opened her arms and taken him into her bed without even knowing his name. "We met when she came to Devon in February."

"She met you as Blood Hall's gardener?" The amazement had not quite left Maxwell's face. At Lyngate's nod he chuckled. "Gad, I knew the girl had democratic tendencies but . . ."

"We can't all be marquesses," Jos said lightly, but the fire of battle was barely banked in his gaze. "Nor famous beauties."

Maxwell grew thoughtful, rubbing his chin with a forefinger. "Julianna's not the usual aristocrat's daughter. She can be difficult, but it's because she's strong and bright, and possessed of a sharp tongue." He glanced at the young man standing above him. "It's proved a hazard to many a man's too high opinion of himself." Lyngate's answering chuckle was oddly reassuring. "So she's laid her sharp tongue across your pride."

"Flailed me to the quick the first morning." Jos smiled fondly at the memory. "She found my manner excessively arrogant and uncouth . . . for a gardener."

Maxwell could well imagine she did, for there was a natural arrogance in Lyngate that would not long remain hidden in any situation. "Do sit down, Lyngate. There's no reason to make melodrama of the matter."

As the young man took his seat, the marquess's mind took flight in quick calculation that made his extemporized speeches in Parliament famous. His dear sweet Gillie. He had been forced to watch in a kind of helpless vexation while she had been mishandled through two London Seasons. Regina had done her best but Julianna was nothing if not stubborn. She so badly needed a strong man, but one with the sense to give her her head most times. Was Lyngate that confident in himself? Even so, how would they live, or had Lyngate given more consideration to that than his bride? The time had come to test the young man's mettle. "What can you offer her?"

"Little at present," Jos admitted, "but I've prospects."

"I'll just bet you do." Maxwell suddenly thumped the arm of his chair. "Lord, but you've got nerve! But if you think I'll be brought into your scheme then you'd best recalculate. Julianna has a small inheritance put by for her as a dowry, but it won't long keep you in style. As for what you've no doubt heard I've promised her, that depends upon the stipulation that I approve of her marriage. I doubt I can be persuaded to approve of a man who'd spy on and betray men who trusted and respected him."

Jos was prepared for each of the marquess's objections but the last thrust, the one that called into account his integrity, cut him in an unexpected way. Even so, his gaze remained cool, the strong lines of his face impassive. "Just so we understand one another. I am ruthless in pursuit of what I desire. I desire Lady Julianna. She's old enough to know her own mind. We don't need even her parents' blessing in the matter, though it would go easier for her if we had it. But we'll live without it, and your generous dowry."

"You seem admirably confident," Maxwell observed. "I wonder what Julianna would say about the prospect of wedding a rascal from debtor's prison."

"She knows," Jos answered shortly but in grudging admiration for how well informed the marquess seemed to be.

"And still she would wed you?" The marquess's skepticism showed plainly on his handsome face. "Is she that besotted with your devilishly handsome face?"

"I cannot speak for her," Jos answered coolly. "I can tell you my feelings. I love her, simply and completely."

"Then I must hear Julianna's version, and soon. She must come to London at once."

"Whatever you say, my lord, but I must tell you that it's in our best interest that we marry quickly."

"Is it, indeed?" Maxwell thundered, his orator's voice rising to the occasion of his anger. "How so?"

Jos's expression darkened, his nostrils flaring slightly with some emotion the marquess could not guess at. "Lady Julianna carries my child."

The words were spoken so low Maxwell had to let them play back in his mind before he understood them. "You bastard," he said low, the power of his rage more terrible for being controlled.

"I love her."

Maxwell held the young man's stare, undecided whether to curse or praise him for the impudence of those words. "It would seem you've managed affairs to your liking thus far. So I'm moved to wonder why you expected to add my blessing to your match."

"I'm not a man who enjoys deceit." Though a muscle jumped in his jaw, Jos didn't elaborate on the slur that the marquess had just made against his character. "We've been a bit hasty, perhaps. The devil will no doubt have his due in the matter, but that's between us. I came to ask for your blessing because I need your help." The marquess's continued amazement reached a new level as Lyngate suddenly blushed. "She refuses to wed me."

"She won't—" Maxwell shook his head. "I must be getting old. Things were simpler in my day."

"Were they?" Amusement infused Jos's expression once more. "I've heard rumors that you wed a lady once accused of murdering her first husband. You must have loved her very much to have been led by your heart rather than appearances."

Touché, my boy, Maxwell thought. He could remember like it was yesterday: the terrible, wonderful, frightening joys of love. The doubts and impracticalities had been nothing compared to the wildfire passion of his desire for Regina. Did this man feel as much for Julianna? He hoped so. Julianna had waited a long time for love. But how to bring them together if she was not certain? A child. *A great-grandchild!* God's grace! He was living too long!

"What reason does she give for refusing to marry you?"

Jos's smile was rueful. "She says we're strangers."

"Does she, by God! Very intimate strangers for all that." He made a steeple of his fingers and rested his chin upon them. "I don't as a rule become embroiled in another man's private folly. My children married where they would, God bless them. But Gillie has my heart, as you must know, you young rapscallion! I'll not have her hurt again."

"Again? Who's hurt again?"

Both gentlemen sprang to their feet, startled to hear a lady's low-pitched voice in the room.

Lady Regina stood in the doorway, a vision in gold and white. She came quickly into the room, smiling first at her husband and then at the handsome young stranger with him. "Good afternoon, gentlemen. I'm sorry to disturb you but Molly thought you might like a fresh pot of tea." She paused beside her husband to prompt him with a significant glance.

"Regina dear, may I present the Honorable Adrian Lyngate. Mr. Lyngate, my wife, the Marchioness of Ilfracombe."

"Delighted, my lady," Jos said as he took her extended hand.

"How charmingly you do that," Regina said as he saluted her hand. "Maxwell never was any good at saluting hands. I told him the continentals have all the charm. English lads are too brusque and boisterous for such manners. But I see I must amend my general opinion." As she spoke she deposited the pot of tea she had brought in on the tray and then settled herself between the two men. "Now who exactly are you, Mr. Lyngate, aside from the man who would marry my granddaughter?"

She had turned her enormous green eyes on him so quickly Jos didn't have time to dissemble. "Blood Hall's gardener."

Lady Regina turned her elegant head toward her husband. "Did I not tell you? And I hadn't yet seen him."

"You've been listening at keyholes again," Maxwell grumbled.

"Of course," she answered sweetly. "It's the only sure way I know to deprive the servants of the opportunity. But I missed a good deal of it. You lied to me about the time of the interview." She turned back to Jos with a perfectly disarming smile. "My husband thinks I'm much too inquisitive for my own good. He's usually right. Now, be so good as to begin again at the beginning, Mr. Lyngate."

A little bewildered by her velvet-fist approach, Jos looked to the marquess for a clue as to how to proceed, but the man was staring moodily at a point in the distance. Given little choice, Jos repeated the essentials.

When he was done, Lady Regina was staring moodily at a distant point, approximating her husband's posture and expression.

"Well, do let's hear a woman's point of view," Maxwell said after a bit of prolonged silence.

Lady Regina touched a hand to her snowy white hair, piled most becomingly upon her head. "Are you aware, Mr. Lyngate, that Julianna was subjected to a most unpleasant experience at the hands of a London gentleman just before she retired to Blood Hall?"

Wary now, Jos said, "I was aware that she was unhappy."

"Ah." Lady Regina's extraordinary green gaze came to rest on him. "You should know the rest. I'm told the Duke of Montrose paid particular attention to my granddaughter beginning at a house party during the Christmas holidays. Afterward he continued to visit her here in London, in this very house. It was properly done, of course."

"Of course," Jos echoed.

"However, it seems that a previous commitment on the duke's part resulted in his being forced to withdrew from Julianna's company. In short, he married elsewhere."

"Not every romance produces wedding vows," Jos said neutrally.

"So true," Regina said wistfully. "But it was the manner of the duke's withdrawal that leaves one dissatisfied. Money is so often involved in disgraceful behavior. He was looking to marry well—few would blame him—yet he chose a rather unpleasant method to achieve his aims." She paused to gaze significantly at Jos. "He romanced a lady in the fall but her father would not give his consent. Yet as the duke moved on to Julianna, he'd left behind a 'token' of his affection for the previous lady that came embarrassingly to fruition."

"You don't say?" Maxwell exclaimed. "You never told me that!"

Lady Regina patted her husband's large hand. "I just found out the whole this morning. You know how Lady Wyndyme must be the first with all news. The Countess of Montrose gave birth last week in Paris. The babe's premature but hardly five months so."

"I see." Jos sat grimly a moment, stricken anew by the outward similarities of the duke's ruthless use of seduction to marry a fortune and his own situation. Perhaps Julianna thought herself trapped by the child she carried. Perhaps she thought he had used her as the duke had used his now lady wife for his own purposes. Damn! If only he had stopped to think. She had told him the story months ago, but it did not mean anything to him until now.

He rose abruptly to his feet. "I thank you for your time, my lord, my lady. You've given me much to think over."

Maxwell rose to his feet. "Don't act until we've talked again, Lyngate. I won't have Julianna forced into something she does not want."

"Then we are in agreement," Jos answered, and shook the hand offered him.

"If you love her, you'll find a way to convince her of it," Lady Regina offered with an encouraging smile. When he was gone she turned to her husband. "I like him. He's perfect for her!"

"You like all handsome young men with good manners," Maxwell groused, but he curved an arm about her waist to bring her closer to him. "What a tangle."

She turned in his arm and snaked her own about his neck. "I predict that we'll waltz at their wedding within a month."

Maxwell gazed down fondly into his wife's face, seeing the young girl of twenty-one that he had met and wed. "They'll be no happier than we, Genna. I wish them half so much."

Regina submitted to the wonder of his kiss, grateful that time had not mellowed its power.

"When did you receive this?" Jos looked across the desktop at the marquess.

"The letter came this morning." The marquess's tone was grim. "I blame Jed for giving the money to her, but he did right to let me know about it. Why do you suppose Julianna wanted the money?"

For a moment Jos's heart had contracted in sorrow. She was running away, of course, just as she had threatened she might. But then his gaze lowered again to the amount that Julianna had borrowed from the Little Hangman mining offices. "Four pounds won't take her very far," he murmured.

"My thoughts exactly," Maxwell answered. "I don't think she's running away. Julianna's got more backbone than that. It's for something else. Why does that disturb me?"

Jos was experiencing the same sense of unease. "I can't say but I intend to find out."

"Wait a bit," Maxwell said as Jos rose from his chair. "Let's think about it. What does four pounds represent to you?"

"The price of three pairs of trousers," Jos responded, beginning to pace slowly. "A presentable pair of boots. Nearly two months' wages for a farming family of seven. A month's wages for a highly skilled miner."

"Ha!" Maxwell held up a finger. "I think you're nearing the truth. That's a good deal of money to a miner."

Jos paused. "Blackmail, do you mean?"

"Or something near it. Perhaps Julianna got into her head some idea of placating the miners. I don't like it. You shouldn't have left her behind."

Jos's jaw tightened. "She didn't want to come to London. She didn't want anyone else to know about us, and the truth is, I hoped we would work it out ourselves before we told her family."

"This letter was written two days ago. God knows what Julianna's got up to in that amount of time. Someone must take her in hand."

Jos smiled grimly. "I don't think anyone will ever have Julianna in hand. Nor would I want it that way."

Maxwell eyed him dispassionately. "So long as you know it." He cleared his throat. "I may have been short with you yesterday."

"No more than I deserved," Jos answered.

"That goes without saying."

The two men held one another's level gaze a moment, neither man elaborating on his thoughts, but a subtle understanding was reached between them.

"I'll take care of her, my lord," Jos said at last, the

faintest glimmer of a smile edging into his concern. "I'll elope with her to Gretna Green, if need be, for I want us decently wed before the end of the month."

Maxwell didn't reply to this, only thought that he hoped Lyngate would be able to bring Julianna around to his way of thinking without an elopement because he was rather looking forward to waltzing at her wedding.

Chapter Twenty-one

❧

Julianna gazed down at the small boy standing barefoot in Blood Hall's entry. He was small and ragged, thin and so pale he looked like a ghost. But the black eyes in his sharp-featured face gleamed with cunning—malice? Or fear? She could not decide. "Would you repeat what you've just said?"

"Me da sa' to brin' his first lot to the new mine shaft on Sunday afternoon. Or else."

"Is your father Rob Wheal?"

"Aye."

Poor child, she thought. "What is your name?

"Pike."

"How old are you, Pike?"

He dropped his eyes and tried to dig a dirty toe into the slate floor. "Da said no' to talk to ye, else he'd wallop me."

"Very well. You needn't talk to me." Julianna did not make the mistake of touching him as she might another child. She recognized the look in his eyes, after all, for she felt the same in his father's presence. It was fear. "If you go around to the kitchen door, my housekeeper will give you something to eat."

He looked up at her, hunger plain in his eyes, but he

didn't reply. "Your father need not ever know," she added with a brief smile.

That was all the encouragement he needed. He scooted out of the door as if his father were already in pursuit.

"Sunday," Julianna murmured as she closed the door on the dark of late evening. Tomorrow was Sunday. She had waited several days for Wheal to contact her, but she supposed he had to work out the logistics himself. But why did he want her to go to the mine? The mine was closed on Sunday, yet there were dozens of desolate places on the moors where they would not have been observed. She did not like mines. After the cave-in in the spring, she had thought she would never go near one again. Perhaps he had sensed her horror of the place that day and wanted to intimidate her further. Well, he was not the only one with methods of intimidation.

She went upstairs quickly, locking her bedroom door behind herself. When she had lit a lamp, she pulled a sack out from under her bed and opened it. Inside it were four pounds sterling and one of her grandfather's dueling pistols. She did not trust Wheal not to try to take advantage of her again. Once she had paid the blackmail, she would be even more in debt to him. This time she would be ready for him.

She sat on the bed and began very carefully to load the pistol.

Julianna made her way down the narrow path, leaving the pony cart tethered at the top of the headland cliff. The day had grown late, the sun a huge glowing cinder hanging a few inches above the horizon, as she descended to the sand. It was the only way to reach the new entrance, called an *adit,* to the mine that had been opened not too far above the shoreline.

She had nearly not come. She had waited all afternoon in sweaty anxiety, hoping that something, anything, would occur to prevent the necessity of doing this. But finally her courage had returned and she had set out. Now to keep it from failing again, she concentrated on the day and not the task before her.

The air was salty and clean. High on the cliff above stood the Little Hangman Mine engine house. Ahead of her in the distance was Combe Martin, the whitewashed walls of the village glowing gold and peach in the setting sunlight. Above her head gulls drifted closer, their shrill cries as compelling as any street vendor's. But she had not brought crumbs for the gulls; nor was she out for her own pleasure.

After a few minutes she glanced toward the opening to the mine, dug since the cave-in to allow men new access to the area that had been sealed off. She did not see Wheal or any indication that he had been here. The only traces in the smooth sand were being made by her footsteps. She was very late. Perhaps he had grown tired of waiting and left.

Finally she began climbing up away from the sand and into the furze growing on higher ground. As she lifted the edges of her cape with one hand, she was careful to keep her other hand hidden beneath. She only wanted to frighten Wheal enough so that he would think twice about opening his mouth to the other miners. Once Jos returned, she was certain he would know how to handle Wheal. But he was not here now, and she had only her own wits to aid her.

Yet as she drew ever nearer to the dark cave of the

mine shaft, she could only wrestle with the urge to flee from the appointment ahead.

He stepped out of the shadow of the mine mouth when she was within ten feet of the entrance. Beneath his miner's hat, his hateful face had a wide grin on it. "So ye thought better'n not t' come." He placed a hand palm-flat against the side of the entrance and leaned his weight on it. "Well, where is it?"

Julianna lifted her chin. He would get nothing from her but a piece of her mind. She was not afraid of what he might say about her, but she had to prevent him from spreading lies about Jos and the Kingsblood family or disaster would surely follow for all of them.

"I came to tell you that I won't pay you!" She flung the words at him and saw him straighten, his face darkening with fury.

"Ye don't know Rob Wheal if ye think I'd let ye get away with that." He moved toward her slowly. "Ye and me, we had a deal."

"You threatened me," she retorted. "I promised you nothing."

"Two pounds a week, ye promised!" He sounded like a thwarted child but she wasn't deceived. He was tall and strong and very angry.

"Stay away from me if you care for your life," she said, taking a backward step.

"Nae, I don't think I will," he said, beginning to grin again. "One way t'other, I'll get me due. If there be no silver there's always a kiss and cuddle to be had."

He rushed at her. She was ready and whipped her pistol free, pointing it at him. He stopped short, surprise making his expression ludicrous. "It's loaded," she warned, "and I know how to use it."

"Now ye don't want to do that." His voice sounded placating but she could see in the sunset's reflected light that he was furious. "All I want is me due, promised fair and square. Ye won't kill a man for his enterprising ways."

Julianna calculated the moment and then delivered her final dangerous threat. "I can see that you're locked up for tampering with the mine. I know that you, not Jos, set that first explosion." She glanced beyond him into the mine interior. "What were you doing in there just now?"

He looked back over his shoulder and then at her. "Why don't ye come in and see?" His smile turned sly. "Mebbe there be a nice surprise inside for them as comin' to work on the morrow."

"Even you aren't that stupid," she responded.

His face drained of color. "That's what ye think, do ye? Rob Wheal's stupid! A no-account 'cause he ain't o' yer class!" He came toward her then, uncaring in his rage that she pointed a pistol at him. "Ye London slut! Think I can't do ye fine? Ye've a bit o' liken' for me else ye'd not o' come! Come here!"

Julianna lurched away, for suddenly she knew she could not shoot an unarmed man. She gained the furze ahead of him but then he was on her so quickly that they collided and the force of it sent them both sprawling. The impact of his weight knocked the breath from her. The pistol fell from her nerveless fingers as her lungs spasmed painfully to draw in air.

Stunned, she lay inert while he scrambled off her and then yanked her to her feet. And then his arms were about her and his mouth engulfed hers, shutting off desperately needed air. His hands were everywhere, on her back, her bodice, kneading her hips. She fought madly with fists and feet, but darkness rushed over her as consciousness began to fail. When he released her, she sagged bonelessly to the ground.

"That's better," she heard him say, his voice almost drowned by the roaring in her ears. And then he was lifting her again and she couldn't stop him or even see him through the thick fog of her half-fainting state.

"Better get inside lest someone come along and see us," he said thickly against her ear. "Then we'll see, Lady High-and-Mighty, what ye're made of."

She felt like a rag doll in his arms. He carried her quickly and easily through the adit and into the darkness beyond. He went a long way in, his iron boot heels ringing confidently on the hard surface of the dug-out cliff. The shaft floor sloped gently downward so that the last of the sunlight shone brightly on the ceiling at the far end. He stopped once, leaning her up against the cold surface of the mine wall while he put a match to the candles stuck into the brim of his miner's hat. Any attempt to flee was useless, for he had her by one arm the entire time.

When he lifted her again, she decided to conserve her slowly returning strength. She had lost her spectacles and pistol when she fell. If someone came past the mine, he would be certain to notice them and the footsteps in the sand, she told herself, buying courage with the slimmest coins of hope.

Her fear had almost subsided when suddenly he let her slide from his arms and she found not solid ground beneath her feet but space. He was lowering her down a narrow shaft sunk into the floor of the main entrance.

With a scream, she grabbed his sleeve. "No! Please, no!"

"So ye like me a bit better now, do ye?" he teased as she clutched frantically at him. "Ye'll have a chance to show me properly once we're out o' sight," he said, and tore her hands free.

Her free fall into blackness lasted only a second, but the terror of the moment far outweighed the measure of time. As she gained her footing in the dank, cold space, she heard footsteps and then saw the candlelight as Wheal lowered himself in after her. It was not a long fall, she saw that now. The drop was a mere nine feet into the bottom of the second shaft. A tall man might easily jump and grab hold of the rim. But Rob was turning to her, his face a terrifying mask of sharp yellow light and black shadows cast by the candle on his hat brim.

"Now ye can grab me again and see what it's like t' hold a real man."

She did not back up because there was nowhere to go. Three walls gleamed wetly in the light of his pitiful small candle. Where the open end of the shaft behind him led she could not see. It must go deeper into the hillside and away from the light and air of the day. She swallowed and wiped a thick curtain of hair from her face. Her bonnet was gone. "I have money," she said, hating the weakness in her voice. "I can pay you."

"Oh, ye'll do that," he answered, greatly enjoying her discomfort. "But I want else besides silver."

She backed away from his grinning jack-o'-lantern face in spite of her resolve. Suddenly she was up to her ankles in water. Distracted, she looked down. "Why is it so wet? Aren't the pumps working?"

He glanced down too. "There be an underground stream 'twixt this level and the main mine beneath." His engineer's mind set in gear, he continued to talk. "Hear that hiss? 'Tis the stream in these walls. Work's been stopped here till 'tis made certain the water won't break through." He threw out his arms. "Come here, lass. 'Tis dry up behind me. Don't want t' ruin yer fancy dress, now do ye?"

Julianna took another step backward. "Stay away from me. You can't think you'll get away free. You'll be arrested!"

He nodded. "That's as may be. But mebbe when we're done, ye'll no want anyone to know."

She took one more desperate step back and felt icy water swirl up to her calves. "I took precautions. I wrote a note."

His eyes widened. "Ye lie. Ye'd want none to know ye'd come t' meet the likes o' me."

It was true. At the last minute she had decided not to leave a note—but he would not know that. "I did it because I thought you might try to harm me." She waded in the water, feeling the strong current running past her ankles. "If I'm not back before nightfall, they'll know where to come looking for me and who to blame if I'm hurt." She plumbed desperately her pocket until the bundle of coins came free. "Here!" she cried, tossing the handkerchief at him. "Four pounds. Take it and leave me alone!"

He caught it up handily. "I knew ye'd come round." He glanced at the small bundle, his fingers feeling through the linen for the exact shape and number of coins therein, then his eyes came hungrily back to her. "Ye done right by Rob Wheal, so he'll do right by ye. Ye keep yer sweet secrets a bit longer, Lady High-and-Mighty. There'll come a time when ye'll be seekin' me out. Yer ponce won't be back, ye can be certain o' that! He's naught but a coward."

He swung away so quickly and her relief was so great, she failed to anticipate what his next move might be. But he jumped up and caught the rim of the hole in one hand. Possessed of a strength she could never match, he lifted himself up to where he could grab hold of the rim with his other hand and slowly began heaving himself up and out of the hole, taking the candlelight on his hat with him.

"No! Wait!" Julianna rushed at him, catching him by the lower legs with both arms. "Don't leave me down here!"

"Dammit!" she heard him mutter. "Let go, woman!" He tried to kick her away, but she had locked her arms too tightly about him to give him any room. "Let me go!"

Panicked beyond reason, she hung on grimly. The thought of being left in the overwhelming darkness was worse than even his threat of abuse.

They both heard it at the same moment—a deep groan inside the walls of the hillside.

For a space of seconds the silence was so absolute Julianna could hear the drip of water somewhere in the distant darkness and her own heart thumping erratically within her chest. And then they heard it again, the sound of shifting rock.

The floor gave way beneath her feet. With a scream of fright Julianna felt her weight suddenly transferred to Wheal's legs. The unexpected jerk of a hundred plus pounds on his ankles caught him off balance and his grip slipped.

They fell together, her high-pitched scream and his

hoarse cry piercing the blackness of the cave's eternal night.

The water was numbingly cold as it closed over them, but Julianna would not let go of the man she hated. She found his belt and hung on. Like one double-bodied being they were swept along in the current, rising to the top like flotsam, choking in the rumbling darkness, rising and falling repeatedly.

So this is how I die, she thought in dazed surprise as the water carried her along. *Down a mine. Alone. Without telling him I love him. Unfair! Unfair! Jos! Our child! Please forgive me!*

"What the devil do you mean she didn't come back last night?"

Mrs. Mead cowered before the angry expression of Blood Hall's erstwhile gardener and tried to adjust her thinking. He had handed her a letter from the marquess saying that he was to be treated as an honored guest. He certainly looked and sounded like a gentleman. Son of an earl? Well, well.

"Her ladyship went out with the pony cart about four o'clock yesterday afternoon. Said she had someone to see. I didn't ask who or where. You know her ladyship's moods. When she didn't come home at dark, me and Tom went out to look for her, but where's a body to look when the one that's lost could be anywhere?"

Jos regarded her grimly. "Has she said anything in the last days about needing to see someone in Combe Martin or Ilfracombe? Did she act nervous, frightened, secretive?"

"Well, now, sir, she's been some distracted these last weeks." Mrs. Mead didn't quite hide her disapproval as she said, "You came as a bit of a shock to our young lady, what with your changed name and manners, and all."

Jos smiled and said cryptically, "There are more shocks to come. But first we must find her."

He paused and pushed his hands impatiently through his hair. The marquess had hired the coach that had driven him straight through from London to Blood Hall without pausing except to change horses. Having a marquess for a relative might prove useful. He had made the journey in little more than twenty-four hours, but he felt as if he had ridden the entire way tied to the back of a mule. Yet none of that mattered now. Julianna was missing. "We must organize a search party. Have Tom send out to the mine for volunteers. I'll pay twice the daily wage."

"That should bring more than a few," Mrs. Mead answered.

"Good. Now hurry. Someone may have seen her pony cart yesterday or this morning."

"Where are you going?" Mrs. Mead asked in surprise as he started up the main stairway, taking two steps at a time.

"To Lady Julianna's room," he called back over his shoulder.

"Well!" the housekeeper said, clucking her tongue as she went out to deliver Mr. Lyngate's message to her husband.

Jos went through the entire contents of the room in a methodical fashion, searching for any clue as to what had been in her mind when she left here the day before. The one thing he had not let himself consider was the idea that Julianna might have taken the money she had borrowed from the miners' wages in order to pay some quack to rid her of the child. Surely she would not do that. There must be some other reason she had disappeared. The clue he finally discovered disturbed him more than he expected. Under her bed was a leather-tooled case that contained a pair of dueling pistols. One was missing.

"Gillie, Gillie," he murmured as he touched the empty space with trembling fingers. She had gone off to do something foolish, something dangerous. What could it be? And whom did it involve?

"Wheal!" He shot to his feet.

He had reached the first landing before he heard voices and looked down to find Jed Coleman in the entry with two other men.

"Jos!" Jed hailed. "One of my men found her ladyship's pony cart up on the headland above Little Hangman Mine this morning."

Jos ran down the last steps. "Where is she?"

"We ain't seen her ladyship," one of the other men answered. "Thought she'd be here."

Jos's face seemed to turn to stone. "No, she's not been seen since yesterday afternoon. We've got to find her. She may have been thrown from the cart and injured. Or she may have been taken by force." His gaze swung to Jed. "When is the last time you saw Wheal?"

"He didn't come to work this morning, if that's what you want to know," Jed answered grimly. The two men's gazes met in silent understanding.

"Have you checked the mine?" Jos asked impatiently.

"The mine's being worked on every level. There was a minor slide during the night but nothing serious. If Wheal or Lady Julianna were holed up in there, they'd have been found by now."

"Then we'll begin a search. Every cottage between here and Ilfracombe should be checked. I suspect Wheal's kidnapped Lady Julianna. Yet he can't have gotten far. Someone must have seen something."

Jed nodded and ushered the other two men out.

No one saw the bleak look that came into Jos's face or the moment when fear spasmed his expression. "God, Gillie! If he's hurt you or the babe . . ."

But he couldn't think of that, only of finding her. Otherwise he would go mad.

Julianna awakened with a sense of unreality. No dream had ever been more opaque, no nightmare more complete. Pain radiated from the base of her skull outward along the nerves of her body. The endless sounds still reverberated inside her mind. Someone was moaning, softly so as not to wake the dead. Was it her, or someone else?

The dead.

Her eyelids snapped back. She felt them move but that was the only sense of reality in the inky black air surrounding her. She felt tears leaking out of her again. Always tears and more tears. Useless. Unnecessary. She was already wet to the bone. So much water. She lay in a puddle. The general numbness of her body was better than the pain that had preceded it. The water was a faint hiss now. The tidal thrust that had lifted and tossed her now lay below the rock beneath where she sprawled.

Wheal had saved her!

Even in the free-fall into the black abyss he had not given up to the mindless terror of the moment. He had found a shelf of rock as the surging water carried them along, and grabbed hold, dragging her nearly inert body with his onto the narrow precipice. The water had churned about them and then sped on toward the new avenue that had been opened by the rock slide. Wheal had held on to her, cursing her, damning her, yet holding her against the drag of the unseen currents. Finally the flood had ebbed.

Canny as a fox, sure-footed at a goat, he had moved through the impenetrable gloom with the instincts of a cat. She understood then why men admired him. He had a fearlessness of the dark and danger that instinctively she knew was unmatched. She had waded along behind him, her fingers clenched on his thick belt. She had not liked him any better, but her admiration had known no bounds. Her grandfather had once said it took ability and guts to work a mine. Wheal had both.

They had begun to walk, wading in thigh-high water. He had known the way, even without a light or marker. He didn't speak to her again. She had known that his every ounce of concentration had been bent upon their survival. When the faint glow at the top of the shaft had appeared suddenly, it had seemed like a miracle. Then she had realized he must have seen it long before she. It was the opening down which he had lowered her.

This time he had boosted her up first, his crude curses bullying her when her battered body failed to heed his commands to climb. He had pushed and shoved, taken indecent advantage of her by thrusting his hands under her skirt and boldly caressing her thighs and buttocks. And finally she had begun to climb.

The sun had set. The light inside the main shaft had turned to dusky shades of lavender and green. He had come up quickly behind her, his ugly face a sight she had never thought she would be glad to see. He had been

bleeding in several places. His hands were raw. Half his
shirt was gone and a long track of skin was missing from
one shoulder, but he had bounded to his feet like a
schoolboy who had survived a prank.

"Come on then, Lady High-and-Mighty," he had said
cheerfully, and reached into his pocket to produce the
soggy handkerchief with the coins. "Got what I come
for."

But she had had no strength left. She had tried to rise
but pain stabbed down through her ankle so that she
cried out.

He had moved a few feet ahead of her, jeering at her
for not following him. And then disaster.

The earth had moved. She had seen Wheal's eyes
bulge and then he had run toward the exit. It had happened so quickly she didn't have a chance to scream. The
second rock slide had been as deafening as the thunder
of the stream had been. Wheal had disappeared into that
fall.

Then it was over, except for the choking dust and ringing in her ears and the terror of knowing that she had
been buried.

Julianna closed her eyes. It was better with her eyes
closed, for then she had a little control over the blackness by which she was swallowed.

Time passed. Lots of time, interrupted by half-waking
weeping fits and piercing cold, and pain.

They would find her. Wheal had gotten away. She told
herself that a hundred times. They would come and dig
her out. All she had to do was lie there and wait. She
would be freed. And then Jos would be there, and she
would tell him the words she had withheld from him,

words he deserved. And then she would never leave him again.

She slept again and awakened. There was something new in the darkness with her. The roaring in her head had subsided. There were sounds outside herself. The flat rhythmic *chink, chink, chink* were the sounds of someone digging.

She sat up and began crawling on her hands and knees toward the place she remembered as the blocked entrance. Her knees beneath her skirts were sore, but she didn't care as she scrambled through the gloom. Finally she found the slope of stones that blocked her path. She began frantically to claw at them, crying out and calling to the men who surely were working to free her.

The smaller stones fell away easily before her digging. The sound of their shifting heartened her. Wheal had gotten free and brought men to help free her. The dirty bit of fabric came under her hand as she dug. She tugged at it and it came free with a small spill of stones. It was knotted in one corner, the shape of four sterling pieces pushed against the material.

She dropped it. But as she started to dig again, she touched another shape. With a howl of horror she scuttled away from the thing she had felt but could not see: a cold human hand.

She drew herself up into a tight ball and waited for the terror to subside. But its talons had sunk too deeply.

Wheal was dead.

No one was digging for her.

As she leaned her body back against the wall, she realized that the sounds she was hearing came from behind her, from one of the old mine shafts. It must be day. Men were working but they did not know she lay just a few feet away, a solid wall of stone between them.

She might well die before they discovered her. The terror scored down deep and she went with it, her last thought not for herself but for Jos. Once she had rejected love for fear of losing it. Now she knew that in her selfishness she had committed a greater error. Nothing could be worse than to die having never shared that love while she had the chance.

She slept and she dreamed.

She was in the rose garden, not the place she remembered but the garden as it had been when she saw it last, barren of blossoms, wild and tangled, choking on itself. The darkness held an oppression never before felt. And then she understood. She knew what it was. Death stalked the garden.

The presence was neither shrouded nor disguised in some mortal terror from the grave. There was only a brilliant void in the depths of the darkness, an absence of being so complete that starlight seemed too vivid for the eye after gazing upon it.

"What do you want?"

The presence moved languidly, emptiness sliding over an infinity of shadows. But finally she saw something take shape in the far corner of the garden.

Two figures pale as candle wax entered the garden. She knew them, the captain and his lady. They bent over a man lying prostrate on the flagstones.

Even as she tried to turn away, a stronger force compelled Julianna to move closer and see what she feared to look upon. As she neared them she seemed to feel the man's failing pulse as her own, hear his shallow too-rapid breaths as hers, until finally she saw the red sea foam of pain break over his white lips. He was dying.

"Jos!" she whispered brokenly.

She heard the words of the figures bending over him as sighs in her mind. *Death has come for him. We must not interfere. Very well. But he will be on your conscience.*

They lifted him then and carried him between them out of the garden. And then she knew. They had saved his life.

The debt must be paid.

She heard, no, felt the declaration as a riff of pain across her heart. And again she understood. The spirits had cheated Death of its prey. But not for long. Even if Jos lived a hundred years, the moment would come again.

She turned back to the void. "We are mortal," she whispered. "You will have your due."

The balance must be made.

"And so it will. Who escapes you?"

A life for a life.

And then she knew she was awake again, lying in the mine. She might die here, lone, afraid, and helpless. Had the apparition of the captain's lady appeared to warn her that Death stalked her life? These last weeks she had been afraid of losing the keen edge of passion to the dull predictability of daily life. How paltry a concern that now seemed when the desire to face the uncertainties of life with Jos was all that stood between her and hopelessness. Life with Jos, whatever its form, was all that she now wanted.

Suddenly she did not feel so helpless, or so alone. She had Jos's love and the promise of their child with her in this place. Love affirmed life. She had only begun to understand that. And nothing, not even Death, would defeat her.

"Not yet!" she shouted, and heard the words reecho in the sealed chamber. "Not today. I defy you in the name of love!"

Even as she closed her eyes, the scintillating blackness seemed to fold in on itself, leaving behind only ordinary darkness.

Jos rode through the gates of Blood Hall at dusk, his face drawn with fatigue and disappointment, and the urgent sense of time running out. With the help of half a dozen men, he had combed the moorlands of the area in search of Julianna and Wheal, but no one had seen either of them. Not even Wheal's wife would say where she thought he might have gone. Jos sensed that she was holding back but that she was also more afraid of Wheal than she was of the marquess's representative.

Jos pulled up short as he saw Mrs. Mead rush out the front door, but then he saw the look of expectancy on her face. He shook his head and dismounted. Too weary to eat and afraid he would drink himself into a stupor if he chose liquor, he turned away from the house and headed without conscious thought toward the rose garden. He had begun to think of it as a sanctuary from the outside world long before Julianna entered his life. He needed that reassurance now, somewhere where he could think in peace. Something was missing in the puzzle of Gillie's disappearance. What was it?

The extent of the disarray surprised him when he opened the gate. Even in the dim light of dusk, he could easily see that the garden had been battered by what seemed to have been gale-force winds. One short month ago he had left it in perfect order. Now chaos ruled. Picking his way carefully through the debris, he moved to the center of the garden, watching and listening for any familiar sound. There was none.

"I know you're about," he said softly. "I need your help. Lady Julianna's disappeared and we've no way to discover her whereabouts. For pity's sake, help me!"

The silence was stunning. The gloom of the garden's shadows was without a single thread of mystery. Ordinary. Something had changed. He had never been a superstitious man, but life or his imagination had taught him differently these last months. Perhaps he had saved his own life. He did not think so. There had been voices in the dark, hands helping him when he could not see, feeding him when he could not lift his head. Dreams? Perhaps. Delirium? Possibly. But now the silence of this prosaic place contained in it the unnerving sense of absence. How could there be this feeling of loss unless there had once been a presence?

"Fool!" He turned on his heel. He was snatching at straws. Worry and weariness were making him behave absurdly.

But as he took a step toward the gate, something moved at the edge of his vision. He did not feel a touch, the sensation was much too light for that. He did not turn around. But he moved his right hand with a suddenness that caught the unseen intruder by surprise. The surprise was shared. Jos had half expected to trap nothing but ether. Instead, he had caught the thin, bony shape of a wrist in his hard fingers.

He held it in a merciless grip as he dragged the bundle attached to it about to face him. What he hauled before him was the face and shape of small, dirty boy. "Well?"

he demanded, too tired and worried to be even-tempered. "What do you have to say for yourself before I break your neck!"

The bellow of rage reduced the boy instantly to abject terror. "Don't murder me, sir! Please!"

Jos had no intention of any such thing, but the disappointment was so acute he continued to grip the boy's wrist. "Who the devil are you?" He shook the boy by the arm when he refused to speak. "Your name, damn you!"

"Pike."

"Pike," Jos repeated, his rage subsiding as he gazed down at the thin bag of bones and skin that made up the child before him. "What are you doing here? And don't tell me your purpose was to steal from me. You might have waited weeks for the opportunity."

The boy looked at him with round eyes, his mouth puckered in obstinancy, but when Jos raised his hand threateningly he burst out, "I'm runnin' away!"

Jos lowered his hand. "From who?"

"Me da."

With a pricking along his spine, Jos knew before he asked. "Who's your father?" The boy lowered his head but Jos didn't have the heart to frighten him again. "Is it Rob Wheal?" The jerk of recognition in the boy was his answer. "Why are you hiding here, Pike? Did Lady Julianna promise you shelter?"

His head shot up. "Nae. 'Tis on account o' the spirits!"

"What spirits?"

" 'Tis said this place be haunted. Me da says so. He won't set foot inside the gates on account 'tis a haunted place, full o' devils."

Jos stared at the boy. "So you thought you'd be safe

from him here. That's clever thinking, Pike, but why do you need to hide?"

Pike began to tremble. "On account he said he'd peel the skin o' me back iffin' the lady o' the hous' dinna' come. She was to meet him yesterday afternoon, only when she didn't come, he sent me to fetch her. But the housekeeper said she'd gone."

The blood began to beat thickly in Jos's veins. "Where was she to meet your father?"

"At th' new adit dug out by th' beach below Little Hangman headland."

Jos breathed deeply. "Thank you, Pike. You may have saved a lady's life. And have no fear, your father will never touch you again. I promise. Now go along to the kitchen door and tell the housekeeper I said you are to be fed and given a place to sleep." He gave Pike shove. "Go! Quickly."

When the boy had run out of the gate, Jos stood a moment to gather his wits. Gillie had gone to meet Wheal at the mine and had not come back. He rejected the touch of fear that Wheal had murdered her and left her to be found. But something had happened.

He was running toward the stable before his thoughts caught up with him. If only he would be in time.

Chapter
Twenty-two

At the top of Little Hangman cliff, Jos paused to catch his breath. The night was dark. With sunset, a fringe of lead-colored, low-riding clouds had gathered on the horizon, showing faintly red underbellies where the departed sun still licked at them. Below him the beach was lost in the gloom, the only demarcation the faintly luminous curl of the sea when it broke foaming onto the shore. It was not the time of day to begin what he was contemplating, but he had no choice. It might mean Julianna's life.

Somewhere under his feet in a corner of the cavernous burrows of Little Hangman Mine Julianna lay trapped. He knew it with a certainty that made him begin the steep descent to the new adit with only a burning torch to guide him instead of waiting for Jed and the others to catch up with him. Whether Wheal was to blame or other circumstances, he did not know or care. Finding her before it was too late was the only clear thought in his mind.

He made the descent to the beach quickly, half sliding, half running in the furze and weeds until his boots hit the smooth surface of sand. Even as he veered off to his left he heard the voices of men above and behind him and the yellow glare of a dozen more torches.

From the moment Wheal's son told him where Julianna had gone, he hadn't been able to get the image of a cave-in out of his mind. Had Blood Hall's ghosts put it there, or was it only vapor from his worst nightmare? The next moment he realized that the answer didn't matter. What was was. Conjecture or truth, he would soon know.

He picked up his pace, running until his lungs ached and his heart pounded. *I'm coming for you, Gillie! Wait for me!*

His eyes searched the cliff face until finally he saw it, the pithy hole in the gray and umber shadows of dusk. He began the climb at the same pace he had covered the beach, the motion causing the torch he bore to cast fitful shadows on the ground before him.

He might have passed it by in the darkness. So small a thing, really. But the flame from his torch licked against the broken glass lying in the grass and winked back at him. He knew what it was even before he touched it. Julianna's spectacles. His heart contracted in a queer combination of joy and pain. She had been here. He was right.

The sound of the men coming up the beach drew his attention. As he turned toward them yet another object glinted in the grass. This time he found the pistol that had been missing from its case. He stood up slowly, looking into the darkness that yawned open before him. And then he went inside.

Jed watched in dismay as Jos entered the mine. "Damn fool!" he muttered. Though he had seen Jos at work underground and knew his nerve to be steady and his instincts for survival to be good, Jos didn't possess the experience necessary to do something as risky as enter an unfamiliar mine alone.

Jed gained the summit breathing heavily. "Ye men, stay here!" he directed those coming up behind him. "I'm going in." But he had only reached the arched entry when he saw Jos running back toward him from inside.

"There's been a slide!" Jos cried as he neared the mine foreman. "I hear water running somewhere. They must be trapped."

"Now, lad," Jed began in a patronizing tone. "Because there's been a slide, it don't follow there's folks in there."

Jos held up the spectacles he still carried, his face grim.

Jed shook his head slowly, his eyes saddened. "Sorry I am to see that. Still, there's naught to do done till dawn and the full crew comes on. If ye heard water 'tis most likely the underground stream that's slowed our excavation. We've been waiting for a new engine so we can pump it out before the pressure breaks a wall in the lower levels."

Jos's face was pale and grim in the harsh torchlight. "The slide's come from the ceiling and there's water seeping under it. If they're in there, they won't last long. We must dig now."

As Jos moved to pass him, Jed put a hand on his arm. "I know what you're feeling, lad, but ye can't do it, not till we've had time to buttress the remaining walls."

Jos jerked away. "Julianna's in there! I'm going to get her out."

The look on the young man's face gave away far more than he realized, Jed thought. But even so, Jed was the mine foreman, first and last. "I won't order men to risk their lives without preparation." He gave Jos a long, level gaze. "Lady Julianna could be dead."

Jos stepped back from Jed's bleak expression. "Do what you must. I will."

Jos saw that one of the men with Jed held a pick and he reached for it. As he turned to reenter the mine, Jed planted his broad frame in his path. "Don't be daft, man! What good 'twill do ye to kill yerself?"

"Keep away from me," Jos said in low voice. "I'm not asking any to help me but, by God, if you try and stop me, I'll kill you."

Jed met the younger man's stare and saw in it agony, fear, and worry, but not the madness of a man pushed by grief past reason. He stepped aside.

Jos reentered the mine and, staking his torch in the rubble, began digging. A few minutes later he heard footsteps behind him and swung around, pick lifted in preparation for a battle. But in their torchlight, he saw that Jed and the two men coming toward him carried picks and shovels and buckets.

A brief smile sketched Jed's face. "You're a fool. But it seems there's more than one of ye abroad this night."

Jos didn't reply, just turned back to the task at hand and began digging.

They worked far into the night, halting occasionally when the digging caused a curtain of rock to slide forward. It was grim, dusty work, the progress necessarily slow and methodical. One mistake and every man knew this place might mark his grave.

Finally one of Jed's spadefuls uncovered something. It was an iron boot heel. He silently nudged the man beside him who in turn pulled on Jos's sleeve.

Jos raised his eyes from the sight to meet Jed's steady gaze. "Wheal?"

Jed nodded once.

Jos closed his eyes briefly, let out his breath in a long sigh, and then turned back to his labor.

They concentrated on the place where the body lay, the work going faster now that the men had the incentive of knowing, however grimly, what they were seeking was mostly likely to be found there.

Julianna heard the sound of men working, but it had been going on so long that she no longer knew which direction the noises came from or if they were closer or farther away than before. She lay huddled in the corner, shivering from the cold and damp, and breathing the thin air that was fast running out.

And then she heard it, the rumbling of falling rock. She cowered against the chiseled rock face at the back of the cavern, gasping and choking on the rising dust. Next she was blinking in disbelief against the light of a dozen torches. She dimly heard a chorus of coarse but joyous male voices and then arms were enfolding her.

She lifted her head weakly. "Tell him," she whispered. "Tell Jos I love him."

"He knows, Gillie," a familiar voice said close by her ear. "Gillie," the voice murmured, "oh, Gillie . . . love!"

"What a shame," Lady Regina replied mildly to Julianna's comment that several of her new gowns no longer fit. "After all the trouble we went to not long ago. Oh, well, Miss Sophie will just have to return and complete a whole new wardrobe for you and later one for the babe." She clapped her hands. "It will be such fun. Caps and gowns and booties and blankets! We must get out the knitting needles. Gillie? Are you listening to me?"

Julianna turned her head away from her bedroom window. "Yes, Grandmama, I'm listening."

"Are you certain you're feeling well? Perhaps you should not be up so soon. I can send for Dr.—"

"No!" Julianna took a deep breath. "No, Grandmama. That won't be necessary. All that is wrong with me is inactivity. It's been three weeks since I've set foot beyond the front door. If I'm not soon allowed out of this house, I shall go mad."

Behind her severe expression, Lady Regina was beaming. This was the first burst of spirit Julianna had shown since she was carried up out of the mine. She and the marquess had arrived within hours of Gillie's rescue. Even now she could not suppress a shiver at the thought of how close her granddaughter had come to death. But for the courage of Jos Lyngate, Gillie would be dead.

Lady Regina smiled to herself. She rather liked the young man, even if she didn't approve of his courting methods. Even now the marquess was finishing the legal work on the marriage contract. Nearly everything was in readiness for the wedding, which was to take place in two days. In fact, they lacked only one thing: a bride's consent.

Julianna had been as lifeless as a fading rose these last days, though the physician had assured her that she was fully recovering from her ordeal and that the child she carried was perfectly fine as well. Only one other thing ailed her granddaughter, and that was a matter of the heart.

"Mr. Lyngate came again this morning."

Julianna pressed her lips together. He came every morning, and every afternoon, and sometimes he came again in the evenings. He came every day but never at night, and never to her room by way of the secret passage. It seemed he had decided to end that part of their lives. Yet that is what she waited for: one last secret tryst. Only then would she willingly submit to the wedding preparations that continued about her.

He had been constantly by her bedside the first days when she lay exhausted and half dead from exposure. But once she awakened and looked at him in love and joy, he had not been back to her bedroom. It was a matter of propriety, he'd said. Well, she didn't want him to be right and proper. And so she had avoided him when he came to the house, but she always watched him leave from an upstairs window. Her love had never been stronger, but neither had her determination to share with him in secret one last time the joy they had known in this room. She would marry the Honorable Adrian Joshua Lyngate, but her heart would also belong to the gruff, earthy, passionate gardener named Jos.

She was vexed beyond words to realize that at the very moment when she most needed him, he had lost the ability to read her mind, to ferret out her desires even before she knew what they were. She wanted back the wild, wicked nights of their first happiness, and she would not be content until he realized it.

"Where are you, Gillie?"

Julianna blinked. "I beg your pardon?"

"You are so far away." Lady Regina rose from the rocker and came to stand beside her tall granddaughter at the window. "What do you see out there? Ah, the sea. I'd forgotten that on certain rare days, the air is so clear that a silver sliver of the sea can be seen from this room." She looked up, pretending not to see the tears that had slipped down both of Julianna's cheeks. "My, how I love the sea. The air would do wonders for your complexion. Blow away the last of the sickroom pallor. How would you like to go for a ride, to see the sea?"

Julianna nearly shook her head, but she didn't. Suddenly she wanted very much to be away from Blood Hall and all the memories that these walls held. "Yes, I should like that."

"Good." Lady Regina patted her waist. "I'll go down and have Mrs. Mead fix up a picnic basket and send one of the footmen to the stables with the message that your pony cart is to be hitched up. I'll send Molly up to help you change. Wear the yellow muslin. It's an especially warm day and you won't want to become overheated."

"Yes, Grandmama." Not wanting to spoil her grandmother's obvious pleasure that she was at last able to maneuver Julianna into some activity, Julianna dutifully removed the yellow muslin gown from the armoire and, with Molly's help, changed into it. Still, she was amazed when, a quarter of an hour later, she descended the stairway into the entry to find a liveried footman waiting with a basket on one arm and a quilt in the other. Beside him, her grandmother held aloft an unopened parasol of yellow organdy with multicolored streamers.

"I hope you put on your walking boots, Gillie," Lady Regina said as she came toward her. "Mrs. Mead has packed a most delightful lunch. There's even a bottle of cider from the cellar and fresh strawberry pie. Here's a parasol. Now remember, you're not to tire yourself but you should take the sea air."

In an amazingly short time Julianna was handed up

into the cart, the footman beside her, and off riding across the open ground beyond the gates of Blood Hall.

The heart-stirring blue sky was high and wide. Thick white clouds shouldered together on the far horizon like brilliant drifts of snow. This was no longer the stark Devonshire moorlands of deep winter or early spring. The heathery, boulder-strewn hillsides baked beneath the radiant power of a near-summer sun. The fresh clear air raced to meet them, lifting and exhilarating her spirits. Behind them the cart wheels raised little dust plumes.

There was a man coming toward them on the lane that led toward the cliffs and the sea beyond. Julianna shielded her spectacles from the sun's glare to watch his progress. He wore a tweed coat and trousers, and upon his head he wore a low-riding, wide-brimmed hat. He lifted his head and she saw his face.

Julianna nearly cried out her surprise, forgetting the caution with which she had restrained herself these last days.

It was Jos Trevelyn, not Adrian Lyngate.

He paused and stepped off the path. She was amazed when the footman reined in the pony beside him. But before she could question his action, he was stepping up to the cart beside her.

He doffed his cap. "Good day, Lady Julianna."

"Good day," she managed over the swift joy that had shot through her like an arrow.

He smiled that oh-so-sweetly remembered smile. "Are you better? I heard you had taken to your bed for good."

"Hardly," she answered tartly, and felt her cheeks sting. He was teasing her about her refusal to see him.

He crossed his forearms and leaned on the edge of the seat beside her, gazing up into her face in frank appreciation. "There's color in your face. And I'd say you're no longer sickening. Life looks good on you."

Julianna looked away from him. "And you," she said softly. Oh, had he at last guessed why she refused to see him, or was it mere coincidence that they'd met like this? She did not want appear too glad to see him, yet she could not keep from turning back to him. She saw now that he looked worn. Hollows carved out the space beneath his eyes and lines scored the sides of his mouth. "Have you been ill as well?"

"Only sickening for the sight of you," he answered, and stepped back from the cart. "I'll take the reins now, Liam," he said to the footman.

With a frown, Julianna turned to see the footman step quickly down. "What are you doing?"

Liam flushed. "The marchioness said I was to see you into Mr. Lyngate's care." He bowed slightly and then set off on foot at a rapid pace, as if he feared that she would delay or embarrass him if he did not get right away.

Julianna swung around to face Jos, amusement brightening her eyes. "You're behind this."

"Absolutely," he answered, and reached across her lap for the reins. He tied them quickly to the seat, saying "You wouldn't let me come to you so I've had you brought to me."

Julianna fought the giddy delight sparked by his revelation. He wanted her! Even so, she crossed her arms primly and said, "Very well. It would seem I'm your hostage for the moment. What do you plan to do with me?"

He looked up at her with an expression that made her wish she had chosen her words more carefully. "Do you want an honest answer? Here and now?"

She did not reply because she could not be certain yet

that the footman was beyond their hearing, and the reply might have shocked him mightily.

Content with her silence, Jos climbed into the cart and stepped up close behind her. A moment later, his arms snaked about her waist and drew her back hard in against his chest.

She balked at the intimacy. "What do you think you're doing?"

"Trying to remember the feel of you," he answered, and buried his nose in the soft skin behind her right ear. "You smell the same, Gillie. So sweet."

She stiffened, trying to dig her elbows into his ribs to hold him off, but his hands at her waist moved, sliding up her rib cage to enclosed her breasts in warm possession.

"Don't! Stop! Stop that!" Her cries came in quick gasps between giggles, but he held her tight. His lips found her earlobe, nibbled the tender fullness, and then his teeth framed it and tugged.

The swift response of her body at once pleased and embarrassed her. Because of her pregnancy, she no longer wore heavily boned stays. His clever fingers quickly found the shape of her nipples through her light-weight corset, and he crushed them tenderly between his thumbs and forefingers, rendering sweet bursts of desire that found an answering pleasure much lower down.

She twisted in his grasp, sliding forward to slip off the seat. He moved one hand from her breast and caught her low down, below her navel, pressing her back onto the seat, and her hips to his groin.

His hand dug into her lap, seeking the shape of her. "Lord, Gillie," she heard him whisper in exasperation. "How many petticoats are you wearing?"

"Enough," she assured him, but she had begun to

doubt it. Despite the layers, she felt his fingers kneading her lower belly, pushing pleasure into her skin and rubbing the deep-down need his simplest touch could bring forth.

"Let me go, Jos. Please!" It was a ragged plea of surrender and he knew it.

He released her slowly, begrudging the loss of the feel of her in his arms, even for a moment. When she was free, he reached forward and brought her chin around so that he could look into her eyes. What he saw there both soothed and discomforted him. There was more than a share of arrogance and pride in her gaze, courage as well, but there was also a melting tenderness that she revealed to him alone. He had nearly lost her. The trembling shock of that was still with him, and it might always be so, for life was fragile and uncertain.

He put his mouth on hers.

For a length of minutes time seemed suspended, the moors newborn and yet ancient, and he found his own small bit of eternity in her kiss.

When he broke it, Julianna moved a little away from him but there seemed to be no place in her world for anything but him: his taste and touch and smell and the look in his hot blue eyes.

He laughed then, the sound of it as bold and audacious and fine as the day into which it was released. "Come, wench, before we shame the day with our needs."

He reached past her and freed the reins. Snapping them smartly over the pony's back, he sent them quickly down the lane that led to the sea.

When they reached the cliff top, he helped her dismount. After he had gathered the picnic basket and blan-

ket, he offered her his hand to lead her down the steep,
narrow path that led to the sheltered cove below. When
her feet touched the sand, he turned and smiled at her.
"Over here," he said, nodding in the direction of a narrow overhang that jutted out over a portion of the beach.
It was a natural shelter away from the wind, closed from
view to all but those who came by sea. He set the basket
in the sea grass and spread the blanket over the sand,
weighting the corners with stones he gathered.

Julianna watched him silently, not offering aid he did
not need. Instead, she devoured him with greedy eyes,
taking in every aspect of him denied her these last weeks.
She envied the hair that grew at his nape and hugged the
strong column of his neck. She grew jealous of the tendrils that caressed the edge of his cheek each time the
wind whipped them. She followed with covetousness the
scalloped lines beneath his cheeks that marked the border of his newly shaved beard.

When he drew off his jacket in response to the heat,
she begrudged the linen shirt that clung to the hard muscles of his broad shoulders and back and lay wantonly
across his chest. She took umbrage against the trousers
that scooped into the tight curves of his buttocks and
stroked his long thighs as he bent to pick up another
stone. She felt enmity toward the thick belt that rode
intimately above his lean hips. She took particular and
instant dislike to the row of buttons that marked so coyly
the place covering his groin.

He had never before seemed so real to her, so finite
and full of life. How splendidly male and desirable, and
self-contained he seemed.

When he was done, she turned away and bit her lip,
near weeping for the foolishness of her thoughts, but

fully aware of their effect on her heart and body. She wanted him, wanted him so badly she ached. She dug her nails into her palms to distract herself with a different kind of pain. When he came up behind her, she held her breath.

"Come walk with me, Gillie," he said in a careless voice. He caught her hand and drew her out into the sunshine.

They walked a long time, the sun on their faces and the wind in their hair. Whenever they paused, he took another article of clothing from her. First he removed her shoes and stockings, later her shawl, finally he removed her bonnet and very slowly unbraided every plait that made up her coronet.

When the wind whipped the black hair from his hands and spread it out behind her like an ebony banner, he stepped back and smiled. "I've been wanting to do that since the first night I saw you lying so trusting in your bed."

His voice sounded odd but his smile was so reckless that Julianna thought he could not be as affected by the memory as she.

When he caught her arm again, swinging their joined hands as children often do, she again matched her steps to his longer strides and gave up to the simple joys of the bright day and the surging sea, and his company.

Finally they returned to the spot where the blanket had been laid and he pulled her down beside him, grinning. "Feed me, Gillie."

And she did. The feast that emerged from the basket seemed more than enough for half a dozen men, but she had never before seen his appetite given rein. He ate three roasted squab with his fingers, consumed a jar of fresh peas, a loaf of bread, and half a round of cheese without hardly a breath. More amazed than hungry, she sat back and watched, her elbows braced on her knees and her chin in her hands.

When he was done, he stretched back on the blanket and folded his arms beneath his head.

"You may burst, you know," she said with a grin.

He looked at her, the blue of his eyes mere slits of sky between the tangle of his tawny lashes. The lines of his face bowed in amusement. And then he unfolded one arm and stretched it out toward her. "Come lie with me, Gillie."

For a moment she could not move, could not find the courage to do what she had wanted to do since the moment she saw him sketched in silhouette against the May sky. And then her hand was reaching out to him. He pulled her down beside him and into the curve made by his arm and shoulder. Yet when he did nothing more, she thought he could not feel as she did. She could not have been more wrong.

Jos had never been more aware of anything in his life than he was of the woman beside him. His arm beneath her trembled from her sweet weight pressed into it. His nostrils quivered with the fragrance rising off her sun-warmed skin. He had watched her for an hour on the beach, jealous of the way the breeze carelessly caressed her face, envious of the way her gown pressed wantonly against her until her nipples stood out boldly through the fabric. Hunger for her had licked at his groin until his trousers grew so tight each glimpse of her soft cheek and tender lip stiffened him to the point of pain.

Yet he held himself apart, deliberately delaying until he saw in her eyes a longing as desperate as his own. He had not been able to understand what fueled her persistent contrariness in avoiding him until he had remembered how she had continued to welcome "Jos" into her bed even when she was angry with "Adrian." He smiled. His prim Gillie was a wanton at heart. Since Jos could not now to come to her at Blood Hall, he had devised this meeting.

He turned to her, his face only inches from hers, and touched her cheek with a finger. How wide her eyes were, as wide and green as the sea beyond them. "Gillie?" he said softly.

Julianna understood the unspoken question. Heat rose to burn beneath the skin where he touched her. When his fingers spread to frame her cheek and chin, she lifted her face and closed her eyes.

He kissed her and she tasted sunshine.

He did not hurry them. They had all the time in the world. Wherever his hands touched her a blush rushed, warm and tingling. Kiss melted into kiss until lips throbbed and teeth ached and the blending was so complete that they were left gasping when the separation came.

He stood and drew her to her feet and into his arms. Impatient now, she raised her hands to his cheeks, holding his warm face to hers, and kissed him with all the tremulous hope and joy and love she held within her. When she heard in triumph his groan of pleasure, her arms slipped around his neck, the fingers entwining protectively at his nape to keep his head bent to her kiss.

His hands found the span of her shoulders and then swept down her back in a molding caress that brought their bodies into sensuous alignment. His hands rose again, moving down her spine as they worked free the hooks and buttons rowed up there.

His hands, strong and gentle, slipped her gown from her where it lay forgotten even before it landed in a whispering puddle of yellow muslin. Next came the myriad of petticoats. When the final bit of linen slipped past her breasts and then her hips, and she stood naked before him, Julianna stepped back away from him.

She did not speak and neither did he. Yet she did not look away from the blaze of his gaze that fed her courage and his desire. She watched him with serious eyes, saw herself in his gaze, and found that the expanding darkness engulfing the blue sky was flattery enough.

He undressed himself, each keenly aware that they had never before seen one another in the light of day. When he was naked, he stood as silent and serious under her regard as she had his.

She saw that he was made of muscle and hard bones. She knew the feel of his dense, lush skin but not the colors from brown to shades of peach and cream. She had imagined the wide planes of his chest, the ripple of his ribs and the concave slip of his belly, but not the fine bright red-gold hairs that added texture to his body. Nor had she considered the shade of the copper curls at the base of his belly, nor the flushed thrust of his turgid flesh. When her gaze lifted again to his face, her wide green eyes held this new knowledge and the glory of the lesson learned.

They moved together quickly then, smiling and pleased as children. Yet there was nothing childish about the passion that flamed between them. Lips, hands, tongues, and intertwining limbs, they made discoveries of

one another in the next hour that would be often repeated but be never again so fresh.

He came into her quickly and knew the source of the
peace that had been eluding him these last weeks. Here
is where he belonged, with and in her, as often as he
could manage it, and for as long as strength would allow.

The moment of fulfillment, the devastating joy, crested
over them as her soft cries of pleasure rose above his
deeper grunts of release.

"I was afraid you no longer wanted me, not like this,"
Julianna whispered through joyous laughter when the
shape of the world had become fixed once more.

"Madwoman!" he chided, and kissed her cheek. "How
could I not?"

She placed a finger to his kiss-bruised lips. "You spoke
only of duty when you told my grandmother you would
marry me."

He laughed, the sound of it unfettered and free as the
gulls skimming past on the sea breeze. "Would you
rather I'd have told her that I wanted her granddaughter
for the taste of her lips and feel of her thighs when she
straddles me?"

"Oh." It was such a small word she nearly swallowed
it.

"Only 'oh,' Gillie?" He suddenly tightened his arms
about her as if he feared she would leap up and run
away. "I nearly got you killed! I never should have left
you with Wheal still about. A hundred times I've cursed
myself for the stupidity of—"

She stopped his words with a hard, lingering kiss. "No
more recriminations," she whispered when the kiss
ended. "I love you. You love me. It is enough."

"Yes, more than enough," he answered, and kissed her again.

They lay a long time in the sand and one another's arms, and traded whispers until dusk. They traded their deepest secrets, never to be told to any other and, perhaps, never to be mentioned again. She told him about her dream of Death and how she had fought it. He told her of his own dreams and how he would rather be with her under any circumstances than to be without her for even one more minute.

Later their conversation became more practical. He told her how her grandfather had offered him a position in his government offices, but that he had recently inherited a small estate in Cornwall belonging to his mother's deceased brother and the life of a country squire held more appeal to him. She told him how a life in the country had always been more to her liking than one in London, and that she has always believed that children should have freedom to grow wild and free where dirty hands and faces are not frowned upon.

Finally, when the crimson sun lay half melted in the western sea, he drew her to him and kissed her softly and said, "Don't make me wait any longer, Gillie. Say you'll marry me."

She looked at him with eyes of love and courage and belief. "I will marry you, Jos Trevelyn Adrian Lyngate, and bear your children. God help the future, and what people will say."

He smiled then, the smile that cut so deeply into her heart and spilled a generous measure of the love she bore him into her veins. "They will sa' th' mad spinster o' th' moors wed herself t' a randy gardener, and lived t' know th' joys o' country ways!"

Epilogue

Lady Regina Kingsblood, Marquess of Ilfracombe, entered the rose garden shortly after midnight, a silk wrapper covering her ball gown. Despite the warmth of the summer night, she felt a slight chill as she closed the gate behind her. Moonlight spilled through the trees in silver coins upon the flagstones. At first she heard nothing as she stood in the shadows waiting, but soon she detected the first notes of the haunting melody that always invaded her mind if she waited long enough.

In the place at the center of the garden where moonlight pooled unimpeded by tree or shrub, a pair of dancers waltzed into view. They came in steps lighter than heartbeats, in silhouettes more fragile than mere mirage, their entrance more gentle than a cloud-shadow passing over the moors.

Regina knew no surprise, no fear, no hesitation in witnessing their entrance for she knew their images well. Since the Restoration nearly two hundred years earlier, they had abided here, a tribute to lovers who dared defy religion and man.

The lady's petite blond beauty was as familiar as was the man's broad sun-darkened features and dark, cropped hair. She wore a gown of pale-gold silk, deeply decolletaged and with wide panniers of an age two centuries removed from the present. He wore a seventeenth-century soldier's doublet of leather, and breeches, jack-boots, and wide gauntleted gloves.

The gay music grew until it was nearly a physical pitch.

Lady Regina approached them cautiously and then waited for them to become aware of her presence.

They did so at once, two pale faces turning in unison to stare at her.

She smiled. "Good evening, Captain. My lady."

They did not reply but she did not expect it. "I've only come to thank you for this night."

She turned her face up toward the second-story window that overlooked the garden. Light spilled from the house and so did music. "I know you hear it, the laughter and the joy. Jos and Gillie were wed today. I don't know how, but I feel you had a part in their coming together. Thank you for that."

She smiled. "And, Captain, I believe I owe you an apology from my last visit. I only wanted your happiness as you so long ago provided for mine. You need not fear for us, your mortal kinsmen, any longer. We have learned the lessons that you sought to teach us.

"Oh, those who follow us may yet make unnecessary muddles of their lives, even resist and reject love's snare, for that is your legacy to us too, is it not? Those doubts come from human frailty. Only by triumphing over them do we realize the true gift of love." More quietly she added, "You have earned your peace."

For a moment longer they stood in perfect rapt stillness. Then, billowing forth like white fire, an incandescent vapor began filling the garden, eclipsing her view.

They emerged from the shimmering waves of spume as delicate, translucent creatures. Light passing through them, broken by the prisms of their beings, cascaded into the garden, striking jewel bright through the darkness, subduing all before it.

The voice came rich and deep, a surging against the senses, palpably masculine but softer than moonlight.

Your apology is accepted, Marchioness. But you are wrong. As long as the name Kingsblood lives, as long as blood runs hot in those mortal veins, we must endure. It is our fate. When you are weary of the world, come again, and we will give you peace.

And then they were gone: light, sound, and silence.

The gate creaked, the sound of it as sharp as a cricket's chirp. "Genna? Genna?"

"Here, Maxwell."

Maxwell Kingsblood stepped into a garden flooded only by moonlight. "I should have known," he said in resignation. "But why tonight, Genna, when we celebrate a wedding?"

Regina went to her husband and wrapped her arms about his waist and pressed her tear-damp cheek to his shirt front. "I was remembering another time, another wedding. Ours," she said quietly.

His embrace tightened about her. "I know. None of the other weddings since have been the same. But there's something in the air tonight, I feel it too."

"It's magic," Regina said, and lifted back her head to look up into the face of the man she had loved for more than forty-five years. "It is a night for lovers."

He kissed her softly, sweetly, and with the approval of his unseen audience.

"You're not still brooding over the fact that I nearly died here last year?" he asked her when they drew apart.

Regina put her whole heart into her smile. "One and all, I expect that we shall presently meet with Eternity."

"Does that frighten you, my love?"

She thought of what the spirits had promised and shook her head. "Less than I'd imagined, my lord."

From the window above them she heard the sounds of the orchestra in the Great Hall as it began a new tune. "You promised me a waltz this night, my lord."

"So I did," he replied, and wrapped an arm about her slender waist to draw her near. "We will dance in honor of Gillie and Jos, and for all those who have known true love."

And so they danced in the garden, mortal and spirit, in time and tune to the joy of new love and of ancient happiness.